A MOTHER'S LOVE

Collier Paget-Browne leaned over the cradle and slipped his finger into the tiny fist of his newborn baby girl, and namesake.

"You're mine, all mine. I swear you'll never want for anything, my daughter, especially love, for I'll love you enough for both your mother and me."

Collier failed to notice his wife, Elinor, standing in the doorway, her lovely face grim. She finally spoke.

"You'd better love her enough for both of us, for as God is my witness, she shall have no love from me. Ever!"

8/91

Nomi Berger

ACE BOOKS, NEW YORK

An Ace Book

Published by arrangement with the author

ISBN: 0-441-14517-5

First Ace Printing: February 1983

Manufactured in the United States of America
Ace Books, 200 Madison Avenue, New York, New York 10016.

With love and gratitude
to my parents
whose devotion has
kept the dream alive

The desire of the moth for the star,
    Of the night for the morrow,
The devotion to something afar
    From the sphere of our sorrow...

To———, 1821
Percy Bysshe Shelley

Collier

~

1920 – 1929

Chapter One

It was the hottest July on record.

Or so it seemed to the four hundred people sweltering inside Boston's Trinity Church that Sunday morning in 1920. The stained-glass windows of Henry Hobson Richardson's great Episcopal cathedral trapped the eleven o'clock sun and spun its rays into a jewel-toned web around the gathering below. It might have been a scene woven into some medieval tapestry, one holy moment preserved forever, if not for the restless shifting of the congregation.

Some of the men, their faces flushed, swabbed their foreheads with the backs of their hands. Others tugged at their shirts or at their stiff Celluloid collars which were slowly beginning to wilt. The women fared no better in their little toque hats and wrist-length gloves. They either patted their faces with their delicately scented lawn handkerchiefs or waved them in the air as ineffectual fans to cool themselves. When Reverend Wallace Gibbing finally began the service, the four hundred congregants offered him their silent thanks. In precisely twelve minutes, their ordeal would be over.

"Hath this Child been already baptized, or no?"

"No." Collier Paget-Browne's deep voice resonated in the restive stillness.

Motes of dust floated upward, radiating in iridescent spokes from the heads of the two men and two women standing to the left of the wooden lectern from which Phillips Brooks had preached during his twenty-one years as Trinity's rector. Positioned beneath the cathedral's dome, bathed in its celestial aura, the four seemed blessed with a tranquility denied the rest of the congregation. Entire pews undulated with an anxious rhythm as people shifted, first to their left, then to their right, before settling again into resigned discomfort.

"Dearly beloved, forasmuch as our Savior Christ saith, None can enter into the kingdom of God, except he be regenerate and born anew of Water..."

3

They were all here today. The descendents of those eight hundred Puritans who had quit England for America three hundred years before. Here they stood, dutiful representatives of the Lowells and the Lodges, the Forbeses and Amorys, the Hemenways and Frothinghams, gathered together to honor the child of a man who was only second-generation Boston.

". . . Suffer the little children to come unto me, and forbid them not; for of such is the kingdom of God."

At six feet three inches, Collier Paget-Browne towered over the others standing before the marble and alabaster baptismal font. He seemed transfixed by the sight of his daughter, lost within the folds of her white satin baptismal dress, and cradled by her godmother, Collier's sixty-year-old cousin, Alice Forsythe Sample. He swallowed hard, forcing down the growing ache inside. How he yearned to hold his daughter himself, to feel the warmth of her little body against his chest, her tiny form molding itself to the shape of his large, strong hands. She belonged with him. She was his. *His*. God, how the word had the ring of Heaven to it.

"How can a man be born when he is old? Can he enter the second time into his mother's womb, and be born?"

Elinor Addison Sargent Paget-Browne stood stiffly beside her husband and concentrated on the drop of sweat on the tip of the minister's nose. What a sight she must be. She plucked at the bodice of her apricot crepe dress in an attempt to free it from her sticky skin. The dress would be completely ruined. She glared up at her husband, cursing him for her discomfort, but he scarcely noticed. His black eyes were consuming his child. Elinor's blue eyes narrowed, turning frosty, and her chest constricted in cold fury.

"Give thy Holy Spirit to this Child, that she may be born again, and be made an heir of everlasting salvation . . ."

Dinah Wicks wriggled uncomfortably in her seat in the last row. She was sure everyone could smell her cheap perfume and her new pink dress. And here she'd expected to look just like the ladies in all those la-di-da magazines she read. But as she straightened her white straw hat with the pink tulle rose pinned to its crown, she knew she looked all wrong. Give her time, though. She'd fit in fine. She was wise to their games now.

". . . sanctify this Water to the mystical washing away of sin; and grant that this Child, now to be baptized therein, may receive the fullness of thy grace . . ."

Reverend Gibbing nodded to Alice Sample. With a smile, the woman held out her godchild to him. The infant immediately began to whimper, her whimpers reaching a crescendo in a shrill howl as the minister took her in his arms. Collier lunged forward. Reverend Gibbing shook his head and waved the anxious father back to his place.

"Name this Child."

Elinor's lips remained tightly pursed. She fingered the triple strand of pearls around her neck.

"Collier." The name reverberated through the nave. "Collier Paget-Browne II."

The fanning stopped. The air grew still. Four hundred pairs of eyes opened wide. The echo of Paget-Browne's deep voice took a long time to die. Recovering from his own astonishment, Reverend Gibbing hastily repeated the girl's given names. Alice Sample removed the infant's lacy cap and gently smoothed down the damp tufts of her fine blond hair. The minister dipped a sterling silver shell into the font and slowly began to pour the holy water over the top of the baby's head. She howled louder, spitting out the water as it streamed down her face, balling her tiny fists and kicking her little feet in protest.

"I baptize thee In the Name of the Father, and of the Son, and of the Holy Ghost. Amen."

As Paget-Browne watched his daughter, his chest swelled with pride; the warmth of ownership spread through him. She'd be a fighter, this one. She was his creation, by God. He glanced at the crucifix suspended above him as if to beg forgiveness for his blasphemy. But he couldn't help himself. She *was* his creation.

Reverend Gibbing picked up a small white towel and dabbed at the water pooling in the creases of fat around the infant's neck. Once again Alice Sample held out her arms. But Paget-Browne was through waiting. He, not Alice, took the crying child into his arms. The sound of congregants sucking in their breath echoed in the cathedral like the roar of the ocean drawing back from the shore. But Paget-Browne heard nothing but his daughter's cries. He cradled her against him, and with his love and his will he commanded her to be still. The squalling infant gradually quieted down. She unclenched her fists. Then she opened her eyes and looked up at him.

He could have sworn she was smiling at him. What did

doctors know when they said a child's earliest smiles were due mainly to gas? He smiled back at her. She closed her eyes, and he rocked her in his arms until she was asleep.

The congregants rose to leave, filing out of the church and down the steps into Copley Square. Paget-Browne, carrying his sleeping child, had just reached the outer foyer when he suddenly stopped. His heartbeat quickened and a warning trickle of fear shivered down his spine. *What the devil was she doing here?* She had given him her word. Why had she come back? She was smiling at him now. That absurdly vacant smile of hers. He wanted to run.

"Hold it right there, sir."

It was a reporter from the Boston *Evening Transcript* with a photographer at his side. Paget-Browne turned as a burst of light exploded in his face.

"Thank you, sir. Now hold still for another one, please."

The baby woke up and began to cry. Cursing under his breath, Paget-Browne shielded her face with his hand. He elbowed his way past the photographer and dashed out the door.

"Were you disappointed that it wasn't a boy, sir?"

"What name did you give the baby?"

"Where's your wife, Mr. Paget-Browne? We'd like some shots of her and the child."

The *Globe,* the *American,* the *Daily Record.* They were all there, trapping him, bombarding him with their questions, giving him no time even to answer them. He caught a glimpse of Elinor as a separate group of newsmen began to close in on her and he watched as she held her purse up in front of her face.

"You'd better get used to this, my precious," he murmured to his child. "You belong to them now." *And Heaven help you, my Collier, Heaven help you.*

"Mrs. Paget-Browne, how about a picture?"

Elinor turned her back on the men advancing on her.

"Smile for us, Mrs. Paget-Browne ... look this way, please ... this way ... that's better ... a big smile now ... come on, Mrs. Paget-Browne, we're hot too, but this won't take long...."

"How about a shot of her holding the baby?"

Paget-Browne looked down at his wife. She refused to meet his eyes. He held out his daughter as if she were a human sacrifice being offered up to some fearsome god.

"That's it . . . marvelous . . . big smile now . . . excellent . . . just a few more . . ."

Perspiration slid from beneath the wide brim of Elinor's beige straw hat and slithered along her cheeks and down her neck. She could taste the salt on her lips and smell the heat of the sun itself. It was all too much. The straps of her pumps were cutting into her ankles. She needed to sit down. But she continued to stand and smile obediently through clenched teeth, while the laughter curdled deep inside her.

Dinah hesitated on the top step. She smoothed out the wrinkles in her skirt, conscious of how it clung to her and provoked second glances from the men following their wives out of the church. As she watched Paget-Browne posing for the photographers, she couldn't hold back a giggle. He'd looked so scared. Silly man. How could he think she'd come back to stir up trouble when he'd given her the chance she'd waited for all her nineteen years? She opened her purse and checked the time printed on her railway ticket. In two hours she'd be on her way back to New York City. She started slowly down the steps.

"Hey, get that girl out of there!"

A man seized Dinah by the shoulders and shoved her out of the way of a photographer. She stumbled and nearly lost her balance. It was several minutes before she felt calm enough to begin inching her way down the stairs again. Paget-Browne's dark eyes suddenly stopped her. *Don't worry,* her message read, *I've kept my word. I'm going away again.* The connection broke. She reached the sidewalk at last. Now she would be safe again.

The interior of the three-story Paget-Browne mansion on Commonwealth Avenue had been converted into a magnificent floral bower, an exuberant tangle of yellow roses, white daisies, and delicate white baby's breath. The guests swirled through the house like a great human wave, the restless tide slowing just long enough for each guest to fill a green and gold Sevres luncheon plate at the elaborate buffet and then move on. With Elinor trailing several steps behind him, Paget-Browne circled each of the formal reception rooms, acknowledging the good wishes of his friends and the unspoken homage being paid to him and to his precious namesake. By their presence here today, these very proper Bostonians were once more affirming his membership in their exclusive club: the one marked "Reserved—Bluebloods and Brahmins Only." And now his daughter, by virtue of her name, would find her own membership secure.

"Dare I even suggest that you've managed to outdo yourself today, old man?"

Avery Leggett, Paget-Browne's attorney, reached out to shake his hand.

"In the twenty years we've known each other, Avery, when have you ever accused me of modesty?" Paget-Browne gave his friend a broad wink. "Wait until you see what I've planned for her wedding."

Avery Leggett roared approvingly. "A toast, Collier," he said, "to you and to that beautiful little girl of yours." He raised his glass of champagne and Paget-Browne obligingly raised his. "You know, one almost forgets this blasted Prohibition nonsense on occasions such as this. Cheers."

Paget-Browne drained his glass and set it down. He tugged a cigar from the inside pocket of his white linen jacket and bent to catch the light Avery offered him.

"Any regrets, old man?" Avery asked as he snapped his lighter shut.

"How could there be?" Paget-Browne drew on the cigar. "You've seen her."

"Except for Elinor's hair, she's you, all right."

"Damned right she is." Paget-Browne thought of the bits of himself so perfectly reproduced in his daughter and he began to smile. But Avery Leggett wasn't smiling. Even the pale gray eyes behind his rimless spectacles had lost some of their earlier humor. "You think I'm a fool, don't you, Avery? You think I'm mad if I fasten the future of Paget-Browne Enterprises to the bib of a pinafore."

Avery Leggett looked uncomfortable. "Empires are unwieldy things, my friend, and better left to men."

"Damnit, Avery, she's more than a girl. She's a Paget-Browne."

"But I'm afraid it will take more than your name to turn her into the son you've needed."

Paget-Browne was shaking as he stubbed out his cigar. "Give me enough time with her, Avery, and I'll give you something more than equal to any man."

Suddenly the room seemed too warm, the people too close. Paget-Browne tugged at the collar of his shirt. The strain of the last months made his very bones ache with fatigue. He needed some peace. And time. Time to devote to the six-week-old infant being put to bed in the nursery one floor above him. He headed for the door.

Avery caught hold of his sleeve. "You haven't forgotten our appointment tomorrow, have you? I'll expect you at ten to sign the revised will."

"I'll be there, Avery," he promised. "At ten." He impatiently shook himself free and bounded up the stairs for another look at his child.

He tiptoed into the nursery, breathing in that special sweetness found only in infants' rooms. There she lay, in the white wicker cradle he himself had once slept in, now freshly painted and draped in yellow silk caught in plump, puffed bows. He leaned over the cradle and slipped the index finger of his right hand into her tiny fist and felt it tighten around him.

There was no mistaking it. She was his mirror image. But then, he reasoned, how could it have been otherwise? Her eyes, an eerie blend of the black of her father and the blue of her mother, were indigo, the opalescent navy of moon-kissed ocean waves. Her mouth was wide, its fullness softening her firm, square jaw and the defiance of her boldly upturned nose. Yes, hers was a strong beauty and she would wear it well.

"We certainly gave them something to talk about today, didn't we, my precious?" he crooned. "You're mine, aren't you, Collier, all mine?" The moist little hand gripped his finger more tightly. "I swear you'll never want for anything, my daughter, especially love, for I'll love you enough for both your mother and me."

He failed to notice Elinor standing there in the doorway, her lovely face grim. The tension which had etched fine lines around her eyes had also worked to set her mouth in a permanent frown. She absently stroked her carefully marcelled blond hair, thankful that her hat hadn't mussed it too badly. The diamond on her left hand blazed in the spill of sunlight drenching the white organdy curtains at the nursery windows. She had always loved the seven-carat stone, known in the gem world as the Sample Diamond, famed for the pink fire which breathed such strange life into it. She had worn it during the six years of her marriage as a declaration of her victory at having captured a man like Collier Paget-Browne. But now the ring meant defeat. It represented duplicity and dishonor. Like her marriage, the Sample Diamond was nothing more than a sham.

"Elinor." Paget-Browne was beckoning to her, but she stared defiantly back at him and remained where she was. "Come here, darling, come have a look at her."

Elinor gripped the door frame as if for moral support and refused to move. It was he who finally capitulated. He walked to her, and gazing down at her from his great height, he thought how small she was, how fragile. He reached out to touch her smooth, golden hair. She flinched and he drew his hand back.

"We're finally a family, Ellie," he said to her then.

"We were a family before."

"We were a couple before, damn it. It wasn't enough. I needed this child."

"This child." Her voice was sneering. "This precious heir of yours."

"Yes, my heir!" He thrust his face into hers and she backed away from him. "Why else would I have gotten married when I did, if not to ensure myself of an heir?"

"But you had no right to force me . . ." Her voice trailed off momentarily, but she quickly recovered. "There was more than enough time to start a family."

"There was precious little time!"

"You're wrong! I'm only twenty-six years old."

"And I am fifty-one!" he thundered. "How dare you speak to me of time!"

The baby whimpered in her sleep and Paget-Browne lowered his voice. "Dear God, why can't I make you understand? You know nothing of a man's compulsion to reproduce himself, to give his name to a child of his blood, to leave behind some proof of his very existence in this world. Believe me, Elinor, we men are a vain lot. We'd blanket the entire earth with our seed if we could be assured of it falling on fertile ground."

Elinor's returning gaze was scornful. "You have a daughter, Collier, not a son. She may bear your almighty name now, but as soon as she marries, she'll forfeit it."

He recoiled from her words as if he had been slapped in the face. "Not her." He shook his head. "Not my child. She'll find a way of preserving it."

But his denial brought him little comfort. What if Avery and Elinor were right? What if his daughter preferred the dreams of a girl to those of a man, choosing to serve and not to rule? Was he nothing more than some deranged Pygmalion to some unsuspecting Galatea? He saw the name of Paget-Browne lying tattered before the feet of a little girl and fear rose like bile in his throat.

Elinor watched with satisfaction as her husband's face contorted in pain. Doubt did not become him. It made him ugly and weak, but more than that it made him human. She allowed herself a semblance of a smile. How ordinary he could be, how vulnerable. As most men were. By his own admission, their vanity was their undoing. How much easier to lead them. What she wouldn't give now for a son.

"Ellie." He whispered her name as if it were a plea, and reached out to touch her, only to have her push him away.

"How dare you touch me after her!" she hissed.

He dropped his arms to his sides and when he spoke again, his voice was thick with pain. "She's part of our past, Ellie. All that matters now is you and me and our little girl."

"Then you'd better remember what you've promised our little girl, Collier. You'd better love her enough for both of us, for as God is my witness, she shall have no love from me. Ever!" And she turned and walked out of the room.

Paget-Browne let her go. Then he tiptoed back to the cradle and peered down at his sleeping child. "You're all I have now, Collier," he whispered to her, "and you're all I shall ever want. Sleep well, my precious one, for I doubt you'll ever find such peace again."

Deep in her sleep, his daughter yawned, and one small thumb worked its way into her mouth.

"If only your grandfather Andrew had lived to see you, Collier, he would have understood. In fact, he would have cursed me for having waited so blasted long."

Andrew Paget-Browne had just turned twenty-four when he left Yorkshire in 1860 to dig a fortune out of the ground in South America. He was a millionaire at twenty-seven. The diamond mines of the Brazilian province of Minas Gerais had been very good to Andrew, but he eventually moved on to Bahia, joining up with a forty-year-old American named Henry Latham Sample. The two men worked alongside their Indian laborers to carve a mighty empire out of the stubborn carbon rock, and they were multimillionaires long before Cecil John

Rhodes, the sickly son of a British vicar, left Hertfordshire to settle in Natal, South Africa. By the time Rhodes formed De Beers Consolidated Mines, Andrew had already bought out Henry Latham to gain complete control of the largest diamond producing and exporting company in South America.

Although the death of Andrew's father had left him with a title and a crumbling estate, he turned his back on England and sailed instead to America, settling in Henry's native Boston and marrying Henry's seventeen-year-old daughter, Dierdre. For a wedding present, Andrew built his bride the white stone mansion on Commonwealth Avenue, and for their first anniversary, she presented him with a son. Virtually assured of the continuity of the name of Paget-Browne, Andrew instilled in his son Collier what every transplanted English nobleman already possessed—a fierce loyalty to his noble name.

The adored and much-fussed-over Collier, secure in his exalted position as only child and heir to the Paget-Browne mining fortune, grew into adolescence devoted to solitary pursuits. Pursuits which dismayed the conventionalist in his mother and delighted the adventurer in his father. For young Collier was a creator, a craftsman blessed with the patience for minute detail and obsessed with the act of creation itself. While his boyhood friends submitted themselves to the battering of the playing field, Collier haunted the public library to study the sketches of everything from the Yankee clipper ship to the sewing machine. Then he would barricade himself in his basement workshop and reconstruct them from memory in perfect miniature.

At eighteen, he agreed to a Harvard education in exchange for a sailboat and a horse-drawn sleigh so that he could indulge his second passion—for speed. But when graduation liberated him four years later, he was ready to begin building again. He wanted it to be something grand this time. Perhaps an empire of his own. America was rapidly entering the age of the modern machine, and Collier decided that he would hold together the inventions of men far more creative than he. He, Collier Paget-Browne, intended to construct his empire out of nuts and bolts.

He borrowed five thousand dollars from his father and rented a warehouse near the harbor. He hired designers and craftsmen, foremen and workers, invested in molds and machinery, and within the year his first factory was in operation. From one factory, there sprang another and then another, spreading like

India ink on a blotter, fanning out across the country. Collier saw his hallmark—the initials P–B—stamped on billions of screws, nuts, bolts, rivets, nailheads, and washers, and he watched his empire stretch and grow.

The years passed, and Collier soon found himself alone. His parents were dead. He was one of the world's wealthiest men and he was already forty-five years old. He gathered the family's scattered interests under the grand umbrella title of Paget-Browne Enterprises and then began to brood because he was the last of his line. He had no heir. He didn't even have a wife. There had never been time.

He decided to make time. The mothers of Boston's eligible daughters held their breath. From the previous season's array of delicate "buds"—those debutantes presented in the fall of 1913—Collier plucked the comeliest of them all. She was twenty-year-old Elinor Addison Sargent of the Sargent banking family.

A casualty of Simmons College in her sophomore year, Elinor had found life a marvelous adventure with the restrictions of a formal education lifted from her fine-boned, ivory shoulders. Like Collier, she was an only child, but she was treated by her father as nothing more than a delightful ornament, a pleasant diversion, to be petted and pampered and then ever-so-politely dismissed. Blessed with that invincible combination of money, beauty and poise, her greatest asset was her ability to smooth over the inevitable lapses in dinner party conversations by chatting sweetly and superficially about any number of topics. Problems were nuisances Elinor delegated to others. Frustrations were temporary inconveniences she circumvented with a dimpled smile, a pretty pout or the determined stamping of one size five foot.

Whatever Elinor casually discarded, others picked up, whether a taffeta slip, the surviving earring of a formerly matched pair or the heart of some lovesick young man. Elinor so far had returned five fraternity pins and three engagement rings, but never the love of any of the young men who pursued her. She dedicated herself instead to perfecting the art of self-indulgence, devoting her time to afternoon teas, fittings with her dressmaker, tennis, dinner parties and just the right number of charitable benefits to give a proper balance to her life.

When she was chosen to be the bride of Collier Paget-Browne, she considered it his good fortune and her just reward.

In the dashing millionaire, she saw a man more than able to care for her in the way her devoted father had always done. As Collier declared his intentions on the maroon velvet Victorian loveseat in the parlor of the Sargent home, Elinor was envisioning the room as the viewing room for her engagement and wedding gifts. When Collier moved to kiss her and seal their betrothal, she cooly presented him with her right cheek because a photographer had once told her that her right side was her best. And when they exchanged vows before a congregation of three hundred inside Trinity Church on a day dismally timed to coincide with the start of World War I, while Elinor dreamed of redecorating the great stone house on Commonwealth Avenue, Collier was imagining them sprawled together across his damask-draped, ancestral bed, working hard at producing his heir.

Now as he looked down at what he had created, flesh born of his flesh, that ultimate extension of himself, Collier Paget-Browne finally knew what it was to love. It was a love so intense that its heat seemed to scorch his very soul. It had taken him six years, but now that he had a living guarantee of his own immortality, he had no intention of loosening his hold on the finite world. He intended to make good his promise to his child. He would love and nurture her, school and guide her, and prepare her for the role which she would one day, by nature's own decree, assume.

Resisting the impulse to wake her up and hold her in his arms, Paget-Browne left the nursery and quietly, but firmly, closed the door behind him.

Chapter Two

America was balanced precariously atop the roller coaster, not daring to look down. Stocks soared in a bull market. Ernest Hemingway, F. Scott Fitzgerald, William Faulkner and Carl Sandburg ushered in the gilded age of literature, and a movie kingdom called Hollywood sprang up in the hills of California. The twenties flaunted its flappers, its bootleg whiskey and its speakeasies. Music gave birth to the blues, to the voice of Bessie Smith and to the husky horn of Louis Armstrong. On May 20, 1927, Charles A. Lindbergh flew his *Spirit of St. Louis* solo from Roosevelt Field in New York to Le Bourget Field outside Paris in thirty-three hours and thirty minutes. The country nearly drowned in the sea of champagne and tickertape that followed.

It was a golden time for golden people, and nowhere was that more evident than in the burgeoning first families of America. Dearborn had its Fords. Battlecreek had the Kelloggs and the Posts. Rochester had the Eastmans, and New York the Astors. But nowhere was royalty more exquisitely in flower than in Boston, alive and embodied in a six-year-old golden sheath of a girl named Collier Paget-Browne II.

Paget-Browne had kept his promise to his daughter, bending and arcing his love protectively around her to insulate her from the unruly world outside. Her life purred with the well-oiled synchronization of a Rolls Royce engine and moved with the precision workings of a Swiss watch. A mood anticipated, a wish expressed, were promises swiftly and grandly kept. Father and daughter were inseparable.

The weekdays were hers, the weekends theirs, and together they agreed that spring was their favorite season. Fridays he would take her out of school so that she could accompany him to the afternoon symphony at the Huntington Avenue Auditorium. Saturday mornings they would shop at Quincy Market for fresh cheeses, fruits and vegetables before going down to the waterfront for freshly caught haddock, scrod and sea bass.

Saturday afternoons meant a sail in a swan boat on the artificial lake in the Common and then a visit to Louisburg Square so that Collier could feed shelled walnuts to the squirrels. On Sundays, they would walk through the Public Garden, and Paget-Browne would invariably lead her over to the bench where Ralph Waldo Emerson and Walt Whitman had sat on the day they first met. Paget-Browne would puff on one of his favorite cigars, and Collier would suck on hers, taking care not to tear the cellophane wrapping so that her father could smoke it afterward.

But in spite of the radiance of their father-daughter times, Collier was lonely, and she longed to be what she was forbidden to be: ordinary. For Collier believed, with a child's innocence, that in sameness lay safety, and in anonymity, the guarantee of acceptance.

"Why do those pesty men always follow me around, asking me questions and taking my picture?" she would constantly demand of her father.

And as always, he would try to explain it to her. "It's simply because they're curious about you, darling. You're a Paget-Browne, you know."

"Is that so important, Daddy?"

"It is to me, my angel." And he would smile that gentle smile of his. "The name of Paget-Browne has always meant a great deal to the men in our family."

"But I'm not a man, Daddy." It still didn't make sense. But it obviously made sense to her father because his smile would vanish and his eyes would suddenly grow sad and empty. Terrified that she had hurt him in some way, she would wrap her arms around his neck and hug him until she was certain the hurt was gone.

"I know you're not a man, my precious," he would murmur as he stroked her hair. "You're my beautiful little girl, and I love you very, very much."

Collier wondered if her father would love her as much if he knew about her secret game—the one in which she gave herself a simple name like Mary Browne. With a name as fancy as Collier Paget-Browne II, she knew she was frightening everyone away, everyone but those pesty men with their cameras and their notepads and all their questions.

She wondered if her father would love her at all if he knew she preferred playing with the other girls at Emaline Price's

School to visiting his factories or sitting in his big office, while he talked to important men like her Uncle Avery about things she couldn't understand.

Her treacherous thoughts upset her. They made her feel so ashamed. She was failing her beloved father by even thinking them. And so, she would promise herself to work especially hard at pleasing him and keeping that unhappy, faraway look out of his eyes. Usually, she was successful.

Just as Paget-Browne had kept his promise to his daughter, Elinor had kept hers. She gave the child nothing. She considered her an intruder in what was once a wonderfully contented household. Outwardly she treated Collier with icy disdain, while inwardly, resentment looped and coiled itself around her heart. But with time Elinor became so practiced at dissembling that she was soon able to pass for the perfect model of devoted wife and mother.

The rewards for her continuing performance were many; she made certain of it. She convinced her husband to buy her a cottage in Nahant where she could spend her summers. Twice a year she would travel to Europe and return with the latest in haute couture. Then she would go to New York for the jewelry to complete her wardrobe. Whenever she happened to be in residence in Boston, she would host a series of gala dinners and formal teas which the society columns lavishly described as "the absolute end in elegance and extravagance."

Because Elinor valued her husband's name as much as he did, she never once sidestepped the boundaries of propriety. She had no intention of allowing anything as frivolous as a flirtation or a fling to close the doors which the name of Paget-Browne held open for her. If she could, she would drain his mighty name dry. Her husband was a fool, frittering away his remaining years as he doddered toward old age on the arm of his precious child. She, Elinor, would continue to live as she had always lived, and she knew she could do it better without him.

To Collier, Elinor was nothing more than a beautiful shadow, a vague presence slipping in and out of her life. She was a small, exquisite stranger whose skin seemed alive with sparkling jewels and who left each room she entered smelling faintly of lilacs. Collier strained to find some hint of her mother in herself, but it seemed all they shared in common was the color of their hair. She often wondered how a kiss from Elinor's

carefully painted mouth would feel against her own cheek or
how her mother's arms might hold her. Those slim white arms
had never once opened wide to her. Her mother always managed to find a way to keep her at a distance.

"You're filthy, child; just look at those clothes. Go upstairs
immediately and have Isabel change your dress." Isabel was
Collier's maid.

"I haven't got time for your lessons now; I'm already late
for my tennis game. Ask Elma to listen to them." Elma was
the housekeeper.

"If you're hungry, have Clementine fix you something to
eat. Your father and I will be having dinner at his club tonight."
Clementine was their cook.

"Just because your father's out of town doesn't mean I'm
supposed to be driving you to school in the morning. That's
Michael's job." Michael was the family chauffeur.

But Collier, aching with a young girl's need for her mother's
love, refused to give up.

"I've made something very special for you this year," she
confided proudly to Elinor on her thirty-third birthday as the
family sat down to a birthday brunch on the terrace.

Elinor acknowledged her daughter's words with the briefest
of nods and began to butter a scone for herself.

Collier squirmed in her seat. The back of her dress was
sticking to the chair. It was too warm, even for the end of
May. She cast nervous glances back and forth between the
presents stacked on a nearby wicker table and her father, who
was staring absently out at the rose garden. She finally caught
his eye. He winked at her and she managed a weak smile in
return. She finally picked up her fork and speared a tomato
slice with it. It was no use. She couldn't eat. She put down
her fork again.

She hoped her mother liked her gift. She had worked very
hard all week at Emaline Price's School, cutting sheets of
colored paper into the shapes of leaves and flower petals and
then pasting them onto a large green mat. When the picture
was finished, her father drove her to Logan's department store
where she picked out a gold-painted wooden frame, some pink
and green striped wrapping paper and a fat pink bow. Then
she locked her bedroom door and worked until dinner time to
wrap up her mother's present.

"Are you ready to open your gifts now, Mother?" Collier

asked as the maids began to clear the table.

"But you haven't even touched your food, darling," her father said. "Aren't you feeling well?"

"I'm just not hungry, Daddy."

She was looking at him with such pleading eyes that he finally signaled one of the maids to take her plate away.

Collier's heart was hammering wildly as she watched her mother open her gifts. Why was she taking so long? Why didn't she hurry and open the one in the pink and green striped paper? She fidgeted in her chair, plucking anxiously at the folds of her dress, and waited. Hers was now the only one left. She caught her breath and held it in. Her chest tightened in anticipation as Elinor tossed the pink bow onto the grass and ripped open the wrapping.

Out of the tightly pursed lips came a tight little "Thank you."

Collier's chest ached even more. Then she noticed that her mother's mouth was twitching and that the lines around her nose had eased. She was smiling! She liked her gift! Collier was able to breathe again.

The following morning, Collier bolted down her breakfast and went out to the garden to clip some peonies for Miss Deering, her favorite teacher at school. On her way back to the house, she noticed Clementine emptying the trash into one of the large metal bins near the kitchen door. A glint of gold caught her eye.

The tears congealed in a solid lump in her throat. Nausea scalded the back of her tongue. Her mouth opened and closed in silent gulps of agony as she clutched her stomach.

Her beautiful picture was lying in a crumpled ball next to some orange peels and an empty cereal box. Beside the picture lay the broken gold frame.

Collier threw up all over Miss Deering's bright pink peonies.

It was a smoldering August night. While the rest of the city scratched and clawed at the heat, Paget-Browne sought refuge in the coolness of his basement workshop. He was just putting the finishing touches on the miniature of a Curtiss biplane when he suddenly felt the terrible heat of the night enter his body and flare through his veins. It narrowed and darkened his world until all he could see was the end of it.

"You're absolutely certain?" he asked again, staring at Elinor who sat serene and composed in the workshop's only chair.

"Yes, I'm certain. I'm pregnant."

Trembling fingers set the tiny plane down on his workbench. "There's no possibility of it being a mistake?"

"A mistake?" Elinor's voice was mocking. "Is that what you'd prefer?"

"No, no, of course not. I'm sorry, Ellie." He combed his fingers through his hair. "I'm just surprised, that's all. Forgive me. I'll need a little time to adjust to the idea."

"You completely amaze me, my dear," Elinor remarked coldly, watching him through narrowed eyes. "I thought you'd be delighted by the news."

Still stunned, he could only shake his head. "It's almost impossible to believe, after all these years." *Oh Collier, my beloved daughter,* he moaned inwardly. *I never thought to share you. Never.*

"Who knows? Maybe this time you'll have the son you've always wanted." Elinor was enjoying this. Taunting him. Watching his pain.

Paget-Browne stared miserably at her. He read the victory in her icy blue eyes and his heart sank. She had played her highest card and won. Seeking to dilute his love for his daughter, she was giving him another child to love. He tried hard to mask his anguish, saying, with forced lightness,

"We could have ourselves a veritable dynasty before we're through, couldn't we, Ellie?"

She veiled her disgust with a faint, enigmatic smile. Dynasty indeed. By virtue of this pregnancy, her wifely role would be fulfilled once and for all. From now on, there would be no more pretense. No more degradation. No more of the love-making she had always despised.

She had suffered her husband's assaults on her flesh until the birth of their daughter, and then she had suggested separate bedrooms. He even had the audacity to look relieved. He seemed completely content now that he had his heir. Through the years, his demands on her body could have been counted on the fingers of both of her small white hands.

In the past year, it was she herself who initiated the couplings which saw his seed embedded within her reluctant womb at last. His surprise at her sudden boldness in no way hampered his performance though. In fact, if anything, he had surpassed himself. The arrogant fool. Measuring the proof of his manliness by his ability to pound himself into oblivion as much as three times in one night.

How blunted his performances might have been if he knew how she gritted her teeth to keep from laughing in his face while he grunted and sweated above her. He was no better than some rutting barnyard animal, splattering her cool skin with his hot sweat, crushing her body with his as he worked so efficiently at satisfying himself. How crushed he would have been knowing that what kept her from screaming out against the humiliation of it all was her determination to present him with a son. She needed a son. For only with a son would she be able to repay them. Both her husband and his precious namesake.

Now it was done. Finally. She proudly patted her small flat belly, convinced that it was a boy with whom she shared her body now. Her body. Her son. The heir he had always wanted.

Satisfied, she stood to leave. He startled her by reaching out for her hand.

His heart twisted wretchedly as she turned her face away.

"Dear Elinor," he murmured gently, "thank you for your news." He pressed a light kiss onto her wrist. "It makes me want to weep."

Yes, he needed to weep. For everything that he was about to lose.

Suddenly, Paget-Browne was a man running out of time. He felt that he was entered in a race he had never sought. He would wake up at night, his chest heaving, his body drenched in sweat, certain that he had reached the end of that race and lost. Slipping out of bed, he would tie on his robe and tiptoe down the hallway to his daughter's room. He would stand in the doorway and watch as she slept in her large, canopied bed. She was all but lost behind the yellow silk draperies, and her golden hair lay tumbled across her face like a protective mantle. His love for her threatened to explode inside him and he would curse himself for waking her, just to feel her sleep-dampened young body close to his.

Collier, trapped within her own terror, would wake to find her father standing over her and she would hold out her arms to him. He would pull her close and she would cling to him, burying her face in the quilted satin collar of his dressing gown. She would breathe in the comforting smell of his skin and know that for a while she was safe. But whenever she managed to put her fear into words, she knew she wasn't safe at all. She was going to lose him. And all because her mother hated her and wanted her father's love to go to someone else.

"Collier, my darling Collier, listen to me," Paget-Browne would plead with her. "You're my firstborn child, and because you are, you hold a very special place in my heart. The love I'll give to your brother or your sister will never diminish my love for you. Do you understand me, Collier?"

"I understand you, Daddy," she would answer in a solemn voice.

"I swear to you that nothing is ever going to change between us. Ever."

The knot in her stomach would refuse to loosen and the chill running through her body would intensify. "I think you're wrong, Daddy. I think everything's going to change when the baby comes."

It took Elinor seven hours of painful labor to force her son into the world. He had chosen the coldest night of the year to be born, when a bone-chilling wind swept off the Charles and the city of Boston lay cowering in the path of an invading blizzard. In the recovery room at St. Margaret's, Elinor began drifting toward sleep. She had done it. She had given her husband the male heir he had always wanted. Her place was secure at last.

She now had someone of her own to love. She had a son. He would be hers. All hers. And she would shape and mold him as her husband had done with his daughter. Just as the girl bore his mighty name, so the boy would carry hers. He would be christened Addison Sargent Paget-Browne. Little Collier be damned! Her reign was nearly over.

When Paget-Browne learned he had a son, he knew that the strenuous battle he had waged within himself was over at last. The sigh he released was the sigh of a man who has been holding his breath for a very long time. He thought of Collier then. She was waiting at home for some word from him, waiting too for the reassurance that, in spite of this unwelcome intrusion in their lives, he would still love her.

He put on his overcoat and tugged on his gloves as he walked briskly toward the elevator. Before seeing his son or visiting his wife, he had to see his daughter. He would bring her back to the hospital and together they would take that first look at his boy.

He backed the car slowly out of the parking lot. Nuggets of snow pelted the windshield, and the wipers began to falter under the weight of the heavy, wet flakes. He used his glove to clear the fogged window and peered out into a night so white that the traffic lights were no more than indistinct slashes of red and amber and green.

Well, my daughter, he thought with grim determination, *it seems we'll all have to learn something about sharing now. But I won't forget what I've promised you, precious. You're still my firstborn.*

He reached into the breast pocket of his coat for a cigar. He lit it and then fanned at the smoke which immediately enveloped him. Rolling down his side window to clear the air, he coughed as a gust of wind and a volley of sharp, little snowflakes lashed at his face.

"Damn! Now I'll have to sit down with Avery again and change my blasted will," he grumbled out loud as he drew on his cigar. *But don't worry, my Collier, there's more than enough there for both of you.*

He turned onto Commonwealth and shifted gears. The Pierce-Arrow slowed, then picked up speed, shimmying for one uncertain moment before it straightened out again. Through the driving snow, Paget-Browne could barely discern the shape of the car just ahead of him. Impatiently he slammed his hand on the horn.

Something was wrong.

The red taillights were coming closer. The car had obviously stalled. With his hand still on the horn, Paget-Browne swung out of his lane. The tires screeched as they lost their grip on the icy street. He fought with the wheel to steady the car. But now two brilliant shafts of yellow light were aimed at him. They blinded him and scalded him and sought to divide him in two as he struggled to escape.

The splintering collision ricocheted through his brain. He screamed against the pain and the shattering glass and the twisting metal. He tasted blood and gagged at the stench of his own burning skin and his singed hair and the crumbling cigar.

"Collier!" he whimpered as the blood rose to fill his throat. He tried to hold on to the beauty of her face as it always

looked when he woke her up in the middle of the night. He
saw her smile and reach out to him. He felt her arms tighten
around him.

With a final, shuddering sigh, he closed his eyes.

The explosion of Collier's seven-year-old world hurled agony in a thousand molten arrows at her. The arrows pierced
her body and then penetrated her soul. Her world lay in fragments and there was no one who could put it back together for
her. He was gone. The sun in her universe had been extin-
guished. She was alone in a cold and hostile darkness.

She stumbled blindly through her inky hell, deaf to the
remaining sounds of life. But the sounds persisted. They were
ugly, intrusive sounds. The sounds of an infant crying. Soon
the sounds turned the terrible numbness into hate. How dare
he be alive when her father was dead! How could her mother
love him when it was his fault that his own father had been
killed! The hatred corroded her body and stained her insides
black.

Then the anger took hold. Quietly, insidiously, it seeped in
through her toes and journeyed upward through her bloodstream. It gathered momentum until it was raging and whining
like a locomotive out of control. As if caught at the epicenter
of a violent earthquake, Collier shuddered and shook. She could
not eat. She could not fall asleep at night. Her days and her
nights flowed into one another and emerged as one long, un-
ending twilight.

Then, one morning shortly before dawn the anger crested.
The bilious wave reared up in front of her and sent Collier
screaming down the hall to her father's room. It was just as
he had left it, with everything still in its proper place. But it
was not going to stay that way for long.

Collier had overheard her mother telling Kendal the butler
that as soon as she was out of bed and strong enough, the room
would be dismantled, his clothing sent to the Men's Mission
on Channel Street, the books, furniture and artwork to be put
into storage.

Collier began to choke on her pain. Soon every trace of her
father would disappear from the house, just as he himself had
disappeared from her life.

"Daddy?" she whimpered, half expecting him to answer
her. "Daddy," she called again, louder this time. "Daddy, I

miss you. Why did you leave me all alone? Why did you have to go away?"

She began to cry then. The tears surged out of her in great heaving spurts, plucking loose some of the grief which had clogged her aching heart.

"You promised you'd always love me," she sobbed. "You promised you'd be with me while I was growing up. But you lied to me, Daddy. You lied!"

Her face was streaked with tears and her nose had started to run.

"And you lied about the baby, Daddy. You said nothing was going to change. But everything's changed, just as I said it would. Now he has her to love him and I have no one. No one, do you hear me? No one!"

With a defiant scream, Collier threw herself across her father's bed. She dug her fingers into the damask spread and rolled from side to side, wrapping it around her like a bulky crimson cape. She slid off the bed and brought the spread down on top of her. Kicking herself free, she tore the blankets and the sheets from the bed and tossed them onto the floor. One by one, she took the pillows and ripped them open, spinning round and round, flapping her arms in the air, coating herself and the entire room in thousands of bits of feathers and down.

She grabbed hold of the lamp on one of his nightstands and sent it crashing to the floor. Then she broke all of the other lamps in the room. She took his books from the walnut bookcases lining one wall and flung them into the air in all directions. They bounced off the windows, glanced off the walls and knocked several oil paintings from their hooks. The Bible slammed into the antique pier glass near the door and the mirror shattered, spraying the room with hundreds of silvery shards.

She heard someone pounding on the door, but her rampage continued. She was safe; the door was locked.

She ran into his bathroom and swept the shelves clean of his bottles of cologne, his bars of scented soap, his shaving brush and china mug and his razor. Then she dumped his towels onto the white tiled floor and went into his dressing room. Out came his shoes and socks, his underwear, sweaters, shirts and cravats. Down from the shelves came his ties and his scarves. She opened his armoire and pulled down his jackets and his trousers and added them to the pile on the floor.

"Liar! Liar! I hate you, hate you, hate you!" She could

hardly breathe now; her chest ached, her voice was hoarse and her throat hurt when she tried to swallow.

"I hate you, Daddy, and I'll always hate you! I'll never forgive you for leaving me. You liar, you had no right to go and die!"

Two firemen finally broke down the door with an ax.

They found Collier, covered in feathers, curled up on the floor at the foot of the stripped four poster bed. Draped over her shoulders was her father's navy blue flannel blazer. While her left hand stroked the crimson and gold Paget-Browne family crest on the breast pocket of the blazer, her right hand slowly worked its way up to her mouth.

Before he could be stopped, a reporter for the *Evening Transcript* burst into the room and snapped off several photos.

That afternoon, when Boston sat down to five o'clock tea and the evening edition of the *Transcript,* they were treated to a front-page photograph of Collier Paget-Browne II, heir to the vast Paget-Browne fortune, crouching beside her father's bed and sucking on her royal young thumb.

Chapter Three

America bordered October 29, 1929 in black and memorialized it as the day their joy ride ended. It was the day that the stock market crashed. Like a drunk with delirium tremens, the country lurched and stumbled along a path strewn with broken bodies, shattered hopes and empires built on worthless bits of paper.

The country plunged into despair, tunneling downward toward the Great Depression. Millions of Americans found themselves out of work, standing in line for jobs, for food and for clothing. Banks failed. Factories closed. Insurance companies collapsed. Business deals were canceled, respected partnerships crumbled and noble cartels disintegrated. Young dreams faltered. Older ones simply gave up and died.

In Boston, October 29 would be remembered as the final day of the spectacular trial of *Paget-Browne* v. *Paget-Browne*.

In Addison's name, Elinor had launched a suit against her late husband's estate in an attempt to break the terms of his will. Her son had been excluded from that will, and Elinor was determined to prove that Addison, and not Collier, was the rightful heir to the Paget-Browne fortune, conservatively estimated to be one hundred million dollars.

Nearly two years had elapsed since Elinor had sat in Avery Leggett's office, ignoring the view of Boston Harbor in favor of glaring at the man who had been her husband's closest friend. At sixty-three, Avery Leggett resembled a clean-shaven Santa Claus, with a remarkably unlined, ruddy face, a thatch of snow white hair and bushy white eyebrows. But in spite of his grandfatherly appearance, he could just as easily have been the devil incarnate or the messenger in some Greek drama who is murdered for being the bearer of bad news.

"There's been some ghastly mistake!" Elinor's outraged howls were like those of an animal gored in a trap.

Avery had lied to her. Either that or his eyesight had finally failed. He might even have missed a complete page.

"It's not possible! It simply isn't possible!" She hoped her husband was roasting in hell.

She flung her black velvet hat with its heavy black veiling onto the chair beside her. Baring her teeth, she balled her hands into fists and readied herself for a fight.

"How dare he do this to me! How dare he deny his own son! He's given her everything and left us with nothing."

"For God's sake, Elinor," Leggett pleaded with her, "please try to calm down."

"Calm down!" she shouted at him. "How am I supposed to stay calm when my husband has betrayed me and left me penniless?"

"My dear Elinor, I would hardly call you penniless." Leggett glanced down at the document he was holding, searching for the appropriate page. "In case you've already forgotten, Collier left you a one million dollar trust, the interest of which is payable to you for as long as you live. He also left you the house on Commonwealth Avenue, the summer cottage in Nahant, and a separate allowance to pay the staff's salaries in both houses. He willed you his entire fleet of antique cars and his two private airplanes. And finally, his estate is to pay off any and all of your outstanding debts which were owing at the time of his death."

"But I have a son! He's left nothing to his son."

"If you would care to examine the date on this document, my dear," Leggett said as he leaned across the desk, "you'll see for yourself that it reads July 27, 1920. You had no son then, Elinor, only a daughter."

She angrily slapped the papers out of his hand. "You'll never convince me that this was his final will. You've all conspired to cheat my son out of his rightful inheritance, and I won't let you get away with it."

Avery Leggett's gray eyes widened in surprise. "Are you accusing me of fraud, Elinor?"

"Such a harsh word, Avery," she clucked sarcastically. "I much prefer *complicity.*"

His fist came down hard on the desk. "Damn it, Elinor, I swear to you that this was and is the only existing will of Collier Paget-Browne!"

Elinor remained unmoved and unconvinced. Her husband had cheated her son. He had cheated her. It was finished between them now. The time for hallowing his almighty name was past. What he had escaped during his lifetime, he would suffer now in death: the humiliation of his name.

"There's no point in continuing this discussion, Avery," she told him then, her voice cold and flat. "As far as I'm concerned, there's only one option left to me, and I fully intend to use it."

"And what might that be?" he demanded.

"I'm going to break the will."

"But there's no earthly reason for such a move," he blustered, half rising from his chair. "This will is a legal document, drawn up according to Collier's wishes, duly signed and sealed in the presence of two witnesses and registered with the courts. You have no grounds whatsoever for contesting and without adequate grounds, no respectable lawyer would even consider such a case."

Elinor faced him calmly, a sly smile on her face. "Then I won't hire a respectable lawyer."

True to her word, Elinor had proceeded directly to the bottom of the legal barrel and scraped up an attorney by the name of Wendel Percy. He was a man who thrived on scandal, fed off the misfortunes of others and lived solely for the pleasure of performing inside a crowded courtroom. His legal confreres despised him. They deplored his lack of ethics, his refusal to ever settle out of court and the histrionics which marked each of his trials. They had even sought and failed on numerous occasions to have him disbarred.

The legal world may have abhorred him, but the public supported him. They loved a good show, and for twenty-seven years Wendel Percy had been playing to please his public. Even the newspapers were indebted to him. Wherever Wendel Percy appeared, scandal followed, and scandal sold papers. Most of his trials made the front page.

In accepting Elinor's case, Wendel Percy knew he was about to take over the front pages once more.

It was the final day of the trial. Avery Leggett had rested the defense's case that morning, but Percy had been granted permission to reopen the prosecution due to the sudden appearance of his only uncalled witness. If there had been any doubt as to his supremacy in matters most foul, this trial would settle the issue once and for all. The fee itself had already made it more than worth his while, but with the help of his final witness, he was about to shake the city of Boston to its very proper core.

He stroked his precisely waxed red moustache. Under the

pretext of shuffling the notes laid out in front of him, he glanced past the invisible boundary separating defense and prosecution into civilized adversaries, for another glimpse of the nine-year-old girl who was his client's avowed enemy.

As always, Percy's breath caught in an audible wheeze. He felt that if he stood next to her, he would be mortally stung by the emanations which formed an eerily visible aura around her. She had a dignity and a kind of beauty which would have been unsettling even in a woman, but the combination was much more powerful because she was still a child. To him, Collier Paget-Browne II was the avenging Artemis or worse, the sorceress Circe, who had it in her power to change him from a man into the swine he was.

Collier clasped her hands together and watched as the knuckles whitened. Her heart was thumping in an awkward rhythm, but she forced herself to sit perfectly still, with her chin thrust out, her legs crossed at the ankles and her back arrow-straight. Her whole body was aching from having held the rigid pose for so long, but she had no other choice. From the outset of the trial, she had been determined to prove how brave and grownup she was. The patricians of Boston would never laugh at her again.

Collier blinked her eyes, forcing back a sudden rush of tears. Had her father loved her too much? Would he have loved Addison more than her if he had lived? And Elinor—had he ever loved her mother at all? She blinked again. She should have paid more attention to the conversations between her father and men like Uncle Avery. She should have shown a greater interest in his factories. How was she supposed to take control of his empire when she wasn't quite sure what an empire was?

She stole a hasty glance at Avery Leggett. She knew that even he had warned her father: Empires were for men to run, not women. And she wasn't even a woman yet. Collier straightened her shoulders and pulled herself even taller in her chair. It was no use. Sitting up straight wouldn't make her into a woman.

She couldn't disappoint her father. Hadn't he proved he trusted her by leaving everything in her care? She began to feel a bit better. He had given her his name, hadn't he? She found herself smiling. She was so proud of that name now. She had even stopped playing her secret game. She didn't want to be called Mary plain-old-Browne anymore.

She thought of Addison again. Although he too carried his father's name, the poor little boy had gotten nothing from him but his black hair. Everything else had come from Elinor. All those bits of her mother which Collier had looked for in herself were there in Addison. Like Elinor, he was small and pretty, with the same heart-shaped face, frosty blue eyes, snub nose and pointed chin. And whenever he cried or whined or just needed to be loved, Elinor would open her arms for him.

The loud rapping of the gavel snapped Collier to attention. Judge Patrick Landon MacMillan was back on the bench, calling the court into session. Collier drew a deep breath and braced herself.

Wendel Percy got up from his seat, leaving Collier with a clear view of her mother's arrogant profile. Contempt coagulated deep in Collier's chest. She swallowed hard, then she coughed. Elinor turned her head, and for one brief, ghastly moment, their eyes locked.

Her indigo eyes darkening, Collier proudly stared her mother down. Elinor would never win. She would never succeed in destroying what two generations of Paget-Brownes had built. Collier would not permit it. She had not been born a Paget-Browne to lose everything now.

Collier heard a sudden intake of breath, the urgent whisperings from the spectators behind her. Then she saw what the others had seen first. An elegant young woman with blond hair and the slow, pronounced walk of the very pregnant was moving toward the witness stand. She glided past Collier in a blur of mauve silk and a flash of amethysts and pearls, leaving a hint of lily-of-the-valley behind her.

Once again Collier's eyes met Elinor's. But this time there was triumph emblazoned across the glacial surface of Elinor's face. Collier felt the first stirrings of panic. She was in danger. And all because of this beautiful woman who could have been her mother's twin.

"My name is Diana West Taggert," the woman was saying in a softly modulated voice, a voice so tentative that Collier had to lean forward in her seat to hear her.

"And you're the wife of Lloyd Taggert, the financier?"

"Yes."

"And you live where, Mrs. Taggert?"

"In Philadelphia."

"Did you come here today of your own free will?"

"I'm not certain that I understand—"

"Did you come into court willingly, Mrs. Taggert?"

She was beginning to feel dizzy. "I . . . no, I don't really know why I'm here at all—"

"Your Honor, let the record show that Mrs. Taggert has been declared and admitted here today as a hostile witness."

The judge made a notation on the papers in front of him. "Duly recorded, counselor."

Wendel Percy glanced over at Collier, hoping to catch her off guard. Her returning gaze never wavered. Percy smiled. He would break her yet. He turned back to the woman fidgeting on the stand.

"Would you tell the court your real name, please?"

Diana Taggert opened her mouth and then quickly closed it. She was getting one of her headaches again. She shifted in her seat as Percy repeated his question. The pain in her head was growing stronger.

"I've already told you my name. It's Diana—"

"Do you know what the penalty is for perjury, Mrs. Taggert?"

She shook her head. The pounding worsened.

"Jail!"

The baby kicked and Diana pressed her hands against her swollen belly. Would her baby be born in prison? She needed another pill. She fumbled with the catch on her purse and then gave up, clasping her hands tightly together in her lap. The man with the stiffly waxed moustache was weaving in and out of focus now. She blinked her eyes and tried to concentrate on what he was saying to her.

"Isn't your real name Dinah Wicks?"

She swallowed hard and found that her throat was dry. She moistened her lips with the tip of her tongue and swallowed again. She needed Lloyd. Why hadn't he come with her? She was getting confused again. She began taking deep breaths to steady herself. She mustn't forget who she was.

"Will the witness please answer counsel's question."

Now even the judge was speaking to her.

"I . . . what was the question?" She had never told anyone the truth, not even Lloyd. Whatever she had done before moving to New York so many years before had nothing to do with her life now.

"Did you know the late Collier Paget-Browne?"

She took a deep breath. "No."

"She's lying!" Elinor was out of her chair.

"Mrs. Paget-Browne, would you please sit down!" Judge MacMillan ordered with an angry bang of his gavel.

"She's lying!" Elinor insisted. "Make her tell you the truth!"

"Mr. Percy, I must ask you to control your client or I'll order her removed from this courtroom."

Elinor sat down again and glared over at Collier. The girl flinched. Fear had doubled itself into a fist that was jabbing away at her stomach. She was afraid that she was going to be sick.

"Mrs. Taggert, did you ever engage in sexual relations with the late Collier Paget-Browne?"

"Objection!"

"Overruled."

There were gasps and shouts of indignation from the crowded courtroom.

Percy and Elinor exchanged smiles.

Collier folded her arms across her chest and began to rock back and forth, moaning softly to herself.

Diana finally managed to open her purse. She slid a white tablet into her mouth. The baby kicked. Lloyd would never forgive her for going to prison. Even when she had shown him the subpoena, she still hadn't told him the truth. She tried to focus on the angry man pacing up and down in front of her, but she was seeing him through a darkening fog.

"Mrs. Taggert, did Collier Paget-Browne pay you the sum of ten thousand dollars to bear him a child?"

The courtroom erupted in shocked protest.

Avery Leggett was on his feet, shouting.

Collier's dress was plastered to her body. Her sweater was too tight. She was smothering. She tried to pull it off.

Diana was losing control. She was going to break down again. Leland! Who would take care of her beloved five-year-old son?

Above the pandemonium, Wendel Percy continued his questioning. "Do you know that your daughter is present in this courtroom today?"

"I don't have a daughter."

"Yes, you do. She's sitting less than thirty feet away from you right now."

Collier gasped as tiny charges of agony exploded inside her brain.

"I have a son." Diana Taggert was sobbing now. "His name

is Lloyd. I mean Leland." She began to giggle. How could
Lloyd be Leland? Where was her son? She needed to see her
son.

"I fail to see the humor in my questions, Mrs. Taggert,"
Percy barked at her.

Collier was suffocating. She opened the top button on her
dress. She still couldn't breathe. Avery passed her a glass of
water, but she pushed it away. How could she swallow any
water when she couldn't even catch her breath?

"Your Honor, I would like to enter into evidence this Agreement of Intent, signed by the late Collier Paget-Browne and
Dinah Wicks on September 24, 1919. Its terms are self-evident,
and if you compare Dinah Wicks's signature on the document
with the signature of Diana Taggert on these cancelled checks,
you'll find them to be identical."

A searing pain knifed through her. They were killing her.
They were killing her baby. She had to save her baby. She
opened her mouth to tell them what they wanted to know, but
all that came out was a muffled groan of pain.

"Mrs. Taggert, did you not enter the Marie Chisholm Home
in Juniper, New Hampshire on January 15, 1920? And did you
not give birth there to a girl on June 7 of that same year?"
Percy was relentless.

Collier gripped the edges of her chair to keep from running
out of the courtroom.

Diana tried once again to force out the words which would
release her and save her baby.

"Mrs. Taggert, I have several witnesses who are prepared
to swear that you were a patient at the Marie Chisholm Home
and that you were registered there under the name of Elinor
Browne. Only three people knew about this little charade—
you and the Paget-Brownes. And because it was presumed that
the real Elinor could not conceive, she was to pass off your
child as hers, while you took their money and agreed to disappear from their lives. Isn't this true, Mrs. Taggert?"

Collier began to cry. Her life had been a lie and everyone
had worked to keep the lie alive. From her pain, she knew that
she was dying, and if she died, the lie would end. It no longer
mattered if they saw her cry. The woman in Collier withered
and the child slumped forward in defeat.

Then something stirred inside her. Suddenly, Collier wanted
to scream. She wanted to hear the sound of her voice just to
prove to herself that she was still alive. She wanted to live.

She wanted to tell them that she understood about the lie and that no one would ever lie to her again. Her poor father. He must have been such a desperate man. And Elinor—she was nothing but a stranger after all.

Angry now, she wiped away her tears and looked up at the sobbing woman on the witness stand. Was she supposed to call this newest stranger "Mother" now?

"I'm sorry, Mrs. Taggert, but I can't hear you," Wendel Percy was saying. "Could you speak up, please?"

"Yes," Diana Taggert repeated. Was she shouting? She was convinced that she had only whispered it. Had they even heard her? "Yes, yes, yes. Everything you said is true."

There. It was out. Now they would leave her alone.

"I have no further questions of this witness, Your Honor. The prosecution rests."

Diana tried to stand up, using the arms of the chair for leverage. She was too weak. She gave up and simply slid out of the chair onto the floor. The pain was all around her now, pirouetting on spindly red legs in and out of her belly. Someone was leaning over her, trying to grab hold of her arms. She struck him with her purse.

Collier was out of her chair and running. Avery Leggett called her name, but all she could hear were the screams of the woman slumped on the floor. A bailiff was trying to hold her now. Collier shoved him out of the way, got down on her knees and pulled Diana into her arms. "Don't cry," she whispered. "They won't hurt you anymore. Please don't cry. I promise they'll never hurt you again."

Lights burst in brilliant crystalline flashes all around them. Collier blinked and tried to shield Diana's eyes with her hand. The photographers edged closer, circling them as jackals circle their prey. Collier looked at Diana, and for one brief moment, she saw in her face what she had never once seen in Elinor's. She saw love.

"My baby." It came out as a strangled sob. Through a graying mist, Diana peered up and saw a face. His face. So it was true. This was her child, *their* child. She held out her arms to Collier and raised herself so that she could kiss the girl's face.

Diana shuddered. A sticky wetness seeped slowly out from between her legs. She closed her eyes. As she held onto her daughter, she released her hold on her son.

• • •

The trial was over. Judge Patrick Landon MacMillan found in favor of the defense and ordered that the will stand as written. Despite the questionable circumstances surrounding her birth, Collier Paget-Browne II was still her father's designated heir and, as such, was legally entitled to his estate.

Mortified, Wendel Percy closed his office for a month and sailed to Europe to recover from his defeat and the loss of much of his own notoriety.

When Diana West Taggert recovered from the ordeal of a still-birth she returned to Philadelphia to enter a private sanatorium. Lloyd Taggert immediately instituted divorce proceedings against his wife, demanding sole custody of their son Leland.

Elinor barricaded herself inside the great stone house on Commonwealth Avenue. With the curtains drawn to protect her from the reporters and photographers who were laying seige to the place, she continued to plot her revenge.

She had gambled and lost, but she would never give in. If her husband only knew how she blessed him now for dying. His death had freed her. It had released her from the vile secret which had been her nemesis for nine years. Oh, the self-righteous Brahmins were snickering now, but they would forget soon enough. They would welcome her back. She was no longer Elinor, loving wife of that dashing Paget-Browne, widow of one of Boston's uncrowned nobility. She was Elinor, betrayed wife and martyred widow of an adulterer and a cad.

"You'll be my weapon now, my little darling," she would croon to her son as she prepared him for bed each evening. Her words became the lullaby which put him to sleep each night. "I'm going to teach you how to love a sister who steals her own brother's birthright from him. And some day, when you're old enough, you'll know how to love her all by yourself."

The pale blue eyes regarding her so solemnly would widen, and his small mouth would stretch into a grin.

"You do understand me, don't you, Addison?" Elinor would smile back at him and trace the shape of his face with the tips of her fingers. "Sleep well, my prince, and grow up big and strong. There's a kingdom here that belongs to you, just waiting for you to come and claim it."

It was now time to finally do something about Collier.

• • •

On a bleak November afternoon, Collier was summoned to her mother's sitting room. It was with a mixture of curiosity and dread that she paused outside the door and waited for her heart to stop beating so wildly. What could the woman possibly want? Neither of them had spoken since the trial. Collier was frightened. Something was going to happen to her and she didn't know how to prepare for it. She drew herself up straight, squared her shoulders and finally made herself open the door.

Elinor was sitting on a sofa in front of the fireplace, her hands folded in her lap, her face a frozen mask.

"Sit!" she commanded, pointing to a small silk slipper chair.

Startled, Collier quickly obeyed.

Elinor wet her lips. "I've decided to send you to live with your godmother Alice Sample in Newport. We'll all be better off with this arrangement and Alice has already agreed to it."

Collier leaped up from her chair, knocking it over onto its side. "But I don't want to live with Cousin Alice," she cried. She was sounding like a child. She caught herself in time and when she spoke again, her voice was tightly controlled. "I don't want to live in Newport. I want to stay in Boston. This is still my home and I don't intend to be thrown out of it."

Elinor felt the hackles rise on the back of her neck. "This is not your home. It's mine. It's one of the few things your father saw fit to leave me," she said with a disdainful sniff. "And since this is my home, I can decide who lives here and who does not."

Collier studied the pale little woman surrounded by her pale, watered-silk furniture and felt only revulsion at her weak display of strength. "This is my father's house," she told her, as her pride stirred and chased away the fear. "This house belongs to the Paget-Brownes."

"It's mine!" Elinor shouted.

"Then I'll ask Uncle Avery to buy the house from you," Collier replied calmly. "I'm sure you'd much prefer to have the money anyway."

Elinor started. There was too much of him in his child. That same arrogance. That same infuriating self-assurance. That stubborn pride. None of it diminished by the events of the past months. She got up from the sofa and her face was flushed with her mounting anger.

"Let me warn you, little girl, our battle has just begun. I intend to see you broken before I'm through with you."

"Broken?" Collier repeated, her eyes smoldering now with a dark flame. "You'll never break me. Nothing you do will ever hurt me again."

The cords were standing out in Elinor's neck. "Your father used me and humiliated me. The fool! He couldn't wait. I gave him the son he wanted, didn't I?" She stopped long enough to catch her breath and then she went on. "I'm going to destroy your father, Collier. I'm going to destroy him through you. And then I'll give my son back what you've stolen from him."

"Never!" Collier retorted. "You'll never destroy us. I won't let you. You'll never slander our name again."

"You're only a child," Elinor snarled at her, "and your threats are those of a child. I have nothing whatever to fear from you."

"And I have less to fear from you." Collier was suddenly amused by Elinor's rage. The woman was throwing a tantrum. The more agitated she became, the calmer it made Collier. How easy it was to maintain control while others lost theirs. Her father had taught her well and that made her smile.

Elinor snapped. With a furious howl, she hurried over to her writing desk, unlocked the middle drawer and drew out a bulging brown envelope. She thrust it into Collier's hands.

"Be grateful that you *are* just a child, my dear Collier, for childhood is probably all you'll ever have."

Collier stared down at the envelope she was holding and her resolve wavered slightly.

"It took nearly a year to track down your mother," Elinor continued, her voice heavy with contempt. "Perhaps you'd like to find out more about her. Despite the expensive finishing school, the elegant name she chose for herself and her society marriage, she's still just a shopgirl from nowhere."

Collier began to tremble.

"You saw your mother," Elinor said, a sly smile on her face. "Well, my dear, what you saw in her, you'll see in yourself one day."

Collier's throat tightened. She was shivering uncontrollably now. The memory of that wretched woman in the courtroom ran through her mind like the reel of a motion picture. The doctors had forbidden Collier to visit her mother, warning her that Diana wouldn't even recognize her. She wondered if she would ever see her real mother again. Now her mouth was dry and her hands were shaking. What was going to happen to her?

What was Elinor threatening her with?

Terrified, she backed away from Elinor, inching toward the door. Elinor went after her and pinned her up against the wall.

"As I said before, Collier, I have nothing to fear from you. I promised you that I would see you broken and I shall. Nature will do it for me. And once you've been dashed to pieces, Addison and I will be there to collect what is rightfully ours." She smacked the envelope Collier was still holding. "Look at the reports of the detective I hired. Read the medical records from the Magnolia County Hospital in Weldon, Arkansas. Find out about the sickness of the women in your mother's family. It's had many names, Collier. It's been called dementia praecox and melancholia, and now it's being called schizophrenia. But its meaning has never changed. It still means madness!"

Collier dropped the envelope. She leaned back against the wall to keep from falling down. A sudden rush of black noise roared through her ears.

"Your father certainly chose poorly when he used Dinah Wicks to carry his precious seed," Elinor sneered. "She brought a blight with her which you will eventually inherit."

"NO!" The scream spiraled upward from the depths of Collier's soul, rupturing the air around her and sending Elinor reeling backward.

Collier's cries echoed through the house as she ran down the hallway to her bedroom. She bolted the door behind her. Then she flung open the doors of her clothes closet and shut herself inside.

She pulled her father's navy blue blazer off its hanger and slipped it on over her dress. She took one of his favorite cigars out of the breast pocket and tucked it into the corner of her mouth. Then she sat down on the floor in the dark, drew her knees up to her chest and rested her head on her arms.

Breathing deeply, she inhaled the scent of him which still lived in the wool fibers of his jacket and in the sweet harshness of his unsmoked cigars. The pain swelled up, filling her entire body, until Collier knew it would be impossible to contain it all.

"I am not mad. . . . I am not mad. . . . I am not mad. . . ." She kept repeating the words over and over again. Elinor would never see her mad. Elinor would never win. *Never. Never. Never.*

Collier rocked back and forth, back and forth, repeating the words out loud. She burrowed deeper inside her father's jacket as she rocked. The jagged edges of her fear began to blur and the sharpness of her pain diminished as she continued her familiar healing ritual. Only this secret ceremony ever brought her the kind of peace she needed. In the dark, close to her father, she could be safe for a while.

Suddenly, she stopped. She pulled the cigar from her mouth. What a fool she was! She began to laugh, an empty, high-pitched laugh of sheer terror.

Her ritual itself was nothing short of madness!

Collier sat shivering in the backseat of the unfamiliar Cord and tucked the plaid wool lap blanket around her knees. Graham, Cousin Alice's elderly chauffeur, started the car. As they drew away from the curb, Collier refused to turn and look back at her home. She concentrated on the wiry gray hair curling below the brim of Graham's cap and pretended that she didn't care. She knew that Elinor would be watching from the window in Addison's nursery. To defy them, Collier threw back her shoulders, proudly set her jaw and continued to stare straight ahead.

It had been snowing all morning, that first wet December snow which soaks the ground and collects in slushy puddles near the curb. The snowflakes frosted the windows until Collier felt herself being sealed off from the world, locked away inside a moving tomb.

She twisted around in her seat and cleared a patch in the rear window with one of her mittens. She couldn't help herself. She had to see her home one more time.

Milo

1938 – 1945

Chapter Four

"Neville Chamberlain is weak. He's preaching appeasement."

"The devil he is!"

"Don't take my word for it. Your own newspapers are saying exactly the same thing."

"My papers are as bad as the whole damned lot of them, bickering about which would be costlier, peace or war."

"You might not be taking this very seriously, Sir Gilbert, but I am. Germany's a real threat to us now." The girl who was speaking flicked the ash from her cigar into the palm of her hand. "Even the Red Cross agrees with me. They've just begun classes in the proper handling of gas masks."

"Bloody alarmists!"

She was beginning to get annoyed. "Are there any ashtrays around?" she asked him in an effort to defuse the situation.

With the head of his cane, he indicated a round metal cylinder just behind her.

"Filthy things," he muttered, watching her stoop to put out the cigar. The girl's a ruddy giant, he thought, just as her father was. But she's a looker, all right. "Disgusting habit," he mumbled. Barely pardonable in a man, but completely inexcusable in a woman.

"Did Alice approve of your smoking those bloody things?" he asked.

Collier had to laugh. "Poor Cousin Alice. Even if she didn't approve, she never showed it. I was a Paget-Browne and that made everything I did not only acceptable, but expected."

"You're your father's child, all right," Sir Gilbert Hall grumbled, trying to keep a straight face. What a marvelously willful young creature she was. He cleared his throat and steered the conversation back to the talk of war. "It's really rather nervy of you, my dear Collier, preaching to us British about appeasement when you're tucked safely away on the far side of the pond. You damned Yanks never did know your place and it's obvious that you still don't."

"Hitler's going to provoke a war, Sir Gilbert, whether you're willing to admit it or not. And then even we damned Yanks won't be safe anymore."

"Hitler!" Sir Gilbert scoffed. "The man's mind isn't equal to the size of his mouth. He's all bluster and no balls, my girl. We've little to fear from him, I can promise you that. Now let's forget this beastly war business, shall we, and have another go round of this exhibition."

Collier stifled a yawn. Although it was the annual exhibit of London's Royal Academy, she found the whole thing boring. Too many paintings of the Coronation. The critics had been right: Most of the works didn't even look royal.

"Why don't we go over to the Leicester Galleries instead?" she bent to whisper in Sir Gilbert's ear. "Wyndham Lewis's portrait of T. S. Eliot has just been hung there and it's supposed to be wonderful."

"Wonderful?" Sir Gilbert's eyes were round. "If it's so bloody wonderful, why was it rejected by the Royal Academy? This Lewis fellow obviously knows nothing about art. Even the letters to the *Times* ridiculed it. Modern art, indeed."

"Do you really believe that calling something modern is a good enough reason to make fun of it?"

She was losing her temper. Gazing down at the man who had promised her godmother Alice not to let her fall into the hands of Jack the Ripper while she was in England, Collier felt instantly contrite. Sir Gilbert Hall was seventy years old. His opinions were two generations behind hers. Impulsively she took him by the arm and led him over to a group of watercolors.

"Now these are good," she said, searching in her catalog for the name of the artist.

"Too derivative," sniffed Sir Gilbert. "I'm suprised they've been hung here at all."

Collier circled the name of Milo Racine on page twenty-one of her catalog and then moved on to an oil painting of an elderly flower vendor seated on a step in Piccadilly.

She immediately thought of Alice. The old woman had been devastated by Collier's decision to go to Europe. They had fought right up to the afternoon that Collier sailed. . . .

"But you can't just pick up and run off, child," Alice admonished her. "You'll be missing your graduation if you do."

"Then the school will just have to mail the diploma to me."

"And what about your birthday this year? I'd planned on a lovely lawn party and I thought we could hire one of those bands you enjoy so much."

"We'll celebrate before I sail. Just the two of us, as always."

"But your coming-out party. There are still so many details to be worked out."

"I don't want any parties at all. There may be a war in Europe soon and I want to see as much of the Continent as I can before that happens."

"But if you leave now, how do you expect to be properly introduced into society? How will you ever find friends among the best families if you insist on breaking all the rules?"

"I don't give a damn about rules. When were any of these so-called best families ever interested in me? What rules were they following when they never replied to the invitations you sent out over the years? Didn't it matter to you that we had to spend all my birthdays alone, giving the staff the afternoon off so they wouldn't find out and gossip about it? Do you still think we fooled anyone? And when did the children of these *best* families ever include me in any of their games at school or choose me to be on any of their teams or ever once try to cheat from my exams? They all cut me out of their world when I was nine years old. If they're that interested in me now, let them come to me. . . ."

"Collier, my girl, you're dreaming."

"I'm sorry, Sir Gilbert, what were you saying?"

"I was simply asking how it feels to be eighteen and one of the richest young women in America?"

"I'll let you know that at one minute past midnight tonight."

"So I'm still to be your escort for this rowdy bash you've planned for yourself?"

"I don't think I'd be able to find anyone I like as much on such short notice, do you?"

"Now there's a bit of left-handed flattery if I've ever heard it," he chuckled. "But why the dickens did you have to choose some bloody old restaurant in Soho? It's hardly suitable for the occasion, my girl. Think of the riffraff mucking about down there."

"I suppose you'd prefer Buckingham Palace where I'd have my pick of every eligible but bankrupt prince, baron and earl."

"Well, they'd be a damn sight more respectable than a gaggle of unwashed bohemians."

"Come on, Sir Gilbert, where's your spirit of adventure? How can you call yourself an old friend of the Paget-Brownes with such a stuffy attitude about everything?"

He tried to look stern but his eyes were twinkling. "Friendship had absolutely nothing to do with it. Your father and I were merely mild competitors over the years, nothing more. Lucky for both of us, he stuck to his nuts and bolts and kept his hands off my newspapers."

"Maybe you won't be as lucky with me," she teased him.

"So you're already planning a takeover of the Hall chain, are you? I think I'd do well to keep an eye on you, my dear Collier."

"I don't think you have anything to worry about, Sir Gilbert. I'm not really interested in the business of building empires." She tucked her arm through his as they left Burlington House to wait for his car to be brought round. "To me, business is nothing more than shuffling stacks of paper from one side of a desk to the other. Shift one pile and a company changes hands. Shift another pile and the executives change places. I'm afraid I'm going to be a terrible disappointment to my father after all because I think I'm going to follow Uncle Avery's advice. I'm going to leave things just as they are and let father's hand-picked men continue to run Paget-Browne Enterprises. I have other plans for myself."

"And just how do you intend to leave your mark on the world, then?"

Her indigo eyes lightened mischievously. "I don't intend to even touch this world. I plan to build myself a new one."

Collier had been a half hour late and Sir Gilbert was properly put out. Now even the Bentley seemed to be conspiring against him as the driver cautiously navigated through the unfamiliar streets of Soho.

"It was damned cheeky of you to sneak away like that this afternoon," Sir Gilbert said, his voice taut with annoyance.

Collier continued to stare out the car window.

"Here you were supposed to be resting up for this evening and off you go to some obscure little gallery to see the works of a group of bloody anarchists."

"They're not anarchists, Sir Gilbert. They've just decided

to break away from tradition. Monet did it. Picasso's doing it. You wouldn't call *them* anarchists, would you? Well, these men aren't either. Their work is exciting and downright refreshing."

"Refreshing, my foot!"

She turned to face him and her cheeks were flushed with her rising anger. "You don't know the first thing about it! I always thought you believed in progress. If advances are being made in science and medicine, why can't they be made in the arts as well? The paintings I saw this afternoon at the Raleigh Gallery are unlike anything I've ever seen before. They burn with a kind of life-force which is almost palpable. We're going to see a very exciting movement grow out of these works, Sir Gilbert, I can sense it."

"Balderdash! I've seen some of these new artists' works. They confuse me and give me a bloody headache. Art is supposed to hallow nature, not make a mockery of it. These paintings look like nothing more than some blasted fool's effort to wipe off his brushes on canvas instead of on a rag. They're outrages! Nothing but an affront to good taste and decency. And I hope to Heaven that you're not going to consider buying any of them and hanging them in my home."

"As a matter of fact, I bought three of the paintings I saw this afternoon. But I won't hang them in your place, Sir Gilbert." She reached over and patted his hand. "I'll wait until I find a home of my own."

He looked as if he were about to say something, so she quickly headed him off.

"Let's forget about art and concentrate on celebrating, okay? After all, it isn't every night that a girl turns eighteen and gets her hands on a ten million dollar trust."

"Just don't go spending it all on useless art," he muttered, determined to have the final say in the matter.

The car finally pulled to a stop outside the Restaurant de Paris on Dean Street. As soon as Collier stepped onto the curb, the glare of flashbulbs lit up the night. She gave the photographers her widest smile and obliged the reporters by slowly turning around in front of them so that they could scribble down the details of the antique lace gown she was wearing.

"Why are you still wearing your hair in the Gibson Girl style, Miss Paget-Browne?" asked one of the women reporters. "Why not the shingle or the bob?"

"I obviously prefer it the way it is. Why should I let someone else tell me how to wear my hair? They'll only change their minds again next year."

"Are you at all handicapped by your height? Do you find men intimidated by it?"

"If any man is frightened off by my height, he's not worth meeting in the first place."

"Why don't you ever wear any jewelry?"

"And have someone try to steal it? Why bother?" The only piece of jewelry she ever wore was her father's gold pocket watch on a heavy gold chain around her neck.

"Shall we go in, my dear?" Sir Gilbert asked, taking hold of Collier's arm. "Bloody boors," he mumbled to her. "Even if I did recognize several chaps from one of my own bloody rags."

Collier had rented the entire restaurant for the evening and the guests were an eclectic mixture of Sir Gilbert's friends, the people Collier herself had met in her three weeks in London, and the friends both groups had invited. The evening reminded her of one long game of musical chairs, as the guests moved from table to table, keeping their plates and glasses full. This was the first party she had ever thrown for herself, and like everyone else who was preoccupied with the talk of war, Collier pretended that she had nothing on her mind but having a good time. She circulated among her guests, playing the part of the gracious hostess, picking up on fragments of each group's conversations.

"Thank goodness for pieces of fluff like Raymond Massey's *Idiot's Delight* at the Apollo."

"Not to mention *Amphitryon 38* with the Lunts at the Lyric."

"Didn't catch that one yet."

"Oh, do. It gives us all a chance to laugh about the gloomy prospect of war."

"What did you make of Noel Coward's *Operette* at Her Majesty's?"

"The reviews were simply poisonous."

"Did you catch Augustus John's exhibit at the Tooth Gallery?"

"Did I. My advice is to let sleeping bohemians lie. His landscapes were simply dreadful."

"I must say I adored Pavel Tchelitchev's *Phenomena*. I hear it took him three years to paint it."

"The *Observer* loved it."

"Well, the *Sunday Times* hated it."

"Do you always believe what the papers say?"

Collier turned around. The man was obviously speaking to her and she hadn't even been aware of him standing there.

"I beg your pardon?"

"For what?"

His speckled brown eyes were boring into her.

"I didn't hear what you said to me."

"You must have heard something. Why else would you have turned around?"

He was laughing at her. Even his nostrils had an arrogant flare to them. She squared her shoulders and tried to stare him down.

"You act as if you don't even know who I am," he said.

"Should I know you?"

"I'm at your party, aren't I?"

"That doesn't mean anything. I hardly know anyone here."

"Collier!" Sir Gilbert was gesturing to her.

"In a minute," she called back to him. She was intrigued by the brash young man who was talking to her.

"Well, Lady Bountiful, since you're obviously baffled, I'd better introduce myself."

"Collier, some of my friends have asked to meet you." Sir Gilbert reached Collier's side just as the young man was sweeping her a deep bow, the fringes of the long, peacock blue scarf he was wearing around his neck brushing the floor.

"My name's Milo Racine," he announced grandly. "Thanks to you, my rent's now paid up for the next few months, not to mention all the back rent I owed."

"Is this the chap whose paintings you bought this afternoon?" Sir Gilbert looked as if he were about to suffer a stroke.

"Apparently it is," Collier answered airily. "But if I'd realized it sooner, I might have changed my mind."

"Can the grateful artist at least shake the hand of his patron?" Milo Racine interrupted their exchange.

"Now really," blustered Sir Gilbert as Collier cooly extended her right hand.

Instead of shaking her hand, Milo Racine pressed her open palm to his lips. Collier immediately pulled away. His touch was unsettling. Too personal. Too familiar. She was suddenly flustered, suddenly unsure of herself. She was grateful to Sir Gilbert for hastily leading her off to meet his friends.

She tried to remember their names as she was introduced to them, but all she could think about was Milo Racine. He had her at a disadvantage. She knew very little about the games played between a man and a woman. No mother had ever warned her about them. No girlfriends had ever teased her about them. All she knew was what her instincts were telling her.

They were telling her to run. To run as fast and as far as she could from the impudent young man whose bold stare made her heart race, whose angry paintings fascinated her, and whose touch had left a permanent scar on her skin.

"I really am grateful to you, you know," murmured the deep voice close to her ear.

Collier jumped. Milo Racine was standing behind her again, grinning at her. He really was a sight. Dressed in a wine colored velvet smoking jacket, baggy black trousers and rubber-soled canvas shoes, with the ridiculously long scarf wound around his neck, he had completed the picture by letting an empty cigarette holder dangle from the corner of his mouth.

She noticed that the backs of his hands were covered with coarse black hair. His hands looked strong, almost cruel, and she found herself wondering if hands like his knew anything about being tender.

"Why are you wearing a smoking jacket to a formal dinner party?" she finally managed to ask him.

"This may be just a smoking jacket to you, but it's formal dressing to me."

"Then why aren't you wearing a shirt under it?"

"Because it would get in the way of my scarf."

She let out a sigh of exasperation. "I think you're just trying to shock people with your idea of how a bohemian should dress."

"I dress the same way I paint, concentrating on texture and contrast. By wearing a silk scarf which is cool, a velvet jacket which is warm and wool pants which are scratchy, I'm aware of each fabric touching my skin. Each texture registers its own sensation, and I never take any of the feelings for granted that way."

His voice was beginning to affect Collier in a strange way. She felt as if someone were running a feather up and down her spine. She shuddered. There was a peculiar tingling between her legs, reminding her of those times when she woke up from a dream, throbbing with a sense of incompleteness, waiting for something unknown to be fulfilled.

She cleared her throat to ease the tightness in it. "Why were your paintings at the Raleigh Gallery so different from those exhibited at the Royal Academy?" she asked. "Your watercolors at the Academy had such a delicate quality to them, while the oils were painted in such vivid splashes of color that they seemed almost defiant."

"Let's just say I paint for the places that exhibit me and for the people who pay me to give them what they want. The Royal Academy will get my best impression of a Constable or a Turner, some snotty aristocrat will be happy with a portrait of himself resembling a Gainsborough, and a middle-class merchant will expect a Reubens rendition of his fat wife and fat children. Whatever I make doing that kind of work buys the oils and the canvases for places like the Raleigh Gallery. But they don't sell and I don't want to starve for the sake of my art. It isn't as noble as it sounds. I know I'm going to make it one day, and when I do, no matter what I paint, there's going to be a market for it, and all because of the name Milo Racine in the corner."

"If that's true, my three paintings should be priceless one day."

"Your investment's safe enough, but don't get greedy. Artists appreciate in value after they're dead. Since I'm only twenty-four, I've got a lot of painting years ahead of me."

"You're American, aren't you?"

"I was born in Hungary. My parents left in 1919, just as Béla Kun was aligning the country with Russia and turning it into a dictatorship. All the members of my family who stayed behind were killed. We were what's glamorously called *émigrés,* but emigrants is a much more honest name for it. We moved around for a while and finally settled in Wisconsin, hence my chosen name Racine. My father's a butcher. My mother raised three daughters who are all married now and busy raising their own daughters."

He paused a moment. "Tell me. Have you ever heard of Arshile Gorky?"

Collier shook her head.

"You will. He paints too. He's Armenian, but he's living in New York now. I met him while I was going to art school there. I talked to him only once, but I felt as if our souls had

actually touched. We're so much alike. Even our histories are
similar. The Armenians were slaughtered by the Turks and then
Armenia was annexed to Russia one year after we left Hungary.
Do you know what Gorky means? It means 'bitter' and that's
the name he took for himself."

Collier found herself fascinated into silence. She wanted to
hear more. She wanted him to continue, but just then a group
of noisy guests converged on them and Milo Racine abruptly
stopped talking.

"Marvelous party, darling," cooed a woman whom Collier
hadn't even met. "We're off to the Ritz now. Why don't you
join us there later and bring this darling bohemian with you?
He'll add such a delightful dash of color to the place."

She gave Milo's trailing scarf a playful tug and her friends
burst out laughing. Milo said nothing. He simply pulled the
end of his scarf out of her hand and flung it across his shoulder.
The heavy fringe slapped the woman across the face. She took
a startled step back and let out a little cry of surprise.

"What bloody gall," exclaimed one of the men in the group.

Collier put her hand over her mouth to hide her smile.

"You certainly know how to break up a party," she told
Milo after the woman and her friends had gone.

"Each to his own methods," he scowled.

"Collier, my girl!"

It was Sir Gilbert. He pointed to the large clock on the wall
above the bar and then, to Collier's dismay, he began to motion
for everyone to be silent.

"It's midnight, ladies and gentlemen," he announced. "And
I should like to offer a toast to our young hostess. To you,
Collier—a happy, happy birthday."

Everyone picked up the cry and raised their glasses. It seemed
to serve as a cue for the photographers and reporters still sta-
tioned outside. They burst into the restaurant, notepads opened,
pencils poised, flashbulbs popping.

Collier gritted her teeth. Then she turned to the silent young
man standing next to her. "Get me out of here. Please!" she
urged.

For a moment, he seemed confused. Then he said, "I know
just the place."

He grabbed her hand and pulled her after him while he
shielded her with his own body.

"Give us a smile, Miss Paget-Browne."

"Come on, love, it's only a smile."

"Who's the bloke with you? Is he anyone important?"

"Just a few words about your party, please, Miss Paget-Browne."

Collier kept her head down, her purse raised to protect her face while Milo Racine led her out of the restaurant by way of the kitchen.

Chapter Five

"So this is a studio," Collier remarked, hoping that the sound of her voice would ease the tension in the room.

Milo was standing with his back to the window, his arms folded across his chest, a bemused look on his face.

"I always thought the idea of a northern exposure was invented by biographers to add to an artist's mystique. As if light from the north gave a work some magical quality." Collier glanced nervously around the large, cluttered room.

It even smelled the way she'd imagined an artist's studio would smell—a not unpleasant mingling of pigments, linseed oil and turpentine.

"I make you nervous, don't I?" Milo commented with a smile.

She wanted to ask him to put his jacket back on. She was too conscious of the tangle of thick black hair on his chest. A slow flush began to spread upward from the base of her neck.

Milo pushed himself away from the window and went over to a battered pine curio cabinet standing in a corner of the room. He opened one of the glass doors, took out a bottle filled with a deep green liquid and held it out to her.

"What is it?" she asked him.

"Absinthe."

She burst out laughing. "Absinthe? You really are a cliché, aren't you?"

She immediately regretted her words. Milo's face darkened, his brows knitting together, his features puckering into an ugly scowl. Collier glanced anxiously toward the door. Suddenly, he threw back his head and roared with laughter.

She glared at him, damning herself for giving him such control over her. Unconsciously, she squared her shoulders and crossed the room to stand in front of him. Saying nothing, she took a glass from the cabinet and held it out to him.

She took a sip of the liqueur. It had a strange, bittersweet taste, faintly reminiscent of the licorice her father used to buy her at the penny-candy stores on the Cape. The memory saddened her and she took her glass and went to stand in front of the window.

"Do you think Chamberlain is an appeaser?" she asked Milo in a subdued voice.

"I don't really care."

"Why not?"

"Why should I?"

He was standing behind her again. She could feel him there though he wasn't even touching her.

"Chamberlain's got no real control. None of us do. Why settle for being ineffectual in a big world when you can control a small world of your own. That's how I try to live: in the world inside my head where I'm in complete control. I might live outside your big world, but everytime I paint something, I'm giving you back a new version of it."

He poured himself another glass of absinthe. "If you're interested in the real history of the world, take a close look at my paintings. It's all there. The pain, the absurdity, the injustice, the futility. Of course the critics will tell you that I can't draw and that my paintings consist of meaningless blobs and patches of color. But they're wrong. They have no vision. One day I'll get them to see."

Collier leaned her head against the window, watching as her breath fogged the pane. "What do your parents think of your work?"

He let out a snort of derisive laughter. "My parents think art stopped somewhere between the Middle Ages and the Renaissance. Take them into a church and they believe God painted the frescoes himself. But at least they gave me a chance. They paid for art school and for a year in Paris. I took a few courses at the Sorbonne, but I was bored. They had nothing to teach me. I don't want to paint like Delacroix or David or Ingres. What I'm doing is unique and there aren't any classes to teach you how to break with tradition."

He set down the bottle on the windowsill and placed his hands on her shoulders, gently turning her around. "A modern woman dressed in antique lace. You're the ideal study in contrasts," he said softly, running the tip of his finger across the high neck of her gown.

His breath was warm against her cheeks. His hands cupped her face and she closed her eyes. His breathing quickened,

burning her skin. With a frightened cry, she broke away from
him and went to stand on the far side of the room.

"I'd better leave," she said.

"I thought you wanted to celebrate your birthday." His tone
was lightly mocking.

"I already have."

"Suit yourself." He poured himself some more absinthe.

He obviously didn't care whether she stayed or not. The
nerve of him. She was no longer frightened. She was angry.

"I'm leaving, Mr. Racine. Right now."

He drained his glass and reached for the bottle again.

"I'd appreciate it if you'd come downstairs and find me a
taxi."

He didn't move.

"Well?" She leveled her coldest stare at him.

"You might be used to ordering servants around, but I'm
not one of them." He raised his glass to her. "I'm not very
good at following orders, even if they come from my very own
patron saint."

"I'm not your patron saint," she snapped. "As a matter of
fact, I might even decide to return your paintings."

"You wouldn't."

"Wouldn't I?"

He slammed the bottle of absinthe down on the windowsill.
"See what happens when money's talking? Monkeys like me
still know how to jump." He yanked his jacket from the back
of a chair and put it on. "I'll get your damned taxi for you."

He opened the door and held it. "Come on."

As soon as she started down the stairs, she heard him slam
the door shut. Halfway down, convinced that he'd gone back
inside, Collier stopped and looked back over her shoulder. Milo
slammed right into her. She would have fallen backwards down
the stairs if he hadn't grabbed her by the shoulders and forced
her up against the wall.

"That was a pretty stupid thing to do. You trying to break
your neck?" ·

She managed to shake her head. She felt like a fool. Her
heart was beating so rapidly that she found it difficult to catch
her breath. She closed her eyes and waited. It was inevitable
now. She braced herself, her heart still racing, whether from
her near fall or his closeness, she couldn't tell. She waited. He
took his hands away. His breath was no longer warm against
her cheeks.

"I'll get you that taxi now," he told her.

She opened her eyes. He had already reached the bottom step. Shakily, she started back down the stairs herself. The bastard. He had managed to turn the whole thing around. It was his victory now, not hers.

Milo Racine awoke feelings in Collier which her daydreams had only hinted at. He re-defined her girlish fantasies and gave direction to her mind's romantic wanderings. Her usually clear thought processes were muddied. She lived by sensation alone. Her heightened sensitivity was like a troublesome itch—the more she scratched it, the more enflamed it became. A delicious mixture of pleasure and pain. And all the time, she waited. Waited to be released.

On an innocent June evening, just eight days after their first meeting, her wait was finally over.

She and Milo were dawdling over dinner in a small Italian restaurant in Soho called Vittorio's. Neither of them was hungry. Neither one spoke very much. Although Milo had consumed most of the wine on his own, it was Collier who kept excusing herself to go to the Powder Room. Her nervousness was overwhelming. It was as if they had reached some unspoken agreement over their first mouthful of spaghetti. Tonight was the night.

Milo finally put an end to the mounting tension between them.

"This is hell," he muttered, tossing his napkin onto the table.

"But I thought you liked Vittorio's spaghetti," Collier protested innocently.

"You know damn well that wasn't what I meant." He was glowering at her.

"The end of your scarf's trailing in the sauce," she told him in a shaky voice.

He acted as if he hadn't heard her as he pushed back his chair and stood up.

"Now you have sauce on your jacket."

He ignored her remark and hauled her out of her seat.

"But I haven't finished my wine yet," she whispered, reaching for her glass.

He got a firm grip on her arm. She put the glass down.

"I think I have to go to the Powder Room again."

"Later," his voice was gruff. "At my place."

"I don't think I can wait."

"Neither can I," he told her through clenched teeth as he steered her toward the door.

By the time they reached his studio, Collier had forgotten all about going to the bathroom.

She wondered if the first time was always like this—the initial awkwardness, the groping and fumbling, the feeling that they were wearing too many clothes. Suddenly, neither of them could remember how to work a zipper or unfasten a button. She heard something tear. Milo muttered something under his breath. They fumbled some more.

A sudden chill made her realize that, by some miracle, she was no longer dressed. Neither was Milo. They stood, two naked strangers, facing each other in the middle of the room. She folded her arms in front of her chest, grateful for the darkness. With only the faint glow of the street lamp outside his window, neither of them could see the other clearly.

Milo began to kiss her, edging her closer to his metal cot. The bed, which had always looked so benign before, now seemed threatening and foreign to her. Only the pressure of his mouth on hers kept her from voicing a feeble protest. She felt the scratchy wool blanket bite into her back as he lay her down on the cot and stretched out beside her.

His tongue began to explore the sensitive recesses of her ear, sending a long shiver down to the tips of her fingers. Her flesh came alive at his touch, and her body slowly caught fire. His lips left a trail of heat behind them as they moved down the slender column of her neck to the generous swell of her breasts.

While he sucked one breast into his mouth, he gently fondled the other one, flicking his thumb back and forth across its tender nipple. Fascinated, Collier watched him. Was that her nipple peaking so saucily in response to his caresses? She felt herself blushing. But a wonderful tingle was starting up between her legs. She concentrated on that tingle, feeling it spread through her body to meet the sensations fanning out from Milo's hungry mouth.

Shouldn't she be doing something to him? She started to sit up, only to have him push her down. With a sigh, she lay back again. He began moving lower, kissing his way across her belly until he grazed the top of her thighs. Instinctively, she squeezed her legs shut. Gripping the sides of his head with both hands, she tried vainly to stop him.

"What are you doing?" she gasped, as a tiny flicker of heat spun off his tongue and made her twitch.

"Nothing," he murmured, plunging his tongue inside her again.

"Yes, you are." Her voice was growing weaker. "No," she whimpered, tensing, raising her knees and arching her back.

"Yes." It was a warm rush of air against her.

"N-o-ooo . . ." Was that her moaning?

Beads of perspiration dotted her forehead and collected in the valley between her breasts. Milo was in complete control of her body now. Mesmerized, she followed his lead. His tongue and her body moved in time to the same rhythm. When he slowed down, she slowed down. When he speeded up, so did she. Her fingers were buried deep in his hair, urging him on, while some small part of her wished she could see his face. She felt strangely alone. Alone with her sensations. Building and ebbing, building and ebbing. He coaxed her up to the edge and tugged her back. Over and over again, until she thought her tautly strung muscles would snap from the strain. There had to be an end to these delicious feelings, and she wondered what it would be.

And then she found out. It burst upon her in a sudden stinging, excruciating wave of ecstasy. No amount of self-control could silence the cry being wrenched from her now. It unfurled from somewhere deep inside her, growing stronger and higher in pitch as wave upon wave of shocked pleasure coarsed through her body. The spasms shook her, thrilled her and swelled her up, until her skin was glossed with a slick, rosy glow. The invading flush thrust her nipples into the air and sent a quivering soreness to that place between her legs where Milo's tongue had slowed to a soothing, gentle lapping.

Sprawled out before him, with her legs open, her mouth slack, her heart thumping rapidly in her chest, Collier felt more vulnerable and more exposed than at any other time in her life. Sobbing and weak, her entire body twitching and trembling, she had just enough strength in her arms to raise his head and look at his face.

"We're not through yet," he told her.

His mouth tasted of her, damp and sweet, as it closed over hers. She sighed and put her arms around his neck. He kissed her tenderly a few more minutes. Then he finally showed her what to do.

She shivered as he molded her right hand to that extension of himself, which pulsed and jumped with a life of its own.

"That's it," he encouraged her. "Move your hand back and forth. That's right. A little bit faster now."

Numbly, she obeyed. She was grateful when he stopped talking and started kissing her again. She did as she was told, sliding her hand up and down the length of him, feeling his shaft thicken and swell. As her confidence grew, she began to experiment, slowing her pace so that his breathing eased, then working faster and hearing his breathing quicken again.

It was Milo who was moaning now. Roughly, he pushed her hand away. Had she hurt him? Had she done something wrong? Disappointed, she opened her eyes. But then she saw what he was doing. She let out a startled cry as he guided himself between her legs.

She raised herself expectantly, wondering how she was going to take all of him, but Milo showed her how. He eased himself into her bit by bit and she rose to meet him. Some primeval instinct told her to wrap her legs around his waist, and she did.

"Oh God," he gasped. "God."

Pleased, she tightened her grip on him.

She waited for the pain she knew was coming. But when it did come, it was no more than a brief sting. A blunt pain dampened and muffled by the intense pleasure of it all. Relieved, giddy with triumph, Collier hung onto Milo as that special feeling began to build inside her once more. Her breathing grew ragged. His breathing echoed hoarsely in her ears.

He tunnelled deeper into her and she grasped him by the buttocks and tried to force him even deeper. Greedily, she sought to devour him, to envelope him so completely that she would never be without him again. She cried out as he withdrew, but it was only to tease her. He dipped into her ever so slightly and then pulled back, dipped again and pulled back, coaxing a whimper from her and then a long, tremulous shudder. When he plunged inside her again, she smiled and sighed and drove him in further.

He was riding her faster now, stabbing at her with short, hard strokes. With his head thrown back, his nostrils flaring, his mouth open, he drove himself closer and closer to completion. She tried to hold her breath, to make the moment last forever. But when his body suddenly stiffened and he called out her name, she knew she was losing him.

He heaved and shook and flooded her with a surprising new

warmth. She clung desperately to him, arching her back, willing him to respond. But it was over. Her breath caught in her throat. Over. She didn't want it to be over.

He collapsed on top of her, all soft and warm, limp and moist. His lips were on her breast, his fingers in her hair. She cradled him in her arms and blinked away her tears. So this was how it was. This was how it would be from now on. She was seized with a sudden, terrible sadness. First times never come again, she thought. They only happen once. Was this the reason for her sadness? The reason for her inexplicable loneliness?

After awhile, Milo stirred. Raising himself on one elbow, he brushed her hair back from her face and smiled down at her. She forced herself to smile back at him. He began to kiss her again, and she responded weakly. As his kisses grew more intense, she could feel him growing stiff and hard along her belly. Growing on his own, without her even stroking him.

In the face of this marvelous discovery, her loneliness was quickly forgotten. She began to return his kisses boldly, aware of a new kind of power within her.

He's a selfish, egotistical, arrogant, mean-tempered bastard and I absolutely despise him!"

Collier gave the leg of the sofa a savage kick, and then let out a yelp of pain.

"What the blazes did the bohemian do now?" demanded Sir Gilbert from behind his newspaper.

"He just backed out of taking me to the opera tonight."

"And that's the reason for this ridiculous display of pique?"

"Not only that," Collier continued angrily, "but I ordered him a suit from Burberry's as a surprise and had it delivered to him this morning. Do you know what he did?" she demanded. "He told me that he cut up the suit and then burned it. Now he's accusing me of trying to turn him into a high society freak. He's a maniac!"

She stopped in front of Sir Gilbert's wing chair and glared down at him. "Tell me, am I supposed to enjoy being seen in a box at the opera with a man who refuses to even wear a shirt under his jacket?"

"Certainly not," Sir Gilbert sniffed. "Most undignified of him. But then you're not given to conventional dress yourself, my dear Collier."

"I at least know how to dress for the opera!"

"Well, why not give Tolly or Kit a ring? Either of them would be delighted to take you this evening. Or how about Edgar?"

Collier made a face. "Tolly's a bore. Kit's not much better and Edgar's too short."

She went back to pacing the library floor. "I'd even managed to get his exact measurements. I ordered shirts and ties to go with the suit. The ungrateful bastard! What a stupid thing to do. I could strangle him!"

"Good God, Collier, simmer down. You're positively red in the face. Next you'll be frothing at the mouth and thrashing about on the floor like some bloody lunatic."

Lunatic. The word triggered an alarm in Collier's brain. Suddenly, she stopped pacing and ran out of the room with her hands over her ears.

Locking herself inside her bedroom closet, she slipped the navy blue blazer over her shoulders and sat down in the dark with her head in her hands.

He's stubborn and selfish and completely impossible. But so am I, aren't I, Daddy? We spark and there's a flare-up and then we make up and forget about what started it just long enough for it to start all over again. But I want him, Daddy, I want him.

It had been exactly sixty-three days since she'd met Milo, and all through the summer, he'd been pulling her one way, with Sir Gilbert pulling the other, while she walked a tenuous line between them both.

Sir Gilbert had trotted out every available man in London to meet her. Some were young, moneyed and full of promise. Others were older with even more money and their promises already fulfilled. She was escorted to the races at Ascot and Goodwood, to various charity balls and to tennis tournaments held at private country clubs. She went yachting at Cowes and hunting grouse on the moors, and all she could think about was Milo Racine.

Irascible, impossible, demanding Milo. With his outlandish outfits, the jangling clash of the colors he wore and the French cigarettes he'd begun to smoke. Together they romped through Soho, roamed galleries even a native Londoner didn't know about, and attended the theatre, where for the price of two top seats, they bought five of the cheapest instead, so that three of

Milo's artist friends could go with them.

He bought her nosegays of violets from the vendors in front of the Eros statue in Piccadilly and always managed to misplace his wallet when it came time to pay for them. He forced her to walk in the rain whenever she suggested hailing a taxi instead. He cooked spaghetti for her on the hot plate in his studio and occasionally allowed her to treat him to dinner at Gennaro's Rendezvous or the Restaurant de Paris.

And to Collier's continual amazement, they fought about almost everything.

"What the hell do you need a car for?" he shouted when she arrived at the studio one morning in the Austin Healey she had just bought. "It doesn't even have a top. Some smart invention for English weather."

"The top rolls up, you fool."

"But you'd be drenched before you could get it up."

"And I always thought you liked walking in the rain."

"Walking in it is one thing, sitting in it is something else."

"Just watch your scarf," she warned him as he finally got into the car. "Isadora Duncan already proved that scarves and sports cars can be a lethal combination."

They would fight because she refused to pose for him.

"You're always happy to pose for the papers, so why won't you pose for me?"

"Because I don't want to spend my whole life posing for people."

"I'll pay you for it."

"You couldn't afford me."

"Then do it for art's sake."

"And end up like the Demoiselles d'Avignon, with my face and body chopped into jagged pieces and scattered all over the place?"

"I'm not imitating Picasso anymore. I'm doing Kandinsky now."

The only thing they never argued about was sex. In Milo's arms, Collier had re-discovered some of the closeness she had known as a child. Just as her father's love had once nurtured and protected her, now it was Milo's love which would nourish her.

When they made love, even the roots of her hair seemed alive with a special electricity. Milo played her as one plays a finely-tuned instrument, strumming, teasing, leading. With

Milo, Collier lost all sense of herself. All she knew was feeling. She was possessed. She had been taken over by a devil who rode her and used her up and then threw her down, exhausted, sated, and completely content.

Having grown up alone, Collier had learned independence early. Now, with Milo in her life, she found herself strangely helpless and weak. *Don't abuse this power I've given you,* she would silently plead with him. *Don't turn it against me. Please.* She despised this weakness in herself and she would try anything to get her independence back. She would even pick a fight with him and storm out of his studio, vowing never to see him again. But she would always go back, the penitent child, fearful that this time she had finally succeeded in freeing herself and losing him. Fearful of finding that she had already been replaced.

Oh, Daddy, if this is how love feels, I don't think I like it. It hurts so much of the time and at other times it feels so wonderful and in between I wonder what's going to come of it at all. She was beginning to get a headache. Her muscles were cramping and when she got to her feet, she felt light-headed and faint. She took off the blazer and hung it up. Then she opened the closet door.

"So that's where you hide yourself!" boomed Sir Gilbert from the doorway of her bedroom. "There's a call for you. Your young bohemian."

"Tell him I'm out."

"I've already told him you were here."

"Then tell him you were wrong!"

"I doubt he'd believe me. Besides, he was nattering away about borrowing a suit from a friend of his and—"

The rest of his sentence was left hanging as Collier lunged for the telephone next to her bed.

"I'm at the Dutton Gallery picking up a check," Milo told her. "They sold three more of my paintings this week. You're good luck for me, you know."

"Why?"

"Because of your name."

Collier felt a slight sinking in the pit of her stomach.

"The word's out that you discovered this great talent, and anyone who thinks he knows something about art is suddenly interested in owning a Milo Racine. I guess I'd better hang onto you for a while. You can be my talisman. What do you say?"

She had nothing to say. All the feelings were coming to-gether in a solid lump in her throat. She was hardly aware of the dial tone ringing in her ears. That was another infuriating habit of his. Milo never said good-bye at the end of a con-versation. He simply hung up.

She slammed down the phone. "Damn you, Milo Racine! Damn you to hell!"

"Well, now do you believe me, Sir Gilbert? Your wonderful Neville Chamberlain has turned out to be an appeaser after all."

Collier and Sir Gilbert were having a brandy at the bar of the old Vic Theatre between acts of Tyrone Guthrie's pro-duction of *Hamlet*. Neither Alec Guinness's brilliant prince nor the unconventional, modern-dress costumes had as great an impact on the audience as the newly signed Munich Agreement between France and Great Britain.

"Czechoslovakia has been abandoned now by being forced to cede Moravia and Bohemia to Germany," Collier went on. "And this is only the beginning."

Sir Gilbert was watching her carefully as she puffed on her cigar. Thank Heaven he had been wise enough not to marry. He could never have handled fatherhood.

"You read too much, my girl, that's your problem. Beautiful young women shouldn't fill their heads with all this bothersome business. Leave that to the men."

Collier blew a perfect smoke ring into his face. "And what are we women supposed to do with our heads? Use them to find a man to marry us and do the thinking for us, while we put our brains to sleep along with a brood of children?"

"God help me, Collier, save such twaddle for that bohemian of yours. You don't know the first thing about being a woman and enjoying it. Look at you! Men's trousers all the time now. Those confounded cigars, that blasted little car of yours! When will you call a halt to this ridiculous rebellion?"

"This is not a rebellion! I'm living the way I want to live. You said it yourself, I'm my father's child, and when did he ever allow people to tell him what to do!"

The lights in the foyer were beginning to flash.

Collier angrily stubbed out her cigar and followed Sir Gilbert back to their seats. God, the man was cranky. She should have gone with Milo to the Wynn Gallery instead of coming to the theatre. It was the final night of his one-man show at the gallery and he had been selling well. The *Observer* called his works "supreme fantasies of the unconscious." The *Times* condemned him for "too much emphasis on free association" and the *Telegraph* labeled the paintings "automatic, a kind of organic surrealism."

But Milo no longer cared what the critics were saying. He was selling.

While the cast was taking its curtain calls, Collier left the theatre and drove down to the Wynn. When she pushed open the gallery door, she noticed that most of the lights had already been turned off and that the front rooms were deserted.

"Milo?" she called.

Her heart began to pound; she could hear it echoing in her ears.

"Milo?"

"In here," came his muffled voice. "In the office."

She walked slowly through the darkened gallery toward the office in the back. She imagined him in the arms of one of his models all tangled up in one of his scarves. She slowed her steps even more to give them time.

"Collier?"

The office door was open. The lights were on. The room seemed too bright after the dimness of the gallery.

She steadied herself in the doorway and took a deep breath.

"What took you so long? I've nearly finished all the champagne myself."

Milo was sitting cross-legged on the floor, a yellow scarf wrapped around his forehead, the ends trailing down across his chest, making him look like a carelessly wrapped mummy. His brown hair was hanging in his eyes and he was grinning.

"Smile," he leered up at her. "Your protégé has been declared a success."

"You have?" her voice was hardly more than a squeak.

"I have." He nodded his head up and down. "C'm'ere." He patted the space beside him on the floor.

Collier hitched up her trousers, kicked off her shoes and sat down beside him.

"Here, have a swig."

She swallowed some of the lukewarm champagne and handed the bottle back to him.

"Now give us a kiss."

She hesitated. He caught hold of her by the collar of her shirt and pulled her toward him until their foreheads were touching.

"I sold every one of my paintings."

She wanted to throw her arms around him but she felt too weak. All she could do was sag against his shoulder.

"I think I'd better keep you around permanently, just to make sure this isn't a fluke or anything. How about getting married?"

She gasped. "Do you really mean that, Milo?"

"Cross my heart and all that."

"You're drunk!"

"So what?"

"You don't even know what you're saying."

"I do so. I asked if you felt like getting married."

Something seemed to shrivel up inside of her. Was this how it was supposed to happen? He was asking her to marry him as casually as he had asked her to have some of his champagne.

"No answer?"

"Ask me tomorrow when you're sober."

"If I do, will you say yes?"

"You'll find out tomorrow."

The following afternoon, when he was sober, Milo again asked Collier to marry him. Without admitting that her answer had gone back and forth between yes and no all during that long night, she told him yes.

They were married in a small Anglican church just outside of London on a rainy November morning. Milo wore a royal blue velvet smoking jacket over a pair of dove gray trousers. As his sole concession to propriety, he tied his emerald green scarf in a large bow to cover his chest. Collier wore a floor-length royal blue silk skirt with an emerald green blouse tied gypsy fashion above her waist. Red roses were entwined all through her hair.

"Well, at least you've managed to color coordinate this circus," grumbled Sir Gilbert as he led Collier up the aisle.

Milo presented Collier with an elaborate silver and gold wedding band made by one of his friends. Because he had no intention of wearing a ring, Collier's gift to him was a solid gold cigarette holder and a matching cigarette case with his initials spelled out in tiny diamonds on the cover.

When they came out of the church, the reporters and the photographers were waiting. Clutching Milo's arm, Collier began to run through the rain to her car.

"Mrs. Racine!"

Collier nearly tripped over the hem of her skirt.

"Mrs. Racine!"

She could hear them all splashing through the muddy grass behind her.

"Miss Paget-Browne."

Collier turned her head for a moment and the flashbulbs went off in her face.

Chapter Six

In 1939, London put on her brightest smile and pretended that all was well. The city's restaurants and nightclubs were filled. The Sadler's Wells Ballet performed *Checkmate* and *The Rake's Progress*. The highlight of the opera season was *The Bartered Bride*, while a magnificent production of *Wuthering Heights* and Clare Boothe's controversial play, *The Women*, performed nightly before sell-out crowds. People threw formal dinner parties, laughed at jokes about Chamberlain and Hitler, and drank only the finest brandy.

Milo's one-man show at the Leicester Gallery closed with only three paintings sold.

One day, the signs and banners began to appear. First in Piccadilly. Then at Marble Arch. Finally, in Trafalgar Square.

WE'VE GOT TO BE PREPARED!

ENGLAND EXPECTS THAT YOU WILL ENROLL TODAY!

BE PREPARED! NATIONAL SERVICE! HAVE YOU OFFERED YOURS?

Milo tore down that particular banner from the statue of Eros in Piccadilly, cut off the first four words and hung the part asking HAVE YOU OFFERED YOURS? above their four-poster Queen Anne bed.

He mounted the same show at the Dutton Gallery and sold exactly one painting.

The laughter grew forced.

The stores of brandy trickled out and the lights on the theatre marquees began to dim. In the spring, marches were organized to protest the talk of conscription. Civilians began drilling. The Red Cross recruited women to roll bandages, to train as nurses and ambulance drivers, and to ready their households for possible billeting. Factories were ordered to begin producing airplanes immediately.

Milo mounted a new show at the Wynn Gallery. It closed without even one painting being sold.

The laughter finally died altogether.

Milo was desperate. In June, he barricaded himself inside

the bedroom he used as his studio. When he emerged, he was ready to mount another show, but he needed reassurance. He asked Collier to charter a plane so that three of his American friends who were still studying in Paris could fly to London and spend a weekend with them.

Collier was only too pleased to cooperate.

"To hell with what's happening in Paris, I've just seen some photos of Gorky's latest work in *Art* magazine," Milo said, standing in the middle of the living room and lecturing to his friends who lay sprawled about on the floor. "The man's a genius. Ten years from now, they'll be calling him the founder of a whole new school of painting."

Collier let out a little laugh. "I thought you'd already claimed that title, Milo."

He ignored her and went on talking. "Gorky is the supreme fantasist. He's taking Kandinsky amd Miró and Masson and surpassing all of them."

Collier studied the faces of his three friends, wondering if she would have them sorted out by the end of the weekend. Theo, Burt and Wylie. She lit a fresh cigar and gave up trying to figure out which one was which.

"What about de Kooning?" asked Theo. Or was it Burt?

"Did you know that conscription started on June 30?" Collier leaned back in her chair and addressed the ceiling.

"Too derivative."

"What about Jackson Pollock then?" put in Wylie.

"The RAF is sending bombers on daylight demo flights over London now," Collier said, blowing a smoke ring into the air.

"Gorky can paint circles around Pollock."

"You should come back to the States with us, Milo," said Burt. "Europe's finished. It's our turn now."

Collier yawned. "The *Telegraph* has crucified Chamberlain for signing the Munich Agreement, but the *Times* is still supporting him."

"You know, everything here looks like it came from a museum," commented Wylie, holding up a Tiffany paperweight to his eye and squinting through it.

"Except for the Milo Racines, of course," Burt laughed.

The ash from Milo's cigarette dropped onto the carpet. Collier gritted her teeth.

"Collier believes in one-stop shopping," Milo explained. "She bought out most of the Antique Dealers Fair at Grosvenor

House last year." He carefully avoided meeting Collier's eyes.

"Is that true?" Theo asked her.

Collier shrugged. "It seemed to be the fastest way to furnish this place. Besides, everything we bought was a good investment."

Milo raised his glass to her in mock salute. "When Collier talks investments, gentlemen, you should all be taking notes. She can make you rich. Look at me. She's made me rich. I can't keep up with the demand for my work. Her name works like a charm. My advice to you three gentlemen is to find yourselves a lady with a name like Collier Paget-Browne and wham!—instant wealth and fame!"

In the uncomfortable hush that followed this outburst, Collier got up and went into the kitchen. Was it her fault that no one was buying his latest paintings? Was it her fault that his work had gone from innovative to obscene? Who wanted to hang a painting of a huge stylized pink breast in their living room? Or one with a fat pink tongue lolling out of one corner of a big red mouth? Or a pair of open legs leading off the canvas?

She stared out of the window at the back garden. It was only July, but the flowers and herbs she had planted were already wilting. She poured herself a glass of cold water. Her head hurt, and her stomach had been queasy all morning.

As she drank the water, her mind began to wander. Czechoslovakia was now a vassal state of Germany. Chamberlain didn't want to risk becoming involved in a war with people he knew nothing about. Italy had just seized Albania. Milo was competing with an Armenian ex-patriate named Arshile Gorky for immortality, and she had the sickening feeling that she might be pregnant.

She looked balefully around her. The flat was too large, too grand. It had been a mistake. Not at first, of course. In the beginning, she and Milo had used the five bedrooms, four bathrooms, living room, dining room, library and servants' quarters for playing hide-and-seek. They had even incorporated the game into their lovemaking. The flat had been fun then. But as the months had passed, all the fun had gone out of it. It was used less for their games and more as a battlefield, with Milo leading the assault and Collier in retreat.

With each unsuccessful exhibition, Milo's frustration mounted and his drinking increased. He would rail at the critics, at the galleries, and at the buyers who were no longer buying him. When he was through blaming them, he would train his venom on her. Stunned, Collier would sit, frozen in a chair, and allow him to carry on—shouting, crying, brandishing a bottle of gin as if it were a sword. Arguing or sympathizing with him had no effect. Trying to reason with him got her nowhere.

She eventually learned to leave the room the moment his tantrums began. While he raged up and down the flat, Collier would curl up in a ball on their bed and let the tears course silently down her cheeks. She ached for him, but she felt helpless in the face of his terrible anger. She hurt for him and for his defeats, but she was powerless to turn those defeats around. His art was his life. As long as he was appreciated, he could preen and strut and rejoice in being alive. Without that recognition, he fell apart. He was nothing. To Milo, being nothing was worse than being dead.

When the house grew quiet again, Collier would dry her eyes, wash her face and go looking for him. She usually found him sprawled in a chair in the living room or stretched out on a bed in one of the guest rooms. Red-eyed, puffy-faced, he would look up at her with a drunken smile and wave his empty bottle at her like a white flag of truce. She would smooth back his hair from his face, pull him into her arms and begin to kiss him. All she ever did was kiss him, because when Milo got drunk, he became impotent.

When Milo's verbal abuse finally turned physical, Collier began to lock herself in her bathroom. He never made a move to touch her. He preferred to take out his hostility on her property instead, and he always ravaged the room he was in at the time of his outburst. Their bedroom was the only room he spared. Lamps would be dashed on the floor, chairs and sofas overturned, beds collapsed, tables knocked over, every visible piece of china, glass and porcelain smashed. Books would be ripped to shreds, drawers emptied, waste baskets upset and mirrors broken.

To Collier, huddled on the cold bathroom floor, Milo's rampages reminded her of the havoc she had wrought upon her father's bedroom so long ago. She remembered the shame she had felt afterward, the remorse at having systematically destroyed the possessions of the man she had loved so dearly. But her tantrum had nothing to do with love at the time. At that moment, she had hated her father, hated him for abandoning her.

Did Milo hate her then? In spite of the fact that she was still with him, that she refused to abandon him? She shuddered to think what the answer might be.

Collier soon found that she had used up most of her sympathy. Even her pity was nearly gone and was being replaced by disgust. What she had once considered to be love was slowly turning into hate. She even stopped crying. Her growing contempt for Milo had dried up all her tears. During his rages, she would simply sit in the bathroom with the water running in the sink, humming to herself, while she waited for him to wear himself out.

There were no soft kisses for him anymore. She made no attempts to soothe him either. The morning after one of his rampages, Collier would clean up the mess he had made (she had finally stopped trying to keep servants) and go out and replace whatever he had broken.

She sighed and put her glass in the sink. She had never felt such despair before. How she prayed that Milo's latest works would sell. She doubted whether either of them could survive another defeat. He still blamed her for his most recent failed exhibit. He stubbornly maintained that if she hadn't hidden in his studio underneath a large white cloth during one of their half-hearted attempts at hide-and-seek, the whole thing might never have started. . . .

"You made it too easy this time, Collier," he called out to her from the doorway of the studio. "Your nipples just gave you away. They're sticking out a mile."

She shook with laughter as he began to peel the sheet off her body with agonizing slowness, revealing only one small part of her body at a time. Growing impatient, she started to sit up.

"Don't move!" he barked at her.

His harsh tone took her by surprise. She quickly lay down again.

"You've just given me a great idea."

Saying this, he reached for one of his sketchpads and started to draw.

What resulted was a series of twenty canvases, all highly stylized representations of various parts of her body. They were all superbly drafted and painted with a stark, geometric clarity in strong primary colors.

The Leicester Gallery had turned the series down, as did the Raleigh and the Dutton. The Wynn finally agreed to mount the show, but only for one week. The critics lambasted him. People who had bought his works before came to the exhibit out of curiosity, but when the show closed, not one of the paintings had been sold.

"The goddamned morons! They're cretins, all of them!" Milo raved when he brought all the paintings home again. "What the hell do they know? Paint them the same old thing and they make you a hero. Try something new and they crucify you."

"They haven't just singled you out for criticism, Milo," she tried to assure him. "They've done the same thing to every other artist and every art movement in history. In the end, no one remembers the critics, they remember the artists."

"In the end! What the hell kind of satisfaction am I supposed to get from being accepted then? I'll be dead!"

"You'll have done a lot more experimenting before that ever happens. Picasso keeps changing his styles in spite of what the critics say, so why can't you? Oh, Milo, you've got such a wonderful talent. Please don't allow this one setback to stifle your creativity. Put the paintings away for now and forget about them. Start something new." She put her arms around his neck and inhaled the smell of the paint which seemed to live in his skin. "Want to play hide-and-seek?" she whispered in his ear.

"That's what started this fiasco in the first place."

"Maybe we can come up with something new this time."

"Let's get drunk first." He pushed her out of the way and headed for the liquor cabinet.

"And then we'll play?"

"Then we'll see."

Between them, they finished a bottle of gin. Collier passed out on the sofa. Milo collapsed on the rug at her feet. When Collier woke up the next morning, Milo was bending over her, a wildly ecstatic expression on his face, moving something back and forth across her belly. It tickled her and felt like a giant moustache. She took a look at herself. He was painting her entire body dark blue.

"Matches your eyes," he explained, sitting back on his heels and exposing his huge erection.

"Don't you dare paint that blue"—she pointed—"if you're thinking of making love to me."

Milo tossed the brush into the air and climbed on top of her. . . .

"Collier!"

She was shaken from her thoughts. Milo was ready for his unveiling.

"Coming!" she called out to him from the kitchen. Then she put on her best hostess smile and headed for his studio.

Ten of the paintings were set up on individual easels, while another five were leaning against one wall. Each was draped in a white cloth.

"Behold, gentlemen and lady," Milo announced. "The latest works of genius from that genius himself—Milo Racine!" He whisked off the first of the cloths. "Walk around. Take your time. Look at them from every angle. And then you may all kneel in homage before me."

Collier shoved her hands into the pockets of her trousers to keep from biting her nails. She watched the three young men slowly circling the room and waited for something to register on their faces.

"Well, do we break out the champagne or do I treat myself to hemlock for one?" Milo demanded, his face tense.

"Fantastic!" Burt was the first to break the silence.

Collier wondered if she should begin to let out her breath.

"It's genius, Milo, it really is," murmured Theo.

Wylie said nothing. Instead he went down on one knee and bowed his head to Milo.

Milo hauled him to his feet. "Yahoo! Bring on the Philistines! Little David is ready at last!"

Slightly weak with relief, Collier left to get the champagne.

Milo followed her out of the room. "I was right in inviting them here, wasn't I? Thanks for doing this for me. I'll pay you back, I promise."

Smiling now, Collier put her arms around his waist. "We're partners, Milo, equals. I wish you'd remember that and stop trying to figure out who owes who what. I've never kept score and I never will."

"Do you think the work's really good?"

He had been asking her that all week, ever since he had

allowed her into the studio to see the paintings. How she pitied him for his vulnerability. She pitied his neediness almost as much as she admired his talent, and she was thankful that she herself had no talent. It demanded too much. It asked too many questions, gave too few answers and caused too much pain.

She gave him a hug now and said, "Your work's more than good, Milo. It's inspired."

But the Forden Gallery, despite its prestigious name, failed to convince its clients that the work was inspired. Even the critics disagreed with Collier's assessment of Milo's latest efforts. No one was interested in buying canvases with either horizontal, diagonal or vertical bands of color running into one another. The strident colors he had used—fuchsia, chartreuse, yellow, orange and teal blue—were too violent, too much like the mood of the country. Untitled, the paintings appeared directionless in a time when people needed direction.

In desperation, Collier telephoned everyone she knew in the city and talked them into going down to the gallery. She would join them there, walk them through the exhibition and pitch Milo's genius to them. But no one was buying. Three days before the exhibit closed, Collier telephoned the gallery, disguising her voice and using an assumed name, and instructed them to place red "SOLD" stickers on two of the paintings. Even that failed to generate any response.

Once again, Milo brought his paintings home.

"They still want Gainsboroughs," he said bitterly as he poured himself a tumbler of gin.

Collier was perched uneasily on the edge of the sofa, watching him get progressively drunker.

"They still want pretty portraits and pastoral scenes. Well, I can't pretend that everything's safe and pretty right now. I'm scared. They're scared. Why can't they admit that they're scared and stop looking for pretty answers?"

"Because once they've looked at the fear, what are they supposed to do with it?" she asked him. "Put it away again in some convenient little cubbyhole? People don't want to admit that they're frightened because if they pretend that everything's all right, they can actually believe it awhile longer."

"You sound as if you're on their side now!"

"I'm not on their side. I'm on our side."

"I trusted you."

"I know you did, but you also trusted Theo and Wylie and

Burt." She got up from the sofa and began to pace the floor. "I'm not God, Milo, I'm only your wife."

"Don't shout at me. I'm going through enough without you shouting at me too!"

"I damn well will shout at you. You shout at me whenever you feel like it. I'm getting tired of this, Milo. I don't have the solutions to every one of your creative crises. I can't make everything work out for you by just wanting it to work out. I wish I could, but I can't. You're the artist, not me."

Milo was on his feet now. "You're right, I *am* the artist. And what the hell are you? A spoiled rich bitch who's never had to fight for a damned thing in her whole life, whose daddy gave her everything and made sure nothing ever went wrong. You can buy and sell half the goddamned world and all you had to do was be born some rich man's brat!"

She stared at Milo as if she had never seen him before. Then with an outraged scream, she drew back her hand and slapped him across the face. He stood there looking stunned while she charged down the hall to their bedroom.

"You bitch, you're going to get it now!" he shouted.

Collier began to run. She slammed their bedroom door and then hurried toward the adjoining bathroom. Milo caught up with her before she could turn the lock on the door.

"No, Milo, no," she whimpered, as he slapped her and her hands went up to protect her face.

"You lousy bitch, I could kill you for what you did!"

"NO!"

She sank her teeth into his arm as he grabbed her by the shoulders and started to shake her.

He wrestled her to the floor of the bathroom. Her head slammed against the cold tiles and she screamed out in pain. He slapped her across the face and again she tried to protect herself. Each time she covered her face, he forced her hands apart and slapped her again.

He aimed a punch at her groin and she doubled up in agony. She crossed her arms in front of her belly, but he pushed them out of the way.

Her bottom lip was cut and a thin stream of blood trickled into her mouth. She began to cough. She was certain that she was going to choke.

Suddenly, something black and warm fluttered by and hovered over her. As it circled her, she reached up and pulled it down. Milo wouldn't be able to find her now.

He was holding out his arms to her, calling her name. She began to run toward him. The sun was behind him, shining into her eyes as she ran. Soon she would be safe again.

"Daddy!" Collier screamed as she collided with the sun. There was nothing now but the blackness.

"Why didn't you tell me you were pregnant?"

Collier looked up through swollen eyes and wished Milo would go away. It still hurt too much to move, and so she forced herself to lie very, very still.

"Why the hell didn't you tell me, Collier?"

She hoped Sir Gilbert wouldn't find out. How would she ever convince him that she had been attacked on the street by two boys after her purse? Even the doctors hadn't seemed convinced.

Registered under the name of Mrs. Racine, she had been praying each day since her admission to the hospital that no one would recognize her and leak the news to the press. Recognize her? Not even the press would recognize her now.

Her insides hurt—less from the beating than from her overwhelming sense of betrayal and despair. She had lost more than a five-week fetus. She had lost her faith in her husband, and she wondered what would happen if she couldn't get it back.

"Collier?" Milo was now sitting on the edge of the bed. "Why didn't you tell me you were pregnant?"

She wet her lips with the tip of her tongue. "Would it have made any difference?" she whispered.

For a moment he didn't answer. "You should have told me," he said then. "You had no right to keep it from me."

"I wasn't even sure. I only suspected it."

Suddenly, she heard the sound of muffled sobs. She turned her head just enough to see Milo, his head in his hands, his shoulders heaving.

"I'm sorry," he cried. "I never meant to hurt you. But you shouldn't have slapped me. I needed help that night, I needed support. I'm sorry. I'll never hurt you again, I promise." He grabbed hold of her hand, and his brimming eyes were pleading. "Say you forgive me, Collier. Please. I couldn't stand it if I thought you'd hold this against me now. Please say that you forgive me. I swear I'll never do anything to hurt you again."

Poor Milo. She had no strength left to give him. She needed it all for herself.

Just then, a young nurse came into the room carrying a small metal tray. "I'm afraid I must ask you to leave now, Mr. Racine," she told him in her most efficient tone.

Collier watched as Milo hastily wiped his eyes with the end of his cerise scarf before getting up from the bed. She quickly closed her eyes and tried not to flinch when he bent over and kissed her on the cheek. She waited until she heard the door swing shut before opening her eyes again.

"It must be marvelous to be married to an artist," bubbled the girl as she gently lifted Collier's head and plumped up her pillows. "My boyfriend and I went to one of his shows last year and we both think he's brilliant."

She poured some water from a plastic pitcher into a small paper cup and handed it, along with a fat red pill, to Collier.

"I looked ever so closely at his hands just now, and I could tell they were the hands of a true artist. They're so expressive, aren't they, and they look ever so gentle."

Collier nearly choked as she swallowed the pill. The twisted smile she gave the nurse cracked open the cut on her bottom lip and it began to bleed again.

One week after Collier returned from the hospital, Milo told her that he wanted them to move back to the States.

"Things are closing in here," he explained to her as they sat at the table after dinner. "Burt was right. If half the artists in Europe are leaving, I'd be a fool to stay."

Collier put down her teacup and began to think about what he was saying.

Home.

Yes, she wanted to go home.

"Wylie wrote to me about the artists' colony down in Rockport, Massachussetts," Milo was saying. "Should we try it? It's close to Boston."

She gave him a wan smile. Poor, dear, frightened Milo. Trying to please her. Trying to make up for what he had done to her. He had been her shadow all week. A man with an air of nervous expectancy about him. Dancing about in reverent attendance. She was already beginning to miss the old Milo. The one whose spark of unpredictability had ignited her own life.

"I suppose I could buy a place in Gloucester or Rocky

Neck." She was beginning to warm to the idea. "My father used to take me to Gloucester every August for two weeks. We both loved it there. The ocean was almost too cold for swimming, but the lobster tasted better there than any place else in New England."

Yes, Gloucester would be ideal. Milo could paint there and she would be close enough to Boston and to the head office of Paget-Browne Enterprises. According to the terms of her father's will, she was to assume the presidency of the company on her twenty-first birthday. She had less than two years to decide on the role she intended to play. Two years to decide what to do with her life.

Her look told him that she had made up her mind.

"Why don't we try Gloucester?" she suggested.

He seemed skeptical. "Both of us?"

"Both of us."

"Collier, I—"

She knew what was coming. "I don't want to talk about it anymore," she told him as she started to get up. He immediately jumped up and took her by the arm to steady her. "I think I'll go in and place a call to Uncle Avery," she said.

But Milo had other plans. He put his arms around her waist and kissed the tip of her upturned nose. "God, you're beautiful," he murmured, his voice husky." He kissed her nose again. "You don't know how badly I want things to be the way they used to be. Once we get back to the States, couldn't we pretend all of this never happened, Collier? Couldn't we start over and—"

She put a finger to his lips to silence him. "Ssh," she whispered. "No more."

When he kissed her on the mouth, she felt a sudden stir of passion. She had been terrified of never feeling anything for him again. Now she was being proven wrong. She wanted him. In spite of everything that had happened, she still wanted him. She still craved what he could give her. With a happy cry, she started kissing him back.

Milo picked her up in his arms and carried her into the bedroom. Avery would have to wait. Milo couldn't. As he quickly undressed her, Collier found she couldn't wait either. His body felt lean and hard against hers, and she felt especially soft and yielding. As they began to explore one another's bodies, it was as if they were discovering each other all over again.

It seemed to Collier that the events of the preceding months had happened to someone else and not to her.

Surely the mouth kissing her so tenderly now was not the same mouth that had shouted so many hurtful things. The hands caressing her could not have been the hands which had beaten and bruised her so badly. This wasn't the same man. She gave a slight, involuntary shudder. This was the old Milo again.

At her shudder, Milo tensed. "Am I hurting you?" he asked. She shook her head. "No," she smiled. "It feels wonderful." "Are you sure?"

"Yes, I'm sure."

He continued to nuzzle her, burrowing deeper into the gentle curve where her neck and shoulder met. Then he began to nip lightly at her skin, making little sucking sounds as he slowly circled her breasts. Collier bit down hard on her bottom lip. Her breasts were still quite sensitive. Feeling her tense, Milo stopped his playful biting and made his kisses soft and feathery instead. Collier immediately relaxed.

He covered her entire body with wispy butterfly kisses. Every part of her knew his touch, the warm, moist path left by his tongue, the tender imprint of his mouth. A light film of perspiration misted Collier's skin. Her legs were taut and partly opened to him. Her hands formed fists at her sides. The special electricity they had once passed between them was there again, sparking each time his lips came in contact with her skin. Collier did nothing but revel in the return of these glorious sensations.

She felt moist and dry, hot and cold. But nowhere was she wetter or hotter than in that secret place between her legs where Milo's tongue was working another of its miracles. She wanted him in her, but she also wanted him to continue licking her. She wanted him on top of her and she wanted him to take her from behind at the same time. Delirious, her head thrashing from side to side, she wanted everything from him and then some. She wanted him to never stop.

She moaned. He was starting to slide inside her. Make it last, she wanted to beg him. Don't ever let it end. Hungrily, she sucked him into her. She clamped her legs around him, her muscles locking him to her. She wanted to squeeze him to death. She wanted to drain all the life from him. Feeling her violent urgency, Milo abruptly pulled out.

"No, Milo, no," she whimpered in frustration.

He kissed her hard to silence her. She bit his bottom lip. He only kissed her harder and ground his body into hers. She finally understood. He was prolonging it for her. With a grateful sob, she molded her body to his and returned his kiss.

He rolled her over onto her side and slid one of his legs up between hers. She began to rub herself against his knee. The warmth from the friction spread through her, making her weak. His hardness was against her belly as they rocked back and forth on top of the bed. He shifted his position, flinging his leg across her hip. Stiff and heavy, he began to penetrate her again.

"Let me get on top of you," she whispered up to him.

Straddling him, his hardness rubbing her from behind, she let her hair fall in front of her face like a silken curtain between them. She trailed her hair up and down the length of his chest, and when she touched his small, brown nipples, she found them taut and puckered. With trembling hands, he pushed her hair back from her face and brought her head down close to his. Her breasts flattened out against his chest and when they kissed, she heard him groan.

She looked into his eyes and lost herself in their limpid brownness. There was a vulnerability to Milo she had never noticed before. Suddenly, she wanted him inside her. She needed him to fill her up, to make her whole again. It had been so long since she had felt whole.

She eased him into her. A shaft of molten fire. The glow radiated outward from that deepest part of her, igniting her whole body. He caught hold of her by the hips, bouncing her up and down, driving himself into her as far as he could.

She forgot who she was or where she was. Once again she had given him permission to transport her. To take her out of herself and beyond herself. As her thoughts took flight, so did her body. She was free again. His fierce heat was growing even hotter. A sob tore loose from her. With a hoarse intake of breath, he came—flooding her, draining himself.

He brought her to her own completion seconds later. She was lost outside herself. She was a pinwheel, throwing off shimmering bursts of ecstasy over and over and over again. She came down very gradually from the heights and coasted with him back to earth again.

The air was cold on her steaming flesh. Exhausted, she let him pull her down beside him. He held her in his arms and stroked her while the heat cooled and her head grew clear again.

It was another three hours before she finally placed her call to Avery Leggett.

When Collier and Milo docked in New York, Avery was there to meet them.

"Well, you certainly timed your arrival rather dramatically," he told Collier as he ushered them toward his waiting limousine.

"What are you talking about?" Collier demanded, casting a puzzled glance at Milo.

"It looks like war, my pet," Avery replied grimly. "Germany's just marched into Poland."

Chapter Seven

~~~~~~~

"Bless me, Father, for I have sinned."

"The Lord be in your heart and upon your lips that you may truly and humbly confess your sins: In the Name of the Father, and of the Son, and of the Holy Spirit. Amen."

"I confess to Almighty God, to his Church and to you, that I have sinned by my own fault in thought, in word and in deed. I shouted at the cook yesterday for burning my pancakes. I told everyone in my class at school that I'd seen Sally Ann Plough kissing Doug Turnbull at the skating rink. I forgot to feed my two goldfish and they were both floating upside down in their bowl this morning."

"And do you feel remorse for what you have confessed to me, my son?"

"I do, Father."

"Then for your penance, you will read the first five chapters of Matthew this evening before you go to bed so that you will better learn the meaning of compassion."

"Yes, Father."

"Our Lord Jesus Christ, who offered himself to be sacrificed for us to the Father, and who conferred power on his Church to forgive sins, absolves you through my ministry by the grace of the Holy Spirit, and restores you in the perfect peace of the Church. Amen. Go in peace, my son, and pray for me, a sinner."

Twelve-year-old Addison Sargent Paget-Browne picked up his prayerbook and stepped out of the confessional. He felt much better now. But then he always felt better after confession. The first five chapters of Matthew. He wondered if he'd been given them before. He'd been given so many chapters over the years that he'd lost track of them all. He straightened his tie, checked to see that the buttons on his jacket were fastened and then headed up the aisle to join his mother.

Darn! She was standing in the foyer talking to Sally Ann Plough and her parents. Sally Ann saw him coming and promptly stuck out her tongue at him. Addison snickered. She'd asked for it. If she'd only let him copy the answers from her arithmetic paper, he wouldn't have had to get back at her. Doug Turnbull was stupid, sneaking off to kiss someone like Sally Ann Plough. She was a ninny. All girls were ninnies, sniffling over the littlest things and then running to their daddies for protection.

Addison didn't need any daddy to protect him. So far he'd done all right on his own. But he wished he'd hurry up and grow. It was getting harder for him to defend himself when all the boys his age were already taller than he was. They were still calling him a sissy, and all because his mother came with the chauffeur to drive him to and from school every day. He really didn't care what he was called. It was too long a walk to school, especially in the winter. The wind made his ears red and gave him earaches. The other boys were jealous of him, just like his mother said. He was a Paget-Browne and they weren't.

"There you are, darling," his mother smiled, holding out her arms to him. "Come say hello to the Ploughs and little Sally Ann," she told him while he nestled closer to the small dead animals hanging around her neck.

"I don't want to say hello to Sally Ann," he muttered.

"But why not?"

"She's a girl."

"That's no reason to be impolite, Addison."

It was a good enough reason for him. His sister Collier was a girl. He hated girls.

Sally Ann Plough began to giggle.

Addison whirled around, his blue eyes blazing. He could have punched her. Instead, with the pressure of his mother's hands on his shoulders, he allowed his anger to cool down until even his eyes seemed to frost over.

With a small whimper of fright, Sally Ann moved closer to her father.

She was such a baby, Addison thought. She wasn't even pretty now.

Before Addison could fully enjoy his new power over her, the Ploughs each seized one of their daughter's hands and hurried her out of the church.

"That was rude, darling," Elinor scolded her son as she helped him into his overcoat. "You really should be nicer to her, you know. Mr. Plough is a very rich and important man."

"As important as we are?" Addison asked. He was already starting to shiver as they walked down the steps toward the car.

"You know your father was one of the richest and most important men in Boston."

"Then the Ploughs should be nicer to me."

"But you still have to make friends with the best families, dear, including the Ploughs."

Addison slid onto the back seat beside his mother and let the chauffeur close the door. "I don't want to think about all that now, Mother," he complained in a cross voice. "I'm cold and I'm hungry."

He pulled the wool lap blanket up to his chin. He despised the cold. When he was as rich as his father had been, he would move south. No more snow and cold for him then. No more sitting up in bed with a cough which made his ribs ache, while his mother rubbed some smelly ointment all over his chest.

His mother was staring out the window. He wriggled closer to her and reached up to rub his hand across her cheek. She turned to him and smiled.

"Do you think you could give me my birthday present before the party starts this afternoon?" he asked her. "I hate opening up your gift in front of other people. It's much more fun when we're alone."

"You're so very thoughtful, Addison my darling," Elinor murmured, kissing the top of his head. "But I wouldn't want you to expect something especially grand and then be disappointed afterward."

"You couldn't disappoint me, Mother. You're the best present-giver in the whole world."

She ruffled his dark hair with her fingers. "All right, dear, you can have your present when we get home."

He gave her his best smile.

Then he slid across the seat again and rested his head against the door. He looked out at the people walking with their heads bent against the wind, their eyes partly closed against the snow which had started falling again. What if the snow got worse and no one was able to come to his party? What would happen to all his presents?

His stomach began to churn and he could even feel his face getting warm. He thought about it for a few minutes and came up with a solution. He'd simply have his mother send the chauffeur to collect the gifts for him.

As soon as he walked into the house, Addison left his coat on a chair for the butler to put away and bolted up the stairs. Opening his bedroom door, he was pleased to find his costume neatly laid out at the foot of his bed. All of his birthday parties had been costume parties for the past six years, and this year he and his mother had chosen a circus theme. He was going as the ringmaster.

Both the living room and dining room had been draped with white sheets and decorated with colored balloons and crepe-paper streamers to make the rooms look like tents. The butler and the maids who would be serving the refreshments had all been given clown costumes to wear, and all the children invited to the party would be dressed as circus performers. Addison picked up the long black whip which came with his costume and flicked it just to hear it snap. His parties were always the best. Everyone said so.

He put down the whip and took a look at the time. He was late. He hastily checked the hallway for some sign of his mother and then locked the door to his room. From the bottom drawer of his desk, he took out the square metal box with the tiny brass padlock, opened it and threw back the lid.

Inside the box lay several neatly folded newspaper clippings, a pair of scissors, a small notepad, a pencil and a ruler. He seated himself at his desk and unfolded the first clipping. He hadn't had time to make the proper notes this morning because his mother had hurried him off to church. Under the heading HEIRESS TOASTS NEW DECADE, he read all about Collier Paget-Browne's lavish party to welcome the year 1940. He let the hatred simmer inside him as he went through each clipping.

Once he had finished them, he picked up his pencil and his ruler and began underlining the key words in each of the articles. Champagne. Caviar. Diamond and ruby ring. Rolls Royce Silver Cloud. Sable coat. Pearl choker. Sailboat. Then he opened his notebook to a fresh page, dated it and very carefully copied down each of the words he had underlined. He stumbled over the spelling of several artists' names, but he knew they each had to be included in his list. They had to be important if they were guests in her home.

His notepad was beginning to fill up. It was so much easier now that she was back in the country again. In Gloucester. Just thirty miles away. He could read about her almost every day now.

"See, I'm keeping a list, smarty-pants sister," he said to her photograph. "I know how rich you are and I know how you're spending my money. I'm keeping this list so I'll know exactly how much you owe me when you pay me back one day."

His list complete, he put everything back in the box, locked it and put it away in his drawer again. "I know all about your mother too. I know she's crazy and that one day you'll be crazy too and all I have to do is wait."

He wiped his hands on his trousers and pulled the telephone closer to him. Picking up the receiver, he asked the operator to place his call. Then he sat up straight and tried to keep his breathing regular so that he could hear her when she came to the phone.

By the fifth ring, his heart was thudding so loudly in his chest that he was afraid he wouldn't be able to hear her at all. What if she wasn't there? It was his birthday. She just had to be in. His face was getting red from the exertion of trying to breathe normally and sit very still.

"Hello?"

It was her!

"Yes, this is Miss Paget-Browne."

How he hated her for having his name.

"Hello?"

"Go ahead, please," said the operator.

Addison's heart was threatening to leap out of his chest. He thought of all the things he wanted to say to her.

"Hello! Operator!"

I hate you. I hate you and I wish you were dead. I hate you for cheating me and spending my money.

"Go ahead, please."

He wanted to tell the operator to shut up. She was blocking out her voice at the other end.

"Hello? Is there someone there?"

I hate you and I'll make you pay me back even if I have to wait until I'm an old man.

Darn her! She'd hung up.

His entire body was trembling. Trembling like the time he'd stuck his finger into the electric socket in his room and felt a terrible snap, while his finger turned black and his insides had twitched and jumped.

"One day," he vowed, putting down the receiver, "one day I'll tell you face to face how much I hate you."

"Addison?"

His mother was trying the door.

"Addison, why is this door locked?"

He was furious at her for interrupting him, but he finally let her into his room.

"You're so flushed," she exclaimed, pressing her hand against his forehead. "You're not catching cold, are you?"

He shook his head as he backed away from her. "I'm just excited about my party," he lied, wondering why she hadn't brought him his present. "Was my gift too big to bring upstairs?"

"As a matter of fact, I have it right here." She patted the pocket of her dress.

"In there?" his voice quavered. Disappointment drained the triumph out of his phone call. He thrust his hands into the pockets of his trousers so she wouldn't see how tightly his fists were clenched.

Elinor held out a tiny blue velvet box with a big blue bow on top of it and Addison's frown deepened. As if the bow could make up for the size of the box. He chewed on the inside of his cheek in an effort to control his mounting anger.

"Here, darling," his mother was smiling at him. "Happy birthday."

He thrust out his bottom lip and refused to take his hands out of his pockets.

"Don't you even want to open it, dear?"

No, he didn't want to open it. He thought of the list he'd just written down in his notepad, and his eyes filled with tears.

"Addison, darling, what's wrong?"

"Nothing!"

He snatched the box out of her hands and tossed the bow onto the floor. Then he pressed on the little pearlized button and watched the lid of the box pop open. Sticking up from the white satin lining was a heavy gold ring with the Paget-Browne family crest on it. Addison batted his eyelashes to hold back his tears.

"It was your father's ring, Addison. I asked the jeweler to make it smaller so that you could wear it now," his mother explained as she took the ring and slipped it onto the third finger of his right hand. "See, it fits you perfectly. You're the head of the household now, so I thought you should start wearing it. I hope you like it, darling."

"It's beautiful, Mother, thank you," he replied in a stiff,

little voice, staring down at the crest which should have meant something to him. But it meant nothing. How could it? All he had was a name and a crest. She had the name and all of his money. Suddenly, he couldn't hold himself back any longer.

"It isn't beautiful!" he cried, pulling off the ring and hurling it across the room. "It isn't beautiful and it isn't fair! It isn't fair, I tell you!"

"Addison, lower your voice, dear, the servants will hear you."

"Who cares if a bunch of servants hear me? You said I'm the head of the household, didn't you? Well, let them hear me, then!"

"Addison—"

"You say I'm the head of the household, but I'm the head of nothing!" he shrieked. "I have nothing and she has everything! Why should I be happy with a stupid old ring when she can buy herself new rings and big cars and sailboats and have huge parties? I don't want a stupid ring with a crest that doesn't mean anything. I want what she stole from me! I want what's supposed to be mine!

"Addison, hush, darling, please." Elinor tried to grab hold of him, but he danced away from her. "I've never seen you act this way before. What's happened? Why are you behaving like this?"

"Because we're poor! I know the man from the bank is always calling you. I know that we owe everybody money because we're trying to pretend that we're richer than everyone else. Get her to help us, Mother! Make her share some of her money with us. Make her, make her, make her!"

Elinor finally caught hold of him by the shoulders and shook him until he thought his head would snap off. "Don't you think I've tried! Don't you think I've spoken to her lawyers, written her letters, explained our situation to her. But do you think she cares? No! She's never answered any of my letters. Only Avery Leggett answers them. And what do we get from him? Nothing. I *have* tried. I've even sold the two airplanes and the fleet of cars your father left me. Now I've put the house in Nahant up for sale. One day you'll get what's coming to you, Addison, I promise you that. I've never broken any of my promises to you, have I?"

Reluctantly, he shook his head.

"Then pick up that ring and come downstairs for lunch. You

have a party this afternoon and you're the host. Remember that." Her face softened. "Now try to be happy, my darling. It's your birthday."

"I'll try," he agreed, wiping his running nose with the back of his hand.

"For God's sake, Addison," she slapped his hand away, "use your handkerchief."

He took out his handkerchief and blew his nose. Then he got down on his hands and knees to reach the ring which had rolled under one of the radiators. "Some day," he told the ring, "I'll have everything else that goes with this crest. My mother's promised."

Chapter Eight

Gloucester is one of the oldest colonies on the Eastern Sea-board, older than either Greenwich or Provincetown. Its brown granite shoreline is rocky and desolate except for broad patches of sandy beaches. The sea shimmers blue-green in the sunlight and flattens into steely gray on a cloudy day. The starkness of the coast is broken by the occasional woody slope. Its trees provide the lumber for many of the peak-roofed, shingled cottages dotting the town and stretching around the harbor. The east wind from the sea keeps the air cool. Indian summers are brief and hot, the autumns clear and crisp.

December in New England is always bleak, but to Collier, December in Gloucester was a particularly ugly time. The trees were stripped of their autumn colors, the sea was a dirty gray, and the air hovered between dampness and bitterness. Everything seemed to exist in a suspended state, waiting for the first purifying snowfall of the season.

Collier had never seen Gloucester bleaker than on this Sunday in December. She hated Sundays. The entire world seemed to close down then. Even the house seemed colder to her today. Neither the roaring fire in the fieldstone fireplace in their bedroom nor the quart of mulled wine she and Milo had been drinking all afternoon had helped warm her.

She sat up in bed, drew the blankets up to her chin and frowned into her half-empty mug. "I've run out of things to toast," she complained.

"I've got one," Milo said. "Here's to the second anniversary of the bombing of Pearl Harbor!"

"Milo!"

"All right then. How about toasting the rheumatic fever I had as a kid that's kept you from becoming a war widow!"

"I'll drink to that," she quickly agreed, clanking mugs with him and finishing the last of her wine.

"All gone." Milo turned his mug upside down and put on a woeful face. "Let's ring for room service."

"I gave the staff the afternoon off, remember?"

"Oh, yeah. Well, then you be a good girl and go make us some more of this heavenly elixir."

"Uh-uh. Too cold."

"I can't bribe you?"

"Nope." She burrowed closer to him under the covers. "I'm freezing. Can't we just cuddle for a while?"

"I'm not even feeling a buzz," he complained, pushing her away from him. "I'm going downstairs to get myself some gin."

"I thought you wanted to do some painting later on."

"Why waste my time? The basement's already filled with the Milo Racines no one wants."

"Then we'll try a gallery this time," she teased him.

"What kind of a crack is that?" he demanded. "Shit, Collier, do you think I've been trying to stock our basement these past four years? Of course I want them hung in a gallery, but no one will take them!"

She decided to take a chance. "Then it might be the perfect time to give your London paintings an airing."

"No!"

"Oh, Milo, there are sixty-four marvelous paintings crated and stored in Boston. Why won't you agree to show them here? This isn't England, you know, and so much has been happening in art these past few years."

"I said no. Do you enjoy seeing me humiliated? Do you want me to take out a bunch of second-rate paintings and hang them and stay second-rate forever?"

"You're not second-rate and neither are your paintings!"

"The answer's still no."

"Then let's hang them in the house. God knows there's enough room."

"Well, if you do, make sure they're in rooms you can lock!" He threw off the covers and got out of bed.

Collier lay back in bed and watched him put on one of his embroidered silk robes. What a mass of contradictions he was. At home, he dressed the part of a dandy, a country gentleman. For the townspeople and the tourists, he still played the bohemian artist, wearing his outlandish clothes and posturing in front of his easel, which he would set up on one of the wharves. He had even taken his outrageous dress a step further by piercing one of his ears and wearing a one-carat diamond stud in it.

His affectations had finally alienated him from all of the serious artists on the Cape, artists who still believed that art had something to do with integrity and with struggle. Milo no longer had to struggle. He had allowed Collier's money to cushion him and provide him with luxuries no artist, no matter how successful, could ever have afforded on his own. The good life had drained the fight out of Milo. It had also diluted his genius.

When he came back into the room, Collier was standing at the window, trying to pull her thoughts together. She was restless. Bored. Angry with herself for doing nothing over the past four years except be the wife of Milo Racine.

At twenty-one, she had come into the second of three ten-million dollar trusts—the third would come to her when she turned twenty-five—and had become president of Paget-Browne Enterprises. But she had kept her promise to Sir Gilbert Hall and left the running of the vast organization to the three vice presidents who had been running it for nearly twenty years.

Milo propped himself up in bed again and poured some gin into his mug.

"Want some?" he offered.

She shook her head. Listlessly, she traced her finger back and forth across the windowpane.

"Just what the hell do you want then?"

"I've decided to do the one thing I'm good at," Collier replied.

He raised a skeptical eyebrow.

"I'm going to begin collecting art."

Before he could interrupt her, she went on.

"I discovered you, didn't I? Well, there must be a lot more Milo Racines in the world waiting to be discovered. I want to find them and sponsor them. Did you know that eight years ago, the Whitney Museum in New York took a chance on a group of unknowns and mounted the first exhibit of abstract paintings in this country? Nothing much came out of the exhibit, but the names of those artists read like a *Who's Who* in American art today. Hans Hofmann, Mark Rothko, Robert Motherwell, Clyfford Still. Even your friend Gorky and his imitators, as you called them, Pollock and de Kooning. Separately, these men have very little power. Collectively, they can form one of the most important art movements of this century. I intend to see that this movement happens, and that it's the first of many such movements."

"Sounds pretty grandiose to me." Milo yawned, filling his mug again.

"Why? You predicted it yourself four years ago."

"I was only referring to Gorky," he snapped.

Puzzled by his hostility, she tried another tack. "As much as I love it here, Milo, I've never been accepted. No one has ever made me feel as if I belonged here. As an artist, you've been able to fit in better. But not me. Even after four years in this place, people still keep their distance from me."

"Well, you can hardly blame them, can you? What the hell do a bunch of fishermen and their wives have in common with an heiress? If you want to fit in some place, you should be living in Palm Beach or Newport."

She finally lost her temper. "All right, then, let's move! Pack up your brushes and your paints and let's go. You'll fit in just as well in Palm Beach as I will, Milo, with your new Jaguar, your custom-made clothes and your taste for sixty-year-old brandy."

He opened his mouth to say something and then just as quickly shut it. Collier turned away from him in disgust. The pattern of her life had been woven into a noose tightening around her throat. It was always the same. Angry words. Milo's silence. A two-day binge. Repentant speeches. A burst of artistic energy. A spate of passionate lovemaking. Then another spark, another conflagration. She wished she had the strength to do without him. Not yet. She wasn't ready. But soon, maybe soon.

She gazed out the window, across the narrow arm of the harbor where the Eastern Point lighthouse sat perched on its own bed of rocks. She had almost forgotten. Today was Jennifer Howe's sixth birthday and Collier had promised the little girl that she would stop by. She went into her dressing room to put on her clothes.

"Where you goin'?" Milo called from the bed, his words increasingly slurred.

"It's Jenny's birthday and she and Orrin are expecting me," she called back to him.

"Well, there you are! You can stop snivelin' about havin' no friends. You have good old Orrin and that little kid of his."

"Why don't you come with me? You know how much Jenny likes you."

"She just likes me for my paintings."

Collier laughed. "You'd better watch out for her, Milo.

She's talented. She might grow up to be your stiffest competition."

"Not if she sticks to fingerpaints, she won't."

Collier pulled on a pair of high rubber boots and then tucked her long hair under a woolen cap. She slipped into her navy blue pea jacket, fished out her mittens and went back into the bedroom to give Milo a light peck on the mouth.

"Why don't you stay here and we'll ask a few people in?" he mumbled, trying to pull her down onto the bed.

"I promised them, Milo. I can't disappoint them."

His face turned sullen. "Okay, forget it. I can party just as well without you."

Something clutched at her insides. It was that familiar lurching feeling she got whenever he used that tone with her. She tried to shrug it off, but it settled inside her stomach like a sodden lump of dough. Letting go of his hand, she went over to her dresser, picked up the large, gift-wrapped present she was bringing Jenny, and without even looking at Milo again, she walked stiffly out of the room.

She inhaled that first stinging breath of the damp sea air and felt the heaviness begin to lift. The frozen grass crunched under the weight of her boots as she started down the path leading to the wooden pier, which would take her to the foot of the Eastern Point lighthouse. She glanced back at the house only once, and that was to look at the wide deck off the third floor attic which Milo had been using as his studio.

She walked briskly, breathing in the salty air, thinking of Orrin Howe, the fifty-year-old lighthouse keeper, and his daughter, who was so painfully shy that she used her home in the clouds to keep her out of the reach of the world below. Orrin's wife had been forty when she became pregnant with Jenny, and because her other four births had been stillborn, she had gratefully delivered her only healthy child—then died from the effort.

Jennifer Howe was a beautiful child, with a stream of black hair hanging to her waist and rock-crystal gray eyes. She followed her father everywhere, making certain that he wouldn't slip away from her when she wasn't looking. Orrin Howe loved the sea. He had been a fisherman most of his life, but because of Jennifer, he had given it up, installing them both in the lighthouse, where she was able to keep him safe.

Collier had met them the first summer she and Milo had

spent in Gloucester. She had gone down to the harbor for the town's annual memorial service honoring the fishermen who had died at sea. It had been a simple ceremony, punctuated by muffled sobs and gentle words. After the names of the lost men and their vessels were read, the minister from the local church offered several prayers, and then everyone released the bouquets of flowers they had brought with them, dropping them, flower by flower, into the water of the Squam River.

Collier had been about to leave when she felt something tug at her skirt.

She looked down into the face of Jennifer Howe.

"You're the only one without any flowers," murmured the little girl whose eyes were fixed on Collier's shoes. "My father said I should let you have one of ours."

Collier accepted the single yellow daisy Jennifer was holding up to her. "Let's put it in the water together," Collier suggested.

She invited Orrin and Jennifer back to the house. Milo joined them for lemonade and cake, and then managed to convince Jennifer to go upstairs with him to see his studio. When Collier went up an hour later, she found Jennifer sitting on a pale blue velvet footstool, her face solemn, her hands clasped lightly in her lap while Milo painted her.

The canvas was evolving into a gentle wash of muted colors, of pale blue, ivory and soft gray. All sharp traces of the girl were gone. What remained were pieces of Jennifer Howe, scattered across the canvas like the parts of a jigsaw puzzle, blurred and beautifully out of place.

Milo finally set down his brush and wiped off his hands. "Once the painting's dry, I'll frame it and then you can take it home with you. Okay?" He smiled at the girl as he helped her up from the stool.

"Yes, sir," she mumbled, her face red, her hands clenched, her small body beginning to tremble.

Suddenly, she burst into tears and ran out of the room. Dumbfounded, Collier and Milo stared at each other. Then Collier noticed the dark stain on the pale blue velvet cushion and her heart began to ache. Jennifer had been too shy to even ask to use the bathroom.

It was Collier who eventually took the framed portrait up to the lighthouse. Jennifer refused to come to the door. It took four more visits before Collier saw the child again.

The lighthouse soon became a refuge for Collier, a place to go when she needed to get away from the house, away from Milo, and find some peace. Milo soon began to call her Rapunzel. Through Orrin's telescope, Collier could see the furthest trawlers out on the sea as well as the smallest details of every house along the beach. She even trained her glass toward the rocky bluff on which her own house stood, and watched the gardener trimming the hedges.

It was through that telescope that she witnessed Milo's adultery for the first time. Stunned and horrified, she saw Milo, naked, his skin pale, the hair on his chest so dark by contrast, standing on the deck off his studio with a young girl whose long red hair was being fanned around her shoulders by the wind. His hands were in her hair. His lips explored her face.

Fascinated, mesmerized, she watched Milo cup the girl's small breasts in his hands. She watched as he stroked them and fondled them and finally bent to suck them into his mouth. The girl threw back her head, and arched her back and seemed to be smiling. Their bodies began to move in an unmistakable, undulating rhythm as they slid slowly to the porch floor.

Collier stepped away from the telescope, soaked through with perspiration and shaking.

Milo's betrayal seized her throat and closed it. It twisted her heart into a knot. Her guts became a living thing turned against her. She wanted to die. Her mind, stung by the outrage she felt, wanted only revenge.

She chose neither revenge nor death.

She simply confronted him with it. It was his indifference more than his betrayal which cauterized her bleeding soul.

"Don't act so surprised," he told her. "She wasn't the first and she won't be the last. It's all part of being an artist."

"Being an artist gives you the right to do whatever you want? It allows you to make love to another woman in my house?" She was incredulous.

"Your house! Your studio! Your money! Everything's yours! That's the problem. All I've got are my senses." She stared at him, speechless. "You don't understand, do you? I have to see and touch and taste and smell. Everything! I have to know or I can't paint."

She finally closed her mind to his excuses and her eyes to his excesses and began to think about what to do with the rest of her life. He was the man she had chosen because of his excesses, because of his unpredictability, because of his disregard for convention. She had given him power over her and he had abused it. She had given him parts of herself to care for and he had mishandled them. Now she wanted to take that power back and make herself whole again.

Slightly winded from the long climb up the circular staircase of the lighthouse, Collier waited until she caught her breath and then knocked on the door. Jennifer herself answered it. With a squeal of delight, she threw her arms around Collier's waist and squeezed her until Collier burst out laughing and pretended to be gasping for air.

"I knew you'd come, I just knew it!" Jenny cried, tugging Collier into the living room.

Orrin glanced up from his newspaper and waved.

"I told Daddy you'd be here, didn't I, Daddy? And I even watched you through the telescope as you came up the pier."

"A glass of sherry, Collier?" asked Orrin, folding up the paper and going over to the teawagon he used as a bar.

"Thanks, Orrin, that would be fine," Collier smiled, taking off her cap and shaking out her hair. "Now, young lady," she said, turning to Jennifer, "before you burst, why don't you open up your present?"

"This will be the best present ever, I just know it! Not that your present wasn't wonderful, Daddy," she hurried to explain. "Daddy bought me a yellow raincoat with a hat to go with it. Now I look exactly like him. Don't I, Daddy?"

"That you do, angel," Orrin agreed, handing Collier her sherry.

"Oh, paints!" exclaimed Jennifer, tearing the tissue paper off the first of the twelve glass bottles. "Real waterpaints. And brushes, too! Oh, thank you, Collier, thank you. I told you this would be the best present ever."

She flung her arms around Collier's neck and planted a moist kiss on her mouth. "Next year it'll be oil paints," Collier told her.

Jennifer began to giggle. "Then you'd better tell Milo to watch out, because one day I'm going to be the best painter in the whole world. One day I'll have a studio just as big as his and everyone will buy my paintings and I'll get to be as rich as you." She stopped to draw a breath and then, in a quiet voice, she said, "Do you know what the best part of being a painter is? I can work all by myself and never have to be with anyone if I don't want to."

Collier and Orrin exchanged glances. "Didn't your father tell you that you'll be going to school next year?" she asked.

The child's face fell. "He told me." Her eyes turned dark and stormy and her bottom lip began to quiver. "But I don't see why I have to go to school. I just want to stay up here and paint."

"Don't you want to learn to read and write?"

"I already know how. Daddy's been teaching me."

"But in school you'll be able to learn about history and geography, even music, Jenny. If you want to be a good artist, you'll have to learn as much as you can about the world."

"I don't like the world," she pouted. "I like it up here. I can see everything I want to from here if I use the telescope. I don't see why I have to go down there at all."

Collier pulled the child onto her lap. "You know, Jenny, you're lucky that you have a nice school to go to because you'll be able to make lots of friends. When I was a little girl, I had to move away from my home and go to live with my godmother. I didn't have any friends and I was a very lonely little girl. My godmother loved me, but she couldn't love me enough to make up for the friends I wanted to have. Your father loves you and I love you, but we're not enough for you, either. You have to find some more people to love you so that you can love them back, too."

"But I'm scared," she whimpered, her eyes filling with tears.

"I know you are, darling, but the scary feelings will go away."

"Did your scary feelings go away?"

"Yes, my pet," she lied. "They went away."

"Do you think mine will?"

"I know they will."

Orrin came over and put his hand on his daughter's shoulder.

"Why don't you show Collier your new paintings, Jenny?" he asked her.

The child's face brightened immediately. She slid off Collier's lap and reached for her hand again. "Remember you told me that John Singer Sargent's father was born in Gloucester and that Winslow Homer used to live here? Well, I pretended that they were my grandfathers and I painted pictures of both of them. Daddy and I framed them and hung them up in the hallway. I'm starting a whole collection of pretend family and pretty soon the wall will look just like one of the walls in the museum you took me to."

Collier allowed Jennifer to walk her down the narrow corridor leading to the bedrooms. Just outside of her own room, the child stopped and pointed. Two fingerpainted portraits of her make-believe ancestors were hanging side by side on the wall, with room for at least a dozen more.

It was dark by the time Collier walked back along the wooden pier to her house. As she climbed the front steps, she found herself gritting her teeth and preparing herself. For a party. An orgy. A simple seduction. She expected any one of them.

The house was silent. She slammed the door. She could almost hear bare feet scampering across the wooden floor overhead. She could almost smell the cigarette smoke, the musky scent of sex as she mounted the stairs. She stood in the doorway of their bedroom and peered in.

Milo lay sprawled across the bed, asleep and snoring.

Chapter Nine

During 1944, Collier made fifteen trips to New York. She appeared at the opening of every exhibit featuring the artists who were now being labeled abstract expressionists. She bought, and she challenged others to buy. She allowed herself to be interviewed on the radio and photographed for every major American magazine with her growing collection of paintings. Her name alone generated enough interest to keep the galleries filled and the artists in oils.

Whatever a Paget-Browne could do, an Astor, Gould, Mellon, Rockefeller and Vanderbilt could also do. And so they began to buy, too.

New York exhilarated and excited Collier; Gloucester only depressed her. She found fewer reasons to return home. But on Christmas Eve, she reluctantly checked out of her suite at the Plaza Hotel and drove home to spend the holiday with Milo.

She carried a silver tray of sliced turkey and salads the cook had left them into the living room, and set it down on the coffee table in front of the fireplace. She began to fill a plate for Milo, but he just shook his head and poured himself another glass of gin. Collier put the plate down and went to sit beside him on the sofa.

He was looking old. The drinking had etched so many lines underneath his eyes that whenever she looked at him, she found it impossible to believe he was only thirty. He had not painted in over a year. At his insistence, there were still no Milo Racines hanging in the Gloucester house. Instead, the walls were covered with her growing collection of Rothkos, de Koonings, Pollocks, Hofmanns, Motherwells, Stills and Bazioteses.

"I still think you should exhibit your London paintings, Milo," she told him now, carefully watching his face. "Peggy

Guggenheim has already agreed to mount the exhibit. Won't you at least consider it?"

He barely looked up from his drink. "Second-rate crap from a second-rate hack," he mumbled. "'Derivative. Imitative.' You want them to write that about me? 'Milo Racine hasn't mounted one decent show in four years, so he's imitating now.'"

"They're hardly imitative, Milo. You did them years ago."

"We never should've come back to the States. I was getting known in London. Here I've been nothing."

Collier turned away as he filled his glass again. She stared over at the large spruce Milo had cut down the week before. It was standing in a corner of the room, undecorated, drying out. She could almost hear the needles falling onto the carpet. Neither of them had felt like decorating the tree. Neither of them felt like being happy or pretending that Christmas mattered anymore. Christmas meant family times. And they were no longer a family.

"I'm burned out, Collier," Milo whispered, staring into his glass. "The genius never even hit his stride and now he's burned out. Even little Jenny could beat me now. She still using those fingerpaints you gave her?"

"She's using oils now, Milo," Collier said softly. She got up from the sofa and poured herself a brandy.

"Got one there for me?" asked Milo, setting down his glass.

"I thought you were sticking to gin."

"I'll switch." He gave her a weak smile. "Just to be sociable. Come on, Rapunzel, it's Christmas Eve."

Collier shuddered. Rapunzel. How long had it been since he had called her that? She poured him a brandy and brought it over to him. He downed it in one swallow.

"You want your present now?" he asked her.

She was surprised that he had even remembered. "If you like."

"Sure, why not? That's what Christmas is for, isn't it?" He took a tiny gold box out of his shirt pocket and handed it to her.

She put it down on the coffee table.

"Aren't you even going to open it?"

"As soon as I get yours."

She called out to him from the hall to close his eyes. Then she carried the large oil painting into the living room and propped it up on the mantelpiece.

"Okay, open your eyes."

Milo blinked and began to look around uncertainly. "Where?" he asked, bewildered.

Collier finally had to point.

He got up from the couch and stumbled over to the fireplace. Supporting himself with both hands, he leaned forward and squinted at the name in the corner of the canvas.

"Gorky?" he whispered. "It's a Gorky. You got me a Gorky!"

He began to run the tips of his fingers across the surface of the painting. He traced the outline of each of the dangling free-form shapes which resembled feet and fingers, breasts and penises, kidneys and cow's udders, all of them linked together by fine, black lines, and painted in vivid reds and oranges and blues and greens.

Collier watched him in silence, her heart pounding, her eyes filling with tears at the look of wonder, so like a child's, on his defeated face. Then she finally opened her own present. It was a diamond stud, identical to the one he still wore. With the earring was a small white card. It read: "We're still part of a matched set. Almost. Milo."

"Remember when you said we were equal partners?" Milo asked, coming over to stand beside her. "You were wrong, you know."

To her surprise, he took out the earring he was wearing and placed it, along with hers, in the open palm of his hand.

Collier's brimming eyes spilled over. Her diamond was larger.

She couldn't get to sleep that night. She was hurting again. It was the same ache she had felt when her godmother Alice had died three months before. It was that same kind of emptiness. It began deep in her belly, churning and winding around itself until it erupted in a stinging tide which swept through her body and left it cold and trembling. She reached out for Milo, but all she felt was a cool, empty place beside her in bed.

She was shivering and her teeth began to chatter when she got up and put on her robe. She would make herself a cup of hot milk, water and sugar, Alice's old recipe for getting a wide-awake child back to sleep. It had seldom worked on her as a child, and she didn't know why she expected it to work now.

Milo was sitting on the floor in the living room, rocking

back and forth, the painting on the carpet in front of him. What she first thought was crooning, she quickly realized was crying.

"Milo?"

She put out her hand and touched his shoulder.

He jumped. His ravaged face was streaked with tears, but when he saw her standing there, he clamped his mouth shut and refused to let her hear him cry. As she stood there helplessly, she saw his face begin to change. It turned from its defeated grayness to a pale shade of pink. The color flamed upward from his chest, covering him like a rash, spreading across his features, darkening them. When his anger exploded, red and raging, it stained his whole face crimson.

"You had to give me this, didn't you?" he shouted at her, flinging the painting aside. "You had to remind me! You couldn't just let me be. Always at me, always pushing me to dig out those London paintings, as if they were the best I could do, as if I wasn't capable of anything better. Why one of *his* paintings, Collier, why? He's been like my brother and you've used him to kill me. Abel killing Cain, goddamn you. You've used him to show me what I am. Nothing. A used-up painter whose wife proves I stink by buying up every other artist around. How could you rub my nose in his greatness and remind me that I'm nothing?"

Terrified by his outburst, Collier began backing away from him. "You're wrong, Milo, I never meant the gift that way. How could you accuse me of trying to humiliate you? I've been the one who's tried to build you up all these years, not tear you down. I bought this painting for you because of your love and respect for the man, nothing more. So don't you dare blame your own failure on Gorky, and don't you dare blame it on me!"

With a snarl of fury, Milo sprang to his feet. Collier turned and ran up the stairs. He sprinted after her. She had just reached the first floor landing when he caught up with her. He grabbed her around the waist and threw her down to the floor.

He flung himself on top of her. Whimpering, she covered her face with her hands, but he made no move to pull them away. Instead, he began to rip open her robe. His hands were cold against her skin. He grabbed her breasts and began to knead them between his fingers. She squirmed and bucked, but he had flattened himself across her body and she was pinned beneath him.

With one hand he worked open his trousers. Collier let out a scream and tried to close her legs.

"No, Milo, no. Not after all those others. You've forfeited your right. No!"

"Why not?" he panted. "Don't you want what they've all been getting?"

She worked up a glob of saliva and spat it into his face. He backhanded a slap across her cheek. She closed her eyes against the sting of the slap and that first, dry grating thrust of him inside her. She forced herself to go limp. Each thrust echoed in her brain like the thud of wood on steel. It was the ax breaking down the door to her father's bedroom. It was the gavel pounding over and over again in the courtroom. It was the thud of Diana's body sliding out of the chair and onto the floor. Her head ached. Her teeth felt sore. Milo plundering her body made her want to vomit.

He finally rolled away from her and allowed her to escape. She ran into the bathroom and locked the door. She ran a bath and stood in the tub while it filled up. Then she soaked in the scalding water, soaping herself and scratching a washcloth across her skin until she was sore and red. When she drained the tub and filled it again, she wondered as she soaped herself a second time if she would ever feel clean again.

That night, she threw all of her towels onto the floor and slept on a crumpled heap in the bathroom.

The following morning, Collier drove into Boston. She interrupted Avery Leggett's Christmas dinner with his children and grandchildren to tell him that she intended to divorce Milo. She knew that in the eyes of the Church she would be considered a renegade, forbidden to receive Holy Communion and forbidden to remarry within the Church. But it didn't matter to her. All that mattered was freeing herself from the man she should have let loose years before.

"I don't need him anymore, Uncle Avery," she told the old man as he ushered her into his study. "There was a time when I thought I would actually die if I had to live without him. I once needed him so badly that I was willing to put up with everything he did just so I wouldn't have to be alone. Now it isn't even a question of my needing him. Now I don't even want him."

The gray eyes behind the thick lenses were pensive. "It's the collecting that's saved you, my dear Collier, and I daresay it's going to be your future. I've watched your marriage un-raveling for a long time now, but I've kept quiet. This was a decision you had to reach on your own."

"I'm glad my father can't see me now, Uncle Avery. He'd probably rue the day he ever had a daughter."

"Nonsense. Your father may have wanted to turn you into a son, but he wasn't given the time, and I say thank God. You're becoming the woman you were meant to be, Collier, and your father would have been the first to applaud."

She gave her head a rueful shake. "Sir Gilbert Hall wouldn't have agreed with you. He never knew what to make of me." Dear Sir Gilbert, dead just three weeks after Alice. Collier felt her hold on the familiar slipping out of her hands.

"You're a Paget-Browne, Collier, you were born rebellious. Make the most of it. Heavens knows why you thought you'd be content darning some man's socks and cooking stews in some obscure New England fishing village!"

Collier laughed. "I still can't cook and I've never darned a sock in my life."

"It's good to see you smiling, my girl." Avery covered her hand with his. Then he got serious again. "If you like, I'll begin drawing up the papers for you immediately. No sense wasting time." Collier suddenly looked hesitant. "You're not having second thoughts, are you?"

"He's so lost, Uncle Avery. I almost feel guilty doing this to him."

"Well, you'd better make up your mind, young lady, and be quick about it. You may have all the time in the world, but I'm already seventy-seven years old. Don't ask me to wait around until I'm ninety."

For a few minutes, Collier said nothing. She leaned back in her chair and stared up at the ceiling, blinking her eyes to hold back her tears.

"All right," she finally said, her voice cracking. "Do it."

Avery clapped his hands together. "Good girl. Now I'll get you free of that phony-baloney Mr. Racine if it's the last thing I do."

Collier stood up and gave the old man a hug.

"I'll call you as soon as I've drawn up the papers," he told her.

"Give me a few days," she said. "I'm not exactly sure when I'll be home."

"Another trip to New York?"

Collier shook her head. "Philadelphia. There's someone there I haven't seen in fifteen years. I think it's time."

"Diana Taggert?"

Collier nodded. "Yes. My mother."

Chapter Ten

The Fairwood Clinic in Philadelphia housed thirty-five patients. All of them were wealthy and all of them were completely dependent upon the sheltered life provided for them by the well-paid, European-trained staff. Fairwood was often mistaken for an exclusive country club. Tall black wrought-iron gates swung open onto a long gravel drive leading up to the portico of the three-story French-styled chateau that served as the clinic. The grounds were maintained by a staff of Italian gardeners. White wicker chairs and round tables with green and white striped umbrellas shading them were set out at strategic intervals through the gardens. There was even a tennis court for the patients, which only the staff members used.

Alva Rittenhouse, the head nurse on the second floor where Diana Taggert was a patient, showed Collier to her mother's room. It was large and overlooked the back gardens and a small, oval-shaped swimming pool. The walls were papered in a lively print of tiny violets with bright green leaves. The ruffled curtains at the windows were mauve, as was the chenille spread on the double bed. All the furniture had been painted white, and the two wing chairs in one corner of the room had been upholstered in the same bright green as the leaves on the wallpaper.

As Collier looked at the room more closely, Fairwood's resemblance to a country club abruptly ended. There was a layer of heavy wire mesh between the double panes of glass in the window. The door could be locked only from the outside and there was a small, uncurtained window set high in that door. Fairwood was nothing more than a pretty prison.

"Mrs. Taggert should be coming in from her walk any minute now," said the woman in the simple gray wool dress with the white sweater slung across her shoulders. Then, as if sensing Collier's unasked question, she explained, "We prefer not to wear uniforms here at Fairwood. We found that uniforms tended to frighten the guests. This way they're much more at ease with us and we're more of a family than an institution."

Guests. Collier smirked. Fairwood wouldn't even admit to calling them patients. Would that have frightened them as well?

There was a large photograph set in a sterling-silver frame on the table next to the bed. Collier picked it up and looked at it. It was the picture of a young boy of about five. He was a handsome child, slim, with light hair and smoky colored eyes. This had to be Leland, she thought. Leland Taggert, her own half-brother.

She heard a noise in the doorway. Guiltily, she set the frame back on the table and turned around. She suddenly found herself trembling. Should she sit down? she wondered. Would her height intimidate Diana? The woman seemed so small.

They stood and simply stared at one another, Collier next to the bed, Diana in the doorway. Separated by no more than six feet, the distance between them seemed vast. It was Collier who made the first move. She walked slowly over to Diana and put out her hand to touch the woman's cheek.

"You're so very beautiful," murmured Diana Taggert, closing her eyes and nuzzling Collier's hand with her lips.

Collier shivered. Once again she was hearing that voice. A voice she had heard as a nine-year-old child in a crowded Boston courtroom. The look on Diana's face was the one she had worn on that awful day. It was a look Collier had been searching for ever since.

With a sob, she reached for the small, lovely woman and drew her into her arms. She pressed Diana's head against her chest and felt again the fine blond hair between her fingers.

"I've waited so long," she whispered. "Forgive me. Please forgive me for waiting so long."

Diana Taggert put her arms around the tall, exquisite woman who was her daughter, and silently forgave her. She was so happy today. It had been such a good day for her. She remembered how the poached eggs had tasted at breakfast and how the coffee had scalded the tip of her tongue. She even remembered the shapes of the snowflakes on the dead brown leaf she had picked up on the path during her walk.

"Would you care for some tea, Miss Paget-Browne?" asked Alva Rittenhouse.

"Yes, we'll have some tea," Collier told the nurse. Anything to be rid of her. Anything to be left alone with this woman whose eyes were still so blue and whose lovely face had scarcely changed since that day so long ago. "Would you please bring the tea in here for us?" she asked as Alva Rittenhouse was heading out the door.

The woman stopped, a frown creasing her brow. "Well, we do prefer our guests take their tea in the parlor, but in this case, I think we can make an exception."

"Thank you." Collier gave the woman something she hoped would pass for a polite smile. Of course Alva Rittenhouse's decision to bend the rules had nothing to do with the ten thousand dollar check Collier had given them that morning.

So many things to say, she thought as she settled Diana in one of the wing chairs and then took the one opposite her. She wondered what they should talk about. She worried about how much her mother would even be able to comprehend. She thought of the absurdity of it all. Here they sat, a mother and a daughter, together for the second time in their lives, sitting down to tea as if they were with a group of Main Line matrons. Two strangers, with nothing in common but their blood.

"Do you like it here?" Collier asked, hating the inanity of the question, but hating the silence between them even more.

"It's the only home I've had since . . . since that day, you know, when I lost my baby," Diana replied. She was speaking very slowly, choosing each of her words carefully, reaching for the right ones from a vocabulary long diminished by illness and drugs. She began to stroke the sleeve of her blue wool dress. "My son, Leland, gave me this dress for Christmas. It's a beautiful dress, don't you think?"

Collier nodded. "It matches your eyes."

"Are you married?" Diana asked, studying the strange gold and silver band on Collier's left hand. She wondered what had happened to her own rings. She massaged the finger where the rings had been. They had been so beautiful. Diamonds. Glittering. Sparkling. Throwing off so many different colors.

Collier wondered if her mother had heard the answer to her question. She seemed so preoccupied, rubbing her ring finger and whispering to herself.

A discreet knock came at the door, followed by Alva Rittenhouse with the tea service. She placed the tray on the small table between Collier and Diana, looked closely at Diana for a moment and then left.

"Mother?" The word almost lodged itself in Collier's throat.

Diana glanced up, looking confused. Then she smiled. Collier smiled back.

"Are you all right?" Collier asked her.

Diana nodded her head. "Would you like some tea?" She reached for the teapot and the weight of it made her hand begin to shake. Collier hastily held out her cup.

She forced herself not to cry out. Diana had missed the cup and was pouring the scalding tea onto Collier's hand. With all the control she could manage, Collier set down her cup and took the pot from Diana's trembling hand. The woman was still smiling at her. She hadn't even noticed what she had done.

The back of her hand was stinging. Collier bit down hard on her bottom lip as she dried herself off with a napkin. Then she began to blow on her hand, hoping to cool the pain. Diana was staring at her, the smile gone from her face, a worried frown there instead. Collier quickly lifted up her empty teacup and pretended to take a sip of her tea. Diana began to smile again.

"Do you have any children?" Diana asked her then.

Collier shook her head.

"You should have children," Diana said. "Children are all a woman has, you know. I'm lucky. I have you and I have Leland." She began to toy with the pleats in the skirt of her dress. "Do you like this dress? Leland gave it to me for my birthday."

Collier tried not to show her confusion.

Diana stared over at the photograph on the table and her eyes filled with tears. Alarmed, Collier sprang out of her chair and knelt on the floor at her mother's feet. Silent tears were coursing down Diana's cheeks. Collier took her napkin and patted the tears away.

"Did you say you had children?" Diana mumbled, her voice almost indistinct. "You should have children, you know. Little ones. They're so sweet when they're little."

Collier could feel Diana slipping away from her. Desperately, she cast about for something to say.

"Have you ever been to the ocean, Mother? That's where I live, you know, near the ocean. Would you like to come and visit me there? We could take long walks together on the beach and we could go swimming. It's warm there in the summer, but the breeze is always cool and—"

"Leave here?" Diana's eyes were wide with fright. "But I don't want to leave."

"It would only be for a little while. You'd be staying with me and I'd take care of you."

Diana was shaking her head. "I like it here. I can take long walks here. I even found a leaf all covered with snow on the path this morning." She reached into the pocket of her dress and pulled out the crumbling leaf. "See?" She began to smooth out its tattered edges. "Are there any trees near the ocean?"

"Lots of trees. And there are seagulls and sandpipers and the beach is covered with seashells. We could collect some shells and put them in a glass bowl for you to take back with you. Then whenever you looked at the shells, you'd remember the ocean."

"I like to take walks outside even when it's cold. Sometimes it gets so warm in here." Diana began to fan herself with her napkin. "It's so warm right now. Don't you think it's warm?"

Collier saw a fine line of perspiration forming above her mother's top lip. Was it really that warm? she wondered. She was actually feeling cold.

Diana began to unbutton her dress. She undid the first five buttons and then tried to slide her right arm out of its sleeve. She managed to tug it out part way and then she seemed to get caught. She whimpered in frustration and tried to work herself free, but she couldn't.

They were putting that jacket around her again. They were pinning her arms behind her back.

Collier got off her knees and tried to help her mother, but Diana wriggled away from her.

Someone was trying to pull the jacket tighter. Diana began to scream.

Collier was panicking. "It's all right, Mother, I'm only trying to help you. Shush, Mama, shush, it's Collier, I'm not trying to hurt you, I'm only trying to help."

"What's happening here?"

Alva Rittenhouse suddenly appeared in the doorway.

"Get away from her," she ordered Collier as she swept into the room. "You're frightening her."

Shaken, Collier backed away from her mother's chair. "She was hot. She was trying to take off her dress and I was only trying to help her."

Diana was crying now. They were hurting her again. They'd promised that if she was good, they wouldn't hurt her anymore. But they'd lied. They were always lying to her.

"Leland!" she screamed, twisting in her chair. "Leland, help me! Help me!"

Where was Leland? Where was her son? He was only five.

He was too little to help her. Maybe this tall woman would help her instead. She tried to stand up. The woman's face. It was a face she knew. But that hair. It should have been black. But it wasn't. It was gold and puffed up like a soft pillow. She looked like an angel. An angel who had his face. Now the angel was opening and closing her mouth. Like a fish. She tried to swim over to the angel-fish, but her arms were tired and she was growing weaker. She had to rest for a moment, and so she stopped swimming and closed her eyes.

Collier stood there helplessly as two young orderlies carried Diana over to the bed. Alva Rittenhouse pulled up the covers and tucked Diana in and smoothed back the blond hair which had fallen across her face.

"Such a shame," the woman clucked, shaking her head. "And this was one of her better days."

"Was it my fault?" Collier whispered, her whole body trembling now. "Was it something I said, something I did?"

"Don't blame yourself, dear, it's no one's fault, not even hers. We still don't know how the mind of the schizophrenic really operates. One minute she's as alert and as calm as you please; the next minute, you'd think the whole world was after her the way she'll carry on. I'm only sorry that on your first visit here, you had to see her like this. When her son's here, she's usually pretty calm. He seems to know how to handle her. But then he's had more practice." She patted Collier's arm and Collier didn't know whether to smile, slap her for her insolence or take Diana out of there as fast as she could.

"Could I at least stay with her until she wakes up?"

"That won't be for hours now, and I really don't think it would be such a good idea. She may not even recognize you. No, dear, I think you'd better leave."

So it was back to the beginning again. Collier glanced down at her hand. It was red and throbbing and the skin was starting to pucker. Her legs were still shaking, and she was feeling sick to her stomach. As she gazed down at the sleeping woman, she imagined herself lying there instead. Perhaps madness might not be so bad after all. She would be able to sleep most of the time and never have to worry about being alone or being afraid again. Someone would always be there to take care of her. She wouldn't even have to remember anything about failed marriages or wars or dead babies. Something would always be able to take the pain away.

"I brought some gifts for my mother," she said to Alva

Rittenhouse then, "and I never had the chance to give them to her."

"Could you tell me what you brought her, please? Precautions, you understand."

Collier's temper bubbled closer to the surface, but she held herself in check. "The gifts are in my car. If someone would carry them in for me, you can see for yourself what they are." She strode out of the room with the nurse trailing several steps behind her.

Collier unlocked the trunk of her car, and as she handed the gift-wrapped boxes to the orderly, she told Alva Rittenhouse what was in each box. A cashmere blanket. A silk nightgown with a matching robe. A pair of satin slippers. A satin bed-jacket. A cashmere sweater. Four bottles of perfume.

She had bought every brand of perfume which smelled even remotely of lily-of-the-valley. She had never known the name of the perfume Diana wore. The last box contained a silver and gold picture frame from Tiffany's. Collier tore off the wrapping and lifted the pale blue lid of the box. Then she carefully slid the photograph out of the frame.

"My mother won't like this picture of me," she explained. "She told me she preferred her children little." Collier put the frame back in the box and handed it to the orderly. "I'll send you a photograph of myself as a child, Miss Rittenhouse, and I'd appreciate it if you'd put it into the frame and give it to my mother yourself."

"I'll be glad to, dear," the woman assured her.

Collier locked the trunk again. "Could I go back inside for a few more minutes?" She hated to ask this stranger for permission to see her own mother. She thought about buying Fairwood. Then she wouldn't have to ask permission of anyone again.

The woman hesitated. Collier stared down at her and dared her to refuse. She finally gave in.

"But just for a few minutes," she warned her.

As Collier walked back toward her mother's room, an idea struck her. Why buy Fairwood when it would be simpler to buy Diana a house, either in Philadelphia where she could still be close to the clinic or in Gloucester near her own house. Gloucester. Collier slowed her steps. Once she and Milo were divorced, would she even want to remain in Gloucester? The house would be too big then, too full of memories. She felt the pain begin again.

"Excuse me," she mumbled absently as she collided with a young man heading in the opposite direction.

He glanced back at her once and then kept on walking. Collier looked over her shoulder at him, fighting the impulse to call out to him. He was so rude! Slamming into her like that. And she, like a complete fool, had actually apologized to *him*.

She tiptoed into Diana's room and stood at the foot of the bed watching her mother sleep. She thought of all the questions she had wanted to ask her. How long had she known the man who had paid her to bear him a child? Had she ever really known him at all? Had it been strictly a business deal where feelings were to play no part? What had her own childhood been like? Had she been popular as a girl? Had she loved Lloyd Taggert when she married him or had he just been part of the dream of a shopgirl from nowhere, as Elinor had so cruelly called her? Collier's heart twisted in agony. So many questions, so few answers, so little time to find them.

"I think you'd better leave now, Miss Paget-Browne," Alva Rittenhouse whispered, touching Collier's elbow.

Collier felt defeated. Her shoulders sagged, her arms felt like leaden weights hanging useless at her sides. She bent to kiss her mother's forehead. Then she walked swiftly out of the room. She silently promised her mother and herself that she would be back. And then, one day she would come to take Diana out of there. She would buy her that house, staff it with round-the-clock attendants, and keep her safe. That way, no one would ever be able to hurt Diana again. It had been fifteen years since Collier had first made that promise to her mother, and it was one she intended to keep.

She drove slowly back down the gravel drive and stopped in front of the heavy iron gates. The uniformed guard came out of his small booth and opened the gates just enough for the Bentley to ease through. As the gates clanged shut, Collier winced. There was something so very final about that sound.

Grimly, she headed back to Gloucester.

Two weeks later, Milo was served with Collier's divorce petition. She braced herself for their confrontation. She vowed that none of his arguments would get her to change her mind.

If she began to waver even the slightest bit, she would back down.

"I'm not going to let you do this!" he shouted, waving the blue-backed documents in her face. "You can't divorce me, Collier, you need me, You've always needed me. How the hell are you going to manage on your own? You've said it yourself that you're afraid to be alone. You can't throw me out. I'll change. I'll start painting again. I'll stop drinking. I'll be faithful to you."

"I suggest you hire a lawyer, Milo, and have him get in touch with Avery Leggett," Collier told him in a voice so calm that it surprised even her. Then she started up the stairs to her bedroom.

Milo charged after her. "You can't do this, damn it. You can't! I can make it, I know I can, I still have it in me. Give me a little more time, Collier. It's not as if I haven't been trying. You never understood what it was like for me, you still don't. All I'm asking for is one more chance. Please, Collier, just one more chance."

"Don't lecture me, Milo, because it won't work. I won't accept it anymore." Her eyes were darkening. "I'd advise you to think twice about getting violent now because if I decide to file assault charges against you, you'll find yourself in a mess you'll never be able to get out of. I want this divorce, Milo, and I intend to get it, and if you take the time to read the terms of the petition, you'll see that I'm being pretty damned generous."

"Terms?" he scoffed. "What terms? What the hell do you want from me? I have nothing."

"I'm not asking you for a thing, Milo. I'm giving you seventy thousand dollars, ten thousand dollars for every year we've been married. Avery tried to talk me out of it. He said I was a fool and that I owed you nothing, but I didn't agree with him. God only knows how you're going to live if you don't go back to painting. In exchange for this money, I want all of the London paintings I've been storing for you in Boston."

Milo threw back his head and roared with laughter. "You really are being generous. You're offering me seventy thousand dollars to get out of your life and all you want are some lousy paintings no one else has ever wanted? Woman, you really must be crazy! And I'd be even crazier not to take you up on your offer."

Collier's voice was cold enough to slice him in half. "You have until the day after tomorrow to get out of my house, Milo."

Even as she said it, she could hear Elinor's words, feel Elinor's rage as she ordered a nine-year-old girl out of her own father's house. Collier stopped herself from saying anything more. She simply signaled the end of their discussion and the end of their marriage by very quietly closing her bedroom door in Milo's startled face.

"I think it's only fitting, don't you, my dear," said Avery Leggett to Collier as they sat together over lunch at his club. "The Allies have just liberated Europe and I've just liberated you. Here's to you, my girl, and to your future."

Collier looked up from her hands which were tightly clenched on her lap. Her ring finger was bare now and the skin seemed to be tingling. She raised her glass and gave Avery a wobbly smile.

"And here's to you, Uncle Avery. What would father and I have done without you?"

Prophetically, Collier's divorce was the last thing Avery Leggett ever did. He went to sleep that night and never woke up.

Thaddeus

1948 – 1951

Chapter Eleven

The sun was merciless. It beat down on the Jordan Valley, sucking the oxygen out of the air and leaving it parched and dry. Part of the team was working inside the natural cave tombs, while the other members of the party concentrated on the ruins of several thin-walled houses a hundred yards away. The expedition, sponsored by the British School of Archeology in Athens, had been working at the Tell El Far'ah for two years. Situated near the Arab town of Nablus, the dig was not far from the head of the Wadi Far'ah which served as a highway linking the Jordan Valley with the neighboring hill country.

The leader of the expedition was Thaddeus Jamieson, one of Britain's most renowned archeologists and an expert on the early civilizations of Greece and Palestine. He had spent forty of his fifty-nine years living in makeshift camps such as the one at the Tell El Far'ah. A director of the British School of Archeology in Athens, he had helped uncover Agamemnon's stronghold of Argolis on Mycenae in 1920 and had been part of Winnifred Lamb's expedition to Lesbos in 1929. He had worked with archeologists Blakeway and Hutchinson on Knossos in 1933 and with Pendlebury at Trapeza on Crete in 1936. But this dig was unique. He had never before unearthed such perfectly preserved specimens of the Proto Urban period.

Jamieson snapped open his pocket watch and squinted at the time. It was noon. Time to eat and have a quick nap. But not just yet. He was too excited. He waved to the young woman sitting in a canvas chair just outside the main tent. She appeared to be either dozing or writing, he found it difficult to tell which, and so he finally called out to her to join him.

Collier sighed and put down her pen. Was he mad? It was noon. They should both be out of the sun by now. She wiped her face with a damp handkerchief and got stiffly to her feet. She felt as if she lived with a high fever all day. Her cotton shirt was already soaked and her long skirt was clinging to the backs of her legs. All she could think of was lying in a cold bath. A cool stream. Or a tepid pool. Even the Dead Sea was beginning to appeal to her.

"Come on, darling, you really must see this!" called Jamieson through his cupped hands. "Where's that famous spirit of yours?"

"Where I should be if I had any sense!" she shouted back to him. "In London!"

"Collier, do be a sport. It won't take but a moment!"

"Your moments are notorious for stretching into hours," she muttered to herself as she put on her dark glasses, pulled up her sagging white socks and set off across the narrow stretch of sand to meet him.

"Now there's a good girl." He gave her an affectionate peck on the cheek. "I promise that you won't be sorry."

"You will be if you've dragged me out here to look at another pile of skulls."

Jamieson's hazel eyes were mischievous. "That's precisely what I wanted you to see."

"Taddy." Collier threw him a warning look.

"Oh, do hush and follow me." He took her by the hand and led her through one of the caves to the tomb he had been working on. "Look there." He pointed out the spot to her. "It's the most devilishly confounding thing."

"What is?"

"Don't you see?" His voice was crackling with impatience now. "This chamber was obviously used for multiple burials."

"So?"

"So, my dear Collier, I want you to observe the way each of the skulls and bodies have been separated."

"I just assumed you'd done that while you were working in here," she told him with a shrug. "You know, sorting them into head piles, leg piles, arm piles—"

"Really, Collier, you can be irksome at times. Everything you see is precisely the way we found it. Notice how the heads have been neatly arranged around the room while the remaining bones have simply been tossed in a jumble in the middle. Bloody marvelous, don't you think?"

Again Collier shrugged. "Maybe they were criminals who were all decapitated before they were buried."

"Interesting observation, pet," he said with a smile as he led her into an adjoining chamber. "Here, I want you to have a look at the burnished red slip on some of these vessels." He held up a pitcher with a curved spout for her to examine.

"Remarkable, isn't it, how this glaze has been so perfectly preserved for nearly five thousand years?"

"I'm going to be just as perfectly preserved if I stay out here much longer," she complained. "Please, Taddy"—she tugged at his sleeve—"let's go back now."

"All right, all right," he sighed, carefully setting down the pitcher again.

They walked hand in hand back through the camp to their own tent. Collier ducked her head as she went in and Thaddeus, at six feet two, looking at that moment like a stooped giraffe, followed her in.

"Someone should either invent a higher tent or shorter chairs," grumbled Collier as she tried to get comfortable.

"Do you know what your problem is, my pet?" Thaddeus asked as he popped an orange section into her mouth to silence her. "You're too bloody tall. You need to be cut down a peg or two."

Collier chewed quickly and swallowed. "And I suppose you're going to tell me that you're just the man to do it."

"I am and I shall."

"We'll see," she smiled enigmatically as she began to peel her own orange.

Dear Taddy, she thought, watching him watch her as she peeled her fruit. *Thaddeus, my husband. My protector. My friend.*

She leaned forward and stroked his moustache and his small, trim goatee. Like the fine hair which covered his elegant head, his moustache and beard were light brown with scarcely a trace of gray. It was strange how the color of some men's beards was so different from the hair on their heads. But not Thaddeus Kendal Jamieson's. He would never have tolerated such a discrepancy.

Collier began to munch thoughtfully on her orange. Would she ever have considered marrying a man like Thaddeus Jamieson if her beloved Avery hadn't died? Avery's death had severed her final ties with her past, leaving her even lonelier than her divorce from Milo. All the old people who had been the cherished occupants of her young world were finally gone. . . .

One month after Avery's death, Collier had appointed his nephew and junior partner, John Ender, as her personal attorney and as legal counsel to Paget-Browne Enterprises. And so it was John Ender who now forwarded Elinor's letters to her.

Addison was turning eighteen, she learned, and he was planning to enter Harvard. All of Elinor's assets, except for the house on Commonwealth Avenue, had been sold to provide her son with the kind of lifestyle owed someone bearing the name of Paget-Browne. Now there was his tuition, his room and board, the proper clubs to join, a new wardrobe, a car and a driver since Addison still preferred not to drive himself. Elinor was not asking for assistance, she was demanding it. It was not for her, but for her son.

Collier finally gave in. Whether out of guilt or pride in their shared family name, it no longer mattered. She had not seen Addison in sixteen years, but he was still her brother. He still bore the name of Paget-Browne. He was still the little boy who had nothing, the little boy cheated out of a father and his share of the inheritance she herself had long since taken for granted.

She therefore instructed John Ender to send Addison a monthly check for ten thousand dollars, drawn from her own personal bank account, with the added stipulation that the amount be increased by five thousand dollars on each of his subsequent birthdays. She even went so far as to have it added as a codicil to her will.

The letters finally stopped.

In the winter of 1946, Collier closed the house in Gloucester, stored her entire art collection in the same company warehouse in Boston where her Racines were stored, and for the second time in her life, she fled to Europe. She bypassed England because the memories of her times there with Milo were still too fresh. Instead, she crossed the Channel into France, took a leisurely tour through Italy and ended up in Greece. . . .

"You seem rather up in the clouds, pet. Take care not to upset your plate."

Collier looked up with a start. "I was just thinking about Greece," she told him.

"Any part in particular?"

"Are you fishing for a compliment, sir?"

"Only if it bears some remote resemblance to the truth."

"I was thinking about my first visit to the British School of Archeology in Athens."

"Ah, yes, that fateful first visit."

"You were acting as guide to a bunch of stuffy old British professors of ancient history."

"And you were poking about, making little tourist noises, and completely shattering the serenity of the place."

"Not to mention your own concentration."

"I give the devil his due," he smiled, inclining his head.

"A relic among relics, that's what you called yourself."

"What could I have been thinking of?" he chuckled. "I'm surprised that after such a ridiculous admission, you actually consented to have dinner with me that evening."

"I asked you for dinner, remember?"

He pretended to think about that for a moment. "You did, didn't you? Quite a turnabout for an old trout like myself."

She may have asked him out for dinner that first time, but it was Thaddeus who asked her to marry him. A lifelong bachelor with little patience and less time for what he considered dalliances, a man whose interest in the world stopped somewhere around one thousand B.C., he was more astonished by his proposal than she was.

They had known each other for only three weeks when Thaddeus began making preparations to join up with the school's expedition on the island of Melos. When Collier asked if she could accompany him to the island, he flatly refused. Her suggestion was nothing short of scandalous. His reaction shocked Collier. The man was positively Victorian. She couldn't have cared less about propriety. He was filling a terrible void in her life and she wasn't prepared to let him go. For Thaddeus, marriage was the only honorable solution to their moral dilemma. And Collier, seeing no other way to hold on to the man, accepted his proposal.

She accompanied him to Melos and stayed with him for three months before returning to civilization again. Over the next two years, she spent her time alternating between his various digs and his flat in Chelsea. As much as she adored the man, she abhorred living in tents, being bounced across the desert on the back of a camel, being lurched over rocky roads in an open jeep, being hot, feeling filthy and being bitten by strange insects. She quickly learned that she was much more pleasant company when she was able to combine equal measures of life in London and life in the rough.

With Thaddeus, Collier felt safe. After her roller coaster ride with Milo, her life with Thaddeus was a calm and gentle one. He was what she needed, a kind and comforting presence. If passion was lacking in their relationship, she didn't mind. She had paid too high a price for passion once before. Her body and spirit had been battered and bruised, and what she needed most was a rest.

"I say, Collier, you certainly are off on an unreachable cloud."

"I think the heat's finally melted my brain," she sighed, reaching for her handkerchief again.

"Three weeks back with me and you're already missing London. Is that what it is?"

She shook her head. "I don't miss it, Taddy. Not yet anyway."

"Admit it then, pet, the only reason you prefer Nablus to London is that no one would dare travel this far to tap you for a handout."

She laughed and gave his hand a light squeeze. "Haven't you ever heard that charity begins at home?" she asked with a hint of reproach in her voice.

"So now I'm a charity case, am I?"

"No, you're not. But I'd still like us to have a real home."

"We've got the flat in Chelsea."

"It's nothing more than a place for me to sleep in. You're never there. What I want is to buy us a big house just outside of London, away from the bombed-out buildings and all the noise of reconstruction. Maybe if you had a real home, you wouldn't want to spend as much time away from it."

"You make my life sound like an extended escape from my bloody flat. Well, it's not. Home for me is where I happen to be at the time. As much as you'd like to dress me in the part of a country squire and send me off to ramble about my estate, it just wouldn't do. I'd be no good at that sort of thing, pet. I'd truly be looking for a way to escape then."

Collier went back to picking her orange apart. Thaddeus was right about one thing. In London she was accessible. She was constantly being approached for financial assistance. The demands came by cable, in the mail, over the telephone and through personal visits. There were orphanages to support in Australia and leper colonies in Hawaii. London itself was teeming with starving playwrights, starving artists and starving musicians, all of whom were willing to dedicate all of their future works to her if she became their patron. She was proposed to by men looking for a wealthy wife. She was asked to support dozens of children claiming that she had abandoned them in infancy. She was expected to divide her inheritance with all of the young men and women claiming to be her relatives, showing up at the flat with photographs of her as a child and locks of her baby hair.

And yet, in spite of what Avery Leggett would have called the phony-baloney claims, Collier still managed to find enough causes to champion. She gave five thousand pounds and the use of her name to a wildlife preserve in Kenya. She saved a TB clinic in Switzerland from bankruptcy by wiring them ten thousand pounds. When the building fund of a hospital in Glasgow was two thousand pounds short of their projected goal, Collier made up the difference. A babysitting service for working mothers in Manchester ran out of money, and Collier gave them enough to stay open for another year. When a fire gutted a slum in Liverpool, leaving hundreds of families homeless, Collier organized an emergency relief fund and financed most of the operation herself.

Charities, not art-collecting, took up most of her time now. She sometimes felt that the control she once had over her life was again slipping away from her. She missed her art. She missed the exhilaration of direct involvement. It had been two years since she had even set foot inside an art gallery. The last painting she bought was the Gorky for Milo. Now she was keeping a promise to herself. She vowed she would only support American artists. Her time would come round again. She was convinced of that.

She glanced up, aware of Thaddeus watching her over the top of his week-old newspaper. He was sucking on one of his pipes. As usual, there was no tobacco in the bowl—his way of cutting down on his lifetime habit of smoking.

She gave up on her orange and wiped her sticky hands on her handkerchief. "If you've read the front page, then I think you know what kind of trouble we could be in if we stay here much longer," she told him.

He folded the paper and tossed it onto his cot. "Bloody marvelous, this whole partition business. With just one month to go, the Arabs and the Jews are already at one another's throats. Old Harry's never going to get his truce now."

"I don't blame President Truman for being cautious, but do you realize that while the United States has been maintaining its arms embargo here, the Arabs and the British have been supplying weapons to the Palestinians?"

"Don't blame us for this mess," he argued. "If it weren't

for Balfour, we never would have gotten mixed up in this business in the first place."

"It wasn't Balfour who started the trouble, it was the British refusing to honor the terms of the Balfour Declaration," Collier retaliated. "It wasn't Balfour who imposed the quota system on Jewish emigration in 1945. It wasn't Balfour who locked thousands of Jews into camps behind barbed wire on Cyprus after they'd just survived the German concentration camps. It was the British, Taddy, the British."

"You're starting to sound more like your sensationalist American press every day, pet."

"Oh, come on, Thaddeus, let's face it. The British don't care about Palestine. All they care about is holding on to the Middle East and its oil."

"Well, I'd much rather the British hold on to it than let the bloody Russians steal it from under our noses."

Collier began to back off. "We have exactly one month left, Taddy, because when the British pull out of here on May fifteenth, this entire region could go up like a giant powder keg. I don't think I want to be here if that happens. I don't even know how to fire a pistol, for God's sake."

"Well, then," Thaddeus was smiling again, "I have exactly one month to turn you into a crack shot."

Collier's eyes were darkening. "You and Sir Gilbert Hall. Two damned ostriches. There's going to be a war here, Taddy."

"War," he snorted. "Be sensible, girl. The Jews don't have any bloody weapons, so how can there possibly be a war?"

"What you're saying then is that there's going to be a massacre."

"Don't put words in my mouth," he snapped.

"I think you'd like that, Taddy, I really do. I think the British would like nothing more than to see Israel destroyed."

"It's not quite Israel yet."

"And it probably never will be," she retorted. "Palestinians have been slipping across the border from Syria and Iraq and Transjordan ever since the Resolution for Partition was agreed to last year. And what have the British done? Nothing. They've just sat back and watched it happen."

"Are you quite sure there's no Jewish blood in you, Collier? You really do get awfully emotional about this, you know."

"Damn it, Thaddeus, sometimes your indifference scares the hell out of me. You can't pretend it doesn't matter to you.

Think of all the future dig sites which might be blown up. Think of all the relics you won't be able to uncover because they'll have been smashed to bits and scattered all across this godforsaken land."

"Now you *have* hit a sensitive nerve." He gave her a wry smile. "If that happened, it would be a bloody shame, a damned bloody shame."

Collier looked away from him. This was their only source of friction. Her outrage at injustice and his dismissal of it, her concern over the future and his obsession with the past. She was grateful for one thing, though. He never ended any of their arguments by striking her. He simply rubbed her back a few times, kissed the top of her head and chucked her under the chin.

"Well, I'm off again," he announced as he stood up. "I suppose I'd best hurry things up if we've only one more month before Armageddon."

As Collier sat there, rigid in her chair, Thaddeus came up to her, rubbed her on the back, kissed the top of her head and then ducked on his way out of the tent.

With a sigh of resignation, she opened her writing pad again. She was only halfway through her letter to Jenny, and it had already taken her two days to get that far. Collier felt a sudden pang of loneliness. Jenny was twelve now. She was neither sister nor daughter, but a treasured tie to home. Jenny. Rapunzel. Stepping down from her tower just long enough to go to school each day and then quickly returning to the tower to paint. Jenny. Still protecting herself from the world, peering down at it through her telescope and then trapping each of its chosen moments in oil.

Collier found herself wondering if she herself held the key to Jenny's prison. Had she unwittingly locked the child in her tower by giving her those first paints so long ago, when all she had intended to do was free her?

As the days passed, Collier knew, with a growing sense of dread, that she was about to be proven right. Even Thaddeus was admitting as much to her each time he rubbed her back and kissed the top of her head. He didn't say anything to her, but she could tell by his eyes and by the deepening lines in his face that he had begun to believe her.

As the day of the British departure from Palestine approached, Zionist terrorism began to spread. Fighting broke out in isolated towns and villages, and word had it that the Jews had been receiving arms from Czechoslovakia. At the end of the month, violence flared in the streets of Haifa. Sixty-five thousand Arabs fled, leaving eighty thousand Jews behind and in control of the key port city. In May, as the Arab exodus out of Palestine continued, the rest of the Arab world began to close ranks, uniting in their common cause against their common enemy.

At night, Collier would crawl into Thaddeus's cot just to lie in his arms. It was impossible to make love—the cot could barely support their combined weights—but it didn't matter. She simply needed to be close to him. She needed to be held.

"You really are worried, aren't you, pet?" he asked as she burrowed as close to him as she could. "If there *is* any fighting, we'll be miles away from it, I promise you that. What would either side want with a bunch of old relics anyway?"

"Speak for yourself," she mumbled as she imagined a band of swarthy Arabs in flowing robes, their sabers glinting in the air, helping themselves to their relics and to her body.

"We'll be through here in another month or so," he assured her. "Ah, pet, what a find this has been. Not only will the museums in Athens and London be indebted to me for this excavation, but my own collection will be expanded considerably."

Thaddeus's private collection fo ancient artifacts was one of the finest in the world. Collier had been astounded to find that his entire flat was filled with glass showcases containing the treasures from his many excavations. Every item was meticulously tagged and catalogued and arranged chronologically in each case. There were terra-cotta figurines, bronze swords and daggers, gold jewelry studded with carnelians, onyx, crystal, agate, amber and lapus lazuli; pendants, scarabs, clay goblets, amphoras and pots and great carved seals.

His home was a virtual museum. Its caretaker was a homely elf of a man, a fifty-one-year-old Scotsman by the name of Gulliver, who had been acting as curator, official housesitter, and duster of each precious item for nearly thirty years. Gulliver's was the only furnished room in the entire eight-room flat.

On her first visit to London after leaving Melos, Collier offered Thaddeus's neighbor twenty-five thousand pounds more than his flat was worth to move out. Then she had the adjoining walls knocked down to add some decent living quarters to the place and furnished the rooms with several days' worth of Sotheby's auctions.

"Aren't you the least bit sleepy, Collier?"

She didn't answer him. She lay there beside him and tried to make her breathing regular and even.

He finally nudged her with his elbow. "My right arm has fallen asleep, and if you don't scurry back to your own bed right now, my arm's the only part of me that will get any sleep tonight."

She turned on her flashlight, training it first on the floor and then on her own cot. She very gingerly shook out the sheets to make certain that nothing had crawled into her bed during the time she was out of it. Then she lay down in the dark and stared up at the peaked roof of the tent until she fell asleep.

At midnight on May 15, 1948, the state of Israel was born. On May 16, the combined armies of Egypt, Jordan, Iraq, Lebanon and Saudi Arabia crossed Israel's borders. The forces split up and began to march on the major cities of Haifa, Tel Aviv and Jerusalem.

Collier woke up with a start. Her cot was moving. The entire tent was shaking.

"Thaddeus!" she called as she leaped out of bed.

He was gone.

She stood there, naked and trembling, her long blond hair spilling around her, clutching at herself as if she were defending her virginity.

The tent flap parted. Collier prepared herself.

She closed her eyes, knowing that when she opened them, he would be standing in front of her, his sword in his hand, his dark face beaded with sweat, stinking of camels, his robes gritty with sand and covered with her husband's blood.

She could hear him breathing.

He touched her arm and she began to scream.

Thaddeus grabbed her by the shoulders and started to shake her.

"Stop it, you ninny, stop it this minute! Collier, for God's sake, pull yourself together. We've got to break camp immediately. Syrian planes are shelling the Valley."

Collier opened her eyes. She fell into Thaddeus's arms,

sobbing and shaking so violently that even her teeth were chattering.

"Pull yourself together, damn you! Didn't you hear me?"

It was better than a slap in the face. Collier gulped down her tears and backed away from him. His harshness was frightening her more than the shelling. Yes, she had heard what he said. Too bad he hadn't heard what *she* had been saying all along.

"As soon as we're organized, we'll be leaving for Tel Aviv," Thaddeus said as he hurriedly stuffed his clothes into a knapsack. "In the meantime, I suggest we all pray to whatever god happens to be listening and hope that these Syrians are lousy marksmen. I haven't devoted two years of my life to this place to have it blasted to hell in a matter of seconds."

For one awful moment, Collier actually hated her husband.

Chapter Twelve

On May 29, the Egyptian army pushed north toward the town of Ashdod, which lay just thirty-five kilometers south of Tel Aviv.

In their Tel Aviv hotel room, Collier was pacing the floor and cursing Thaddeus for having trapped them there. She tried to recall all of the vast Paget-Browne holdings, picturing the minute books of each company they controlled, mentally trying to locate an airline somewhere among the pages. No commercial aircraft were flying into or out of Israel now, and because Thaddeus had been convinced that the war between the Arabs and the Jews would be a swift and decisive one, he had stalled for time and thrown away their chances for escape.

As she watched him now, reading a book and chomping on the stem of his pipe, she knew he had refused to leave Israel because of the dig. He wanted to make certain that once the smoke of battle cleared, his flag would still be flying over Tell El Far'ah. She nervously lit a cigar and continued her pacing.

Damn you, Taddy, she cursed him with each shaky step she took. *Couldn't you at least pretend to be nervous?* She couldn't imagine anyone not being terrified. How dare he be so calm? He ate all of his meals on time, slept right through the night, waking precisely at six, took a long walk each morning and then played cards in the afternoon with members of the expedition stuck in the same dingy hotel. He even had the nerve to appear to be enjoying himself.

"You haven't heard a single shot, seen one bloody rocket, watched the street get torn up in front of you or had a building collapse on top of you. So why on earth are you making such a bloody fuss!" he had railed at her one evening. "My God, Collier, compared with the blitz, this is a ruddy holiday. Even camping out in a tent at Nablus was heaven compared to spending the night in a stinking hot bomb shelter with children puking all around you and men wailing like schoolboys."

The room was stifling. She threw open the window and waited for some hint of a breeze to come in. Today was Elinor's birthday. *Happy birthday, Elinor*. Strange the things you think about when you're certain you're about to die. She leaned across the windowsill, straining to hear the sounds of that first spurt of artillery fire. How absurd it was, to have it all end here. In that part of the world where civilization had begun.

She jumped back from the window as a squadron of fighter planes streaked by overhead. If what she had learned from one of the newsmen camped in the hotel lobby was true, these were some of the Messerschmitts which Israel had just bought from Czechoslovakia. *Hurray for our side*. She raised her fist in silent tribute to the planes.

Her relief was only temporary. The fear soon settled down inside of her again. It felt like a lump of wet clay. It moved when she moved. It sat down and it stood up with her. It followed her everywhere and refused to leave her alone.

"'Heiress Dies in Mid-East Conflict,'" she muttered, visualizing the headlines in bold, black print. "'Search Goes On for Missing Heiress. World Mourns Loss of Collier Paget-Browne II.'"

"Is that how you plan on amusing yourself from now on?" demanded Thaddeus, looking up from his book. "Do you enjoy writing your own obituary?"

"Well, at least it got your attention," she returned sourly.

He set the book on the floor and gestured to her. "Come sit with me, pet. At least that way you'll be out of the line of fire. I understand they always aim straight for beautiful blond women leaning out of hotel windows."

Relieved that he could still be tender, she stubbed out her cigar and allowed him to pull her down onto his lap. She rested her head against his chest and listened to the steady thumping of his heart.

"Taddy, I'm so damned scared," she whispered in his ear. "I don't want to die. I'll only be twenty-eight in another nine days. It isn't fair. Twenty-eight isn't old enough to die."

"Do you think fifty-nine is old enough?"

"Don't be smart. I'd give anything to live to see fifty-nine."

"Heaven help us. Think of all the blasted paintings you'll have collected by then and hung in front of a protesting world."

That brought a rush of tears to her eyes. She thought of her paintings sitting in storage until she came back to claim them.

What a waste it had been to even buy them if she was going to die.

"Oh, Taddy, think of all the wonderful new talent I might never see. I'll never know if Milo is painting again. I'll never find out if Jenny is as talented as I think she is." She began to sob. "I still haven't bought that house for my mother. She'll think I've forgotten about her again. Oh, Taddy, I don't want to die. Not here in this hotel whose name I can't even pronounce. They probably won't even be able to identify my body and I'll be thrown into a pit just like those skeletons we found, bits of me going every which way, and someone will say a prayer over me in either Hebrew or Arabic, depending on which side wins, and I'll be sent straight to hell and find Addison waiting for me there. Oh, Taddy, please promise me that I'm not going to die. Promise me, promise me."

She was a child again, clinging to her father, begging him to promise her that nothing would change when the baby came, that he would always love her best. He had promised her all those things over and over again, and in the end, he had broken his promises and left her alone.

"You're not going to die, Collier," Thaddeus told her, brushing the hair out of her eyes and trying to get her to look at him. "Please, pet, don't carry on so. I promise you that you're not going to die. You'll see, you'll spite all of us and go on and on, and only when you're certain that the world is bloody tired of you and your paintings will you even begin to think about dying."

She tightened her grip on his neck and sobbed against the curve of his shoulder. He continued to stroke her hair and croon to her until her tears began to subside. Listening to his words of comfort, feeling his hands in her hair, she gradually allowed some of the fear to lift, and she wondered why someone else's empty promises still had such power over her.

"Why don't you go and wash up," he said, "and change into something fetching. Then we'll go downstairs to the bar and order the finest rot-gut liquor they stock."

Collier obediently climbed off his lap and did exactly as he suggested. She brushed her hair and took the time to wind it into an intricate top knot. She splashed her face with cold water and then slathered lotion all over her face and body to combat the drying effects of the sun, which had given her a dark tan. As she put on her lipstick, she couldn't understand how anyone who looked as healthy as she could feel so wretched. She slipped into her one clean sundress, slid her feet into a pair of high-heeled sandals, and then turned to Thaddeus for his approval.

"You look positively ravishing." He smiled, coming over to her and putting his arms around her. He kissed her on the side of her neck and gently began to massage one of her breasts.

Collier sighed and leaned up against him, feeling her knees begin to weaken.

"What do you say we forget about that drink and stay here instead?" he breathed against the sensitive rim of her ear.

She opened her mouth to his kiss and closed her eyes.

Just then the door to their room was flung open.

"Hey, you two, did you hear the news? There's talk of a ceasefire in the works."

It was one of the young men from the expedition.

"A group of newspapermen just checked in downstairs and that's the latest word from Jerusalem."

Before either Collier or Thaddeus could react, he was out the door again.

"Well, my dear, what did I tell you?" Thaddeus gave Collier a big hug. "Liberation is at hand. No more obituaries for you. Now, how about that drink?"

She felt as if she had just stepped off a spinning top and needed time to get her balance back. Covering her disappointment with a hasty smile, she reluctantly followed Thaddeus out of the room.

As soon as they entered the smoke-filled bar and looked around for a table, they realized that it was hopeless. In a room designed to hold no more than fifty people, at least a hundred were crammed. Some of them were sharing barstools and chairs, others were standing, and some were simply sitting in small groups on the floor. The noise level was deafening, and Collier wanted to turn around and go back up to their room.

"Let's work our way toward the back," Thaddeus shouted in her ear, taking her by the hand and beginning to push through the crowd.

As they threaded their way through the room, Collier clung to Thaddeus's hand and tried to keep her body as close to his as possible. She recognized the faces of several of the reporters she was passing and she ducked her head in the hope that they hadn't recognized her as well.

Suddenly, one of the men reached out and grabbed hold of her arm.

"Hey, look who's here!"

"Miss Paget-Browne, isn't this a bit out-of-the-way for you?"

Collier pulled her arm free and kept on walking.

"The last time I saw her, she was all done up in sables at one of Peggy Guggenheim's openings back in New York."

"How about a couple of photographs, Miss Paget-Browne?"

"Could I ask you a few questions? The folks Stateside would sure like to know how it feels to be right in the middle of history being made."

"Taddy, could you move a little faster?" she shouted at the back of her husband's head.

She was now being pushed and shoved as the newspapermen all tried to get closer to her. Someone caught her around the waist and she was forced to let go of Thaddeus's hand. It was as if a solid wall of men had sprung up all around her. Flashbulbs began to go off in her face and as she blinked her eyes, she kept trying to push past the photographer who seemed intent on blinding her.

"Can I get a few more shots of you? I'm from the Chicago *Trib.*"

"Me first, fella. *Daily News,* Miss Paget-Browne."

"Gentlemen, please!" Her shout was as effective as a whisper.

"This way, Miss Paget-Browne."

"My husband and I—"

"Big smile now."

"There's a war going on. People are being killed. *We* might even be killed. I'm not your story!"

Collier glanced back over her shoulder, hoping for an escape route to miraculously open up behind her. All she saw was that solid wall of men. She stood on tiptoes and tried to locate Thaddeus. Then she tried to move forward again.

Someone had her by the arm now and was holding her back. She could feel the panic rising in her as she struggled to free her arm again.

"Miss Paget-Browne, I'd like to speak to you for a moment."

At last. A civilized voice in all the confusion.

She turned around and found herself staring into a smiling face.

"Would you please let go of me?" she demanded.

"Don't you want to get out of here?"

"I just want to find my husband. Now let go of my arm!"

He shook his head and his face grew serious. Collier began to feel annoyed.

"What are you doing?" she cried as he turned and pulled her after him. "My husband's back there!"

He shoved and punched his way back through the bar and out into the lobby.

"You fool, let go of me this instant! You're only making things worse!"

She finally managed to work her arm free so that she could brush the hair out of her eyes and look around for a way to lose this man.

"Just what are you gaping at?" she snapped at him.

"You."

He grabbed her hand again and pulled her into the elevator behind him.

"Are you crazy! Let me go or I'll shout this place down!"

"I don't think anyone would even hear you."

The door slid shut and Collier flattened herself up against the wall. He was taller than she was. Lanky but strong. And his eyes were a remarkable speckled blend of gray and blue.

"Do you think that your display of gallantry down there merits you an exclusive now?" she asked him coldly, trying to talk above the rapid hammering of her heart.

"I don't want an exclusive," he told her in a strangely gentle voice.

She suddenly thought of Milo. Milo rescuing her from her eighteenth birthday party in Soho. She reached for the nearest button on the wall panel. She had to get out of there.

When the door slid open again, he took her by the arm and led her down the hall. She stumbled and tried to hold back.

She noticed that his sandy brown hair had been streaked blond by the sun. She refused to even think about how handsome he was. His hand on her arm was causing a strange stirring inside of her and her legs were beginning to weaken.

He opened the door to a small bedroom and waited. She grabbed hold of the door frame and refused to move.

"My husband's waiting for me," she said in a quavering voice.

"Five minutes." He held up his hand.

"Any story you want from me—"

"I don't want a story."

There was something in his smile which was reassuring, and she began to relax again. The smile reached his eyes and they grew moist and almost tender.

"You don't remember me at all, do you?" he asked her.

She shook her head.

"That's okay. You really didn't get a good look at me."

She stared up at him, not quite understanding.

"If I'd realized who you were at the time, I would have done something about it sooner."

"Just what are you talking about?" she finally asked him.

"We bumped into each other, literally, in the corridor of the Fairwood Clinic about three years ago."

It took a moment for what he was saying to penetrate her daze.

"You bumped into me and I was the one who apologized." She began to laugh. "Do you mean to tell me that you rescued me downstairs just so you could apologize to me now?"

It was his turn to laugh and the sound of his laughter made the hair rise on the back of her neck.

"I'll apologize if you want me to because it really was my fault. I was pretty upset at the time and I just wanted to get out of there."

She was standing perfectly still and yet she felt as if her entire body was moving. He reached for a long strand of her hair and began to wrap it around his finger.

"Please forgive the dramatics, but I had to get you alone so that I could finally introduce myself to you."

He was smiling at her again. She found herself wanting to smile back, but she was too confused.

"I believe we're related," he told her.

She covered her mouth with her hand.

"I'm Leland Taggert."

Chapter Thirteen

~ ~

She staggered backward as if he had just struck her. Leland. A name sobbed from a witness stand. The boy in the photograph. The man here now in the flesh. The half-brother she had never met. Images through the years of what he would look like, sound like, be like. Dreams of how it would have been to grow up with him, to play and fight with him, and explore all the things children explore when they're growing up together. Leland. Like Addison. Unreachable. Untouchable. Until now.

Collier was reaching out now. She reached out for that other extension of her mother and felt the love of a brother for the first time. They were both crying, but she would never remember who had started crying first. They were both crying and laughing and talking at the same time, while she groped past the pain and the joy of it all to find some cool place out of the sun which was blinding her and melting her into this stranger, this brother of hers. Only in that cool place would the agony begin to lessen. Only then would she be able to breathe again and pretend that she would ever be the same.

All she could think of to say when she found her voice again was, "You don't look a bit like your photograph."

He tightened his grip on her. "Neither do you," he whispered. "No camera's ever caught you as you really are."

"Oh God, Leland," she murmured over and over again, her fingers deep in his thick hair, their bodies pressed closer than two bodies had ever been before. "Leland." If she died tonight, it wouldn't matter. She wouldn't even mind going to hell now. Addison couldn't hurt her now that she had found Leland.

Half-brother and half-sister. Together, could they make a whole?

His lips grazed her ear. He whispered her name and it ricocheted through her brain. One word, two smooth syllables, sounding different than it had ever sounded before. Her skin was on fire, the surface warm and bruised, and the heat of her blood melted all of her vital organs together.

She cupped his face in her hands, searching for traces of Diana and finding them there. His features were stronger than Diana's, but they were softened by that same gentleness which would forever mark him as vulnerable. Her Leland would never know how to be hard or cruel. His compassion was there in his eyes and in his tears, and she ached for the tenderness in him which would keep him bruised and bleeding.

"You first." He offered her his handkerchief.

She dried her tears and then she dried his, tracing the tracks the tears had left on his cheeks, eager to touch and to know each plane and angle of his face.

"I think we could both use a drink," he said.

"Oh God," she groaned. "Not downstairs."

"I have some brandy in a flask somewhere. Just give me a minute."

He emptied a canvas bag onto his bed and dug out a tarnished silver hip-flask in a leather case.

"If you're looking for glasses, forget it," Collier told him. "This is anything but the Ritz."

He unscrewed the cap and handed the flask to her. She took a deep swig and passed the flask back to him. She held the brandy in her mouth and swallowed it slowly, bit by bit, feeling it sting the back of her throat and ignite a tail of fire deep in her belly. They passed the flask back and forth to each other until it was empty. Collier made a face. Leland shrugged his shoulders. He capped the flask and put it back in the canvas bag. Then he cleared a space on the bed and pulled her down beside him.

"Where to begin?" he asked softly, tracing the pale blue vein standing out on the back of her hand.

"You first," she said. "You probably know everything about me from the newspapers."

"I've learned more about you in this past half hour than I could learn in any paper. And I should know. I'm a reporter myself. I work for the Philadelphia *Eagle*." His smile grew impish. "You were the reason I got into this field in the first place, you know."

"I was?"

He nodded. "I was five years old and couldn't have cared less about newspapers and the events in other people's lives. I didn't know any of the people. Besides, a five-year-old boy is only interested in riding his bicycle, playing catch and getting into trouble. Then something happened. Someone I actually knew was in the paper. My mother. Oh, my parents had appeared in the social pages often enough, and my mother would cut out the photographs and show them to me and then she'd paste them into an album she kept. But this time it was different.

"This time it was my father who showed me the clipping. I took a look at my mother. This time she wasn't wearing an evening gown and standing beside my father. She was sitting on some kind of a platform, holding onto a girl who had long, blond hair. My father read the story out loud to me and I started to cry, as much for my mother as for this girl.

"Then I saw another photograph. It was a full-face shot of that same girl. I thought she was the most exquisite girl I'd ever seen. Imagine a young boy's image of someone so pure and sacred that she could only exist in a fairytale. To me, she was a princess who'd been locked in some tower, and I wanted to be the prince who would free her." Leland shook his head and gave a short laugh. "You'll never know how disappointed I was when I found out that this little princess was my half-sister and everything I'd been imagining was politely referred to as incest."

Collier's eyes were filling up again. Impulsively she reached for his hand and pressed it to her cheek. She ached for him. Leland Taggert had been made for broken dreams as surely as she had been made for broken promises.

"Well, that was how it started. Once the initial horror of the whole episode began to pass, I found I was obsessed. I had to find out everything I could about this sister of mine with a name as formidable as Collier Paget-Browne II. I went to the public library and pestered the librarians into digging up every newspaper and magazine article ever written about you."

"I hope you've given that up by now. I stopped reading about myself years ago."

"I've never stopped. And that's why this is all your fault. I've never read a single story which captured the real essence of you or anyone else, for that matter. Everyone's been too busy being impressed by your fortune, what you spend your money on and the outrageous things you do. No one has ever tried to find out about the person actually living behind those magnificent eyes of yours. That's what's always fascinated me." He gently drew the edges of his thumbs across her eyelids.

"I've always wanted to know about the person living inside your head, inside everyone's heads. I'm not interested in the obvious, I'm after what's being left unsaid by the people I'm interviewing. I want to ask the right kind of questions in a way to make them trust themselves with me. I want them to know that I care about them and not about selling papers or winning awards. That's the kind of reporter I intend to be."

"Do your editors always approve of your methods?" she wanted to know.

"My editors are always threatening to fire me. They tell me that if they had to depend on stories like mine to sell their papers, they'd go bankrupt. But right now I don't have to worry about being fired. My father owns the paper I work for."

"Well, I suppose that's something in your favor."

"This has been the only time my father's name has kept a door open for me." He grew angry as he said this. "Everything I've ever done has been on my own, in spite of my father and in spite of his name. After he divorced my mother, he married a woman from good old Main Line stock and they had three boys, bam, bam, bam. Guess who got lost in the shuffle? I learned never to ask my father for anything again. I even put myself through Columbia, and when I got my journalism degree, no one from my dear family even showed up for my graduation. I'd been working on the *Eagle* for nine months when I found out my father owned the paper. Then before I could do anything about changing jobs, I was assigned to cover the war over here. It was probably my father's idea. He's probably hoping I'll get killed and then he'll be able to pretend my mother and I never existed."

Collier was sick at heart. She searched for the words to ease his terrible hurt, but she knew that anything she said would only come out sounding banal. And so, she simply put her arms around him and held him. After a few minutes, he gently drew away from her, and by his smile, she could tell that the pain had passed. At least for a while.

She decided to break the silence. "Is it true about the cease-fire?" she asked him.

Leland shrugged his shoulders. "That's the word right now, but it's really anybody's guess."

He got up from the bed and sauntered over to the window. He moved with a kind of grace which was both self-assured and self-conscious. It was a casual kind of grace, Collier decided, and it would serve to offset his earnestness, his intensity, and lend him some balance.

"It was hell being in Jerusalem," he told her, "really hell. I don't think I handle other people's agonies very well yet. By the time we left there, the food supplies and ammunition were nearly gone. It was practically impossible for medical supplies or equipment to get through. If there's no ceasefire soon, I'm afraid Israel will have had the briefest statehood in history."

Collier suddenly regretted having steered the conversation back to the war. A distance was creeping into his voice and she felt herself being closed out. She went over to him and slipped her arm through his. Just touching him made everything good again.

"That day at Fairwood," she began uncertainly, "was the first time I'd seen my mother since the trial. I'd hoped to spend several days with her, but after an hour she disintegrated right in front of my eyes. I'd just asked her to come to Gloucester for a visit and the thought of leaving the clinic seemed to terrify her. They had to come in and sedate her."

"I know. She was sleeping when I dropped by to visit her."

"No wonder you were in such a hurry to get out of there. It was all my fault."

"No, it wasn't your fault. Didn't they explain her condition to you? There could be any number of reasons for her illness. A mix-up in the signals inside the brain, something going wrong in the womb, an accident at birth, a bad childhood. No one really knows yet."

"All I know is that it runs in the women in her family. Be thankful you're a man, Leland. I might have the privilege of going mad one day."

"If it hasn't manifested itself by now, chances are it never will. You're nothing like our mother, Collier. You've got too much of your father in you to worry about ever going mad."

"Can you promise me that?" As soon as she said it, she wanted to take the question back. "None of the doctors I've spoken to over the years have ever given me that kind of guarantee. I wish I could believe you."

He put his arms around her, and she felt that she had found the anchor she had spent twenty years searching for.

"To think that it took a war half way around the world to finally bring us together," he said as he rubbed the nape of her neck.

"Why didn't we ever try to contact each other before this?"

"Because now was obviously the right time. I guess I'm a fatalist. Maybe it's an old-fashioned notion. I'm sure the existentialists would have a field day with me, but I've always believed that whatever happens was meant to happen and that nothing we do can alter the natural course of events. Then again, maybe we weren't ready before. We were still being formed."

"Do you think we're ready now?"

"In some ways, yes. You'll probably carve out a place for yourself in history and I'll be the one recording that history."

"You sound pretty definite about that," she laughed. "We'd make a good team, you and I. I'll discover the artists and begin to buy up their paintings, you'll write about them and create a demand for their work. Then every art snob will think we've discovered genius, the artists will get rich and they won't have to worry about starving anymore and everyone will be happy. What do you think of my little fantasy?"

"One problem with it. Make an artist too successful too soon and he'll get lazy. He won't feel like creating anymore. I think that some sacrifice and just enough uncertainty can make for exceptional creativity. Take away that slight edge of anxiety and some of that special dedication gets lost. If success comes too quickly, he begins to coast because he knows that even if he decides to sign his name to the rag he uses to clean his brushes, someone will buy it."

Collier let out a sigh. "You make too much sense, Leland. That's the best part about fantasies. They don't have to make any sense." She caught him looking at his watch and her hand flew to her mouth. "My God!" she exclaimed. "Thaddeus will think I've been kidnapped."

"Give us a few more minutes together, Collier. I have to leave again in an hour."

"But you just got here," she protested, her heart beginning to beat wildly.

"I thought we were supposed to be spending the night here, but just as I was going down to the bar before, I found out about some heavy fighting near Jaffa. I'll be heading up that way now to cover it."

She was growing colder with each word he spoke. "You can't leave just like that. We've just found each other. We haven't had any time together. You can't leave now. What if something were to happen to you? It wouldn't be fair, Leland. It would have been better if we'd never had this hour together. I don't think I could stand to live if something happened to you now."

"Nothing's going to happen to me. I'm not one for heroics. I have a lot planned for myself and I don't intend to jeopardize everything by looking for stray bullets."

She felt as if the life preserver she had been tossed was deflating and that she was about to drown. Fearfully she sought to hold onto what he had been giving her, but she was failing. He was leaving her. Just as they had all left her.

"Are you all right?" he asked, his face mirroring his concern.

"I'm fine." And just to prove it, she put on her best Collier Paget-Browne smile, the one she reserved especially for the press.

Leland seemed unconvinced. "You don't have to pretend with me, Collier. Ever."

She shuddered. Even her thoughts would never be safe from the probing eyes of this man.

He pressed a finger to her lips. Her smile faltered.

"That's better. I don't know you well enough yet, but I think I'm beginning to understand you. You were brought up believing the whole world was watching you and that everything you did would be chronicled and scrutinized. I know how important it's been for you to keep your guard up and to prevent anyone from getting past your defenses and using your vulnerability against you. I know just how it feels. I grew up building defenses. I saw rejection and ridicule on the faces of the kids I went to school with. I heard it in the refusals from the girls I asked out. I felt it when every fraternity and club turned down my applications for membership. But it taught me to fight, Collier, and I'm stronger now because of it. Like you, I'm going to make it. You're going to develop into one of the world's leading art patrons, and I'm going to give men like Edward R. Murrow a good run for their money. And then, one day, everyone who's ever slighted us will be choking on their smug little smiles and their holier-than-thou attitudes because they'll have to respect us."

He glanced down at his watch again.

"I suppose you'd better find that husband of yours now and let me get organized here."

Panic washed over her like a chilling wave. She grabbed

hold of his arm. "When am I going to see you again?"

"I don't know. Very soon, I hope."

"Do you have our number in London?"

"I can get it."

"Will you promise to either write me or phone me whenever you can?"

"I promise I will."

She was shaking as he took her in his arms one last time, but she promised herself that when he let her go, she wouldn't cry.

Chapter Fourteen

"Gorky's dead."

Collier tried to get a better grip on the receiver. "What? Who is this?"

She squinted at the time on the clock beside her bed. It was three A.M.

"I had to call you. I had to tell you. You're the only one who'll understand. I'm sick inside, I can't believe it's true. He's dead. He hanged himself in his barn in Sherman, Connecticut."

Collier sat bolt upright in bed. "Milo?"

"Everything went wrong for him in the end. There was a fire in that goddamned barn of his, which destroyed most of his latest paintings. His wife took their two kids and walked out on him. He was operated on for cancer, and then a few months ago, his painting arm was paralyzed in a car accident. The poor bastard. I don't blame him. How could anyone blame him? He had nothing left. Nothing."

"Milo, where are you?" Collier asked as she switched on her bedside lamp. "Where are you calling from?"

"New York," he shouted. "Where the hell else would I be? Didn't you hear what I said, Collier? Gorky's dead. God damn it, the man was only forty-four years old."

She kept trying to put her thoughts together. "I'm sorry, Milo, I'm really very sorry. It must be a terrible shock for you. But he was obviously in so much pain that he couldn't even think about living any longer."

"They'll immortalize him now, you know. They'll finally give him the recognition he's always deserved. Too bad he didn't get it when he was alive."

She heard the clank of a bottle against the receiver.

"But then that's the price you pay for genius. It's hard, you know. People spit in your face and you keep telling yourself it's rain. Then they bury you, and the rain turns to tears and then to gold because they can't sell your paintings fast enough at a high enough price. Quite the joke, isn't it? Do you think the spit's going to turn into gold for me some day?"

"Milo—"

"That painting you gave me will be worth plenty now. But they can offer me a million bucks for it and you know what I'll tell them? I'll tell them they should have paid him that million when he was alive. Maybe it would have saved him. Maybe if they'd paid him, he would have kept on fighting, said to hell with them all, and kept right on painting."

"Milo, are you painting at all?"

"Me?" His laugh was harsh. Once again she heard the clank of a bottle against the receiver. "Sure, I'm painting. I've had some shows in the Village and some of the stuff actually sells. Course I'm not getting that much for them these days, but with the money you gave me, I still make out. Most people come by the galleries just to have a look at the guy who was once married to that rich lady, Collier Paget-Browne. So you see, your name still carries some weight around here."

"Milo—"

"Well, sorry I woke you up. I keep forgetting there's a time difference between the real world and yours. Anyway, I've still got some serious drinking to do."

Then, she was holding on to a dead connection. Poor Gorky. Dead. Poor Milo. Barely alive. That great force which had surged through him, giving him a few short years of creative life, was completely gone now. Again she found herself wondering if she was to blame. Had Leland been speaking of Milo when he said that the combination of success and comfort dilutes an artist's energies, corrupts his ambition and dampens his fighting spirit? Milo had been defiant when she met him, but she had left him a defeated shell.

She turned over onto her stomach, stretching out her hand to touch the smooth, cool place beside her, wishing Thaddeus were there. After that much rumored ceasefire had gone into effect on June 11, she had pleaded with him to return to London with her. Of course he had refused. He saw her safely aboard a commercial flight out of Tel Aviv and then he set out for Nablus again with the rest of his team.

From the safety of their flat in Chelsea, with only Gulliver for companionship, Collier had continued to monitor Israel's battle for survival. She seldom went out. She kept the radio on all day, tuned to the BBC, listening to the news, praying

that the ceasefire would hold and that Thaddeus was still safe
among his ruins.

Unable to sleep now, she got out of bed and walked over
to the window. She stood there, looking out at the small park
across the street. The lamps were bright round dots in the
darkness, and she could barely make out the benches and some
of the formal flower beds. The breeze from the open window
felt warm on her face, but it was cool enough to make her
nipples pucker and cause goosebumps to stand out on her naked
flesh.

She wrapped her arms around herself, imagining Thaddeus
there with her, holding her, touching her. She remembered the
feel of his hands on her breasts, the whistle of his breath in
her ear as they stood together in that hotel room in Tel Aviv
just before hearing the news of the rumored ceasefire.

She began to shiver. If they hadn't gone downstairs to the
bar, if she hadn't lost sight of Thaddeus in the crowd, she never
would have met Leland. Leland. It was he who was holding
her now. The cold she was feeling turned into a strange new
warmth. She thought of the way he said her name, how his
arms closed around her, the tenderness in his gaze when he
looked at her.

"Is it because we have the same blood in our veins?" she
had asked Thaddeus over dinner that night after Leland had
gone. "It's the strangest sensation I've ever known, almost like
touching your own reflection in the mirror and finding out
exactly how you feel. We're not even twins, he's four years
younger than I am, and we had different fathers. We don't
even look particularly alike. And yet, we share something inexplicable and intangible. When we were together, something
passed between us that you could almost see. It was like a life
spark, a fusion, something electrical."

"I think I'd be well advised to keep an eye on you two from
now on, even if he is your half-brother. Bloody shame he
skipped out before I could meet him."

"There will be other times, lots of them. I just know it."

"Have your eyes ever sparkled that way for me, I wonder?"

"Don't tease me, Taddy."

"You're certain you were with your brother and not some
lover you've kept stashed away all this time?"

"Why would I need a lover when I have you?"

His grip on her hand had tightened. She saw a strange change in his face. The thought of her with a lover seemed to excite him. They had left their dinner half-eaten and returned to their hotel room. His erection had been obvious even before he began to unfasten his trousers.

He had made love to her with a ferocity which startled her at first and then aroused her. It had brought back memories of Milo's early lovemaking, something she had never experienced or even expected to feel with Thaddeus. She had wondered if it had been the threat of some unseen competition, the sudden appearance of a younger man in her life which had sparked the passionate lover in him. But the reason hadn't mattered. Thaddeus had made love to her three times that night, only stopping short of a fourth penetration because she begged him. She was just too sore.

Collier moaned now. Her hands had worked their way down between her legs. She stood there at the window, swaying, rubbing herself, as the heat and urgency spiraled upward from her groin. She threw herself onto the bed and ground her hips into the mattress. Her breath was hoarse and wild in her ears. Turning over onto her back, she opened her legs. She touched herself with the tip of her finger, several light, teasing strokes, and the heat exploded all around her. Her body arched and bucked with the exquisite intensity of her orgasm, burning away the tension and leaving her weak and trembling.

She was tingling all over. A light gloss of perspiration covered her body. She licked her top lip and her tongue came away tasting salty. Slowly she turned onto her side and reached for Thaddeus's pillow. She wrapped her arms around it and willed it to respond to her.

The tingling passed and the loneliness rushed in once more. She had two men to miss now, so her loneliness had been doubled. She had received several brief notes from Thaddeus in the two months since her return to London, while Leland had written only once. She knew his letter by heart. The words were imprinted on her mind in the same gently flowing script the letter was written in.

Sis—
This is the first and last time I'll ever call you that, but I couldn't resist seeing how it looked on paper. I've waited twenty-four years for the chance to do it, so I hope you'll forgive me.

As expected, life here is anything but easy. It's the dying that seems easier. Wars should be decreed off-limits to civilians who ask nothing more than the chance to live. Wars should be reserved for professional soldiers, men who honestly believe that what they're doing will actually make a difference in the grand scheme of things.

I haven't taken a shower in three days and I'm beginning to look the way I feel. Lousy. Dirtied by this entire exercise. I know I'll get through it, though. All I have to do is put your face in front of me and it makes the ugliness around me beautiful.

Collier, dear heart, what we had in Tel Aviv is just a beginning. Until we have the time to be together again, know that you are loved and missed.

                                                      Leland

Seeing her name spelled out by his hand was like hearing him say it. Reading his name was like saying it herself. Whenever she thought of his letter or took it out to read again, she felt him there with her. And that made her feel safe.

She tossed the pillow aside and got out of bed. She put on a silk dressing gown and went to the kitchen to make herself some tea. She lit a cigar, quickly fanning away the smoke, hoping that Gulliver wouldn't smell it in his sleep and wake up to give her an argument. He despised smoking. It was probably Gulliver who had gotten Thaddeus to quit.

She must have dozed off sitting at the kitchen table, because the next thing she knew she was being awakened by the door chimes. For a moment, she was completely disoriented. She looked around, not knowing where she was or how she had gotten there. Was the place on fire? She looked for her cigar and noticed it leaning against the rim of the ashtray on the table next to her cup of cold tea. It had burned out less than a third of the way down.

"A cable for you, madam."

Gulliver was standing in the doorway. He was already dressed for the day, wearing his usual black suit with the stiff-collared, white shirt and black velvet bowtie which made him look like a head waiter. As she took the telegram from him, her mouth went dry. Her heart was pounding and her hands were beginning to shake. She stared down at the pale yellow envelope she was holding and wondered where she would find the strength to open it.

Something had happened to either Thaddeus or Leland and she didn't want to know about it.

"Shall I open it for you, madam?"

Dear Gulliver, the master of efficiency, spotless white gloves in place, ready to take over. His bald head looked as if it were polished with the same lemon oil he used on the furniture. His face was so ordinary in its homeliness that she still had trouble remembering what he looked like. She usually lost him when they went marketing together, and she often walked right past him when she was looking for their car.

"I'll do it myself, Gulliver, thank you."

Moving in slow motion, she took a steak knife from one of the kitchen drawers and very neatly slit open the back of the envelope. She withdrew the piece of folded yellow paper and put it down on the table. As she unfolded it, she smoothed out each precise crease in the paper with the palms of her hands, until it was finally spread open in front of her. Then she forced herself to look down and read each of the words taped onto the message.

She burst out laughing.

MONEY LOST IN NEW VENTURE STOP CREDITOR THREATENS SEIZE HOUSE STOP SEND FUNDS STOP FIFTEEN THOUSAND WILL COVER STOP

ADDISON

She was so relieved that, at that moment, she would have wired Addison the moon.

She wondered which particular investment this one was. It seemed Addison was as poor an investor as he was a student. He was barely scraping through Harvard and now it seemed that all the money she was transferring into his account each month was being wasted on get-rich-quick schemes which consistently backfired. There would never be any hard work for Addison Sargent Paget-Browne. No discipline, no dedication, no sacrifice. After all, he was a Paget-Browne and the world owed him. His mother had taught him well.

Later that afternoon, Collier placed an overseas call to Boston and instructed John Ender to transfer the necessary funds into Addison's account immediately.

"How can you even be sure this latest demand is legitimate, Collier?" shouted the irate lawyer. "No one would seize a house like that just for fifteen thousand dollars. They'd go after Elinor's new Rolls Royce first. Let me have someone investigate this one for you."

"Don't waste your time, John. Addison would manage to find some way of convincing you the threat's real enough. Besides, it isn't that much money and I can't take a chance on losing that house."

"If you add this newest claim of his to all the others these past two years, you'll find that you've paid out a great deal of money beyond the agreed-upon stipend. Eighty-five thousand dollars, to be exact. Shall I tell you about the fancy figure he's been cutting around town lately? It seems he's bought himself a new Mercedes Benz and hired the latest in a string of short-lived chauffeurs. Not only that, but he'd make any of you ladies jealous with his wardrobe. So I'd advise you to think twice about this fifteen thousand dollars, Collier. It could be that your little brother is in debt for nothing more than his fancy clothes and his fancy car."

"I appreciate your concern, John, but Addison could never cost me as much as I have. So just arrange to have the money transferred as soon as you can."

"You're only encouraging him, Collier. He's never going to make it on his own if you keep bailing him out all the time. Let him sweat a little. Make him roll up those fancy Brooks Brothers sleeves of his and dirty his hands with some honest effort for a change. I hate seeing you manipulated this way. Your father would have straightened him out quickly enough."

"It was my father who got me into this in the first place, John. Addison is a weight I'll be carrying for the rest of my life."

There was a pause at the other end. "I'm sorry, Collier, that was tactless of me."

"Just arrange for the money to be transferred, and we'll consider this matter closed." Until the next time, she thought wearily as she hung up the phone.

Gulliver made her breakfast which she ate alone in the kitchen. She could hear him walking slowly through the flat, dusting and polishing, as if he were the curator of a grand museum instead of a gentleman's gentleman presiding over one man's private collection which no one ever saw. After a second cup of tea, Collier went into the library to finish the letter she had begun to Jenny the night before. She wanted to post it on her way to the vernissage at the Paladin Gallery in Soho that evening. Glancing down at the engraved invitation on her desk, she was reminded again of Milo's distressing phone call.

She suddenly realized how very much she missed home.

The show was a disappointment and that made her more homesick than ever. She wanted to continue where she had so abruptly left off. She felt strangely out of place in London, strangely out of step. Once again she had the feeling that she was treading water, stagnating, while others had begun to supplant her. Would Thaddeus consider moving to Boston? she wondered. Or New York? As she left the gallery, she began to figure out ways to convince him.

Gulliver was supposed to have called for her at ten sharp. She looked at her watch again. He was already ten minutes late and that was unlike him. She decided to walk down the block. Keeping an eye out for Gulliver, she sauntered down to the corner and back again. Checking the time, she saw that it was ten-twenty.

Halfway up the block for the third time, she saw the car rounding the corner and she waved. Gulliver would miss her. He would be looking for her in front of the gallery. She waved again, hoping to catch his attention. When she saw the car slow down, she stepped off the curb.

The car picked up speed and Collier jumped back.

She snagged the heel of her shoe on the sidewalk and lost her balance. As she fell to the pavement, the black car sped off into the night.

She lay there stunned, her breath coming in ragged gasps, the palms of her hands skinned and bleeding from her attempt to break her fall.

"Are you all right, miss?"

"Somebody get a bobby."

"Bloody close call, miss."

"You daft, stepping in front of a car like that?"

Collier began to shake. She had been looking for a black Jaguar and she had nearly gotten herself killed stepping in front of a Bentley. Her father had taught her about cars and she knew enough to know that the car had been a Bentley. How could she have been so foolish, assuming that the first black car to come along would be theirs?

He had tried to hit her. Of that she was certain. Whoever had been driving that car had deliberately tried to run her down. A curious drumming began in her head.

"Can you stand up, miss?"

"Where's that bobby? The lady's bleedin'."

"I'm all right," Collier told them in a quavering voice, as she got to her knees. "Don't worry about me. I'm fine, really I am. It was my fault, I thought it was my driver."

She was babbling and she knew it, but just the sound of her own voice was convincing her that she really was all right. She finally stood up straight. Her whole body ached and the drumming in her head seemed to have grown worse.

"Madam, whatever's happened?"

It was Gulliver.

"She walked right in front of a bleedin' car, mate."

"She musta been sleepwalkin' or else she was tryin' to get herself killed."

"Lean on me then, madam," Gulliver ordered, as he slipped his arm around Collier's waist. "I'll get you to a hospital straight away."

"No." She shook her head. "I'm fine. Just take me home."

"Are you certain, madam?" He looked as frightened as she felt.

"Yes, I'm certain."

"I do apologize for being late, madam, but when I went round to get the car, I found that one of the tires was flat. It took me these extra twenty-five minutes to change it. I most sincerely apologize."

She waved his words away with a weak flick of her wrist and allowed him to settle her in the back seat of the car. As soon as he closed the door, she opened up the small bar and poured herself a snifter of brandy. As she gulped it down, she began to run those few terrifying seconds over again in her mind.

She saw herself stepping off the curb. She saw the car pick up speed. She watched herself fall backward onto the pavement and saw the crowd of people gathering around her. Had it been coincidence and not a deliberate attempt to run her down? After all, she had put herself in the path of the car in the first place. She had been the one to step off the curb.

In spite of the brandy, she was still trembling. Today was the kind of day people drank to forget about, she thought, as she poured herself another brandy. First Milo's call, then Addison's cable and now this near-miss.

She suddenly thought of Diana, afloat in a world where her

every need was anticipated and met, drifting, always drifting, never having to be accountable to anyone for anything. The despair Collier had begun to feel gave way to panic.

Was she doomed to live in that same netherworld of half-sights and half-sounds as her mother? Unable to take care of herself, to make the simplest decision, needing someone else to do all of the thinking for her? Had Leland been wrong? Was it starting?

She shook her head. No, it would never happen to her. She wouldn't let it. She saw herself locked inside a room where the windows were barred and the door had a window in it and a smiling woman in a dress with a sweater thrown over her shoulders was giving her a pill which promised her oblivion.

The snifter slipped out of her hand. If Gulliver hadn't been there, Collier knew she would have started to cry.

He had witnessed the entire incident. He had even jotted down the exact time in his notepad. What a fool thing to do. She could have gotten herself killed and he would have found himself out of a job. He lit a cigarette and tossed the match onto the sidewalk. He had second thoughts and bent down to pick it up again. He also picked up her half-smoked cigar. He dropped the match and the cigar into the trash bin on the corner.

Any lady who smoked cigars really *was* crazy.

Chapter Fifteen

"Tell her I'm not home!"

Addison slammed his bedroom door and stood in the middle of the room fuming. He could feel the heat of his breath steaming out of his nostrils and onto his face. He was in no mood for the simpering, half-witted chatter of Paige Carlton, even if she was his date for his mother's annual Halloween ball that evening. He was sick and tired of his mother fobbing off one snotty girl after another on him.

It had all started when he graduated from Harvard that spring. He was only twenty-two, for Christ's sake, he mumbled to himself as he paced the floor. He was in no hurry to saddle himself with a wife and a family. He had no time for added responsibilities right now. He was having enough trouble staying solvent himself.

He parted the curtains and looked down at the driveway where Marshall, his chauffeur, was polishing the new Jaguar. God, he loved that car, even more than he'd loved his old Mercedes. That car had been sideswiped by some bum in a Dodge that summer, and even though his mechanic had assured him that it could be repaired, Addison had refused to drive around in an overhauled wreck. So he'd gone out and bought the Jaguar.

It was just like hers, only newer. Bottle green instead of black. Its lines were sleek and curved and proud. Just like her.

Marshall glanced up from his work and caught Addison's eye. Addison gave him a curt nod. Marshall appeared not to have noticed. Addison stood there, hands on his hips, waiting. Marshall looked up again. This time Addison didn't move. Marshall, his short blond hair blowing like feathers in the breeze, tipped an invisible cap to Addison and resumed his polishing.

"My God, you're insolent, Marshall Doyle," Addison muttered. He could feel his face flushing as he watched the young man rubbing his chamois back and forth, back and forth across the top of the hood. It was like watching a man stroking his dog or caressing the leg of a woman. Feeling a stab of heat in his groin, Addison pried himself away from the window.

I'll pay you back for this, you bastard. Tonight when I take Paige home after the party, we'll put on a show for you that will burst your goddamned zipper.

He had been playing this game for four years now, and Marshall was the latest in a parade of faceless young men to allow the game to continue. Addison had never learned to drive. He hated driving. On the road, people were careless maniacs. He much preferred being driven. After hiring his first chauffeur, he had invented his little game and it had added a new dimension to his social life.

Never having to be completely alone with any of the pretty but brainless girls he knew gave him an edge over them. They would think twice before compromising themselves before a silent but observant witness and this made the challenge that much more exciting. Knowing that the eyes of his chauffeur were torn between watching the road and watching the back seat further titillated him. He petted and teased each of his women, drawing his power from being able to end it at their front door, drawing his strength from the hunger in their faces and the lust in the eyes of his driver reflected in the rearview mirror.

That was how the Mercedes had been wrecked. And since the poor chauffeur had broken the rules of the game, losing control of himself and the car, Addison had been forced to fire him.

He checked the time on his watch and then doublechecked it against the clock beside his bed. The man was late. Addison resented being kept waiting, especially by a lackey. He picked up a brush from his dressing table and ran it through his straight black hair. He splashed on some cologne, gave his vest a good tug and then fastened one of the buttons on his blazer. He glanced at his watch again. Damn the bastard! Now he'd be late for church.

"Addison!"

His mother was calling him.

"There's a gentleman here to see you."

At last. Addison checked himself one more time in the mirror and opened his bedroom door.

He was halfway up the stairs, taking them slowly, puffing

slightly when he reached the top. Addison hid his contempt behind a civilized smile and ushered the man into the room which had been his father's study. Waving him to a chair, Addison positioned himself in front of one of the bookcases and crossed his arms in front of him.

The man unzipped the leather case he was carrying, drew out a sheaf of papers and laid them on the table beside him. Addison waited. What he wanted right now was a brief verbal report. He'd go over the details later. The man was just about to light up a cigarette, but the look on Addison's face made him change his mind. He stuck the cigarette back in the package and tucked it away in his coat pocket.

He cleared his throat with a dry, hacking sound and looked Addison straight in the eye. "It's all there in my latest report, Mr. Paget-Browne," he said.

"What is?"

"Nothing."

"What do you mean by 'nothing'?"

"Just like I said. Nothing. Nothing's changed. She's still spending part of her time in London and part of her time with her husband in Greece and Israel."

"What about men?"

"There haven't been any men."

"Has she been buying any art again?"

"Nothing in these last four years."

"What about Leland Taggert?"

"Nothing more than what you already know. He's making a name for himself in Philadelphia, has his own radio show on PHBS twice a week, and a byline in the *Herald* which has put him in direct competition with his old man."

"Never mind about his career," Addison snapped. "What about the two of them?"

The man shrugged. "As far as I can tell, they've only seen each other three times. Once was that time in Tel Aviv and twice in London. The last time was a month ago when he was on his way to Korea."

"Korea?"

"There's a war on over there, remember?"

Addison couldn't countenance sarcasm from an equal let alone from some two-bit detective. He knew damned well about Korea. He got down on his knees every night and thanked God that he was ineligible for the draft. As the sole surviving male in his family, he was needed at home to support his mother.

"You're certain there's nothing between them?" Addison persisted.

"Yes, sir, so far as I can tell."

"You don't sound completely convinced. I thought I was paying you to be sure about these things."

"I'm sure."

"What about her then? Is she showing any more signs of poor judgment or instability? Anything?"

The man shook his head.

Addison swallowed his impatience. One day she'd slip and he'd be ready. What a waste. What a goddamned waste! All that money and she didn't even know how to spend it. She didn't know how to go about being rich and enjoying it. Paintings and charities! What the hell good were they? He thought of the lists he'd made as a child. He'd already worked his way through one third of what he'd written down. She was no fun anymore, no longer a challenge. What a disappointing bore she was turning out to be. And she still had all the money.

The man didn't even deserve to be paid, but Addison had to be careful. He couldn't take any chances. Hirelings were known to turn on their masters. He unlocked the drawer of his desk and took out a sealed white envelope. How would she react, he wondered, if she knew she was paying for surveillance on herself?

After the man had gone, Addison went downstairs and found his mother arranging flowers in a crystal vase in the dining room. He put his arms around her waist and gave her a kiss on the cheek.

"Careful, darling, you'll mess my hair," Elinor cautioned him with a pat on the wrist. She wore her blond hair pulled back in a sleek chignon now, and if there were any white strands among the gold, they were scarcely noticeable.

She set the vase down on the buffet and turned to her son. "Aren't you ever going to tell me who that peculiar man is, dear?"

"I've told you before, Mother, it's business."

"What kind of business is conducted on Sunday?"

"It isn't always on Sunday. I see him whenever he happens to be in town." He wagged a playful finger at her. "Now don't get all inquisitive on me, you know better than that. Just be happy that I'm looking out for the two of us."

She ran her hand over his cheek. "You're everything I'd hoped you'd be, Addison," she said with a loving smile. "But then I knew you would be. After all, you are a Paget-Browne."

The muscle in his left eye began to twitch. "I wish to hell they'd all remember that."

"Who, dear?"

"The other vice presidents, that's who. They treat me as if I weren't there most of the time. I suppose they figure I'm earning my salary just by turning up at their stuffy old board meetings. Five months with my father's own company, and they never let me make a suggestion or even submit a proposal."

"But you're Vice President in charge of Special Projects, aren't you?"

"So what? It's a title, nothing else. She just created the position for me when I graduated. I'm nothing but a name on a door. All I get to do is sign my goddamned name to stacks of papers and piles of minute books while she gets to make all the money. It isn't fair, Mother! I'm sick of being grateful to her for her measly handouts. I want my share of my father's estate and I don't want to wait forever to get it."

"Be patient, Addison. Time is on your side, remember."

"I have been patient, damn it!" he shouted. "But time's proving you wrong, Mother. She's far from a raving lunatic, you know."

"Excuse me, sir, but I've brought the car around," Marshall announced from the doorway. His dark blue suit was buttoned up to his neck and he was holding his cap in his hands.

"I'll be right there," Addison dismissed him coldly.

Elinor caught hold of her son's arm. "Please promise me you'll call Paige back as soon as you get home. Remember, darling, the Carltons are very fond of you and Paige's father is worth millions."

"So you and Paige keep reminding me."

He took his topcoat and hat from the closet in the front hall and went out the front door.

As he sank back against the cushioned seat of the car, he allowed his eyes to meet Marshall's in the mirror. Marshall's eyes were black. Hers were almost black. Her photo on the cover of the June edition of *Life* magazine remained fixed in his mind. Her eyes and the arrogant set of her head had made him want to suck in his breath and then release it very, very slowly. Her beauty diminished him. Her strength weakened him. Her power incapacitated him. He could have loved her if he had been born first.

She was everything he would never be, so he had to hate her for what she was and envy her because of who she was. He felt the ache begin. It was a knot of agony deep in his groin, twisting and turning, worming its way through his organs and into his bloodstream. He shifted around in his seat, looking for a more comfortable position. The edges of his hatred and his love were blurring, beginning and ending in that shuddering heat which throbbed inside him.

He got a tighter grip on his prayerbook. Jesus, he had so much to confess. He needed to confess. He needed peace. He took the handkerchief from the breast pocket of his blazer and wiped his face with it. God, he needed peace.

Stop it, Marshall! You don't know what I'm thinking about. Stop looking at me that way. You're only a chauffeur. If she were yours, Marshall, what would you do that I wouldn't do? Would you lie with her, lie to her, lie about her? Would you try to destroy her because you couldn't have her or be her? Would you hate her and wish she were dead?

He would punish Marshall tonight. And Paige. Pale little Paige. A shadow in the face of that other glorious sun.

The car stopped in front of Trinity Church. Addison didn't wait for Marshall to open the door for him. Shaking, his body drenched in sweat, his stomach churning, he bolted from the car and up the stairs in search of absolution.

Chapter Sixteen

The year 1951 began with the Communist forces of North Korea and China, and the combined forces of the United Nations, zigging and zagging across an arbitrary battleline known as the thirty-eighth parallel. While much of the world sat in front of their television sets, watching history unfold, a smaller world was turning to something more immediate. For those in the art world, history would be made on January 23, when the Museum of Modern Art in New York launched its landmark exhibition entitled "Abstract Painting and Sculpture in America." Abstract expressionism, a term first applied to describe the work of Wassily Kandinsky in 1919, was now the official name of the art movement which had been spearheaded by Arshile Gorky.

It was time for Collier to go home.

She stood in the middle of her bedroom with two empty suitcases lying open at her feet, clothes draped everywhere, trying to decide what to take with her. For someone who didn't care much about fashion, she thought wryly, she had certainly managed to collect a lot of clothes in just five years. She couldn't remember wearing half of them. She glanced at some of the labels: Dior, Chanel, Balmain, Balenciaga, Fath, Worth. She shoved her hands into the pockets of her trousers and frowned. She had no idea how much to pack. She hadn't even decided on how long to stay.

"What the devil do you intend to do with all those bloody clothes?" asked Thaddeus as he came into the room. "You're not being presented at court, you know, you're only going to America."

He slipped his arms around her waist and gave her a tight squeeze. "I wish you weren't going, pet. I'll miss you, you know."

Would he? she wondered. Or was he put out because *she* was leaving this time, not him?

"Why don't you come with me, Taddy? Stay just a couple of days."

"As much as I'd love to, I have a group of eager young archeologists waiting for me in Jericho."

This latest expedition was being sponsored jointly by the British School of Archeology in Jerusalem and the British Academy, but the project was still sorely in need of additional funding. Collier almost wished the funds would dry up completely. That might provide her with the ammunition she needed. She still hadn't been able to convince Thaddeus even to consider leaving London and moving to the States. If this newest venture failed, perhaps she could get him to change his mind.

As she leaned against him, feeling his body touching hers, she was filled with a wistful sadness. The nomadic life they had been leading was finally working against them. Their relationship had begun to change. They were living apart more and more now. Even their times together had begun to feel like a prelude to a more permanent separation. She was restless, but he seemed oblivious to it.

Thaddeus planted a kiss on her forehead and held her out to look at her. "So the young collector has been proven correct, after all, eh? You'll be returning to America the conquering heroine who can say 'I told you so' to every stuffed cuckoo who ever considered himself an art connoisseur. You've really shown them, pet, and I'm proud of you."

She felt strangely shy hearing him talk that way. Shy and pleased and still somewhat shocked. When the invitation to the gala opening had arrived, she had burst into tears. She still took it out of her desk drawer at least a dozen times a day to keep herself believing that it was really true. Rothko, Baziotes, de Kooning, Pollock, Motherwell, Still, Hofmann and, of course, Gorky. Recognition, at last.

"Tell me, pet, will you be giving *Time* and *Look* the interviews they've been asking for?"

"Why not? Anything to further the cause."

"And what about TV and radio?"

"So far, I've only got two interviews set up. One with Edward R. Murrow on the program *See It Now* for CBS and a radio show with Leland."

"In a backwater town like Philadelphia?"

"Uh-uh. New York." At his look of surprise, she said, "Didn't I tell you? Leland phoned me last week to say that he'd landed that job he wanted at WNBC. Not only that, but he's finally getting a byline in the *New York Times*. Philadelphia's in the past now."

"Careful, my girl, you're about to burst those buttons of yours."

Collier's eyes were bright. "Oh, Taddy, I'm so proud of him. He's making it, really making it, just as he said he would."

"And so will you, pet, so will you."

"You sound as if I were the genius behind abstract expressionism, Taddy," she said. "I'm not, you know. I'm just someone who got excited by something at what everyone else considered to be the wrong time. Now, suddenly, it's the right time. I'm being called intuitive, far-sighted, a visionary and God only knows what else, but I'm not. I simply believed in what those artists were doing at the time, and I felt a responsibility toward them and their work. I was just lucky enough to have had the means to do something about it."

"Don't put yourself down for what you've done, pet. What you've just described is someone the art world cannot do without. A patron. You, my dear Collier, are a patron. Be proud of that appellation."

"If I am the patron you say I am, why shouldn't I show them how right I really was? I think I'll take my paintings out of storage, Taddy, and see if I can lease a gallery on Madison Avenue. Then I'll mount my own exhibition to run concurrently with the Museum of Modern Art's exhibit."

"But that means you'll be away for two months."

Collier went on as if she hadn't heard him. "I might even try to drag Milo out of mothballs and have him come into the gallery to talk about his own work. Who knows, it might even stimulate him enough to really take his painting seriously again."

"If you're so intent on salvaging that wastrel's career, I'd advise you not to display all of his works at once. You'll only succeed in knocking down the price of every Racine now in circulation. Feed them out a few at a time."

"I don't think you understand, Taddy. I'm not going to sell my paintings; I'm only going to exhibit them."

"But you could make a bloody fortune out of them now." She stared at him. It took him another moment, but he finally realized the absurdity of what he had said. "I really must be getting on. You're the last person who need ever worry about making fortunes."

He seemed to hesitate for a moment, and then, as if reconsidering, he pulled something out of his pocket and handed it to her.

"Speaking of making one's fortune, what do you think of this ring I've just had made up? It's one of the coins from the Laconian dig. I thought I might begin making up pairs of cufflinks and tie clips from the extra coins I have floating around, give me a chance to wear some of my little treasures. Gulliver has already given me his approval. I shouldn't wonder. He's begun to grumble about all the dusting. The bugger must be getting old."

Collier examined the ring and handed it back to him. "I think it's a terrific idea. At least this way, part of your collection will be portable."

"They'd make bloody effective gifts too, don't you think? If I ever get to the point where I can no longer hold a shovel or get down on my knees with a brush, I can always open up a gift shop."

Collier made a face.

"I agree," he said with a sigh. "But how else are these old bones going to earn a living?"

"You'll continue to lecture, you'll write books, and if worse comes to worse, you'll sell off some of the more important pieces in your collection."

"That, my dear, would be sacrilege."

"You know you don't have to worry, Taddy," she told him in a gentle voice. "I'll take care of you."

"So you'll put me at the head of your favorite-charities list, will you? Thanks, pet. Now I think I'd best leave you to pack."

He gave her a pat on the head, but she refused to let him go that easily. She seized his hand and planted a noisy kiss on the back of it. She felt as if she were seeing his hand for the first time. The dark spots and the thinning skin belonged to an older person's hand, not Thaddeus's. It was with a painful jolt that she realized he was now sixty-two years old—exactly twice her age.

A few minutes later, he was back again, holding up a copy of the London *Times*. "Now here's something which should interest you." He pointed to a front page story. "Didn't you say you'd stayed with a Sir Gilbert Hall when you first came to London in thirty-eight?"

Collier nodded, feeling a strange clutching in her chest.

"Well, according to the *Times,* the old boy's chain of newspapers is about to go belly up. They're in receivership. Five papers, one here in London, two in Wales, one in Scotland and one in Ireland. Labor problems and outdated equipment, it seems. I imagine they couldn't quite keep up with the competition. Pity."

"Let me see that." Collier snatched the paper out of his hands. Along with the story was a photograph of Earle Hall, nephew of the late Sir Gilbert Hall and present owner of the chain, standing in front of the house she remembered so well. Tears welled up in her eyes. She gave Thaddeus back the paper and reached for the telephone.

"What are you doing?" he asked.

She put her hand over the mouthpiece. "I've always felt guilty about not taking more interest in my father's business. Well, I'm about to change that right now. I wonder how the board will feel about expanding into the newspaper field." She gave the overseas operator two numbers.

"And just whom are you calling?"

"John Ender and Leland."

"Why Leland?"

"He's a newspaperman, isn't he? I can't think of a better person to save Sir Gilbert's chain than Leland. How do you think he'd be at building a newspaper empire?"

"I should think you'd bloody well have to ask him."

"That's precisely what I intend to do."

The flight from London to New York's Idlewild Airport was only eleven minutes late. Customs, however, detained Collier for nearly an hour while all of her bags were opened, and the clothes she had never worn were inspected, sniffed, held in the air, and otherwise examined. In exasperation, she offered to give the clothes to the matron who was manhandling them, but when her offer was misconstrued as a bribe, Collier hastily paid them the full duty on the clothes and they released her. She marched, fuming, out the doors and into the arms of her anxious brother.

As soon as he held her, she began to relax. This was how it always was with Leland. Each time she saw him was like the first time all over again. He kissed her on the forehead, on the tip of her nose and on her chin. Then he planted a long, warm kiss on her lips.

"Red's not your color," she told him.

"It tastes good though," he said, wiping off her lipstick with his handkerchief. "God, you look terrific."

"Thank you, sir." She dipped him a light curtsy. "Every woman over thirty deserves to hear that at least once a day."

"Then I'll make sure to remind you every day. Those your bags?" He indicated the three suitcases, one steamer trunk and the small vanity case a porter had on his trolley.

She nodded. He seemed to gulp.

"You certainly came prepared, didn't you?"

"Why not? I plan to take America by storm." She gave her sables a dramatic twirl and lowered her eyes. "It's been five years since these size eleven feet of mine have touched American soil, so indulge me a little."

"I'd like to, but I have a two-seater MG."

She burst out laughing. "You take me in your car and I'll hire a limousine to follow us with the luggage."

"That's what I like best about having money—nothing's an obstacle for very long." He signaled the porter to follow them.

As they stepped out of the terminal, flashbulbs began to go off. A clutch of reporters rushed up to Collier, notepads open, pencils poised, their questions ready. Nothing changes, she thought, except the cameras—they keep getting smaller.

"How does it feel to be back in the States, Miss Paget-Browne?"

"Give me another five minutes, I just arrived."

"You planning on staying long?"

"Just how long is long?"

"Do you think the recognition these artists are getting now has been a long time coming?"

This question she took seriously.

"The fact that they're being recognized at all is extremely important. Whoever made up the rule which states an artist has to die before he can be recognized? If an artist can't gain this recognition during his lifetime, fewer and fewer people will be willing to commit themselves to art."

"Is it true that you and Mr. Jamieson have separated?"

The question caught her offguard. When she answered, it was in a tightly controlled voice: "We're separated only by distance."

She hadn't realized how tightly she had been holding on to Leland's hand until he let her go. He opened the door of a bright red sportscar and motioned for her to get in.

Leland started the car, and Collier began to wonder if that

reporter could have been right without even knowing it. Were she and Thaddeus actually being separated by something more than just distance? Had Thaddeus realized something she had missed?

Suddenly, the car seemed too small. She was getting hot. Her furs were starting to choke her.

"Leland"—she clutched his arm—"could you put the top down for me?"

"In January? Are you nuts?"

"Please!"

The urgency in her tone made him pull the car over to the side of the road. While he tugged back the top and secured it, she took out the pins holding her hair in place. Combing her fingers through her hair, she decided to let the wind do whatever it wanted with it. For the moment, she needed to feel free.

"I don't know many women who'd do what you just did," he told her as he jumped back into the car. "If you really want a breeze, get ready for one."

As Collier watched, the speedometer began to climb. When the needle swung to eighty, she threw back her head and closed her eyes.

"Are you sure you don't have any Paget-Browne blood in your veins?" she shouted to him above the roar of the wind.

"If I do, it's only by association."

"How do you feel about cigars?"

"As long as you're the one smoking them, they're fine."

"You're definitely not a Paget-Browne, then."

The wind made too loud a wail for them to carry on any kind of conversation, so they drove into Manhattan in silence. With the buildings towering over her and closing in around her, Collier gave into the flood of memories her self-imposed exile had held back for so long. She was home again. She breathed in the stinging, sooty, burning city, filling her lungs with its filthy air and her body with its special life.

At the first red light they stopped for, Collier finally asked Leland if he had come to any decision regarding the Hall chain of newspapers.

He actually looked uncomfortable. "As I told you over the phone, Collier, the timing's all wrong. As tempting as it sounds, I can give you three solid reasons for my not getting involved right now."

"I don't think I want to hear them," she said glumly. But she still refused to give up and when she spoke again, she made herself sound as enthusiastic as possible. "Think of it, Leland. You'd be living in London. You'd be in charge of five papers, with the power to do anything you wanted to do. And we'd be able to see each other more often. Do you realize that we've spent exactly nine days together in our entire lives? Every time you leave I feel we're losing another chance, that we're missing out on something precious. I get so angry with you, Leland, and then I get angry with myself for not being able to make you stay."

"But you can't buy me a business in order to keep us together, Collier," he said with a hint of reproach in his voice. "I don't want to follow someone else's game plan. This is *my* life we're talking about. Come on, Collier, don't look like that."

She was sitting straight in her seat, her chin thrust out defiantly, her jaw set.

"Collier, please, try to understand me. I told you I was willing to work for what I wanted, and I'm not afraid to do just that. Look how far I've come these last three years. It wasn't the name of Taggert that did it, and it wasn't because I had Paget-Browne money behind me. It was because of Leland the reporter. Probing, digging, persistent, perfectionist Leland. I'd feel I was selling out my own dreams if I settled for a safe job handed to me by someone else."

"I'd hardly call trying to save a newspaper chain from bankruptcy a safe job," she scowled. "But I understand you, Leland, much more than you think I do, and I respect you for it. Now, what are those three reasons?"

"Korea, WNBC and the *Times*."

"So you're off to Korea again, is that what you're trying to tell me?"

"I guess so."

She was almost afraid to ask. "When?"

"In three days."

She clasped her hands together in her lap and concentrated on the road ahead of her. "Well, at least that gives me three days to work on you. With you or without you, I intend to save that chain. I couldn't stand by and watch Sir Gilbert's empire collapse."

Avery Leggett's words came back to her again: *Empires are unwieldy things and better left to men.* To sons. Sir Gilbert Hall had had no sons.

She thought of Addison. Her father's son. She thought of

her failed attempts to make him independent, the position she had created for him at Paget-Browne Enterprises, having the company pay him a salary instead of her transferring her own money into his account each month. From all the reports she received, Addison didn't want the chance she had given him any more than the ruling board of the company wanted him to have it.

She studied Leland's strong profile and a bitter longing tugged at her heart. "Even if I don't get you to agree to this proposition, I'll eventually get you to agree to something," she told him.

"That sounds ominous. Is that a threat?"

"It's a promise. We Paget-Brownes are stubborn, you know, and if we wait long enough, we usually get what we want."

"Then let's hope I've found the gallery you wanted," he said, tossing a scrap of paper into her lap.

"What's this?"

"A list of some Madison Avenue art galleries. Only one guy seemed interested. His name's Wally Kincaid. Apparently he's just redecorated the place—painting, lighting, carpeting, the works. He was supposed to mount a one-man exhibit this month, but the artist backed out, leaving Kincaid high and dry. He owes everybody money, including the bank, and he's panicking because he hasn't been able to line up a replacement."

"Well, it seems he's found one now. Let's go have a talk with Wally Kincaid right away." Collier could feel the adrenaline pumping through her system. "God, I must look like a mess." She immediately began trying to straighten out her tousled hair. "He'll think he's renting his gallery to a cleaning lady."

"Just fling your sables in his face and show him your checkbook, and he'll forget about your hair."

"Tell me," she mumbled around a mouthful of hairpins, "do you date, Leland?" It was the one area of his life she had never questioned him about.

"Not really. I never have enough time. I'm either working or traveling and most women want more than a part-time lover. I'm trying to build up my career and these years are crucial to me. I don't have the energy for both a career and a relationship right now, so my relationships suffer." He turned to her and gave her a wink. "Besides, next to you, other women are pretty damned dull."

She squeezed his hand. Suddenly, the thought of his leaving began to do strange fluttering things to her stomach. She cast about for some way to plug the hole his leaving would cause, and she came up with Jenny. She would bring Jenny to New York. She told Leland of her intentions.

"Jenny's the little girl from Gloucester?"

"Yes, Jennifer Howe. But she's not a little girl anymore. She's fifteen now, and from her letters, I'd say she's becoming quite an accomplished artist. Stay a few more days and meet her, Leland. I'm sure Orrin would give his permission, and I know you'd like her. She's lovely, very shy, but she's a sheer delight, and she'll just adore you."

"That's quite a buildup," he chuckled. "You're going to make someone a great mother one day."

"Not me."

"Don't be silly. You're still young enough to have children."

"I might be, but Thaddeus isn't."

Leland didn't comment, and Collier noticed how tightly clenched his jaw was. He senses it too, she thought unhappily. Was it that obvious to everyone? She felt as if she were suffering from some terminal disease that everyone knew about but her. They were simply trying to protect her, that's what they would say if she confronted them with her suspicions.

She found she didn't want to talk anymore. She sat up straight again, her back rigid, her arms stiff at her sides, as if she were bracing herself for a blow.

She was still sitting that way, tense and expectant, when they pulled up in front of the Kincaid Gallery. The large bay window, framed by a royal blue awning, was bare except for one large oil painting set on a gold easel against a backdrop of royal blue velvet.

The place smelled of fresh paint. The white walls were bare, the high ceilings pocked with chrome cylinders which were still without lightbulbs. The main room of the gallery led through an archway into a second room of approximately the same size. The only spot of color in the place was the plush royal blue carpeting.

Collier and Leland walked through the gallery to the back where the office was located. There they found a harassed-looking stringbean of a man whose blond hair sprang from his head like a furry halo. With his puckish features and pale blue eyes, he looked like an impish albino. He was dressed in faded jeans and running shoes and his plaid work shirt was open at the neck to reveal a heavy black iron cross.

"I'm Kincaid, I'm desperately busy, so I hope what you came here for won't take too long," he announced in a breathy monotone, as he slammed a drawer shut in his filing cabinet and opened another.

Collier and Leland exchanged amused glances.

"My brother was in here yesterday speaking to you about the possibility of my renting your gallery for two months."

Wally Kincaid rewarded Collier with a blank stare.

"That's why I'm here now," Collier explained patiently. "I'd like to rent your gallery for two months."

"Lady, this is a bad day for jokes. The electrician refuses to finish the lighting system, the phone company's threatening to cut off the damned phone, and my bank manager is sharpening his knife to whack off my balls if I don't show up Monday with some found, stolen or borrowed money."

"I told you he'd think I was a cleaning lady," Collier whispered to Leland.

"Flash him something impressive," he whispered back, indicating her sables.

"I understand you were supposed to mount an exhibition and the artist—"

"Crapped out on me, the bastard. He's had his head inside a bottle for so long, he doesn't know which end of the paintbrush to use anymore. I only did it for his agent who's a friend of mine and because the bum used to be somebody. Twenty-five paintings, that's what they promised me. I turned down two other exhibits because of him, and the lush comes up with six pieces of shit I wouldn't hang in my john. Six! And now I'm up the creek."

"Then I'll repeat my offer to you, Mr. Kincaid. My name is Collier Paget-Browne, and I'll pay you ten thousand dollars if you lease me your gallery for two months."

"If this is a joke, lady, I'll have you arrested for verbal assault."

"Show him your driver's license," muttered Leland, losing his patience.

But Wally Kincaid was hastily slipping a pair of tiny metal-rimmed glasses onto his button nose. "Holy shit! Now that's a face you don't forget. Never mind about the license, I believe you." He took off his glasses and put them back in his shirt pocket. "You're not going to believe this, but that bum I was telling you about was your ex."

Shock waves rippled through Collier. "Milo?"

"Yup. Seems he was miffed because he hadn't been included in the Museum of Modern Art's exhibition, and he wanted to prove how wrong they'd been to leave him out. At least that's how he explained it to me. I felt sorry for him. I thought he might still have something left in him, so I decided to give him a chance. I guess I was wrong."

It was as if cold water had been poured into Collier's veins. She was only vaguely aware of Leland's supporting hand on her arm. "You'll have your Milo Racine exhibit, Mr. Kincaid. Now will you lease me your gallery?"

He looked like a bug squirming on the end of a needle. "You still offering me ten thousand for it?"

"Will you take my personal check?" she asked as she opened her purse.

"Sure." He cleared his throat and wiped his hands on his jeans. "Hey, listen, I'm sorry about what I said about—you know, if I'd known—"

"Don't apologize." Collier tore off the check and handed it to him. "You couldn't tell me anything about Milo Racine I don't already know. I'll be in touch with you, Mr. Kincaid, as soon as I've arranged for the paintings to be sent from Boston."

"And they're all Racines, you said."

"Sixty-four Racines to be precise."

He let out a low whistle. "We don't have that kind of space."

"Then we'll rotate them, Mr. Kincaid. Just leave everything to me."

Collier took Leland's arm and they left the gallery.

"Now that's what I call a shock," Leland said as he helped her back into the car. "I'm sorry, Collier, I really am. I know how this must hurt."

"The poor pathetic man," she whispered, surprised that she could still ache for him after all this time. "He'll have his exhibition, Leland, and I'll see to it that *everyone* comes to it. The company has a printer who'll drop everything to do the invitations for me, and I'll use a messenger service to hand-deliver them. I'll give Milo an opening this city won't forget and I'll do it before the museum's opening. I swear it."

• • •

The Milo Racine Retrospective Exhibition opened with champagne and strawberries at the Kincaid Gallery on January 22, one night before the official opening of the Museum of Modern Art's exhibit. The names of the three hundred guests attending the opening could have filled the social register. There were even several congressmen, senators and cabinet members among them. They came from Philadelphia, Chicago, Boston, Palm Beach and San Francisco. From Racine, Wisconsin came an aging butcher and his wife, their three daughters with their husbands and all ten of their children. And the press turned out to record the event for posterity.

The only one missing was the artist himself.

On the same morning that Collier was meeting with Wally Kincaid, Milo Racine hanged himself in his rented loft in Greenwich Village.

He had used a purple scarf.

Chapter Seventeen

Milo's suicide left Collier both devastated and angry. He had lived such a small part of his dream. He had watched his talent flare and then too quickly falter. And now, just as he had feared, the question of his ultimate contribution was going to be assessed by others after his death. Collier ached for his death just as she had ached for his life, but her anger at his cowardice soon consumed the pain and made her bitter. It was only when she realized that Milo Racine had never been a fighter, that his strength had been a bluff bolstered by his mouth and his fists, that her conflicted feelings gradually sorted themselves out. Soon all she was left with was a gentle regret.

In later years, when she was able to look back at that time from the safety of distance, she saw that it wasn't only Milo's death which finally jolted her out of her own paralysis. It was the week she spent with Jennifer Howe. She had looked at that lovely woman-child, with her rock-crystal eyes and waist-length black hair, and she had seen in Jenny's face what had been missing in her own face for a very long time.

Curiosity.

Collier had simply stopped being curious. And now there was a void inside her which needed to be filled. It wasn't long before she was combing the major art galleries of Manhattan and the obscure galleries of Greenwich Village in search of talent.

And she found it.

What the abstract expressionists had created in oils, a group of sculptors had been translating into bronze and iron and steel: miniature works, giant works, some for display on a coffee table, others to be set outside in a garden, still others to hang from the ceiling as mobiles. They were contorted and twisted abstract concoctions of sheer whimsy, nailed and soldered and welded together, bits and scraps of metal transformed into geometric forms and biomorphic shapes.

Excited by what she saw and allowing her instinct to guide

her once more, Collier bought a number of the large works and some of the smaller works of Alexander Calder, David Smith, Reuben Nakian, David Hare, Theodore Roszak, Seymour Lipton and Frederick Kiesler. The two dozen sculptures were crated and shipped directly to Boston, where they were stored with the rest of her art collection.

Turning to painting, she discovered that there was already a tentative, new movement afoot. As revolutionary as the abstract expressionists had been, this emerging school was even more radical. Their focus was the commercialism beginning to saturate the American way of life. What resulted from their observations were mixed-media works parodying that way of life. Men like Jasper Johns, Larry Rivers and Robert Rauschenberg were managing to blur the line between art and reality. Using everyday objects such as shoes, stuffed animals, flags and auto parts, together with pieces of splintered wood, rope, wire and oils mixed with sand, they were creating what critic Lawrence Alloway had dubbed "junk art."

Once again, Collier bought and bought heavily, dispatching still another full truck to Boston. She didn't have to look in the mirror to see the changes in herself. She could feel them. She was living them. She felt alive again. Alone but alive. And this worried her. She was enduring her separation from Thaddeus too well. Too easily. Not only was she brimming with life, but she felt strangely content. And contentment was something she had done without for too long.

When the exhibition closed at the end of March and Milo's paintings were returned to the company warehouse in Boston, Collier drove to Philadelphia. It was time to do what she had promised to do for six years—buy Diana a house.

Collier and Leland had discussed moving their mother out of Fairwood and into a home of her own many times. It was the only source of friction between them. Whenever Collier broached the subject, Leland would tense up, setting his jaw as stubbornly as she would set hers, and they would argue. Sister and brother would battle lovingly over the woman whose blood they shared, as tenuous as that bloodline was.

After a long visit with Diana in January, the day before Leland had left for Korea, Collier had brought up the subject again. She had pestered her brother all the way back to New York.

"But she's done well at Fairwood," he had argued. "She

has everything she needs and she gets all the attention she could possibly want. I only hope I can find some place to take as good care of me in my old age."

"Don't joke about it, Leland!" she snapped. "I want Diana out of that institution."

"You know it's more like a country club."

"Don't you dare pretend to believe their public relations, it's an institution!"

"I know." He gave her a wink. "Look, Collier, even thinking about moving her into her own home frightens me. I still feel that taking her out of the one place she feels safe in and plunking her down in the middle of a totally new environment is asking for trouble. The move might be just enough of a shock to finally push her over the edge. I don't want to take that chance. I don't want to risk losing her completely. I don't want that kind of responsibility. I couldn't live with the guilt. She's the only family I have."

"That's not true," Collier pouted. "You have me."

He took his hand off the steering wheel and patted her. "I know I have you, dear heart, but it's not the same. Diana's my mother."

"She's my mother too," Collier returned in a low voice, "and I'd never knowingly hurt her, believe me. But I made a promise a long time ago, and I want to keep that promise. I want to take care of her, Leland, really take care of her. I hate Fairwood," she declared vehemently. "I hate everything about the place. I hate being issued those impersonal monthly reports on her condition. They probably write up one report, mimeograph it and send a copy to each patient's family." Leland snickered. "I want to be able to visit her when *I* want to visit, and not when someone else gives me permission," Collier went on. "I know she receives expert medical attention there, but how can she forget for a moment that she's sick? Look at the people around her. Most of them are sicker than she is. Wouldn't that frighten you, Leland?" Without even waiting for him to answer, she continued, "But what I despise most is her room. As pretty as it is, it's nothing but a cage, and some faceless keeper has the power to lock her up and let her out. That's what terrifies me, Leland, and I'm sure it must terrify her." Her fist came down hard on the dashboard. "I'm sick of the whole thing. I want her out of there. I want to give Diana what she needs."

"What *you* think she needs," Leland interjected. "Fairwood already gives her everything she needs."

"They don't give her freedom."

"Spell that out for me."

"Selma Bryce."

"Selma Bryce?" His forehead creased as he tried to place the name. "The new nurse who's taking care of her?"

Collier nodded. "Diana adores her. The woman's marvelous with her and you can tell that Diana feels safe with her. As far as I'm concerned, Selma Bryce is the first *human* being I've ever seen at Fairwood."

"How would you know? This was only your second visit to Fairwood."

At her pained expression, Leland apologized hastily. "I'm sorry, Collier, that was mean. Forgive me."

Collier managed to hide her hurt behind a forced smile. "I like Selma," she said, "and what's more, I trust her." She paused, glanced sideways at her brother and then looked away again. "I asked her if she'd ever consider leaving Fairwood and living fulltime with Diana." She paused again. "She said yes."

Leland's grip tightened on the wheel. "I see," was all he could manage to say.

"Selma Bryce can mean freedom for Diana," Collier persisted.

Leland said nothing. Collier counted up to fifty.

"Suppose my father objects?" he asked her. "After all, he's been footing the bill for Fairwood all these years."

Collier's face darkened. "Your father's got nothing to do with this. This is our decision, Leland, yours and mine. Lloyd Taggert is just one more reason for getting Diana out of that place. The minute that door closes behind her, your dear father can stop paying out his conscience money. I'm sure he won't mind one bit," she continued bitterly. "On the contrary, he'll probably be relieved."

"But you're talking big bucks, Collier," Leland countered, "and right now, I just don't have the kind of money a move like this requires."

"I'm not asking you for money," Collier explained patiently. "I'm prepared to assume full financial responsibility for Diana from now on. All I want from you is your approval and the promise that you'll see her as often as possible. As you pointed out, I haven't been particularly strong in that area." *But I'll change that,* she told herself, *I swear I'll change that now.*

"Some partnership," he snorted. "You pay the bills and I pay the visits."

Collier refused to be put off by his sarcasm. "Oh Leland, please say yes," she begged him. "Please? We've done it your way all these years, couldn't we at least try it my way now? As soon as the exhibition's over, I could drive back to Philadelphia and start looking for a house. Think of the privacy we'll have once Diana's in a place of her own. Whenever we visit, we'll be a real family with a real home. She deserves a real home again, Leland. She hasn't had one in twenty-two years." *And neither have I,* she wanted to add. *Or you. All three of us deserve this house.*

Somewhat embarrassed by her outburst, she lapsed into stony silence. She had to give him time to think it over. Every tense muscle in her body was telling her that she was right. She lit a cigar. This time, she held all the cards. Leland had to agree to it. He simply had to.

She noticed the slight nod of his head and her heart soared. She stubbed out the cigar and waited.

"All right, Collier," he told her in a subdued voice, "we'll give it a try."

With a shriek of delight, she threw her arms around his neck and hugged him. The car swerved sharply as Leland tried to fight her off.

"But I'm warning you," he shouted above the squeal of the tires as he wrestled with the wheel, "at the first sign of any deterioration in her condition, back she goes to Fairwood. Is that understood."

Collier gulped. "It's understood."

"Promise?"

"Promise," she agreed, with a solemn nod of her head.

After spending five days in Philadelphia and being shown dozens of houses, Collier finally decided on a three-bedroom, gray fieldstone bungalow on a quiet, tree-shaded street called Appleview Drive. It was only four blocks from Fairwood, close enough to give Diana the security she needed, but far enough away for her to feel free. As free as she could ever feel.

When Collier took Diana to see the house for the first time, she was convinced that the day itself was on her side. Spring

was now more of a hint than a promise. It was gloriously sunny
and mild, and most of the snow had melted. Several clusters
of purple crocuses had already opened in one of the flower
beds close to the house and Diana's eyes brightened at the sight
of them.

As Collier led her mother up the flagstone path to the front
door, Diana tugged at her sleeve and made her stop. She was
staring down at the crocuses, a look of longing in her blue
eyes. Impulsively, Collier bent down and snapped off one of
the stalks to give to her mother. Diana smiled at her and held
the flower up to her nose.

Watching her, Collier felt a painful tug at her heart. Though
she was fifty, Diana had scarcely changed over the years. There
were very few lines in her pretty face, very little white in the
pale gold of her hair. She was still slim and her slender frame
seemed all the more delicate because of the simple pale blue
or mauve dresses she liked to wear. To Collier, her mother
would always remain more of a pastel shadow than a real
person. A shadow that smelled of lily-of-the-valley and spoke
in a whisper.

Collier's chest constricted with that old familiar ache. It was
the ache born in that Boston courtroom on that day so long
ago. The ache she felt whenever she thought of her mother, a
stranger she would never know. The ache which reminded her
that they would never share what other mothers and daughters
get to share in a lifetime. She chewed on the inside of her
cheek to keep her lips from trembling. *I'm thirty-one years
old*, she thought miserably, *and I keep waiting for a miracle.
I keep waiting for her to be a real mother to me.*

Diana gazed up at her daughter through tear-filled eyes.

"Just one step up," Collier cautioned as she helped Diana
into the foyer. *Please God*, she prayed, *let her like it. Don't
let her be afraid. Please. Please.*

The house was bathed in sunlight. Although the rooms were
empty, Collier had filled them with greenery. Tubs of miniature
trees stood in the corners of each room. African violets lined
the windowsills and pots of chrysanthemums, geraniums, aza-
leas and rhododendrum were set in clusters on the floor.

Diana's eyes were wide, and when she spoke, her voice
was as breathy as a child's. "Is all this for me?" she asked.

"For you and for Selma," Collier told her, glancing over at
the woman hovering near Diana like a benevolent shadow. The

two women were the same height and somehow Collier found that reassuring. Her mother would never feel threatened or overwhelmed by Selma Bryce. On the contrary, she would feel protected. The woman had a stocky build with an ample bosom and a face which could only be described as serene under a cloud of short, curling brown hair. Her warm brown eyes had a saucy glint to them, as if to prove that, in spite of the solidity of the rest of her, she knew something about humor too. At fifty-three, Selma Bryce was a widow with no children of her own. In Diana, she had found herself a lifelong child.

Collier took Diana by the hand and led her into what would be her bedroom. It was a large room facing the back garden, but its most winning feature was the small solarium attached to it. Glassed in on three sides, it was a warm and sheltered spot, with just enough room for a small table and two chairs. Collier had made the little hideaway even more magical by hanging baskets of ivy and philodendron from the ceiling.

Diana gasped and clapped her hands together. Then she crossed the room alone, easily navigated the two steps leading up to the solarium, and touched each one of the plants individually. What a wonderful house! She had never seen so many trees and plants in a house before. She caught hold of a trailing stem of ivy and rubbed it back and forth across her cheek.

Collier joined Diana in the solarium and she wrapped her arms around her mother's narrow waist. Diana sighed and leaned her head against Collier's chest.

"Leland and I love you very much," Collier said gently, "and we want to make you happy. We both think this house can make you happy. So, if you'd like, this can be your home from now on, Mother, and you can do anything you want with it."

Diana thought for a moment, and then, in her little girl's voice, she asked,

"Could my new bedroom have the same kind of wallpaper as my old room?"

"Of course it could," Collier assured her. She was elated. Diana had referred to her room at Fairwood as her old room. Collier felt her heart begin to pound wildly. Diana wanted to move! She wasn't afraid. She was ready.

Diana turned to her daughter. "I think I'd like to live here," she told her shyly. "I'd like this to be my home."

• • •

It took Collier less than a month to decorate the house. She simply hired the workmen she needed, paid them triple their usual hourly wage and put them to work. She showed Diana a number of magazines featuring the homes of the best-known families in America and her mother indicated her preference for American colonial furniture. Collier proceeded to deplete the stock of every antique store in and around Philadelphia in her search for authentic Duncan Phyfe, Shaker and Lambert Hitchcock furniture.

Diana insisted on green carpeting for the entire house because she wanted to pretend that she was always walking on soft grass. Collier carpeted the house in green. She chose the same shade of green for the walls in the hallways, living room and dining room and painted the ceilings and moldings white. The kitchen was papered in a bold yellow daisy pattern and, at Diana's urging, the wallpaper used for all three bedrooms was almost identical to the mauve violet wallpaper in her bedroom at Fairwood.

Collier complied with all of her mother's decisions, agreeing to anything which might keep her feeling safe. To simplify life for Selma, Collier hired a middle-aged Negro couple by the name of Cole to come to the house five full days a week. Delia Cole would cook and do the marketing and the housework. Julius Cole would look after the garden, do all the light maintenance work and on those occasions when Diana could be coaxed out of the house, drive the large Chrysler limousine Collier had bought her mother.

The task of maintaining the greenery inside the house was assigned to Varley's Florist on Sycamore Street. Not only were they to tend the trees and the plants, but they were to keep every vase filled with fresh, cut flowers.

The completion of the house and Leland's return from Korea fell within two days of one another. On a bright April afternoon, Leland arrived in Philadelphia from New York and Collier was at the airport to meet him. He appeared haggard and thin and he hardly spoke at all on the way to Fairwood to pick up Diana and Selma. He seemed preoccupied and distant. Perhaps it was just as well, Collier thought, as she chewed on the end of a cigar she had forgotten to light. She was too nervous for conversation anyway.

Her hands were clammy, her stomach was tied in a knot and she kept fighting down the urge to cry. This would be his first glimpse of the house. What if he didn't like it? What if he didn't approve of the way it was furnished? What if Diana didn't like it? What if she changed her mind about moving and decided to return to Fairwood? She couldn't go back even if she wanted to. Her room had already been reserved for a woman whose family had been on Fairwood's waiting list for two years.

Collier was bristling with agitation by the time the four of them got out of the car in front of the house on Appleview Drive. As they started up the walk, Collier chanced a look at her mother. Her face was flushed, her eyes wide, and she was clinging tightly to Selma's arm. Leland was still lost in thought. He walked slowly, his shoulders stooped. Collier's stomach churned. *God, please let this all work out,* she prayed.

Julius carried Diana's bags to her room and Selma went with him to unpack them. Collier looked at Leland, and then they both looked at Diana. Suddenly, as if on cue, Leland seemed to come to life. He took one of Diana's hands, Collier took the other, and together, they began their tour of the house.

"Think of all the money you'll save on hotel bills from now on," Collier told Leland with false gaiety.

All she got from him as they moved from room to room was the occasional low whistle and a nod. She wanted to strangle him for torturing her. She glanced over at Diana. She seemed to be walking between them in a trance, with a tremulous smile fixed on her face. Collier's nerves were ready to snap.

"Oh, look at the lovely flowers," Diana's soft voice broke the silence. Collier jumped. "They're the same as the ones in the wallpaper."

Collier gave her mother's hand a squeeze, relieved that she was still alert in spite of the masklike quality of her face. They moved finally to the guest bedroom, the only room left to see. Collier noticed Leland watching her and her throat tightened. Here it comes, she thought, bracing herself. *Here it comes now.*

"You've really done quite a job with this place," he told her, "and in such a short time, too. It already has a kind of lived-in quality about it. I like that."

Collier started to unwind slowly, but she still wasn't satisfied. "Do you like the house itself though?" she asked him.

Leland looked at Diana and he nodded. "I think it's going to be perfect for her."

"But do *you* like it?" Collier persisted.

Again, he nodded. "I think it's a great place."

"Honest?"

"Honest."

Collier's body sagged with relief. She wanted to hug her brother until he could not breathe. He had released her. Her ordeal was over. To her surprise, he began to rub her back.

"Take it easy," he soothed her. "You've passed inspection with flying colors. Relax. That's a good girl." A moment later, his voice turned mischievous. "You're paying for the florist, right?"

Collier laughed. "Why? Are you volunteering?"

"I'd be bankrupt within the year," he retorted, giving her a light smack. "But just to prove that I'm not completely selfish, I *have* made my own meager contribution to the house. Be back in a minute." And he bounded out the door.

By the time he returned, Diana was curled up on one of the twin beds with her shoes off, and Collier was sitting cross-legged on the other.

"This is for your room, Mother," Leland told Diana, placing a long, flat package in her lap, and then going to sit down next to Collier.

Diana stared at the package she was holding and said nothing. She made no move either to sit up or to open it.

"Go on, Mother," Leland urged her. "It's for you. Open it."

Diana stirred and finally sat up. She had heard everything he'd said, but for the moment all she wanted to do was hold the present and just look at her son. At her beloved children. She wanted them to know how happy she was today. She wanted to tell them how beautiful her house was. Even more beautiful than the one she'd lived in so long ago. She wished she could recall the words to let them know exactly how she felt, but she'd forgotten most of them. Instead of speaking, she gave her children her widest and warmest smile, and hoped they'd understand.

As Collier watched the radiant smile spreading across Diana's face, she found herself smiling back. *I understand,* she told her, *Leland and I both understand. And we're happy too.* The lump in her throat was back, growing larger. Her unshed tears edged closer to the surface. Desperate to maintain her composure, Collier gave her head a toss and forced herself to focus on her mother's face without blinking.

"This is just like Christmas, isn't it," declared Diana, as she slowly opened her gift. As soon as she saw what it was, she began to tremble with excitement. "My babies!" she exclaimed.

Leland had put together a collage from old snapshots and newspaper photos of himself and Collier, pasting them onto a large piece of plywood and coating the board with shellac. Diana held up the collage for them to admire before turning it around again and hugging it to her chest.

The lump in Collier's throat hardened. The tears sprang to her eyes in spite of her efforts to combat them. She was seeing another collage, one made by a six-year-old girl, reduced to a crumpled ball and a twisted wood frame, lying in a pail of garbage. She rubbed her eyes, brushing the tears away, praying that Diana hadn't noticed. Leland draped his arm protectively around her, pulling her closer to him on the bed.

Just then, Selma appeared in the doorway, clutching two framed photographs. "Where should I put these, dear?" she asked Diana.

Diana thought for a moment before she made up her mind. Suddenly, she knew exactly where to put them. She beckoned to Selma and took the pictures from her.

"Now, Collier," she addressed her daughter, "which bed would you like?"

Collier and Leland exchanged glances. The look in his eyes warned her to go along with whatever game their mother was playing.

Collier cleared her throat. "This one," she replied, indicating the bed she and Leland were sitting on.

Diana nodded her approval. "Then you can have this one," she told Leland, patting the space beside her.

"That's fine with me," he agreed easily.

"Good." She was pleased they'd decided so quickly. "Now I'll know which beds to put you both in. Leland, you'll be sleeping here," she said, placing the silver-framed photograph of the five-year-old Leland on the pillow next to her. Then she stood up and walked over to the other bed. "And you'll sleep here, Collier." She laid the silver and gold framed photo of Collier as a nine-year-old on the pillow and stepped back with a satisfied sigh. "Now we're finally a real family," she told her children as she reached for their hands. "Even when you're not really sleeping here, I can pretend you are."

Collier couldn't control herself any longer. Clinging tightly to her mother's hand, she burst into tears.

Chapter Eighteen

With Diana settled and Leland back in New York, Collier decided to do something completely frivolous. She knew she was stalling for time, but time was something she still needed. She couldn't return to England just yet. And so, she flew to Miami, chartered a yacht and sailed south to the Caribbean.

Their course took them first to the Bahamas, Haiti and Puerto Rico, then to the Leeward and the Windward Islands. They weighed anchor at each of the major islands—the British Virgins, Antigua, Guadeloupe, Martinique, Barbados and Trinidad, so that Collier could go ashore and play the tourist. She wore cotton skirts and halters and flat sandals and carried a large straw bag to hold the bargains she invariably bought at the outdoor markets. When she wasn't sightseeing, she was swimming, either from the side of the boat or off one of the island beaches. She sunbathed, collected shells and snorkelled and each evening she would dine alone on deck, while the crew maintained a respectful distance.

After three weeks, her guilt forced her to place an overseas call to Thaddeus. The following day, he telephoned her from Athens.

"The expedition's running out of funds, blast it all!" he bellowed into her ear. "I'm spending all my time running around like a damned fool trying to raise the capital we need. Wish you were here, pet, you're far more effective at separating the wealthy from their money than I am."

"What you need is a holiday, Taddy," she told him. "If you come down here and spend some time with me, you'll be able to rest and recharge that cranky battery of yours."

He went on as if he hadn't even heard her. "I'm an archeologist, damnit, not a bloody fund raiser. I'm no damned good at this sort of thing."

"Then why not come down here, Taddy? You'd love it. And the only important decisions to make are which island to visit and what kind of fish to eat for dinner. I'll have a ticket delivered to you if you say you'll come."

"I can't get away. Haven't you heard a word I've been saying? I don't need a bloody holiday, lolling about on some boat and visiting obscure little islands whose poverty everyone finds so picturesque. I have no time for fun right now, Collier. I'm trying to save my expedition. Enjoy your trip. Enjoy it for both of us." And with that, he hung up on her.

It was after discovering a tiny, remote island called St. Cristobal, which lay forty miles northwest of Jamaica, that Collier put in a second call to Thaddeus. When he called her back three days later from London, she had used those three days to carry on a debate with herself, airing every argument she could think of and weighing the effects of her decision in the light of reason rather than impulse. But in the end, she knew. It was as if she had been looking for this island all her life.

"I'm buying an island, Taddy."

"What? Are you daft! It sounds to me as if you've been out in that Caribbean sun too long."

"I'm buying the island of St. Cristobal, Taddy."

"Never heard of it."

"Neither had I until we happened to cruise past it. That's the beauty of it, Taddy. The island is quite primitive, with a native population of about three hundred who live on the northern tip in a town called Bonnyport. Their homes are made out of wood and tin, and although they have electricity, there's no running water, and the streets in the town have side gutters to collect sewage."

"Sounds positively ghastly!"

"The rest of the island is completely deserted with only one rough road linking the northern and southern parts."

"What the devil would you want with a deserted island inhabited by a bunch of darkies? I think you'd best turn that pleasure craft of yours around and catch the first plane back here."

"I've found home, Taddy."

"Nonsense, woman. London is your home."

"No, it's not," she contradicted him, "no more than Newport or Gloucester were. I had a real home once—for exactly nine years. Now I've found another one. I want this place, Taddy. I need the privacy I'll be able to find here. I want it to be a permanent home for my art collection and a more permanent home for the two of us. I'm an American, Taddy. I need to be close to the mainland again, close to my mother, close enough to attend all the major art shows, close enough to participate in my country's cultural growth, without being too close. Am I making any sense, Taddy, any sense at all?"

"None whatsoever," he barked. "How the devil does one go about buying an island anyway? Aren't there laws governing this sort of thing?"

"I'm not buying the entire island, only a third of it, the southern tip. I intend to turn a few acres of land into a private compound and leave the rest as it is. It's a paradise, Taddy, and with my owning part of it, at least part of it will stay a paradise. There won't be any tourists or souvenir shops or motels or exclusive country clubs if I have any say in the matter."

"It sounds as if you've been thrown back a century or two. You're certain old Darwin isn't out there, lurking about in the bushes?"

"Taddy, please take me seriously because I'm going through with it. I want you to come down and see the island for yourself. I promise you that after one look at this place, even Jericho will seem light years away. How do you think Gulliver will enjoy dusting in the tropics?"

"He'll positively hate it. And so will I. I'd feel completely cut off from the rest of the world down there. I've never been to the Caribbean, for God's sake. I can't even swim."

"Then we'll find some native girl to teach you. Oh, Taddy, it's such a magnificent island. I know you'll love it."

The silence at the other end of the wire soon began to deafen her. When Thaddeus finally spoke, the coldness in his voice made her shudder.

"I don't appreciate unilateral decisions in a marriage, Collier. They bode rather poorly for the future."

"Taddy—"

"Are you proposing we now divide our time between London and this bloody island of yours?"

"I suppose I was hoping you'd be tired enough of London by now to consider moving down here permanently. You're not going to keep up this pace of yours forever, you know, and the island would be an ideal place to retire—"

"I won't have you retiring and burying me just yet, thank you. I'm not prepared to trade my life for the chance to laze about in a hammock and sip rum or whatever they drink down there."

Her own tone was frosty now. "Before you condemn it, Thaddeus, would you at least come down here and have a look?"

"Let me think about it and I'll ring you back."

"When?"

"When I've bloody well thought about it!"

Once again he hung up on her.

When he called her back two days later, it was to tell her that the British School of Archeology in Athens had just come through with the additional funding for his expedition. He was returning to Jericho immediately. Paradise, he told her, would just have to wait.

It was Leland who saw the island first.

"You're right, Collier, it is a paradise."

They were standing arm-in-arm, at the edge of the cliff overlooking the Caribbean where she would build her home.

"Just tell me where you want your own house and I'll even let you turn the first shovelful of earth," she said.

His low laugh set her teeth on edge. "So you want to hide me away from the world, too. No wonder Thaddeus is balking. Nothing to do here but watch your body turn to flab and your brain to mush."

"It doesn't have to be that way," she argued. "We could all use the island as a base. If I feel the need to get in touch with civilization, I still have the house in Gloucester. If Thaddeus wants to keep the flat in London, he can, and you can still have your apartment in New York."

"But Thaddeus's work is in the Middle East and mine takes up the rest of the globe. We'd both be away much more than we'd be here. What would you do down here all alone?"

"I won't be alone; I'll be busy. I've already discussed some of my plans with Horace Coombes."

"And who is Horace Coombes?"

"He's the equivalent of a prime minister on the island, although he's really more of a mayor. St. Cristobal was part of the British Empire until 1937. I suppose the British couldn't find any reason for holding onto a tiny island with no commerce and no exports, so they freed them to fend for themselves. They haven't advanced one day beyond 1937."

"And you intend to change all that."

She nodded. "I plan to bring down some men from the company and have them meet with Coombes and his town council to work out a plan for the modernization of Bonnyport. I won't use any company money for this project, everything will come out of my own private funds. That way I won't be answerable to the board in Boston. I intend to get the people working on housing, roads and sanitation. I want to build a bigger electrical plant, a water storage tower, and I intend to set up a clinic and a school to replace their so-called infirmary and the two shacks which pass for a school now."

"Are you sure you know what you're doing? Don't you feel a bit like the white missionary carrying the word to Africa? What makes you think your way is the right way?"

"Because of something Thaddeus said. He told me that people come down to these islands, see the poverty here and call it picturesque. What he said hurt me, Leland, because it's true. Horace Coombes could have told me to take my white woman's money and go straight to hell, but he didn't. He's going to speak to his people and if they agree, I'll go ahead with my plans. If they decide against it, I'll still proceed with my purchase, but I'll have to settle for just the compound."

"If this goes through, the news media will have a field day with you."

"They'll never be able to get to me down here."

"I hope you're right."

"I think my father would have been proud of me, Leland. I might even rival him as an empire builder some day. The board has agreed to purchase Sir Gilbert's newspaper chain, and now I'm out to save a Caribbean island whose population hasn't decided on whether or not they want to be saved. You can't say I'm not diversifying."

On July 4, while the United States celebrated Independence Day, Collier handed Horace Coombes a personal check for two hundred thousand dollars and he presented her with a ceremonial tin shovel.

At sixty-one, Horace Coombes had never been off the island he had been born on. He had been his tiny country's only prime minister. He was a portly man with a square face and broad, blunt features, and his thick black hair was heavily salted with gray. Whenever he spoke in his lilting English, Collier imagined she could hear the rumble of the ocean in his voice. A widower, he was a bit of an oddity on an island which boasted about the size of its families. He only had two sons, eighteen-year-old Cleavon and seventeen-year-old Clement. But like all the other families, the Coombeses had turned out for the dedication ceremony at the town hall, wearing the clothes they reserved only for church on Sunday and funerals.

If Collier had thought her purchase would remain a secret, she was wrong. As soon as the news had leaked out, helicopters and private airplanes, yachts and sailboats began to infest the air and the water around the island. She was eventually forced to give in to the media's demands for a story when the islanders themselves, convinced that they were under attack, pleaded with her to protect them.

She agreed to invite a group of newsmen representing the major American television networks, radio stations and newspapers down to the island to cover the ceremony. They flew into Jamaica, where they were met by a yacht Collier had chartered for the day and brought over to Bonnyport. Thaddeus surprised her by flying in from Israel and Leland arrived on his way back from Korea. Now, with the shovel in her hand, Collier began to pose for the photographers.

"I'm devilishly warm," Thaddeus said when the photographers seemed to have finished. "I think a dip would be a bloody marvelous idea right about now." He caught hold of Collier and began to dance her around. "Shall we strip naked and fling ourselves into the sea, pet?"

"You can't swim, remember?"

"Ah, but I have you, my nymph, to rescue me."

"You're drunk, Taddy, and you're making me dizzy."

"Wasn't this little paradise of yours made for fantasies? Well, then, let me fantasize." Throwing back his head, he bellowed, "Heeding the call of the wild, I shall follow my pagan goddess wherever she chooses to lead me."

Collier could hear isolated snickers from the reporters.

"I'll lead you straight back to the yacht and put you to bed if you don't behave," she told him in a strained undertone.

"No doubt my goddess will. Then, while old Arthur naps, young Lancelot may while away the hours with his beloved Guinevere."

"Thaddeus, you'd better lower your voice or everything you say will be written up in the papers tomorrow."

"Indeed, you say, then let us away from this place and make

for Camelot where this aging Arthur may himself play at being Lancelot awhile."

Collier cast a helpless glance in Leland's direction.

"How about a walk, Thaddeus?" Leland put his hand on the older man's shoulder only to have Thaddeus roughly shrug it off.

"No, thank you, sir," he snapped, releasing Collier and giving Leland a light push.

Collier was growing increasingly embarrassed. Several of the photographers had begun to edge closer to the two men.

Leland caught Thaddeus's arm just as he staggered and appeared about to fall down.

"Release me, you young pup," he shouted, aiming a weak punch in the vicinity of Leland's chest.

Leland backed up to avoid the blow and before Thaddeus could swing again, he grabbed hold of the older man's arms and pinned them down at his sides.

Flashbulbs were starting to go off. People began to push forward for a better look. Thaddeus advanced on Leland, lost his balance and fell to the floor.

Collier could hear the catcalls and the whistles now, the loud jeers, and the rhythmic clapping of hundreds of pairs of hands. The laughter grew louder. She could hear Boston laughing again. Laughing, not at them, but at her.

"Stop it!" she screamed. "Stop it! Stop it! Stop it!"

She was shouting as much at the people as at Thaddeus. He had spoiled it for her. He had taken her day and defiled it.

The laughter grew louder. The people moved closer. The flashbulbs were bright and hot in her face. She turned and ran.

She ran out of the town hall and through the narrow, twisting streets. She ran until her lungs began to ache and the stitch in her side grew unbearable. She ran until the perspiration streamed down her face and coated her body and her dress clung to her and she felt faint.

She began to tear at her dress. It was too hot, too scratchy. She had to get out of it. She had to get out of the sun. Crashing through some light underbrush, she headed for the cover of the woods which separated Bonnyport from the sea. She hitched her dress higher as she ran, but it was shrinking, growing tighter, the way her dress had shrunk in the courtroom that day when her mother fell out of her chair and all of Boston began to laugh.

"Collier!"

Uncle Avery was calling her name, but she couldn't stop now, she had to get to her mother.

"Collier!"

Milo was after her. He was going to beat her and she would lose her baby. She clutched her stomach as she ran. She couldn't let him hurt the baby.

"Collier, for God's sake, stop! Collier!"

Daddy! It didn't hurt to run now. He was waiting for her among the trees. He was holding out his arms to her. She could smell his cologne and feel the heat from his lighted cigar.

She was suffocating. She tugged the dress over her head and flung it away from her. She was cooler now, but the light from the tip of his cigar was growing brighter, turning from orange to red. It was blinding her. She was going blind! She closed her eyes and reached out to him. Stumbling into his arms, she dragged him down with her as she fell.

"Collier. Open your eyes and look at me. Collier, please look at me."

From behind her eyelids, she heard his voice. She tried to do as he was telling her, but she knew that the sun would blind her if she did.

"It's Leland, Collier, can you hear me?"

Something warm was being put over her. She was dead! They were covering her with a shroud. *No,* she screamed inside her head. *I'm not dead! I'm not dead! Please wait. Wait!* She raised her hand and ripped away the shroud.

"Collier, lie still, it's only my shirt. Lie still. It's Leland and I'm not going to hurt you."

Her eyes flew open. She could see. She could see him. The sun was gone and Leland was there with her.

"Oh, Leland," she gasped. "I'm going mad. Dear God, I'm going mad. I'm going to end up just like her. Help me, Leland, don't let me go mad. Please don't let me go mad."

"You're not mad, Collier, do you hear me! You're not mad!"

"I am, I know I am. It's because of their laughter. I can't bear to have them laughing at me."

"They weren't laughing at you."

"Yes, they were. Why won't they stop laughing? Why won't they leave me alone and let me live?"

"Because you belong to them, Collier, you and Doris Duke and Gloria Vanderbilt and Barbara Hutton and the Dionne Quintuplets in Canada. You're victims, sideshows, all of you, adored and admired and hated and envied because of who you are. But you're lucky, Collier, you have St. Cristobal now, and you'll have more privacy here than anywhere else in the world."

"But you told me they would always find a way. You told me—"

"Yes, they'll keep trying, for a while anyway. But they'll soon give up and find someone else to hound. And then, one day, when you've thickened that sensitive skin of yours, you'll learn to use them just as they've been using you. Give yourself time, Collier. You have this island now."

"But Thaddeus," she whispered. "He still hasn't agreed to live down here and I can't go back to London again. I'm so tired of following someone else's dreams, Leland. All I want is the time to live my own. Am I wrong? Am I selfish and wrong?"

"No, Collier. You're just growing up."

"But I'm frightened. Everything's changing again."

"Don't let the fear of change keep you from growing, dear heart. You can't stand still just to keep everything as it was. As soon as we begin to ask questions and grope around for a new set of answers, what we've always accepted as the truth is already in jeopardy. The same is true in relationships. The good ones are resilient, they bend and adapt. The bad ones don't. If your relationship with Thaddeus is still good, it will adapt and grow and nothing will break it. But you can't be afraid to test it, Collier, simply because you're afraid of the outcome."

"But I don't want to be alone again."

"How do you know that you're going to be alone again?"

"I can sense it."

"As long as you have this island and your art, Collier, you'll never be alone. And besides, I'll always be around. One of those guest suites has my name on it, remember?"

That made her smile.

And after a few more minutes she was able to sit up again. She suddenly flushed. Leland's pale blue shirt barely covered her torso. Her long legs, brown and bare, were open, indecent, inviting. Her eyes met his and he hastily looked away.

"I think I'd better find your dress," he mumbled, his own face reddening as he got to his feet.

A few minutes later, he was back with her rumpled dress hanging across his arm. While he turned his back, she tossed his shirt aside and got dressed.

"Did you mean it when you said you'd always be around?" she asked as she handed him back his shirt.

"Yes, I meant it."

"Even if you fall madly in love with someone and marry her and have children?"

"I doubt I'll ever fall madly in love with anyone, but even if I do, I can love both of you, can't I?"

A strange new warmth flooded through her. "You really do love me, don't you, Leland?"

She was awed by the sound of the word "love" as she said it aloud. She repeated it to herself as if it were a word she had never heard before. *Love*. It was a word seldom used in either of her marriages. With Milo, love had meant passion, with Thaddeus, comfort. True love still eluded her.

"I do love you, Collier."

He was gripping her shoulders so tightly that she felt the heated imprints of his fingers through her dress.

"I've stored away a lot of love for you, and it's a love you can lean on and count on. Always."

His words frightened her. What he was committing to her was something he should have been committing to some other woman in some future time. What frightened her even more was her reaction to what he was saying. She really didn't want his love to go to anyone else.

Shyly, almost reverently, she reached up and touched his cheek. "I love you, Leland," she told him softly. "I love you, too."

He said nothing more to her. He simply took her hand and led her back.

He could finally let out his breath. He buttoned the leather case over his camera and gave himself five extra minutes just to be safe. He was sweating like a pig. He slapped at a mosquito. He began to curse the mosquito and the heat and the whole, goddamned island. Then he thought about what he'd gotten down on film, and suddenly things didn't look so bad. What he had would be worth a fortune.

Leland

1956 ~ 1961

Chapter Nineteen

"Well, Leland, how do I look?"

Collier did a slow turn in front of him.

"Fabulous. Except that the back of your dress is undone."

She glanced over her shoulder at her reflection in the mirror. "Oh God, you're right. You'd better do me up."

"Then please try to stand still," he advised her as his long fingers tried to work the tiny covered buttons through their individual loops. "Jesus, why couldn't you have worn one of your muumuus; it would have been so much simpler."

"When in civilization, one must try to look civilized."

"Hold still, will you? There's one button here as stubborn as you are. It's refusing to cooperate."

"When have you ever known me to be uncooperative?"

"Scratch 'uncooperative' then, but we'll stick with 'stubborn.' Why are you so nervous? It's not as if you're getting married again, so calm down."

She felt a slight pang at that remark. No, she wasn't getting married again. Two failed attempts were more than enough for her.

"How would you know how it feels to get married?" she asked him, sounding slightly defiant. "Have you ever made it past the fifth date with anyone?"

"That's a professional secret." He fastened the last button and gave her behind a light whack.

"I'll bet the answer is no."

"Something tells me you're trying to get rid of me. I thought you liked having me all to yourself."

Her eyebrows arched. "All to myself? How many days a year do you think this exclusivity adds up to?"

"I don't believe I've ever stopped to count."

"I think it averages out to something like forty-eight and a half days a year."

"That makes it four days and a few hours a month. I'd say you were doing fairly well."

"I'd say I was running neck and neck with NBC. They get you four Sundays a month."

"You've forgotten about those months with five Sundays in them."

"You see, I'm still second."

"But you'll always be first in my heart."   -

Will I? she wondered, as she watched him put on his jacket and straighten his tie. He was so very precious to her, filling those gaps in her life whenever her projects and her traveling wore thin enough for the underlying loneliness to poke through again. He was thirty-two. He was at that age when most men have been married for several years, with children, a house with a mortgage, and a second family car being paid for on the installment plan. But not Leland Taggert. He was too busy being successful.

Besides his weekly radio program on WNBC, he now taped a weekly TV show for NBC called *We The People*. On it, he would interview anyone from President Eisenhower to an unemployed coal miner living in Appalachia. His twice-weekly column, *Profile*, which appeared in *The New York Times*, was already syndicated in one hundred and ten newspapers across the country. Because of his extensive travels, he was a regular contributing editor to *The National Geographic* magazine, *Time*, *Life*, *Look* and *The Saturday Evening Post*.

He still lived out of suitcases and hotel rooms, but whenever he was in the States, he divided his time between his one-bedroom apartment on Manhattan's Upper East Side and Diana's Philadelphia home. His greatest pleasure had been in taking over the monthly payments to Varley's Florist the year before. Whatever time was left over from his hectic routine was spent in seclusion with Collier on St. Cristobal.

"I just thought of something," Collier said. "Who's supplying the scissors?"

"What scissors?"

"For the ribbon-cutting ceremony."

"The social committee, I suppose," he shrugged. "It's part of their job."

"I hope you're right, because after spending over a million dollars and nearly two years on this project, if I was supposed to be responsible for the scissors too—"

"Stop worrying. I promise you that when the time comes, someone will have the scissors."

Collier looked around the hotel room which had become as familiar to her as her own bedroom on the island, and she sighed. As much as she had enjoyed these past two years, dividing her time between St. Cristobal and Boston, it would be a relief to return home and not have to leave again for a long, long time.

Searching for something to keep herself occupied, she swung open the full-length three-way mirror beside the dresser and began fussing with her hair. As always, it was wound in a softly swirling Gibson knot and it looked perfect. Her years in the sun had bleached the golden blond to almost white. Her face was perpetually tanned, and as she studied herself in the mirror and noticed the fine lines around her eyes and mouth, she promised herself that she would try to stay out of the sun more.

"It's time," Leland announced from the window. "The limo's just pulled up in front."

Collier's stomach flip-flopped. She gave her hair a final pat, closed the mirror and picked up her small clutch. "Okay, I'm ready."

In the limousine, she glanced sideways at Leland, wondering if he was as nervous as she was. Moving closer to him, she linked her arm through his. He turned and smiled at her, and gave her hand a squeeze.

"What were you thinking about just then?" she asked.

"I was thinking about how far you've come these past five years, just as I predicted you would." He planted a kiss squarely in the middle of her forehead. "You're quite a lady, Collier, quite a lady."

"This project was your idea, remember?"

"Of course, I remember," he laughed. "It was my devious way of keeping you from enjoying your solitude too much. The only time you ever left your little paradise was to buy more paintings. How else was I to get you back into the stream of things?"

Less than a year after her purchase of the southern tip of St. Cristobal, Collier's marriage to Thaddeus had finally limped to a close. Thaddeus had visited the island only twice that year, and after his second trip, he had refused to come back. She, in turn, had refused to move back to London. The one thing they did agree on was a divorce. The dig at Jericho had been in financial trouble again, and so, in exchange for one-third of his private collection of ancient artifacts, Collier had agreed to subsidize the dig until its completion. Thaddeus had balked at first but eventually gave in.

Saying goodbye to Thaddeus had been like saying goodbye to an old friend.

There was no bitterness and no hostility. Her worst fears about being alone again were never realized—her island kept her too busy.

Their divorce was finalized at the same time that the compound was ready. She moved off the yacht and into her home at last. Then she invited the gentlemen of the press down to the island again. It was her way of thanking them for leaving her alone during the eighteen months it had taken to complete it.

She led them through her house, which was furnished in cane and wicker and upholstered in gay pastel chintzes. The accent pieces were either glass or marble, the lamps porcelain with broad, pleated shades, and the floors were tile. White wooden shutters folded across the floor-to-ceiling windows. Everything in the house had been designed with mildew, insects and hurricanes in mind.

The grounds had been so artfully landscaped that it was impossible to determine where nature left off and human hands took over. Flagstone paths wound past clusters of flowering oleander and hibiscus trees and curved around tiny pools where water lilies floated. She took the press down to the edge of the bluff and showed them the wide steps which had been carved into the rock to provide a natural staircase to the beach below. Then she walked them over to the museum.

This was her proudest moment, and it was here that she and her guests spent the most time. Four of the rooms contained her Racine collection, three held the works of other abstract expressionists, two were devoted to her iron, bronze and steel sculptures, two were for the "junk art" paintings and three were reserved for the eighteen glass showcases filled with ancient artifacts from Thaddeus's digs.

"It looks as if you're about to add another room," commented one of the reporters.

"I intend to expand this museum as long as there is art to fill it," she told him.

"Do you have any particular artists in mind at the moment?"

"Do the names Claes Oldenburg, James Rosenquist, Roy

Lichtenstein or Andy Warhol mean anything to any of you?"

The men looked blank.

"They'll mean something to you some day. I bought a number of their paintings on my last trip to New York and I plan to buy more. The critics haven't discovered them yet, but I'm sure they'll crucify them when they do. These men are really breaking all the rules. They're taking all the snobbery out of art and popularizing it so that even a kindergarten child will be able to look at a painting and know what it is."

By February 1953, Collier had added another three rooms to her museum and filled them with the comic-strip paintings of Roy Lichtenstein, the supermarket parodies of Andy Warhol, the billboard art of James Rosenquist and the mechanical convenience wall-hangings of Claes Oldenburg. Soon, even the critics began to take notice.

Leland invited Collier to be his guest on his opening show of *We The People*. He arrived at the island with an entire TV camera crew and spent the day interviewing her while they toured the museum. The interview was edited down to fifty minutes, allowing ten minutes for the commercials and credits. When the show was aired, it received the highest rating of any show in the history of NBC.

Soon the other networks approached her for interviews. Then came radio, the newspapers and magazines. Remembering what Leland had told her about using the media to her own advantage, Collier agreed to all of their requests. Why be like Thaddeus, she reasoned, greedily hoarding his collection and keeping it hidden? What she was doing was chronicling the major art movements in America. She owed it to her fellow countrymen to share her collection with them.

She spent three exhausting months taping various TV and radio programs and submitting herself to extensive magazine and newspaper interviews. Then a representative of the Museum of Modern Art in New York flew down to the island and spent an entire week with her, photographing each painting, sculpture and artifact. The Museum then compiled and produced a full-color catalog of the collection and sold it in its gift shop. Collier refused her share of the profits from the sale of the catalog and turned the money back to the Museum for its own new expansion program.

In July 1954, Collier invited the press back to the island for what she hoped would be the last time. Instead of disembarking at the dock below the compound, the reporters and photographers got off the launch she had chartered for them at Bonnyport.

It was a beaming Horace Coombes who proudly showed the press what a difference three years had made on St. Cristobal. He took them on a tour of the power plant, the sewage plant and the water tower, the two-story schoolhouse and the large, modern infirmary which was staffed by a team of Jamaican doctors and nurses.

The small town itself had undergone a complete transition. Small shingled bungalows now replaced the wood and tin shacks, and well-tended vegetable gardens had been planted behind each house. No garbage was collecting in the side gutters of the streets and even the narrow sidewalks were free of litter.

"Our children are in school, our men are at work improving the roads, and our women are taking care of their homes. Many are even attending classes themselves to learn how to read and write. It is a beginning our people have awaited for nearly twenty years," announced Horace Coombes from the steps of the town hall. "And we have one remarkable woman to thank for all of this. She has done what even the British Empire could not do for us. Collier Paget-Browne has given us back our dignity. She has given us back our pride."

The car came to a sudden stop at a red light and Collier nearly slid out of her seat.

"Easy, lady." Leland had her by the arm.

"Tell that to the driver," she snapped.

"God, you're tense. Relax."

"I'm sorry," she apologized, leaning back in her seat. "You really would think I was getting married again."

She wished her heart would slow down. It was beating so rapidly that she felt it might burst through the walls of her chest. In another three blocks, they would be rounding the corner and catching their first glimpse of it: The Collier Paget-Browne Center for Fine Arts.

It was exactly twenty-six months ago to the day that Leland had suggested she build such a center.

"So far you've been supporting professionals," he had told her. "Why not set something up to encourage new talent and to school artists who are only beginning?"

Collier had immediately thought of Jenny. Unschooled and

untrained, her work possessed a delightful innocence which would probably be termed "primitive." How much further could she take her art with the proper training? She was painting only miniatures now, using tiny boards no larger than a six-inch square. With great delicacy, she painted fields of flowers, forest scenes, tiny animals, flocks of birds, shell-encrusted rocks. Just as she had once reproduced the world she saw through her father's telescope, she was now creating a world she seemed to be viewing through a microscope.

She had graduated from high school in June and refused to go on to college. With so little money in the family and the sheltered life she was still leading in Gloucester, Jennifer Howe had little opportunity to learn more about her craft or sell to anyone other than the summer tourists and the local gift shops.

Collier had taken Leland's idea and converted it into reality, choosing an acre of land on a hill overlooking Boston's Charles River for the site of the Center. And today, the Center would be formally opened.

"We're here, Collier," Leland said, giving her knee a light pat.

As the limousine drew up to the curb, Collier peered out the window, grateful that the September sun had decided to shine for her. While she waited for the driver to open her door, she just stared at the magnificent building she was about to dedicate. A two-story structure, designed on horizontal planes, it was built entirely of glass, reinforced by vertical and horizontal steel supports. The acre of land on which it sat had already been landscaped with clusters of young maples and birches, flowering shrubs and planted rockeries.

A large crowd had gathered across the street, but they were being controlled quite easily by the security guards Collier had hired. Other limousines were beginning to arrive now, most of them letting their passengers out at the curb, while dozens more cars, some filled with guests, others with members of the press, were being directed into the parking lot behind the building.

With Leland walking beside her, Collier headed up the marble steps, across the marble terrace, and was just about to open one of the glass doors, when she stopped and looked up. Her mouth went dry. Her heart began to race again. On the broad horizontal beam above the entrance, large raised letters in galvanized steel spelled out the words: COLLIER PAGET-BROWNE CENTER FOR FINE ARTS. Here was where she hoped to make her greatest contribution to the world of art.

Leland finally ushered her inside. She walked ahead of him into the cool marbled foyer. The sunlight was streaming in through the glass, warming the interior of the building and casting long, slanting shadows on the walls painted the palest shade of oyster gray.

Crystal slabs with hundreds of small light bulbs inside them hung in jagged clusters from the thirty foot ceiling. An open staircase with a polished chrome railing led up from either end of the foyer to the second floor where the classrooms and studios were located. Through double glass doors on either side of the foyer lay several more studios, an auditorium and a large exhibition hall. The place smelled of fresh paint, polished marble and emptiness. Collier had ordered the walls left bare, the specially constructed platforms and niches left empty. They would all be filled in time by the works of the students themselves.

The foyer was getting crowded. Collier took her place on the second step of one of the staircases. Just behind her swung the red ceremonial ribbon. Leland stood below her on the first step, his right shoulder in easy reach of her left hand. She rested her right hand lightly on the chrome bannister and felt it chill her palm. She smiled, nervously at first and then proudly for the photographers who were now standing and kneeling on the marble floor in front of her.

She kept straining to catch a glimpse of the two people for whom this opening had such a special meaning. Trying not to be too obvious about her growing concern, she stole a furtive glance at her watch. The ceremony was to start at one. Her heart fluttered. What if something had happened to them? Orrin's car was old. What if it had broken down?

Collier pressed her fist to her mouth. Her glove came away smeared with lipstick. She tugged off the gloves and stuffed them into her purse. She'd always hated gloves anyway.

And then she saw them.

She could relax now. She wanted to wave, but she held herself back. Orrin had Jenny by the hand and was pulling her after him, trying to push through to the front of the gathering. Jenny appeared to be holding back. Collier could see her downcast eyes, the shy tilt of her head, the spill of black hair down her back.

They were standing in front now. Collier was certain the

girl was shaking. Her face was flushed. Her dress, gray like her eyes, had a small white collar which only accented the little girl she still was.

But Jennifer Howe was not a little girl. She would be twenty in December. And she had been the first student Collier saw registered at the Center. Their eyes met and the girl's blush deepened.

Collier touched Leland's shoulder and directed his gaze toward Jenny and Orrin. He looked back up at her and mouthed the word "pretty," and Collier nodded. She saw the mayor coming toward her then and she could have wept with relief. He was carrying a pair of scissors.

Afterward Collier could remember little of the ceremony itself. She vaguely remembered snipping the ribbon and feeling pleased that it had fallen away so cleanly. All she could recall of the reception in the exhibition hall was that the room's emptiness had been masked by the extravagant flower arrangements which seemed to fill it. She thought she remembered exchanging the requisite niceties with all the correct people.

But what she was sure she remembered with astonishing clarity and a clutching pain in her belly was the look in Jenny's eyes when she had been introduced to Leland. What had turned the pain into a spasm of agony was the look he gave her back.

As she had watched them take their glasses of champagne and disappear somewhere inside the protective swell of the crowd, Collier remembered how she had felt when her father left her to go to the hospital to see the baby and never came back.

For the first time in a very long time, she felt afraid.

Chapter Twenty

The evening before Collier was to return to St. Cristobal and Leland was to leave for New York, they had dinner in the dining room of their hotel. It was their first meal together since the opening of the Center the week before. Collier had spent that week sitting in on lectures, observing studio classes, meeting with groups of students over lunch and with teachers over coffee. Leland had spent the time taping the activities of the Center for a *We The People* special which would be aired on NBC on three consecutive Sunday evenings.

Collier put down her menu. She wasn't really hungry. She folded her hands in her lap and watched Leland scanning his menu. She was looking for traces of something new in his face, and she wondered what she would do if she found them. When the waiter came to take their order, all Collier could decide on was a shrimp cocktail. She lit up a cigar and ordered a second martini.

"That's quite a switch," commented Leland.

"I have them occasionally." She gave the lemon twist a squeeze and dropped it back into the glass. "My father used to drink martinis once in a while and he'd let me taste them. Of course I thought they were awful, they reminded me of turpentine, but once after eating a lobster dinner, I discovered that a martini made a very effective finger bowl."

Leland laughed and Collier's stomach tightened. She loved the way his eyes crinkled when he laughed. The lines fanning out from the corners of his eyes were more firmly etched now, and they deepened further whenever he smiled. He was wearing his hair longer these days, and his sideburns were longer and fuller too. With his V-neck sweaters, jeans and loafers, he looked more like a college student than a successful media man. He really hadn't changed at all over the years, she thought, except for those lines around his eyes.

She took a deep, burning sip of her drink, and her eyes teared. She was the one who had changed. She felt old.

Away from the island she felt old. She remembered the story of Shangri-la and the white men who lost their way and stumbled upon a timeless civilization living high in the Himalayas. When the men left, taking some of the beautiful young women with them, they watched the women age into wrinkled old crones right in front of their eyes. She ran her fingers over her cheeks, convinced that she could feel the skin wrinkling and beginning to sag. Suddenly her teeth felt loose. Her hands began to tremble and she hastily tucked them away in her lap again.

"Do I look old to you, Leland?"

"What kind of a question is that?"

"It's just a question."

He looked perplexed. "Is something wrong?"

"Just answer me. Do I look old?"

"You look beautiful."

"That's not what I asked you. I asked you if I looked old."

"No, you don't look old. You look young and you look beautiful. You're lucky. You have the kind of beauty that ages well. You'll probably look the same at sixty."

"When I'm sixty and you're fifty-six, will you still tell me I'm beautiful?"

Again he laughed. "I don't see why not. Of course I'll probably be wearing glasses by then, but I don't think my powers of observation will have changed all that much." His eyes narrowed for a moment. "Do you know what your problem is, Collier? You need a man in your life."

"The hell I do."

"The hell you don't. How can you pretend that the way you live is normal or even satisfying? Do you intend to spend the rest of your life playing the benevolent monarch to a people whose lives will go on with or without you, with or without indoor plumbing? Do you want to continue living vicariously through the artists you support? And now, with the Center, you'll have one hundred students to live through, one hundred new reasons not to live for yourself. It's wrong, Collier, because inside this very generous benefactor is a young, very beautiful and very normal woman with normal needs. How do you plan to take care of that part of yourself?"

"Marriage doesn't agree with me, remember?"

"Who said anything about marriage? Have yourself a fling, find yourself a lover."

"Should I place an ad in the paper or would it be more effective if you announced it over the air: 'Lonely heiress seeks sex without strings. Just bring your own bathing suit and she'll supply you with paradise.'"

"It wasn't meant to be a joke."

"Well, I'm taking it as one." She stubbed out her cigar as the waiter put the shrimp cocktail in front of her and she ordered another drink. "I think you'd like to see me tied up with someone again so you wouldn't have to feel obligated to show up every time I get lonely or feel I'm going crazy. I can't say I blame you though. You've been a good sport about it, a much better sport than any of the other men in my life so far."

"There's something going on inside your head and I'm trying to figure out what it is. You're suddenly drinking martinis and you're talking nonsense. This all started when you asked me if you looked old. Now what's going on?"

Collier began her third martini. She felt like a fool. How could she tell him? What could she say that wouldn't make her sound either suspicious, possessive, jealous or afraid?

"Collier, tell me. What is it?"

"I'm frightened," she said in a small voice.

"Of what?"

"I don't know. Yes, I do. It's something I can sense and yet it might not even be real." She couldn't meet his eyes. She concentrated instead on the six plump shrimps arranged in a circle around the cocktail sauce. "Jenny mentioned that she had dinner with you twice this week."

She could feel his eyes boring into the top of her head. Then she heard his laugh.

"Is that what all this was about? I took Jennifer Howe out to dinner and you're suddenly wondering if you look old."

"You called her Jennifer."

"She said she prefers it to Jenny. It makes her feel more grownup."

Collier's cheeks were burning. "She's got a crush on you, Leland. Be careful with her. She's still such a child."

"Not as much as you might think, Collier." A bolt of panic flashed through her. "She's really a very talented young lady. The other night she showed me an album containing the photos of each one of her paintings."

Jenny hadn't shown her any album.

"Apparently she was so reluctant to leave home and board

here in Boston that she wanted to bring her paintings with her. Orrin took color snapshots of each one and pasted them into an album and gave it to her as a going-away present."

Had he also seen her room then? She hadn't been up there yet.

Collier squirted lemon juice all over her shrimp. "I hope my bringing her to Boston wasn't a mistake. I hope I'm not forcing her into something she really doesn't want."

"On the contrary, from what she's told me, you've given her the greatest opportunity of her life. Collier, she worships you. Her eyes have a special light in them reserved for you. I hardly know her, but because she has so much of your vulnerability, I can see why you're the only person she's ever allowed into her life. Give her time and she'll blossom, just as you have. After only a week at the Center, she's already discovered a whole new world for herself."

"And what about you?" she asked softly. "You sound as if you've discovered penicillin."

He set down his knife and fork with a clatter. "Collier, I find Jennifer a very pleasant and a very lovely young lady. We had dinner twice. I think the only reason she accepted my invitations was because I'm your brother."

"Don't hurt her, Leland."

"I don't even know when I'll see her again. I'm leaving for New York tomorrow, remember? I'll be there for a week and then I'm off to Paris, Brussels, Rome and Athens. Then it's a week on the West Coast, two weeks in Hawaii and then back to New York again. Not much time for hurting someone in that schedule."

"I'll never forgive you if you hurt her and I'll never be able to forgive myself for bringing her to Boston. I doubt she'll last the three years at the Center, but I want her to be exposed to the best there is so that, if she has to, she'll be able to make it on her own with the best available skills. I believe in her talent, and I love her as if she were my own daughter, so if you're thinking about playing with her, Leland, think hard. She'll become attached to you and you won't ever be there."

"What worries me is how you're reacting to this, Collier." His tone of voice frightened her. There was something in it she had never heard before. "I don't think you're worried about Jennifer at all. I think you're more concerned about yourself."

Collier slammed her cocktail fork onto her plate. The shrimp slipped off the tines and flopped onto the tablecloth and lay there in a tiny pool of red cocktail sauce. She was trembling with rage as she bent down to pick up her purse from the floor. She hurled her napkin onto her plate and pushed back her chair.

Leland immediately rose to his feet.

"Collier, where are you going?"

She was heading straight for the door.

"Collier!"

With studied dignity, she strode out of the restaurant, got into the limousine and gave the driver Jenny's address. She sat back in the seat, lit a cigar, and refused to even think about what Leland had said or what she would say to Jenny or what she hoped to accomplish by seeing her.

Jennifer was living with a family several blocks from the Center. She had refused to allow Collier to pay the rent on an apartment for her and all Orrin could afford was to board her with a family. Emily and Bernard Harper were retired school-teachers in their late sixties. Their two children lived out of state and they had been renting out their spare rooms to students for nearly twenty-five years. Jenny said she would feel safe with them.

Jenny herself answered the door.

"Collier!" The gray eyes widened in surprise. "What are you doing here? I was just reading a book for my art history course tomorrow morning. Come in, it's so cold at night now."

Darling Jenny, with her words still spilling over themselves. Had nothing changed then? Collier felt awkward towering over the girl in the hallway of the small house, while Jenny looked up at her with that special expression Leland had mentioned. Instinctively Collier put her arms around the small girl and gave her a hug.

"I always feel as if I'm going to crush you," she told her. "Your bones feel as fragile as a bird's."

The girl laughed her delicate tinkle of a laugh and gave Collier two typically Jenny kisses, soft and warm and firmly planted on either side of Collier's neck. Jenny was five feet one and even when she stood on tiptoes, Collier's throat was as high as she could ever reach.

"Is there something wrong, Collier?" she asked, her face clouding over slightly.

Collier shook her head. "No, nothing's wrong. Why?"

"Leland told me that you were having dinner together tonight and it's only eight-thirty. I know how you always like to eat late—"

"We made it an early dinner tonight," Collier cut her off. "We both have to pack and he's leaving at seven tomorrow morning." She glanced around the room. "Where are the Harpers?"

"They went to a movie. They asked me to go with them, but I had all this reading to do. Come." She took Collier by the hand and led her toward the staircase. "I wanted to have some of my artwork up before you saw my room, but I think I'd like to show it to you anyway. It's in the attic. I adore it because it's the only room up there, and I have my own bathroom and a wonderful view of the city. My room opens onto the widow's walk—in the old days the women used to sit up there and look through their telescopes for some sign of their men returning from the sea. Well, my father's promised to buy me a telescope. That way I can pretend that I've never really left the ocean."

"It seems I've taken you out of one tower and you've managed to find yourself another one," Collier remarked as they climbed the stairs to the third floor.

"It's far from being a tower, Collier. It's more like living in a treehouse. I can look down at the world and no one can look back up at me."

The room was large and cheerful and papered in a busy pattern of big yellow bows and tiny clusters of blue forget-me-nots. The curtains and the bedspread were blue. The furniture was painted yellow and the window seat curving around the widow's watch was covered in yellow velvet. Collier found herself glancing about the room for some sign of a photo album, for some sign of Leland's having been there.

"Look out at the city, Collier. Look at all the lights in the houses and the street lights. They're nothing but thousands of tiny white dots just like that game where you're supposed to connect the dots and create different objects out of them."

Collier joined Jenny on the widow's walk. She could hear the breeze and the rustle of the leaves in the trees. The lights of the city winked and sparkled and zigzagged into thousands of broken shapes just as Jenny had said. She breathed in the smell of the night, feeling that strange kind of loneliness that only comes at night. The loneliness that comes when the rush of the day is over and the defenses are gone and the space left is an open invitation for memories.

"All you're missing is the sound of the sea," she said.

"I thought my ears were blocked the first night I spent here. I knew something was missing and then I realized it was the sea. The silence actually hurt my ears and I couldn't get to sleep at all. I lay in bed and tried to imagine how the sea sounded from my bedroom window at home, and I pretended that I could hear the waves crashing against the rocks below the lighthouse. But that didn't work either, so I finally got out of bed and turned on the taps in the sink." She flushed and her eyes dropped. "I don't think the Harpers would be too pleased if they knew I was running the water all night, but it's the only way I've been able to sleep. Leland's suggested I try a glass of brandy."

It was happening again. That stab of fear inside her. Collier nearly winced.

"Jenny," she began, her voice sounding strained. "Tell me how you feel about Leland."

Her eyes dropped again and her hands seemed to be looking for a place to hide. "He's very nice, Collier, and he's very different from anyone I've ever met before. He's so worldly." Her eyes lit up. "He's been to so many of the places my father used to make me read about, places I know I'll never get to see, and he interviews so many of the people I just read about or watch on TV. He's so lucky, Collier, not to be shy, not to be afraid of things. Look at me, I was terrified of coming to Boston, and he's been to China and India and Korea. But I'm changing. I can feel it in myself already. Just being at the Center and speaking to Leland have made me see how different things can be for me. I used to believe only in my painting and now I can't wait to try everything else."

"Do you like him, Jenny?" She couldn't think of her as Jennifer in spite of what Leland said. "Do you think you'll see more of him?"

Again she was flushing. "I know he won't be in Boston again for a while, but he's promised to take me down with him to the island on his next trip. I know I've been an awful coward about visiting you, but if I'm with Leland, maybe I won't be so afraid of flying." She touched Collier's hand with a light, fluttering motion. "I do like him, Collier, and I hope you don't mind. I know how much you love each other, but I'm hoping he has a bit of room left in him to like me a little. I know how busy he is and how dedicated he is to his career, but I'd still like to see him occasionally. Do you know that I've spoken to him on the phone nearly every day this week? He sounds so relaxed when we're talking. It's as if he can forget about his work and where he has to be next and what important person he's going to be interviewing. We laugh about all kinds of things, silly things really, and I begin to forget that he's so much older than I am. It's almost as if we're both children."

"But you're not children, Jenny. In spite of the age difference, you're a woman and he's a man. Don't ever forget that, not for a moment. I want you to be happy, Jenny. I don't want you to be hurt."

The girl looked confused. "I don't believe Leland would deliberately try to hurt me. So far he's been only kind and thoughtful. He's made me feel less lonesome for my father and Gloucester. He's been encouraging me to make friends at the Center and to be excited about finding new ways to express myself through my art. I wouldn't call that hurtful."

Collier pulled Jenny down on the seat beside her and began to stroke her long black hair. She thought back to what Leland had told her that first day in Tel Aviv. She had been the princess then, locked away in her tower, and he had wanted to be the prince with the key to free her. Was Jenny that princess now? Was she herself still Jenny's jailor? And was Leland still the prince, patiently waiting to use that key?

She began to shiver. She was cold. And the cold was coming from deep inside her, from that special place where all the fears lay waiting.

She wanted to go home. She had to get warm again.

She left Jenny and then she did something she hadn't done in the twenty-seven years since she had first left Boston. She had the driver take her past the house on Commonwealth Avenue.

The house looked as large to her as an adult as it had when she was a child. Nothing had changed, except that the twin spruce trees flanking the front door had grown much taller. The lights were on in the living room and in the room which had been Elinor's bedroom. The cold inside Collier grew even colder.

She knew no man had ever moved into the house to take her father's place. Elinor obviously preferred to live alone with her son and her hatred, and then die a Paget-Browne, rather than align herself with a man with a lesser name.

A figure moved behind the drawn window shade in Elinor's room. Another figure came to join it. Elinor and Addison? Elinor and a man? Addison and a woman? There had been so many women in Addison's life. Their names were all names from the city's social register, and yet, Addison was still living with his mother and her obsession. And Collier herself was still paying to keep them out of her life.

As soon as she returned to the hotel, she used the phone in the lobby to call the pilot of her private plane. She wanted the plane fueled and ready for immediate takeoff. She couldn't wait around until morning. There would be no sleep for her in Boston tonight.

The messages she picked up at the desk said that Leland Taggert had telephoned her at nine, nine-thirty, ten and ten-thirty. She crumpled the messages and threw them into the wastebasket in her room. It was nearly eleven. The phone began to ring. She ignored it and kept on packing. As soon as she was ready, she had the driver take her to the airport. She would wait there.

She sat down in the deserted VIP lounge and lit up a cigar. Following Leland's advice to Jenny, she ordered a brandy to steady her nerves. She drank it down quickly and ordered a second. This one she sipped. She finished her cigar and was just about to light another when the queasy feeling in her stomach made her change her mind.

As she walked toward the plane, she realized that it was the first time she had ever walked out on Leland. Walked out angry and hurt and confused and jealous. She added "guilty" to her list of the emotions swirling around inside her head as she began to feel the two brandies and three martinis sloshing around in her stomach. She should have answered the phone. She should have apologized. Apologized for being afraid, for feeling threatened, for wanting to deny him what he had every right to have.

She put her hands over her ears to block out the sound of a plane taking off from the runway. Soon she would be hearing the ocean again. How she envied the thundering roar of the sea as it slammed into the cliffs and spent its anger on the rocks, because as soon as it pulled away again, it was tamed and calm.

As the plane leveled off, Collier stumbled forward to the washroom. She knew she was going to be sick. It would be the first time she had ever been sick on a plane.

All of her love and her guilt and her fear, together with the pain and the longing, poured out of her in one purging rush. And then, like the sea, she waited to feel calm again.

●

Chapter Twenty-one

Addison should have been happy, but he wasn't. He was miserable and someone was going to have to pay for it.

"What am I supposed to do, Mother?" he demanded, pacing up and down in front of Elinor who was curled up defensively on the living room sofa. "I should never have married Mary Beth, never. If you hadn't been so damned persistent about my carrying on our precious family name, I wouldn't be in this mess. We have our damned son now. She's done her duty. Now I want to divorce her."

"Never! I won't abide another scandal."

"But she's got nothing. She's a goddamned liability. She'll drain us dry. I didn't even find out until last week that her father sold his tire business to Paget-Browne Enterprises last year just before he was going to declare bankruptcy. The little bitch! She used me!"

"If you'd spent more time at the company instead of spending money, you might have found out about her father's business last year instead of last week."

"Would I also have found out that her damned old man used every cent of the money the company gave him to pay off his own debts?" he snarled. "I'm trapped now—is that what you're telling me? And am I to stay trapped forever?"

"You trapped yourself, Addison. You were the one who got Mary Beth pregnant, not me."

"I thought she had money," he moaned, running his fingers through his hair. "And I was even stupid enough to think I loved her."

"Love, hah!" snorted Elinor. "What a fool you've been. Look at the marvelous opportunities you've squandered over the years—Paige Carlton, Sue Ellen Harrington, Leslie Rowendale, Margery—"

"I couldn't stand any of them, Mother, fortune or no fortune. And I was damned if I was going to be forced to fulfill my conjugal obligations to those cows with my eyes closed and

220

my teeth clenched. You'd have had me impotent within a month."

"So you decided to act with all the maturity of a schoolboy and elope with a Simmons undergraduate, someone from New York with a prestigious name, and no dowry to go along with her pretty face."

"Now she wants me to buy her a house."

"She has a house. This is our family home, and since she is part of this family, she will remain here where she belongs."

"She says she wants to run her own place from now on. She feels that because this is your house, she has no authority here."

"Then tell her to wait until I'm dead!"

"Mother!"

"I'm sorry, dear." Elinor fluttered him an apologetic smile. "But this isn't easy for me either."

Addison cracked his knuckles and continued pacing the floor. He was beginning to sweat. He opened one of the windows to let in some air. It wasn't helping. He opened a second one. Then he took out a handkerchief and blotted the sides of his nose and the middle of his forehead.

"Don't you intend to visit Mary Beth in the hospital, Addison?" Elinor asked. "If you're going, you'd better leave now. Visiting hours are over at nine."

"I know, I know." He waved his handkerchief at her and then stuffed it back into the pocket of his jacket again. "We've decided to call him Andrew Jeffrey. Andrew after father's father and Jeffrey after Mary Beth's maternal grandfather. Are you pleased, or would you prefer a name from your side of the family instead of father's?"

"Andrew's perfectly acceptable to me, dear. After all, you are continuing the line of Paget-Brownes, not Sargents."

He leaned his forehead against the window frame and sighed. What a joke it was. Eight months of marriage and he was trapped for good. He'd thought he was marrying money and so had she. All she'd brought with her was an insatiable sexual appetite and the experience to satisfy it. Whatever he'd once felt for her—more lust than love—had long since turned to loathing. But he was still trapped.

And he would stay trapped because he needed her and the respectability she lent him. And he would continue to pay for his imprisonment. He would continue to pay for the clothes and the jewelry and the furs and the trips just to keep her at his side and keep him respectable. But he was damned if he was going to touch her again!

"Addison, dear, could you please close the windows, I'm getting chilled," Elinor called out to him. "It's October, for Heaven's sake, not July."

Sometimes he forgot. She was sixty-four now and she'd begun to complain about the cold the way he'd complained about it as a child. He slammed the windows shut with an angry bang. She was overheating the house these days and he found himself walking around the place in a perpetual lather. He even woke up at night, kicking off the covers, his body drenched with sweat. With Mary Beth pressed up against him, he felt as if he were suffocating. Only a long soak in a tub of tepid water could cool him down again.

He took out his handkerchief and wiped off his face. Why had he married the first woman who'd been able to keep him erect? His wife was nothing. She was a twenty-year-old bitch who was four inches taller than he was, with a voluptuous body which now repelled him, strawberry blond hair and startling black eyes. She'd turned his games around on him and led him by the balls through a wedding ceremony.

"I don't think I'll visit Mary Beth tonight, Mother," he said, turning to Elinor with an improvised yawn. "I'm really tired. I think I'll just go upstairs and read for a while."

He kissed her lightly on the cheek and walked from the room. Unbuttoning his shirt, he headed up the stairs, half-giddy at the prospect of spending one more night alone in his own bed. He'd had three nights of blessed solitude so far.

He stripped off his clothes and threw open the window. The sharp autumn air bit into his flesh. He began to shiver. His nipples puckered. His skin was soon covered with gooseflesh. He took a deep breath, held it in for a moment, and then slowly let it out.

The light went on in the room above the garage. The room belonged to Ned Thayer, Addison's new chauffeur. Although the curtains were drawn, Addison knew precisely what was going on behind them. He checked his watch. It wouldn't be long now.

The curtains parted. Ned's blond head appeared at the window. Addison sucked in his stomach and threw out his chest. As always, Ned was wearing his black uniform, his peaked cap tucked respectfully under one arm. He glanced up at Addison's window, checking to see if he was there. *You don't have to check, you bastard,* Addison sneered. *You know damn well I'm here. Get on with it, damn it, get on with it, I'm cold.*

With Addison greedily watching, Ned slowly began to undress. He started with his jacket, unbuttoning it and letting it slide off his shoulders, down his arms and onto the floor. He worked open the knot of his tie, and with one smooth, practiced tug, he slid it from around his neck and let it drop. He then undid each of the buttons of his white shirt, shrugged the shirt off and flexed the heavily corded muscles of his arms. The large, gold crucifix he was wearing shimmered in the light as he postured and posed.

When Ned's black trousers slithered to the floor, Addison began to tremble. He braced himself against the windowsill and spread his legs for support. Then he began to fondle himself. He was already hard. With every stroke, he found himself thinking about Mary Beth, wishing to hell she'd never come home from the hospital. Whenever she was around, he had to use his father's old bedroom, and the view of the garage wasn't nearly as good as the one from his own room. His breathing quickened. He was getting close.

Ned's hands disappeared inside his pale blue undershorts. Addison's mouth fell open. He increased his speed. He wet his lips. They felt dry and cracked. Even his tongue felt dry. How could his mouth be so dry when the rest of him was slick and steamy with sweat?

The blue shorts dropped.

Addison tensed. All he could see was the top of Ned's patch of blond pubic hair. He wanted to see more. He wanted to see all of it. Ned backed slowly away from the window. Addison got his wish. He could see everything now. He let out a low, agonized groan. The groan melted into a whimper. For one delicious moment, he seemed to hang suspended in mid-air. Then he came.

The force of his orgasm drove his body deep into the ledge and slammed his head up against the window. His mouth flattened out against the cold pane. He heaved and panted, his breath fogging the glass. Then, wet, slippery and spent, he slid away from the window and sagged onto the floor. He lay there, gasping and shuddering, until the spasms had played themselves out.

The curtains closed in the room above the garage. Their little game was over for another night.

When he finally found the strength to pick himself up off the floor, Addison limped into the bathroom and sponged himself off. Then he tied on a cashmere robe and sat down at his desk. Opening the top drawer, he pulled out a pair of large scissors and began to trim the article he'd torn out of *Town & Country* magazine. It was a five-page, color spread all about *her*.

He held up the first page of the article and stared into her face. Silently, he vented all of his anger and his frustration and his weariness on her. How he hated that beautiful face of hers which refused to change or even show its age. In two more years, she'd be forty. The bitch. Forty! And he was still waiting. *Damn you, Collier, damn you to hell! You've kept me waiting too long*. He could feel the tears starting. Even worse, the heat was starting up again. He pressed the heel of his hand against his crotch to force the heat back inside.

He was sweating again. The scissors slid out of his hand. With shaking fingers he pasted the article into his scrapbook. He'd just started his seventh book. Seven books filled with bits of *her*. Seven books which he kept locked in his safe along with the reports and the photographs. The heat began to cool as soon as he thought of the photographs.

He leafed through the article and read about the second anniversary of the Collier Paget-Browne Center For Fine Arts. She'd come to Boston for the anniversary and he'd stood with the crowd across the street, just as he'd stood there on the first anniversary and on the day the Center officially opened. He'd stood there and watched her sweep out of her limousine like royalty, her head held high and her chin announcing to all the world that she was better than they were, better than he was, better than he would ever be.

Collier Paget-Browne and her Center. Collier Paget-Browne and her island. Collier Paget-Browne and her museum. Collier Paget-Browne spending his money. A bead of sweat trickled down his chin and plopped onto the photograph of her face. He closed the book and put it back in the safe.

The pain took over from where the heat had left off. He began to strain as it threatened to double him over. Hurrying into his dressing room, he put on a pair of slacks and a sweater. He couldn't get the zipper on his slacks to close so he pulled the sweater down until his aching bulge was covered.

He tiptoed down the stairs. The house was already dark. Elinor went to bed very early now.

He let himself out by the back door. He stood in the driveway in the cold, hoping that the air would soothe his ache and quiet the roaring inside his head. He waited, his hands thrust into the pockets of his slacks, praying to the god which had deserted him to rid him of the evil decaying his body and cleanse him of the blight tainting his soul.

But his god no longer had time for him.

Addison couldn't wait. His agony was pushing him closer and closer to that other door. He raised his hand to knock and then lowered it again. Once more, he waited while the pain throttled him and made his knees begin to buckle. He was breathing in wheezing gasps which echoed eerily in the night like the howls of a crazed wolf. He covered his mouth with his hand to push the noise back in.

When he drew his hand away from his mouth, he doubled it into a fist and pounded it against the door.

Ned opened the door and let Addison in.

Chapter Twenty-two

The year was 1959 and a revolution was taking place one hundred and twenty miles northeast of St. Cristobal on the island of Cuba, pearl of the Antilles. After two years of skirmishes, a tattered but determined band of guerilla soldiers swept out of the Sierra Maestra and put an end to the corrupt presidency of Fulgenzio Batista. In July, Osvaldo Dorticos Torrado was sworn in as president of the country's new socialist government while the nation's true power remained firmly clenched in the fist of its premier, a bearded Goliath by the name of Fidel Castro.

Collier was worried. She was living once again on the fringes of war. As she had once monitored the progress of Israel's battle for survival from the safety of her flat in London, she was now following the activities of Cuba's new regime from the seclusion of her hilltop compound. If Communism could come to Cuba, it could come to any of the islands in the Caribbean, including her own.

She snapped off the radio in her bedroom and got out of her chair. She slid back the glass door leading onto the terrace around the swimming pool and took a deep breath of the humid morning air. A heady blend of frangipani, jasmine and oleander, it was a combination she never tired of. It invigorated her and filled up her senses and made her feel round and ripe.

She glanced at the time. She still had another hour so she slipped her father's watch from around her neck, set it down on a table and climbed down the steps into the pool. She waded toward the deep end, shivering as the cool water rippled around her waist, then climbed higher to cover her chest and shoulders until it finally reached the base of her neck. Kicking her legs out behind her, she started to do a slow crawl.

It was that time of the year again, that special weekend set aside for a visit from the Center's three top students and a handful of selected gallery owners and patrons. As much as Collier's staff grumbled good-naturedly about the extra work and as much as the presence of a dozen extra people in the compound unnerved her, by the end of the third day Collier had to admit that July was just not July anymore without this weekend.

She turned over onto her back and floated, eyes closed, the sun drying the water droplets on her face. As she drifted in the pool, her thoughts drifted with her, sliding into memories which bobbed gently on the currents within her mind.

Leland's words came back to her. *You need a man in your life.* She had continued to do her best to prove him wrong. Over the years celibacy was something she had gotten used to. She seldom gave it a second thought. It was a state of being she had simply come to accept. But there were mornings now when she was shaken awake by the spasms of an orgasm, when she was brought to a climax by a distant dream, by the stroking of a phantom hand. She would lie alone in her bed as the throbbing subsided between her legs and the name she grudgingly gave to the aftermath of her orgasm was loneliness.

She had slept with no man since Thaddeus. For seven years, she had been waking up in the morning with the same empty place beside her, the sheet cool, the second pillow she kept on the bed out of habit, smooth, the case smelling of fresh laundering.

She swam over to the side of the pool, reached for the ladder and hauled herself out of the water. As she toweled herself dry, her thoughts returned to Leland, the one man she had permitted into her life. She had always thought of them as inseparable. In her mind, even their names were linked. Hyphenated. Leland-Collier. Collier-Leland.

But no more.

Not for two years now.

Now it was Leland-Jennifer. Jennifer-Leland.

It had begun with those first two dinners in Boston. After that, Leland had changed his travel route to include Gloucester along with New York, Philadelphia and St. Cristobal. Soon Jenny's letters to Collier had been filled only with talk of Leland. His letters still told her only about his work, while his phone calls had mentioned Jenny but briefly.

At the close of the Center's first year, Jenny had won first prize for one of her batiks. There was no longer any excuse for her to stay away from the island. When she had come down to St. Cristobal with the other two winners for their promised weekend, Leland came with her. She had been holding tightly onto his hand as she stepped from the launch bringing them over from Jamaica. Looking at the two of them together, Collier had known this was how it would be from then on. . . .

"I'm not going back to the Center in the fall," Jenny announced on the final night of their visit.

The three of them were sitting together in the living room after the others had gone to bed.

"I'm going home," she said, her eyes on Leland. Her hand found its way into his as she continued speaking. "I've learned more during my year at the Center than in my entire life. I've experimented with every major art form and now I want to begin to earn my living from my art. You and my father have supported me long enough, Collier. I think it's time your investment showed you both some kind of return."

Had she grown so much in one year? Collier experienced a stab of disbelief which left her breathless. The shyness was still there and the soft, sweet voice hadn't changed that much, but Jenny's tentativeness had been replaced by a new sureness. Were the changes a result of her burgeoning talent or her obvious love for Leland? Without asking, Collier knew that it had to be a combination of them both.

Her Jenny, Leland's Jennifer, had grown up at last. And Collier wondered how adept she herself would be at finally letting go. Leland was studying her carefully, and she wanted to show him what a good sport she could be about everything.

"Are you going to go back to painting at all?" she asked Jenny in a voice which in spite of herself sounded strained.

"I think I'll continue working with batiks and soft wool sculptures for a while," Jenny told her, and then she burst out laughing. "It's so strange, Collier. Whenever I look at the paintings I did before going to the Center, I don't know whether to laugh or throw up. What I think I'd really like to do is burn them all."

"Don't you dare!" Collier cried. "Anything you intend throwing away, you send to me."

"She'll immortalize you, Jen," Leland smiled, ruffling her hair.

Jenny kissed the back of his hand. Collier felt a catch in her throat.

"If I send you some of my paintings, will you hang them

right near your Racines?" Jenny teased, her eyes sparkling.

Collier shook her head. "I'll simply add on another room to the museum. Would you like that?"

"I think you'd better have another look at my work before you contact the builders. You might change your mind."

"Nothing could ever get me to change my mind about raw, unschooled talent," Collier said fiercely. "You've always had talent, Jenny. The Center only refined it and allowed you to branch out. You can work in almost any medium now, and you're talented enough to take any one of them as far as you want. Only one thing bothers me. Do you think it's a good idea to go back to live with your father?"

Jenny tightened her grip on Leland's hand.

"If you surround yourself with everything that's always been safe and familiar to you, if you tuck yourself away from the world again, you might feel less inclined to keep on experimenting," Collier went on. "Besides, there isn't enough room in the lighthouse for you to have the kind of studio you'll need. I still have the house in Gloucester and I'd gladly open it up for you to live in."

Jenny and Leland exchanged glances. Collier waited. It was the kind of exchange which said, "Should you tell her or should I?" Suddenly apprehensive, she took out a cigar and tried to light it.

It was Leland who told her.

"I've just rented a cottage for Jennifer in Rockport. She had her own misgivings about going back to live with Orrin and we thought that having her own place was the best answer. I'm in Boston more often these days because of my new monthly program on WBTO, and this way I'll have one less hotel to worry about."

The flame from Collier's lighted match singed her fingers and she dropped it, still burning, into the ashtray in front of her.

"And, Collier, you'll have a place to stay whenever you visit," Jenny added, her face flushed, her smile growing wider. "The house has four bedrooms and I'm going to use two of them as studios. Then I'll fill up the rest of the house with my work, just as you filled up your house with Milo's work."

Say that you're happy for them, Collier told herself. *Say that it's what they both deserve. Tell them how right they look together.* But she couldn't, so instead she kissed them both.

"You're the two people I love most in this world," she finally managed, "and I couldn't be happier for you."

That had been two years ago. They would be here soon. It had become a tradition of theirs to come down to the island for these weekends in July.

Collier went back to her bedroom to change. She pulled her hair back into a long, damp ponytail, slipped into a muumuu and a pair of sandals and then took a long, careful look at herself in her mirror.

What would it be like to see someone else reflected next to her in the glass? To have someone other than her maid do up the buttons on the back of her dress? To have someone to fight over the covers with in bed? Alone had seemed so right for so long. One glass, one plate, one cup and saucer. Dinner for one. Theatre tickets for one. A room for one.

She turned away from the mirror disgusted with herself. "Is this what your togetherness has done to me?" she addressed the absent Leland. "Has it just made me feel my aloneness more?"

She glanced at the time. The launch was due to arrive from Jamaica soon and she wanted to be there when it did. Although she had recently bought a helicopter and cleared a landing pad for it outside the compound, for visiting parties of more than four people she still preferred using her private plane and the launch.

Jenny was the last one off the boat. And she was alone.

Collier tried to conceal her disappointment and the strained look on Jenny's face further sealed her silence.

"Leland's in Cuba," Jenny said, as Collier steered her toward the beach so that they could be alone. "There's been some talk about the new regime severing all ties with the United States and President Eisenhower's warned all Americans living in Cuba to get out of the country as quickly as possible." She turned to Collier with a wild look of fear in her eyes. "Why is it always Leland they choose for these assignments? I hate these constant separations. I hate never knowing how he is or if I'll ever hear from him again."

"I know," Collier sighed. "I've never gotten used to it either." She took Jenny's face in her hands. "Are you feeling all right? You look awfully tired."

"I am tired," she admitted. "My batiks and wall hangings

are selling so well that I can barely meet the demand. It feels so good to get away from my work."

"There's something else, Jenny, something you're not telling me. What is it?"

Jenny bit down on her lower lip and her whole face seemed to crumble. "I'm alone so much of the time, Collier, and I don't want it that way anymore. Until I went to the Center, I never thought of myself as lonely. But ever since I met Leland, I've found out what loneliness really means." Her gray eyes filled with tears. "He's given me nothing less than what he promised, but he's given me nothing more either. I know he loves me and there's a wonderful peace between us when we're together, but I only get to see him when he can find the time for me which, as you well know, is a day here, a weekend there—never as much as one week at a time."

"I see him even less than you do, Jenny," Collier said in a gentle voice. "And as selfish as this might sound, I couldn't bear to give up any of my time with him, not even for you."

"I'd never ask that of you, Collier, never." Jenny looked distraught. "But I feel there's a bond between you two that no one can ever weaken. Sometimes I think you're the one he loves, not me."

"I'm his sister, Jenny. Leland loves me the way any brother loves his sister. He loves you the way a man loves a woman and there's a big difference between the two."

"I wonder if he even knows the difference when it comes to you."

Collier drew back, stunned. "What are you saying?"

Jenny didn't answer her.

"What did you mean by that?" She felt like shaking the girl.

Tears welled up in Jenny's eyes again. "I don't know," she whispered. "But whatever Leland feels for you doesn't seem natural, Collier, it just doesn't."

"But there's never been anything unnatural between us. What exactly are you accusing us of?"

"I'm not accusing you of anything. But Leland's not free. Something won't allow him to give himself completely to any woman."

"Leland has spent his entire life building a career and establishing a name for himself," Collier explained, keeping a tight rein on her voice. "You've had Leland longer than every other woman put together. Be grateful for what he's giving you, but don't destroy what you have by demanding more than he's capable of giving. If you want him, Jenny, really want him, you might have to settle for that."

"But I don't want to settle," she sobbed. "I want all of him."

Collier pulled the sobbing girl into her arms. "My poor little Jenny," she murmured. "You've been envying me and I've been envying the two of you, and we're both just as lonely. Perhaps all any of us are entitled to in this life are bits and pieces of things, with only a few of the pieces ever fitting together at any one time." She lifted Jenny's face and made the girl look at her. "If Leland is the man you want, give him some more time. But if you decide that having part of him isn't enough for you, then leave him. Find someone who wants as much of you as you want of him."

Throughout the entire weekend, Collier walked herself through the role of the consummate hostess. Deep inside, she felt like nothing more than a hostage. She suddenly felt that her island paradise had been converted into a fortress under seige by the enemy. Her awareness of her own loneliness, coupled with Jenny's unhappiness and Leland's absence had stirred up too many old feelings. Much like the sediment at the bottom of a pond, the feelings had lain there undisturbed inside her. Now, because of one violent splash, they had come bounding to the surface again.

And then, the weekend was over. They all left. Even Jenny, pale and red-eyed and silent.

Collier was alone again.

The following morning, she awoke early and went for a walk through the compound. It was her way of regaining control over her domain. Then she took a leisurely tour of her museum. She went from room to room, tracing the chronology of the artists she had patronized, the men whose genius she had only guessed at, and then promoted. It was like taking a stroll through her past. When she left the museum three hours later and locked the door, her healing was complete.

Amiel, the houseboy, caught up with her just as she was starting across the gardens toward the house.

"Telephone, Miss Collier. It's Mr. Leland."

"Leland!" His name was a cry of joy bursting from her lips.

She began to run. The joy gave way to terror. Something had happened to him. He was hurt. Something had happened to Jenny. They had ended it. She was practically panting by the time she picked up the receiver.

"How would you like a houseguest for a couple of days?" he blurted out without preamble. "I'm bushed. You'll have to send your chopper for me, though. It could be days before I get a flight out of here into Jamaica."

"Yes to everything," she cried. "And, Leland, hurry!"

She filled the hours of waiting by airing out his suite and filling every available vase in the house with flowers. She put several bottles of his favorite Reisling on ice and had Mattie the cook start on the bouillabaise he loved. She showered and took the time to wash and dry her hair and then work it up into its elaborate Gibson knot. Instead of a muumuu, she put on a pair of beige silk slacks and knotted a matching blouse around her waist and then slipped into a pair of high-heeled sandals.

She went out to the landing pad to wait for him. She tucked a red oleander blossom behind her left ear and, as she did with all her guests, she was carrying a spray of the flowers to give him when he arrived.

She felt like a child. Her heart was racing and her palms were moist. As the helicopter set down, she automatically backed away from the dust and the whirring blades. Once the engine was cut and the blades began to slow, the door on the passenger side swung open and Leland stepped down. He stood there for a moment, with bits of grass and earth eddying around him, an attaché case in one hand, a rumpled jacket thrown over his free arm.

She called his name and started to run toward him. The attaché case hit the ground first and the jacket quickly followed. He grabbed her by the waist and spun her around. Then he put her down and locked his arms around her.

His kiss on her mouth had never felt warmer, his arms never stronger. She closed her eyes and breathed in the nearness of him. Only when she was convinced that he was really there with her did she finally let him go.

They had dinner out on the terrace overlooking the pool. In spite of a shower and a shave and the fresh clothes he'd put on, Leland still looked tired and drawn.

"I wired Jennifer from Cuba to let her know I was coming down here," he said.

"You didn't call her?"

He shook his head. "I was too tired to either apologize or argue about it. It seemed simpler just to send a wire."

"What's happened, Leland? She was so unhappy when she was here."

"I know," he sighed, leaning back in his chair. "It's not working out, Collier, at least not the way she wants it to. I can understand her unhappiness because I'm just as unhappy myself. She always insisted she could settle for a full-time career and a part-time love affair. Now she wants the reverse and I don't. We both started out agreeing to play by the same rules, but she's changed them now and I'm still using the old ones."

"And you don't want to change them?"

"No, I don't. I can't." He took a sip of wine and set his glass down again. "I'm very fond of her, Collier, she's been such a delight. She never clung to me and she seemed content with whatever time we could spend together. I even cut back on my traveling to spend more time with her."

Even in the pale flickering candlelight, Collier could see the pain in his face, and she wished she could make the hurt disappear.

"Damn it, Collier, why can't we keep our promises?" he demanded, his voice cracking. "Why can't we keep wanting what we said we wanted at the beginning, without changing, without expecting more?

"Jennifer can't give me what my work's always given me. She can't be anything more than what she is, someone who wants to be an artist and spend the rest of her life in Rockport. She still can't take chances. She still needs life to be safe and ordered and predictable. I can't live on anything short of the edge. Predictability bores me, routine stifles me. Change is what keeps me alive. She's asking me to be satisfied with living a half-life with her. If I settle for that, I'll end up despising her while I watch myself die."

"What do you intend to do, then?"

"Talk to her about it. Again. Tell her I've got to start traveling more and that I've got to pick up the work I've dropped. I hope she'll agree to give it a chance, but if she doesn't, I'd rather end it now before we hate the very things we've loved about each other."

Collier tried to choose her next words very carefully. "What Jenny needs is security. She needs to know that you're coming back to her after each assignment. Marriage would give her that security, Leland."

"I don't want marriage, Collier. You, of all people, should understand. Look how far you've run to keep yourself free."

"I do understand you, Leland," she told him in a weary voice, "but I don't feel that free anymore. I see loneliness as just as much of a trap as marriage. I'm lonely now, Leland, and I wish I could feel something for someone again. I think I'm looking for what you've decided you don't want."

She pushed back her chair and went to sit at the edge of the pool. Leland came and crouched down beside her. Soon his face was floating in the water alongside hers. She splashed at their reflections with her hand and watched as their images wavered, shimmering in and out of focus, until the water finally cleared and their images were whole again.

"I told you that you'd spoiled me for other women, didn't I?" he murmured, his breath warm on her neck.

"Do you think we've been blessed or cursed because of it?"

He didn't say anything.

"Jenny herself said there was a bond between us that no one would ever be able to break."

"It's true, Collier," he said, slipping his arm around her shoulder. "There is."

She actually grew alarmed. "Then what would either of us do without the other?"

"We'll make a pact. Neither of us agrees to go without the other."

Collier laughed. "I think I'd prefer having someone work on keeping us immortal."

She turned to look at him and her face grew serious again. "I'm very sorry about you and Jenny, Leland. The two people I care the most about are being hurt and that hurts me."

"Enough of this," he said, pulling her to her feet. "I'd like to take a long walk on the beach."

He rolled up his slacks and kicked off his loafers.

Hand in hand, he and Collier climbed down the broad stone steps and onto the beach. The sand was warm and dry. The breeze coming in from the ocean was cool. The air was a mixture of dampness and sharpness, and Collier wondered if a thunderstorm might be brewing. July was the month for thunderstorms. Clouds scudded across the sky and as they walked, the wind began to increase in strength.

Collier shivered, drawing closer to Leland for warmth. He put his arm around her waist and she slipped hers around his. The wind rose to a howl and whipped the surface of the waves into peaks of white froth which crashed around their feet and splattered their legs and soaked their clothes.

The night felt wild. Strange. Collier thought of Cuba then and she felt peculiarly disquieted. Even with Leland walking beside her, holding her, she could sense the changes around her.

That vague hint of sulphur before a storm.

An eerie foreboding of some hidden danger.

She glanced back over her shoulder, half expecting there to be someone behind her.

This was her island. Her refuge. Her home. And yet, suddenly and inexplicably, she could feel an evil lurking there.

Chapter Twenty-three

A young man by the name of John Fitzgerald Kennedy was in the White House and he was calling his administration The New Frontier. It promised to be a time dedicated to idealism and peace, and the youth of America found themselves caught up in a new kind of dream.

Peace was a word Collier no longer believed in. It now meant nothing in her small corner of the world where the key word was fear. And the focus of that fear was Cuba. Each ripple emanating from that smoldering island was magnified until it raged with the intensity of a tidal wave, threatening to engulf the entire Caribbean.

On St. Cristobal, Collier's own loneliness was being quickly supplanted by her growing awareness of a much greater sense of isolation: her island's isolation. It was no longer a comfort to be cut off from civilization; it was now a burden. Three weeks after Kennedy's inauguration Cleavon Coombes came to tell Collier that the people of Bonnyport shared that same burden.

Unlike his father, Cleavon was tall and slender, with the delicate features of the white man whose seed had watered down his blackness generations before. At twenty-eight, he was his father's chief advisor in the running of the town government and the only one of his people to have ever left St. Cristobal. Collier had seen the potential in Cleavon, and when he was twenty, she had sent him to Miami and put him through two years of technical school there. He had returned to the island a skilled electrician and a master mechanic.

Now he stretched out in a wicker chair on the patio overlooking the ocean and accepted a tall glass of rum punch from Amiel. Collier took her own glass and sat down in the chair beside him.

"We are an outdated and obsolete people down here," Cleavon told her in his softly modulated voice. "We have nothing but our ignorance to keep us safe and nothing with which to defend ourselves should the need ever arise. We want no Cubans on St. Cristobal, Miss Collier."

"Cuba has too many internal problems to deal with before they can even begin to think about expansionism," she said, hoping that she sounded convincing. "Did it ever occur to you that the very isolation of St. Cristobal might actually protect it? Jamaica or the Bahamas or even Haiti have much more to offer the Cubans than this little island."

"It will take more than our isolation to save us if we were ever threatened," he insisted. "We must find ways to defend ourselves."

"What would you suggest then? Organizing the island's one hundred men into an army, building a few bomb shelters—"

"Perhaps a radar system, an early warning device which would sound an alarm and give us ample time to fling ourselves into the sea."

"Cleavon!"

"I'm sorry, Miss Collier. I have no answer right now, but I intend to find one."

Collier shuddered, imagining the island transformed into an armed camp. Cleavon had finished his drink and was ready to leave. She stood up and walked him to the door. He took her hand, and in the quaint, courtly manner he had learned from his father, he bent to kiss it.

That night Collier put in a call to Leland. She hadn't seen him since he and Jenny had come down to the island for Christmas. She missed him. Especially now, after her conversation with Cleavon. As the phone rang, she tried to anticipate his mood. He and Jenny were still together, still living on their emotional treadmill, which was leading them nowhere. Leland was traveling more and seeing Jenny less. She was working harder and pretending she was still willing to settle.

Orrin had died of a heart attack just after New Year's and Jenny was finally alone for the first time in her life. There would be no more Orrin staying home from the sea to protect her. Now there wasn't even the tower for her to return to. The lighthouse at Eastern Point had passed into other hands.

There was no answer at Jenny's in Rockport and no answer at Leland's apartment in New York. When she tried Diana's number in Philadelphia, she got a busy signal. That didn't worry her. Selma Bryce was fond of chatting on the phone. She tried the number twice more and then gave up and went to bed.

Then in the morning, Leland called *her*. He was in Philadelphia.

"Diana ran away from the house two nights ago," he told her.

Collier gasped.

"Selma notified the police and they found Diana wandering around in her nightgown on the grounds outside Fairwood. She's back at Fairwood now with a slight touch of pneumonia."

Collier's legs gave way and she slumped into a chair. *We've had ten wonderful years together,* she forced herself to remember. *Ten years in which to be a family. I should be grateful.* But right now, she wasn't feeling very grateful. She was angry and sad. She thought of what the three of them had shared over the years, sharing at least some of what other families shared, given the circumstances.

She remembered all their family times. All of them spent with Diana in Philadelphia. The walks through Fairmont Park and through the campus of the University of Pennsylvania. The strolls along the Delaware River wharves. The drives through the country. Picnics on the bank of the Schuykill River. Tea in the solarium off Diana's bedroom. Popcorn in front of the television in the living room.

Collier's eyes filled with tears and she didn't even try to hold them back. "H-how is she?" she stammered, when she could speak again.

"She's going to be all right." Somehow Leland didn't sound convinced. "The pneumonia's mild."

Collier sniffed. She didn't like the sound of Leland's voice. He sounded strained. There was something he wasn't telling her, something he was holding back.

"Are you sure Diana's going to be all right?" she demanded.

He didn't answer her.

"Leland!"

"What?" he mumbled. "I'm sorry, Collier, I—"

"If you think dead space sounds terrible on the air, you should hear how awful it sounds over the phone!"

"Diana's going to be fine, Collier, honest."

"But." She prodded him, knowing there had to be more.

"But she doesn't recognize me anymore. She's completely incoherent."

"No," she cried. "No, no, no." She pounded the arm of her

chair. It wasn't fair. It couldn't be true. It just couldn't be! "She'll come out of it again, won't she?" she asked him.

"The doctors are hopeful."

"Doctors are always hopeful," she muttered, "they're paid to be hopeful."

"Collier—"

"I'm flying up to see her immediately."

"It won't make any difference. She won't know who you are."

Collier stood firm. "I'm still coming."

"Suit yourself," Leland sighed. "We've been lucky, dear heart, we've had ten good years with her. Remember that."

"Don't talk as if they're over and that's all we'll ever have," she snapped at him.

"I'm sorry, Collier, I didn't mean—"

"I know," she answered contritely. "I had no right to lash out at you. It isn't your fault. But I'm just so upset."

"I understand exactly how you feel," he assured her. "I feel the same way. Helpless and angry at the same time. But I'd still advise you to wait a few more days before coming up here. Things might be radically different by then."

She stopped being defensive long enough to consider what he was saying.

"By the way, I'm leaving for Paris and Brussels tomorrow evening," Leland told her in his flat, weary voice. "I'll be gone about three weeks." He paused. "I thought I might stop off to see you on my way back to the States." Once again, he paused. "Jenny and I have finally called it quits."

So that was it. The real reason for the deadness in his voice. Collier got a tighter grip on the receiver.

"Why, Leland? Why now?"

"Because she has an opening at a new gallery in Boston in two weeks and I won't be there. She's just used this as an excuse to give me the ultimatum she's been holding back for a long time."

"Do you want me to speak to her?" she asked.

"What difference would that make? We've been seesawing back and forth for too long now. It's better this way. At least I won't be hurting her anymore."

"But what about you?" she cried. "Aren't *you* hurting?"

"I'm fine."

And then the line went dead.

• • •

At the end of a week, Collier was in Philadelphia.

At the clinic, she found Diana to be much the way Leland had described her. Although the antibiotics were clearing up her pneumonia, Diana seemed more frail and remote than ever. She simply lay in her bed in the infirmary wing with her hands loosely clasped on top of the covers and her eyes vacant and staring. She didn't move. She seldom blinked. Not once did she acknowledge Collier's presence in the room. To Collier, her mother looked like a living corpse already laid out for burial, with only the uneven rise and fall of her chest to prove that she was alive at all.

Collier pulled up a large vinyl chair next to the bed and remained there for the next eighteen hours. Throughout the day, her feelings alternated between anger and despair, anguish and defeat. She hated seeing her mother this way. Helpless. Lost some place where no one else could follow. She was a fragile shell, a fading shadow. To keep herself from crying, Collier kept thinking about the times when Diana's gentle blue eyes had been clear enough to really see her, when those thin, white arms had been strong enough to hold her, and when that whispery voice had called out her name.

She wanted those times back. She wanted her mother back. She would fight to get them both back again. She had kept all her other promises to Diana and she would keep this one too. She swore it.

Collier spent the night sleeping fitfully in the chair beside Diana's bed. In the morning, she looked for some sign of improvement in her mother's condition and found none. She began to despair all over again. The doctors told her it would be senseless to stay on. Alva Rittenhouse agreed with them. So did Selma Bryce. In the end, Collier capitulated. Perhaps it *was* senseless. She forced down the lukewarm coffee and the cold cheese Danish which Selma brought her and said good-bye to the woman. Then she got into her rented Thunderbird sports coupe, roared out through the iron gates and headed for Rockport.

She drove recklessly, collecting three speeding tickets along the way. But she didn't mind the tickets. The one thing Collier missed on her beloved island was a car, and being able to race the wind. Thinking of the island gave her an idea. As soon as

Diana was well enough, Collier would bring her down for a visit. Her mother had never seen St. Cristobal before. She had never wanted to venture any further than the outskirts of Philadelphia. But this time was different. St. Cristobal would heal Diana. It would give her back her life. Collier's spirits lifted. Now all she had to do was convince Leland.

Her good mood lasted until she reached Rockport. But when she got to Jenny's house and found no one home, her spirits fell again. She stood on the porch in the cold and knocked until her knuckles felt bruised. She kept trying the doorknob, hoping it would give, but it didn't. Cursing under her breath, she stamped her feet in an effort to keep the circulation going in her toes. In spite of her long fox cape and high leather boots, she was freezing. All she could think of was getting warm. She went back to the car and sat there with the motor running and the heater on.

The afternoon wore on and there was still no sign of Jenny. Collier was hungry and she was cold. Finally, she gave up and drove back into Boston.

She spent the following two days at the Center, sitting in on a number of lectures and studio classes. She phoned Jenny periodically, with no results. By the afternoon of the second day, she decided it was futile to stay on any longer in Boston. She would just go home. Ringing the room of her pilot, she got no answer and left a message with the hotel operator to have him come to the bar when he returned. She packed her one suitcase, left it on the bed and took the elevator down to the lobby. She stopped at the newsstand to buy some cigars and then headed for the bar.

"Miss Paget-Browne?"

She whirled around.

A tall young man with tousled blond hair and drooping moustache was grinning at her. He was wearing a navy blue duffel coat with the collar turned up. He was hunched over, his hands shoved deep into his pockets, and his nose was red. He looked vaguely familiar.

"Paul Caitlin," he said, holding out one large, reddened hand to her. "I was at the island a couple of years back."

"Of course," she smiled politely as she took his hand. She recalled now that he had been one of the Center's prize-winning sculptors. "How have you been?"

"Not bad," he said with a shrug. "Could be better, if you

want to know the truth. Hey, look, you have time for a drink?"

She hesitated.

· "I was just heading home from a friend's and I knew I'd never make it if I didn't stop in here to warm up." He winked at her. "Come on, have one drink with me. It'd be my way of showing you some northern hospitality."

His smile was so open, his expression so frankly pleading that she found herself taking his arm and allowing him to steer her into the bar. He ordered a beer and she did the same. She hated beer, but she doubted he could afford anything else. Sitting across from her in the booth now, he suddenly seemed uncomfortable and when their drinks arrived, he immediately gulped down half of his. To put him at ease, she asked him about his work.

"Since I graduated from the Center two years ago, I've been in some group shows here in Boston and a few in New York and Baltimore. I've done all right, but I haven't taken off like I thought I would. So to keep the landlord off my back and keep myself in peanut butter, I've been taking on odd jobs to make some extra bread." He quickly drained the rest of his beer and ordered another.

She was curious about him. He was growing increasingly agitated as he talked. She wondered if he might be on drugs.

"What kind of jobs have you been doing?" she asked him.

"Short-order cook, bouncer, chauffeur—you name it, I've tried it."

"Have you thought of applying to the Center for a part-time position? I know they're always looking for studio assistants."

"Yeah, I've applied a few times, but there haven't been any openings in the sculpture studios. I'd be useless at macramé or weaving."

The bitterness in his voice was reminiscent of the tone Milo had used so often and her heart ached for him.

"Hey, no sense my laying all my problems on you," he said with a smile as he finished off his second beer. "I'm having some friends up to my place tonight for a few drinks. Why don't you come by? You can take a look at my latest work and if you find something you like, I'll give you a good price on it."

She declined his invitation with a shake of her head. "I was counting on flying back to the island tonight."

"Come on. Please?" He reached across the table for her

hand. "You'd be surprised at the things I can do with peanut butter. And besides, when was the last time you sat around with a bunch of real, live struggling artists?"

When she finally accepted the invitation, she knew it was because she was hoping to find some of his works good enough to buy.

She arrived at his rooming house at seven, carrying a large wicker hamper filled with a loaf of pâté, three kinds of cheese, two boxes of crackers and four pounds of black grapes. In spite of his boasts, she had her doubts about anyone's ability to do anything with peanut butter.

His room took up half of the second floor of the old frame building. A corner of the room served as his bedroom, one third of it was a combination kitchen, living room and dining room, and the rest was his studio. Welded steel figures of varying sizes covered two wooden trestle tables and several long benches. Several small works in progress were set up on individual wooden stands, while chunks and scraps of metal, boxes of nails and rivets, and large spools of copper wire filled up every available bit of shelf and floor space.

"Hey, you didn't have to bring anything with you," Paul protested as he took the hamper from her.

In spite of his protests, she could see that he was pleased. While he was unpacking the hamper, she began to look over his works.

"I like what you've been doing," she told him. "I think you might make yourself a few easy sales tonight."

"You're not just saying that because you feel I need the bread, are you? I'm not into charity, you know. That's why I do the part-time job number. It saves on the pride."

She put down a small iron figurine. "When I buy art, it isn't charity, Paul, it's an investment in someone's talent. If I say I like your work, you can believe me. Give me until the end of the evening, and I'll let you know which piece I intend to buy."

By eight o'clock, all of Paul's friends had arrived. There were now seven new and indistinguishable faces for Collier to sort out. She was only on her second glass of wine so her lack of perception had nothing to do with being drunk. She settled herself on the sofa and tried to sort out the girls from the boys. They all looked the same. They all had long hair and they all wore work shirts over jeans and boots.

"Looks like your peanut butter's been retired for the night, Paul," laughed one of the girls as she slathered pâté on a cracker and popped it into her mouth.

"Where'd you ever dig up such a groovy chick, man, she's far out." A young man leaned over Collier and stared into her eyes. "Far out, and I don't mean just the eats."

"Hey, treat the lady with respect, asshole," Paul shot back, pulling him away from the sofa. "She's special."

"Care for some weed, special lady?" A hand reached up in front of Collier.

She shook her head and pushed the hand down.

"Hey, what a drag. Don't you do drugs at all?"

"She gets high on nature, man," Paul answered for her.

Collier stifled a yawn and got up to pour herself some more wine.

"Here, let me do that for you." Paul grabbed the glass out of her hand. "You just relax and let me play host, okay?"

She sat down again.

"Ever drop any acid, mama?" asked the young man who had offered her the marijuana. At her startled look, he laughed. "You know. LSD. It's this little magic cube that can take you on a beautiful trip. Really open up your mind for you."

He was making her nervous, but she tried to sound casual as she slipped into the strange jargon they were all using. "As Paul told you before, I get high on nature."

"But how will you ever know if that's as high as you can get?"

"Lay off, will you, Ross." Paul was back with Collier's drink.

His hand was shaking as she took it from him and some wine spilled onto her sweater. She brushed off the wet spots with the back of her hand.

Paul turned up the volume on the stereo just as Collier finished her new glass of wine. There was a speaker in each of the four corners of the room and the bleating trumpet of Miles Davis seemed to envelope her and penetrate all of her senses.

"Want to dance?" Paul was holding out his arms to her.

"No, thanks." Collier shook her head. She suddenly felt dizzy.

"Come on, it's groovy stuff to dance to."

He hauled her to her feet and she wobbled into his arms.

He pressed her up against him and guided her to the center of the room. The room began to spin and she asked him to slow down.

"Can't go any slower than this," he told her.

She looked down at her feet. They were barely moving at all.

As soon as she raised her head, the room tilted again. She stumbled, and Paul tightened his grip on her. She blinked her eyes. Three glasses of white wine, no matter how inexpensive, couldn't be affecting her this way. Her head felt as if it now belonged to someone else. It was growing heavier, too heavy for her neck to support. She stumbled again and rested her head on Paul's shoulder.

She couldn't feel her feet anymore. She wriggled her toes, but she still couldn't feel them. Her whole body was now too weak for her head. She had to let go of her head or else she would collapse. She dropped her head onto the floor with a loud thud. Weightless, she floated out of Paul's arms into the air.

From her perch on the ceiling, she was able to see the entire room. Large pink bodies were sprawled about on the floor, while white puffs of smoke rose in spirals all around them. The smaller black bodies were resting too. But as she looked more closely, she saw them begin to move. The black bodies were moving, changing shapes and moving.

They raised their arms and kicked out their legs. They waved their arms high in the air and stamped their feet in time to the music. Clapping and stomping, they began to dance around the room.

The nails came away. One by one, the nails fell out. The arms and legs were loose now, wobbling, no longer keeping time with the music. They clattered onto the floor, spitting nails in all directions.

Now the wires were moving. They were twisting and writhing, weaving their way across the floor. Collier began to scream. The wires had stretched themselves into glistening copper snakes, growing thinner and longer as they wriggled across the floor and stood up on their tails to reach her.

She shouted for Paul to help her, but she couldn't see him anymore. He had left her alone to fight off the snakes by herself.

And then she saw the flowers. They were just like the flowers on her island. Purple and pink and yellow and white.

The flowers were waving to her. They would help her escape from the snakes. They fluttered near the window, danced and billowed on either side of the open window, and beckoned her over to them.

If she could fly over to the flowers, she would be safe. She began to flap her arms and kick her legs. Once she reached the flowers, she would be home again. Home. It was hot at home. Too hot for the heavy clothes she was wearing. That was why she wasn't able to fly. Her clothes were weighing her down.

She took off her clothes and dropped them on the floor. She was so much lighter now. Now she would be able to fly home and be safe.

She remembered the birds, the seagulls, and how they were able to spread their wings and soar above the tops of the waves. She flapped her wings and tried again, but something was holding her down.

And then she heard the explosions. The hunters were shooting at her. She looked down and saw the great silver bursts of light which sparked and popped and twinkled all around her. She screamed again. They were blinding her and she couldn't see the flowers anymore.

The snakes had reached her feet. They wrapped themselves around her ankles and began to pull her down. She had no strength left to fight them off. She let go of the ceiling and let them pull her down, down, down. The floor rushed up to meet her and she put out her hands to break her fall.

She felt nothing. Only the blackness.

He parked the Thunderbird half a block from the entrance to her hotel. He positioned her in such a way that as soon as he shut the door, she slumped forward against the steering wheel, hitting her head on the horn.

The blaring sound of the horn cut through the night.

He waited in a doorway across the street until the doorman came and pulled her out of the car. Then he walked for three blocks and hailed a cab. He lit a cigarette and blew the smoke out slowly through his nose. He'd develop the film as soon as he got home.

Caitlin had more than earned his five thousand bucks.

• • •

The ringing shook Collier awake. With the receiver half slipping out of her hand, she heard her pilot say that they had one hour to clear Boston before the snowstorm heading east kept them grounded for at least two days. Dropping the receiver back in its cradle, she struggled to sit up straight.

She was strangely light-headed and when she tried to focus, she felt as if she were seeing the room with her head cocked to one side. Her body felt weightless, as if all the blood had been drained out of her and replaced with air. Her mouth was dry and as she steadied herself against the bedside table, she noticed several long scratches on the backs of her hands.

And then she remembered. Paul Caitlin. He had obviously put something in her wine. Or Ross. The one talking about LSD. The evening skidded in and out of focus as she tried to recall what had happened. They had sent her on a trip. The bastards. Why? How had she managed to get back to her hotel?

She located her purse on top of the dresser and checked her wallet. Nothing was missing. All of her clothes were laid out neatly on the chair near the door. Who had undressed her and put her to bed? She was mortified. Her one consolation was that she hadn't bought any of Paul Caitlin's works. At best they were mediocre and she had wanted to help him. What a fool she had been.

A little boy playing little boy's games. All she could think of was punishing him for what he had done. She picked up the phone and asked Information for his number. It was unlisted. She began to get dressed, slipping into the same clothes she had worn the night before. She checked the time. She wouldn't be able to get to Paul's flat and then to the airport in time, and she refused to even consider being snowbound in Boston.

What would Paul even say if she confronted him? He would probably either laugh it off or deny the whole thing. Seeing him again would only make her feel like more of a fool. She tried to keep her temper under control. No one, especially not someone like Paul Caitlin, could get away with making a fool out of her. She lit a cigar and sat down on the bed to think. Then she glanced at her watch again.

The first snowflakes drifting past the window made up her mind for her.

She rang the Bell Captain and asked him to send someone up for her suitcase.

The doors of the art world were about to swing shut on dear

Paul Caitlin. Pulling her address book out of her purse, she opened it to the letter "A". She reached for the phone, took a deep breath, and began to make her calls.

It took nearly four hours to complete the task. Collier put down the phone after her final call and looked out of the window. There was already an inch of snow on the sill. She shoved her address book back in her purse. She had to get out of there right away. She stood up and stretched. Her whole body felt stiff and sore. Even her hands were trembling. Her shirt was soaked through and she had bitten off all of her lipstick. Finding her lipstick and her compact, she hastily repaired the damage.

As she patted her hair back into place, she thought about what she had just done. She had never considered herself a vindictive person. Whenever she acted, it was usually in self-defence. In this case, Paul Caitlin had provoked her and she had been obliged to retaliate. She grimaced, thinking of the phone bill she had just run up. But she shrugged it off. Whatever it cost, the results would be worth it.

It had really been very simple. She had contacted the major galleries in every major city across the country and threatened to withhold her name and all future support if they ever exhibited the works of one Paul Caitlin. From the east coast to the west, north and south, in cities like New York and San Francisco, New Orleans and Seattle, Houston and Chicago, Palm Beach and Boston, the word would already be filtering down. Spreading quickly via the art world's reliable grapevine.

No gallery, large or small, in any city, could risk losing Collier Paget-Browne as either a patron or a potential patron. None of them could risk losing her as a drawing card and a meal ticket. If they lost her, they might also be losing every big name in the American social register. No artist was worth that risk. Especially a yet-to-be-discovered sculptor by the name of Paul Caitlin.

The man was of questionable moral character? How awful. A blight on the illustrious name of the Collier Paget-Browne Center for Fine Arts? How ghastly. An embarrassment to her personally? Dreadful. She found his work offensive? A thousand apologies. Anything to cooperate, Miss Paget-Browne. We do so appreciate your continued interest in our humble gallery. Did you receive an invitation to our upcoming exhibition? You did? Marvelous. And so it had gone.

The few galleries already handling Paul Caitlin wouldn't be

able to return his work to him fast enough. Those who had considered accepting his work for some future show would immediately inform him that they had changed their minds. With the proper apologies, of course.

Collier put on her coat. It was over and done with. She could now return home and forget all about Paul Caitlin. But she doubted that he would ever forget her.

Chapter Twenty-four

At the beginning of April, Collier brought her mother down to St. Cristobal. Although Diana was not emotionally prepared for such a trip, circumstance, and not choice, had prompted Collier's decision. Shortly before Diana's scheduled release from Fairwood, Selma Bryce had fallen on the steps of the clinic and fractured her pelvis. The woman was completely incapacitated and immediately hospitalized. At Collier's insistence—and a twenty-thousand-dollar donation to their building fund—Fairwood agreed to keep Diana on. But as the weeks passed, and Selma's progress seemed maddeningly slow, Collier decided to take her mother out of the clinic and bring her down to the island. Leland agreed without an argument.

On their first morning together, Collier woke her mother up and helped her to dress. Although completely recovered from her bout of pneumonia, Diana was still withdrawn. There was a distant look in her eyes and a vagueness to her movements. Even as Collier walked her out onto the terrace for breakfast, Diana appeared more asleep than awake. It was as if she had decided to stay locked inside her private world for good. But Collier still clung to the hope that her mother's deterioration was only temporary, that one day something would go "click" inside her head and the fog would lift. Time, Collier counselled herself for the one hundredth time that morning, give her time.

She seated Diana at a table near the swimming pool and took the chair opposite her. Does she know where she is, Collier wondered. Does she remember anything I've ever told her about the island? Does she even realize she's in *my* home now? Diana's blue eyes were surprisingly clear, considering how heavily sedated she had been on the flight down. Collier sighed. If only her mother's mind were as clear as her eyes.

Diana unfolded her linen napkin and placed it in her lap. Then she clasped her hands together and continued to stare straight ahead of her. She seemed to be waiting for something.

251

Collier finally realized that Diana was waiting to be served. She had failed to notice the breakfast laid out on the portable tea wagon just behind her. Collier got up and wheeled the cart over to the table.

"What would you like to eat, Mother?" Collier asked, touching Diana lightly on the shoulder.

Diana looked up, startled. Collier pointed out the food to her. After carefully considering all of the silver serving dishes, she settled on several slices of mango and papaya and a hot croissant. She held up her cup and Collier obediently filled it with coffee. Diana raised the steaming cup to her lips, but instead of drinking any, she simply sniffed at it. Then she rewarded Collier with a shy little smile.

"Cream?" Collier held up the silver pitcher and Diana nodded.

"Sugar?" Diana took one teaspoon of sugar, but Collier wanted her to remember that on her own.

Diana frowned as she tried to concentrate. Collier waited patiently, studying her mother's face. She was so pale. Her skin was that translucent white of the sickly and the housebound. Give it time, Collier chastised herself for her impatience, the island would eventually turn that greenish cast to a golden brown.

Diana suddenly brightened. She seemed quite pleased with herself.

"I'll take one teaspoon, thank you," she told her daughter, with a nod of her head for emphasis.

Collier stooped to kiss the top of Diana's head. "Good for you," she murmured, taking this as a sign of her mother's first positive step toward recovery.

They ate their meal in silence, but Collier anxiously monitored all of Diana's movements. She watched in fascination as her mother cut her fruit into precise little chunks and then chewed each piece the same number of times before swallowing it. She repeated this ritual until all the fruit was gone, and then she did the same thing with her croissant. It took a flock of tiny yellow birds flying past the table to finally break her concentration. She let out a frightened squeal when one of the birds landed on the rim of her plate.

"Don't be afraid," Collier told her. "They won't hurt you. They're just hungry."

She spooned some sugar onto the tablecloth and Diana

watched the bird hop off her plate onto the table and begin pecking at the sugar with its sharp, black beak. She laid down her knife and fork and stared at the bird.

"I call them 'sugar birds'," Collier explained, "because they always come by at mealtimes and sugar is all they ever eat. One day, I noticed two lizards eating the sugar the birds had left behind, so I started putting out small mounds for them too. That made the birds jealous." Diana giggled. "Now they're always fighting. The birds drive the lizards off so they can eat first, but as soon as they've flown away, the lizards come back and finish up whatever's left."

Diana clapped her hands. She liked that story. Now there were five tiny yellow birds pecking at the sugar. Gingerly, she picked up her teaspoon, reached into the sugar bowl and added another small mound to Collier's.

"Tippy," murmured Diana, in a voice so low that Collier had to lean forward to hear her. "When I was little, I had a yellow bird named Tippy. I only fed him seeds, but I think he would have liked the sugar better."

Collier wanted to jump up and hug her mother. She had recalled something from her past! She was starting to get better. The island was going to be good for her. It would save her, just as Collier knew it would. Her heart was thumping wildly. Wait until Leland arrived. He would be down within the week. Wait until he saw Diana. She might be completely healed by then.

Diana had finished the last of her coffee and appeared to be growing restless. Collier forgot about the rest of her own meal and helped her mother out of her chair.

"Would you like to take a walk on the beach now?" she asked.

Diana looked down at her short, flowered housecoat and the slippers she was wearing and frowned.

"Just take off your slippers," Collier told her.

Diana gingerly stepped out of them and then just stood there, waiting to be told what to do next.

"We're going to walk through the garden and down to the steps leading to the beach," Collier explained, taking her mother's hand.

She walked her as she would a child. Diana slowed down several times, stopping once to examine a branch of bougainvillea and then to pick up a fallen oleander blossom. As they passed under a hibiscus tree, Collier snapped off one of the yellow, trumpet-shaped flowers and tucked it behind her mother's left ear.

"That's how we wear flowers down here," Collier said, snapping off one for herself.

Diana touched the flower in Collier's hair and then ran her fingers over the one in her own hair and her eyes filled with tears. Impulsively Collier put her arms around her mother and felt the small body tremble. Diana's arms slowly worked their way around Collier's back. They held onto one another that way until Collier felt her mother's arms begin to shake and finally fall away from her. Saying nothing, she took hold of her mother's hand again and led her over to the steps.

Diana stopped, a look of alarm spreading across her features, and refused to move any further. She gazed down at the beach and then back at the steps again, as if gauging the distance between her and safety. She swayed slightly and Collier grasped her by the shoulders to steady her.

"Don't be afraid," she told her in a gentle voice. "The steps are wide and I'll be beside you all the way down. I won't let you fall, Mother, I won't let you hurt yourself. I promise. You'll be safe with me."

"Hold my hand again," Diana whispered, and Collier did.

Diana edged tentatively toward the top step. Collier stayed close to her, holding tightly onto her hand, urging her down, step by step. The strain of their slow descent was making her hand stiff. The muscles in her arm were cramping. She gritted her teeth. Her whole body was slick with perspiration by the time they reached the bottom step. Diana let go of Collier's hand and fell to her knees in the sand.

Leaning forward, she dug her hands deep into the sand. Then she raised her arms in the air and opened her fingers to let the sand stream through them. She giggled like a small child, as over and over again, she scooped up the sand and watched it fall. The only time her smile faltered was when she tried to dig a hole. Each handful of sand she cleared only slid back down and filled up the hole again.

As she watched her mother playing, Collier knew a longing so intense that she could have wept. She pressed her hands to her belly and felt the emptiness there. She had failed as a woman, just as her father had believed he had failed as a man. She was nearly forty-one years old and there would be no child for her now. There would be no heir to leave her father's fortune to, no son to carry on her father's name. She thought of the child Milo had stolen from her and a great cold wave of despair and regret washed over her.

"Collier?"

She looked up. Only then did she realize she was crying. Diana was sitting back on her heels, holding out her arms. Collier got down on her knees and laid her head against her mother's chest. Diana's arms closed around her.

As Collier lay there sobbing, she heard her mother whisper her name again. She cried harder, believing with all her heart that Diana had been returned to her.

Leland arrived at the end of the week and the three of them were a family again. Because of Diana's continuing improvement, Collier showed her mother off the way a child shows off a new toy. But the excitement of Leland's arrival seemed to have tired her out, and so, after their first dinner together, Collier put her to bed early. Then she led her brother out onto the patio for a talk.

She wanted to ask him how he had been managing since his break-up with Jenny, but something in the grave set of his face held her back. He was still hurting. It was obvious that the intensity of his pain had taken him by surprise. And so, she said nothing. He would bring it up himself when he was ready.

They pushed two wicker chairs together and sat down to look out at the sea. The air was still. The moon was riding rather low in the sky, and the slap of the waves against the beach below had a hypnotic effect on Collier. She yawned, stretched her arms above her head and yawned again.

"Am I keeping you up?" Leland asked in a playful tone.

She shook her head. "I'm good for at least another hour," she replied, watching him hide a yawn of his own. She reached out for his hand. "Tell me," she said, her expression earnest, "how do you think Mother looks?"

"I think she looks better than she has in a long time," he replied, giving her hand a squeeze.

Collier began to beam. "She's been eating so well that I think she's put on a pound or two. And don't you think she looks so much healthier with that bit of a tan? I was right to bring her down here, wasn't I, Leland?"

"I'd have to agree with you so far," he said, "but we have no guarantee she'll remain this way."

Collier refused to be discouraged. "It's so good for her here, Leland. She isn't taking as much medication as she takes up north. She's smiling more. She's much more lucid again. She's even carrying on conversations with me now."

"Just how long do you plan on keeping her here?"

Collier was afraid to meet his gaze. "To be honest with you, I'd like her to stay here permanently."

"You know that's impossible," he shouted. At Collier's stern look, he lowered his voice. "Outside of the clinic in Bonnyport, there are no decent medical facilities around. She might be stable now, but what will you do if she gets confused again or becomes violent? You wouldn't be able to handle her by yourself. It could be dangerous for both of you."

"Then I'll hire a medical team from the States to live down here with us."

"Collier, be reasonable."

"She's sixty years old, Leland!" Now Collier was getting angry. "What kind of a life has she led for those sixty years? What kind of a future does she have? A goddamned empty one, that's the kind she has! Well, I want her to have something more. She deserves more. The best thing we ever did was to buy her that house in Philadelphia, but that was ten years ago. It's time we did something else for her, and that means allowing her to live wherever she's happiest. As far as I'm concerned, that's here with me."

"But for how long?" he persisted.

"You said it yourself," she answered warily, "we have no guarantee. But I'm willing to chance it."

"I'm not," Leland declared. "You seem to be forgetting that our mother is a schizophrenic, Collier. Her behaviour will never be predictable. You're setting yourself up for disaster if you think otherwise." He softened his tone, saying, "I don't want you to be hurt, dear heart, you're too vulnerable. Too goddamned vulnerable."

Collier got up and turned her back to him. That way he wouldn't see the torment on her face. But when she spoke again, her voice was cold. "Thank you for the warning, Leland. I promise not to make any decision about this without consulting you first."

"Collier"—Leland was on his feet—"I didn't mean to upset you."

"I'm tired. I'm going to bed."

"I was only trying—"

"I don't want to talk about it anymore tonight."

She left him standing there, staring after her, their discussion unresolved.

In spite of their argument, the days flowed easily into one another, until the morning Cleavon burst onto the terrace and interrupted their breakfast. Startled, Collier leapt up from her chair.

"It's war, Miss Collier!" he shouted. "It has started just as I feared it would."

"What are you talking about?" She could barely get the words out of her mouth.

"Cuba. The Americans have landed on Cuba."

"Holy Christ!" Leland grabbed hold of Cleavon's sleeve. "Tell me everything you know."

The young man cast a pointed look at Collier. "For the past month, we have been monitoring all of the broadcasts throughout the Caribbean on a short-wave radio Miss Collier purchased for us, and this morning, during one of our routine sweeps of the airwaves, we picked up the broadcast from Cuba. It was a catastrophe. A group of Cuban exiles with the support of the United States government landed at *Playa Giron* and were nearly massacred by Cuban troops."

"What's *Playa Giron?*" Collier demanded.

"The Bay of Pigs," Cleavon told her. "I chose not to wait for further details, I felt you should be informed of this as quickly as possible. I must return to town now. My people have been terribly frightened by this and my father will need my help in keeping them calm." He bowed to Collier and began backing toward the door. "I apologize for having disturbed your breakfast."

No sooner was Cleavon out the door than Leland was heading for the phone.

Collier sat down hard in her seat, stunned.

"What's wrong?" Diana whispered, her eyes growing round. "What's happened?"

Collier reached out to pat the hands which were suddenly trying to shred a cloth napkin. "Nothing's wrong, Mother. One of the men from the town came to tell us about some trouble he had heard about, and Leland's just gone into the house to use the telephone."

"Is Leland in trouble?"

"No, dear, no. Leland's not in trouble."

"We're in trouble then." Diana's voice was rising. "Something bad is going to happen and you don't want me to know."

"No, Mother, nothing bad is going to happen, I promise."

Diana pushed Collier's hand away.

"We're safe here," Collier tried again to calm her mother down. "Nothing can hurt you as long as you're with me. This is my island, my home. You're safe here. We all are."

Now Diana was trying to get out of her chair.

Collier began to panic. She could recognize the warning signs. Her mother was slipping again, losing control. *Not now, dear God,* she prayed, *not now. Not so soon. It isn't fair. Give us some more time together. Please don't do this to her now.*

Collier got out of her chair and tried to keep Diana in hers. "Stay where you are, Mother, please. Just stay where you are. I'm going to get you some medicine."

She raced into the house and into the bathroom in her mother's guest suite. Flinging open the medicine chest, she gathered up all the bottles she could find and hurried back out to the terrace.

"Mother!"

Diana was not in her chair. Collier dropped the bottles onto the table and ran into the garden.

"Mother!"

Diana was sitting cross-legged on the ground under one of the large oleanders, sniffing on a flower.

Collier dropped to her knees. Lifting her mother's head, she anxiously searched her face. Her eyes were blank. Her face was masklike again. Even the color seemed to be draining out of it. Collier wanted to scream and cry at the same time, but she did neither. Instead, she scooped her mother up in her arms and carried her into the house.

She put her down on her bed and went out to the terrace for the medication, bumping into Leland as he came out of his own room.

"I'm going to have to leave," he told her brusquely. "Can I borrow the chopper?"

She nodded.

"Please forgive me for running out on you this way, but I've got no choice."

"I know." Her voice was hollow.

Before she could tell him about Diana, he hurried back into his room and started to pack.

Following the list of instructions prepared by the doctors at Fairwood, she gave her mother all the prescribed medication and then got her into bed. She wondered if she should contact Fairwood or even fly in a doctor from Miami. But as she watched Diana drift off to sleep, she decided to wait, hoping the crisis would be short-lived.

She had one of the maids sit with Diana while she went to see Leland off. She couldn't take a chance on leaving her mother completely alone.

"I'm supposed to meet the chopper at the pad in ten minutes," Leland told her as he came out of his room carrying a small suitcase and his portable tape recorder.

She knew this was no time to tell him about Diana, but she was feeling abandoned, first by her mother and now by him. She wanted to tell him that she was frightened—for him, for their mother and for their world which seemed intent on destroying itself. She wanted to tell him not to leave her, not to risk his life for someone else's errors of judgment. She wanted to tell him to stay with her and help her keep their mother safe. But in the end, all she said was, "Now I know how Jenny used to feel."

And then he was gone.

Collier thanked all the gods she could think of. Diana's spell passed quickly and two days later, she was back walking the beach. The color began to return to her face and her eyes grew clearer again. But, in spite of her swift recovery, Collier was still worried about her. She was also worried about Leland. She had received no word from him at all.

Five days after Leland's abrupt departure, Diana seemed to forget all about him. She even stopped asking Collier when he would be coming back. That evening, after their usual early dinner together, Collier sat her mother down in one of the wicker chairs on the patio, so that they could look out at the ocean. Diana loved to watch the movement of the waves. She would sit in her chair without moving a muscle, staring at the sea, until it grew dark and it was time for bed.

As Collier watched her mother sitting there so peacefully, she found herself beginning to make plans. Knowing how much Diana loved lily-of-the-valley perfume, she thought of redecorating her suite in lily-of-the-valley wallpaper, with matching fabric for the curtains, bedspread and reading chair. She wondered if Selma Bryce would approve of the gay floral chintz in the suite she would occupy—*if*, after being discharged from the hospital, she was capable of looking after Diana again, and *if* she agreed to live on St. Cristobal. Collier felt a comforting warmth spread through her. Her dream of keeping Diana with her seemed closer than ever to coming true.

Diana's soft voice cut into Collier's thoughts. "Will you read me some more of my book tonight?" she asked without turning her head.

"Wouldn't you like me to start your other book instead?"

"No. That one's my favorite."

Collier gently squeezed her mother's shoulder. "I'll read whatever you want, you know that."

Diana's obsession was a book called *The Water Babies*, a charming bit of whimsy about two British children who are lost and stumble upon a mermaid kingdom under the sea. It was one of two books Diana had brought down with her—the other was *Alice in Wonderland*—and Collier read to her mother each evening to help her fall asleep.

Tonight, Diana was asleep even before Collier could finish a single chapter. She marked the place and put the book back on the table next to her mother's bed. She bent to kiss Diana on the cheek and then turned out the light.

Collier woke up with a start in the middle of the night. Her nightgown was sticking to her body. Her chest was heaving, her pulse racing.

She had heard something.

Or was it only part of a dream?

She sat up in bed and listened carefully. All she could hear was the easy roll of the waves and the hammering of her heart. She threw back the covers and got out of bed. Opening the sliding glass doors, she stepped out onto the terrace.

The sky was clear. The moon was bright. There were no signs of an approaching storm. The air smelled of jasmine and frangipani. And lily-of-the-valley.

The blood froze in Collier's veins.

She ran back into the house and tore down the hall to Diana's room.

The bed was empty. The door to the terrace was wide open.

Collier went out onto the terrace again, switched on the pool lights and forced herself to look down into the water.

The water was turquoise blue and perfectly clear.

She scanned the area around the pool. Nothing. Running

into the kitchen, she flicked on the intercom connecting the house with the servants' cottages and woke everyone up. Then she raced across the garden, straight for the stone steps leading down to the beach.

"Mother!" she screamed the moment her feet touched the sand. "Mother!"

Mother, please let me find you sitting under one of the palm trees. Let me find you kneeling on the beach, wondering why the sand and the sea are always filling in the holes you dig.

"Mother, answer me! It's Collier. Mother, where are you?"

Mother, don't leave me. Not now. Not now. Dear God, I couldn't bear it.

"Mother! Diana! Please!"

She was running up the beach now, scanning the trees, the shoreline, the waves. She caught the glare of a dozen flashlights high on the cliff outside the compound. The staff was searching, too.

She waded into the water, still calling, praying that Diana would answer her from the shore. She walked through the shallows, following the line of the beach, scanning the shore and then turning her head to squint out at the open sea.

She walked deeper into the ocean. It was soon up to her neck. She began to swim. Her arms were leaden, her legs refused to kick. She swallowed a mouthful of water and began to cough. Her nightgown, light as a silken wisp when dry, was like a suit of armor dragging her down. She ripped off the straps. Then, taking a deep breath, she submerged herself and worked the nightgown down over her hips and kicked herself free of it.

She set out again, cutting cleanly through the waves, swimming up and back, up and back, shouting when she had the breath for it.

Exhausted, she finally swam back to shore. She crawled out of the water on her hands and knees and waited, crouched in that position, until she had the strength to stand up again.

Then she staggered down the beach. The beach she and Diana had walked together nearly every day. As she walked, she searched. Every piece of driftwood became a leg or an arm, every fallen coconut a head or part of a torso, a part of her mother.

She heard voices behind her, turned and saw the beams of their flashlights. She started to run. They had the lights. All she had was the moon and her terror. The wind tore at her matted hair, dried the water on her body and chilled her, so that her teeth chattered and her whole body shook as she ran.

The dark patch in the sand loomed larger as she got closer. She saw the arm, and she knew that this time it wasn't going to be a piece of driftwood. She opened her mouth to scream, but no sound came out. Wordlessly, she collapsed beside the figure lying in the sand.

The hem of Diana's nightgown was floating on the tail of the wave which lapped at her ankles. Her hair was pressed in wet curlicues against her face and her eyes were closed. She glistened with water and with sand, and a large web of seaweed lay across her neck and shoulders like a dark lace shawl.

Collier pulled away the seaweed and smoothed back the hair from her mother's cheeks. Then she tugged Diana into her arms.

"They won't hurt you anymore," she whispered in her mother's ear. "I'll never let them hurt you again. I'll take care of you, just as I promised I would. And you'll never have to leave again. You'll stay with me and you'll be safe here. We'll feed the sugar birds and the lizards, and I'll teach you to swim. I never taught you to swim, did I, but I will now. I promise."

She could sense them standing near her, their lights trained on the sand, leaving her alone in the semi-darkness, alone with her nakedness, alone with her mother, alone with her guilt and her grief.

Then she felt something warm and dry settling around her shoulders. She felt a pair of hands reach out to separate her from her mother.

"No!" she screamed, trying to hold onto her. "Don't touch her. She's my mother. I'll take care of her. I promised her I would take care of her and keep her safe. Please don't take her away. Please!"

No one was listening to her. They kept trying to cover her up. She tried again to fight them off, but there were too many hands now.

"Leland!" she screamed. Where was her brother? She needed her brother. They were trying to smother her and someone was hurting Diana. They were taking Diana away and wrapping her in something white and now they were wrapping her in something too.

"Leland! Help me! Help me, Leland, please!"

She felt a pinprick in her arm, and the last thing she saw was the sneer of contempt on the face of the moon.

When she opened her eyes, it was light. She tried to raise her head, but the pain wouldn't allow her to move. The lead weight on her chest extended all the way down to her feet. She couldn't get one part of her body to move. All she could manage to do was turn her face toward the windows. She could feel the warmth of the sun through the glass and see the green of the trees and the flecks of color that were the oleander bushes. Beyond them lay the sea. Collier turned her head away again. She didn't want to think about the sea.

She had killed her mother.

Somehow she found the strength to draw her knees up to her chest. She curled herself into the fetal position, wishing she could slip back into the womb which had thrust her out into the world in the first place. Then they could start all over again. And maybe this time, Collier would know how to do it right.

Later that afternoon, Cleavon was shown into Collier's room. She had had the shutters closed to muffle the sounds of the sea. The room was hot. She didn't care. She didn't want to hear the sea.

"I have been trying to contact Mr. Leland in Cuba," Cleavon told her in a subdued voice. His dark eyes were moist and his hands were clenched at his sides. "So far I have failed. But I will continue to try. I will also contact his newspaper in New York and leave word for him there."

Collier stared up at the young man and tried to find the words to thank him, but all she could manage was a weak nod.

"My people grieve with you, Miss Collier, and we are all praying for you."

She didn't even hear him leave.

Two days later, Leland returned to St. Cristobal. At sunset, he stood with Collier in a small grove of oleanders overlooking the sea. He kept his arm around her waist while the minister from Bonnyport's one church delivered a brief eulogy. At the end of the service, Leland helped Collier scatter a handful of oleander petals over the top of the simple, dark wood coffin. Then he led her away from the grove before the first spadeful of earth was tossed into Diana's grave.

He took her back to her room and helped her into bed. She

hadn't spoken to him once. All she could do was look into his eyes for the blame she knew she would find there. But she could see only his grief.

He reached down to turn out the light. She pushed his hand away. He left the light on. As he turned to leave, she called out his name and beckoned him over to her. She pointed to the book lying on the table next to her bed and he picked it up.

"Read to me," she whispered.

He sat down on the edge of the bed and turned to the first chapter of *The Water Babies* and began to read.

Chapter Twenty-five

There was a place where the grief and the guilt blended together, and gradually, Collier no longer tried to separate them. She simply lay in bed and gave in to the war being fought within her, refusing to take sides, refusing to even fight back.

Two weeks after Diana's death, Collier finally abandoned the stifling solitude of her bedroom and traded it for brief morning strolls around the compound and afternoon naps beside the pool in the same lounge chair Diana had used. Then, each evening, just before sunset, she would sit on the ground in front of the simple headstone marking her mother's grave, and read aloud one chapter from *The Water Babies*.

With each passing day, the agony which raged through her like a high fever, grew cooler, until it burned itself out. Soon, all that was left of the pain was a gentle wash of remorse. When Collier read the final page of *The Water Babies*, she walked over to the top of the stone steps leading down to the beach, and hurled the book into the sea.

It was time for her to put her life back together again.

She had been out of touch with the world for five weeks, and now she sensed a new urgency in herself. In the face of her mother's death, she realized how much she wanted to live.

She sorted through the mail she had neglected for five weeks and came across an invitation to an opening at the Kincaid Gallery, the gallery where she had mounted Milo's exhibit ten years before. The photograph on the invitation fascinated her. It was a photo of a circular painting, resembling a brilliantly colored archery target, apparently painted in acrylics. She had never heard of the artist before. Ellsworth Kelly. She looked at the date on the invitation. She had missed the opening by four days, but the exhibition itself would still be on.

It was May. New York was green and flamboyant and giddy with sunshine in May. It didn't take her long to make up her mind. She was packed within the hour.

265

• • •

Wally Kincaid no longer owned the gallery on Madison, but the new owner, a young man from New Jersey, had decided to keep the name Kincaid anyway.

"It's much classier than Jerkovic, don't you think?" confided Casimir Jerkovic to Collier, as he led her into the front room filled with Kellys. "I wasn't too sure about these, but I thought I'd take a chance. I've only sold three of them so far. Everyone's been complaining that they're too artificial, that it looks like he used a ruler or some tape to keep his lines so straight. So what if he did! Look at Mondrian, for God's sake. I guess people just aren't ready for the Kellys of this world."

Collier found herself intrigued by the hard-edged perfection of the canvases, their geometric designs and their bold, primary colors. They possessed a startling clarity which vibrated with a strange kind of electricity.

"If you like Kelly," Jerkovic continued, "you'll adore Frank Stella and Leon Polk Smith."

"And where would I find them?" Collier wanted to know.

Jerkovic's smile was almost lascivious. "In the back room."

When Collier left the Kincaid Gallery two hours later, she had purchased four Kellys, five Stellas and three Smiths. She had a good feeling about these new artists, and she had yet to be faulted for her intuition.

She located a pay phone on the corner and called the *New York Times*. Leland, she was told, was in Rockport. Her stomach lurched. Rockport. Had he and Jenny made up? Were they back together again?

Her fingers could barely dial "O." Her voice was suddenly so hoarse that she had to repeat Jenny's number three times before the harassed operator could understand her. She didn't even have any change for the call. She felt like a fool reversing the charges. Jenny answered the phone and without any hesitation, accepted the call. Collier hastily told her where she was and what she was doing there and then asked about Leland.

For a second, Jenny's voice sounded indistinct and then it cleared again. Leland had picked up the extension.

"You're back together again," Collier blurted out.

It was Leland who broke the awkward silence which followed her outburst. "Not quite."

The pitching in Collier's stomach intensified. Out came a

small "Oh." It was half-question and half-exclamation.

"I'm pregnant," Jenny said.

The receiver slipped out of Collier's hand and slammed into the glass. She lunged for it, missed it as it swung past her, then managed to grab it as it bounced off the glass again.

"Are you still there?" Leland demanded.

"I'm sorry. I dropped the phone." Her face was burning.

"I just found out about it." Leland sounded as if he were still in shock.

"I knew about it in February," Jenny put in, "just before my opening in Boston. I went to New York for an abortion and then I changed my mind."

Visions of standing on Jenny's porch in the cold, knocking on the door, flashed through Collier's mind. The empty house, the phone which had kept on ringing. Jenny in some sleazy back room in a tenement, stretched out on a table with a sheet draped over it. Jenny hemorrhaging to death.

"Collier?" It was Jenny again. "I'm fine, really I am. I decided I wanted to keep the baby, and I'm not sorry at all. I want this child very, very much. Just think, I'll finally have someone all my own to love."

Collier searched her blank mind for something to say, but nothing sounded appropriate.

"I'm sorry I waited so long to tell you," Jenny continued, "but up until a few days ago, I didn't even want to tell Leland. Then I decided that since this is his child too, he had a right to know."

"I've asked Jennifer to marry me."

"And I've said no."

Collier wished she had a chair. She needed to sit down.

"Why, Jenny?" she mumbled incoherently. "Why did you say no when this is what you've wanted all along?"

"Because, as I told you that day on the beach, I don't want to settle for the bits and pieces. I want *all* of someone. Leland won't be any different if we're married. I'll still be settling for bits of him and pieces of his time. Well, the piece of him growing inside me is a piece I'll get to keep, and some day I'll find someone who's willing to take on both of us full-time."

"Leland?" Collier wanted to know how he was taking this.

"I'll hang up," Jenny offered, "so the two of you can talk."

"I don't blame her for refusing a second-hand kind of pro-posal," Leland was saying. "I wasn't willing to marry her before, so why should I expect her to be flattered by an offer that's being made simply because she's four months pregnant?"

"I'm not concerned with Jenny's reactions, Leland," she cut him short. "I'm concerned about you. Tell me how you're feeling."

"Confused, hurt, angry," he admitted. "I think I've run the entire gamut of emotions since she phoned and told me about it yesterday. I guess I'll continue swinging back and forth for a while until I get used to the idea that the mother of our child isn't interested in marrying the father." He gave a wry sort of chuckle. "This is quite the switch, isn't it? I'm willing to cut back and settle a bit and Jennifer's not interested. I suppose she figures I might be fine for a while, but that I'll eventually start chafing at the domestic bit and look for another war to cover."

"She's right, though, isn't she?"

"As a matter of fact, there's trouble right now in some godforsaken corner of Southeast Asia no one but the French have cared about. I'm heading over there in ten days."

"Where now?" She could hardly conceal the exasperation in her voice.

"Vietnam," he answered. "The U.S. government has been sending advisors over there for some time now, and there's talk of the area turning into another Korea one day."

"Nothing changes but the name of the country and the names of the victims," she murmured, suddenly feeling very tired and very old.

This time it was Leland who cut her short. "I'm going to be spending the next few days here with Jennifer, so if you're through buying out the galleries in New York, why don't you give Boston a try? You're welcome to stay here, you know that." He turned away from the phone for a moment and then came back on the line again. "Jennifer's nodding her head. She's insisting that you come."

"With both of you insisting like that, I'd be a fool to refuse."

Collier had been in Rockport for three days, and it seemed to her that all she had done so far was stuff herself on shrimp and lobster and sit on a different wharf each day and watch the local artists paint varying views of the same harbor scene. Leland and Jenny were out looking for furniture at a flea market for what would eventually be the baby's room, and Collier was trying to decide whether or not to take a walk along the rocks, when there was a knock at the door.

She swung open the screen door and looked down at a short, squat man with inky black hair and the physique of a onetime boxer.

"Collier Paget-Browne?" the man said.

"Yes?"

Without another word, he thrust a bulky white document, neatly folded in four, into her hand. Nodding to her, he turned and walked back toward the car waiting for him at the curb.

Stunned, she stared after him until the car had driven away. Then she glanced down at the papers she was holding. The bold black words typed out across the legal backing seemed to assume a life of their own as they leapt from the page and fastened themselves around her throat.

It was happening all over again.

She backed into the house and just managed to close the door.

She felt all the air being sucked out of her body.

PAGET-BROWNE v. PAGET-BROWNE

She read the heading over and over again, trying to absorb it.

APPLICATION TO HAVE DEFENDANT DECLARED INCOMPETENT (NON COMPOS MENTIS)

With mounting horror, she turned to the first page of the application.

> . . . that Collier Paget-Browne, hereinafter referred to as DEFENDANT, be committed for an indeterminate length of stay to a mental institution for observation and confinement . . . and that Addison Sargent Paget-Browne, hereinafter referred to as PLAINTIFF, be appointed guardian to DEFENDANT's person and personal assets until such time . . .

The papers dropped from her hands. She covered her ears to muffle her outraged cries, but she could still hear them as they echoed in her brain.

Addison was trying to have her declared insane!

He wanted her locked away so that he and Elinor could gain control of her father's estate.

They wanted her locked away forever while they gloated

over the pieces and collected what they thought was theirs.

A woman wearing a wool dress and a sweater thrown over her shoulders would dole out bits of oblivion to her forever.

Bars on the windows and a window in the door.

She fell to her knees and began crawling toward the bathroom. A wave of nausea spiraled through her, but she fought it back down. The black noise roared in her ears and the great green dots exploded, one after another, behind her eyes. The wave rose up in her throat again, and again she fought it back down.

Her skin was wet and clammy as she collapsed on the cold tile floor, with her head against the porcelain bowl.

She finally gave in to the sickness surging through her.

Chapter Twenty-six

One week later, Collier came face to face with her brother Addison for the first time in her adult life.

The boy of two was now a man of thirty-three. He was as dark as she was fair, as short as she was tall, a replica of his mother as Collier was of her father. Impeccably dressed in a navy blue pin-stripe suit, a white shirt and a navy blue and maroon striped tie, he seemed, to Collier, to be the epitome of moneyed grace and style. The one piece of jewelry he wore was a heavy gold signet ring which she immediately recognized as her father's. As she saw him toying with the ring, her own fingers closed protectively over the watch hanging on the chain around her neck.

They were meeting in court, in the private chambers of Judge Harlan Tewes. Collier, her hands clasped tightly in her lap, sat stiffly to the left of her attorney, John Ender. To John's right was Dirwood Fitzpatrick, Addison's attorney, and next to him sat Addison himself. All of them were facing the balding fifty-five-year-old justice with the darting brown eyes and the professionally passive features.

Just as she had been separated from Elinor by two attorneys and a distance of some twenty feet in a Boston courtroom thirty-two years before, Collier was now separated from Addison by two different attorneys and a distance of only eight feet. But the battlelines defined and drawn were no different. Neither were the reasons for them. Where was Elinor today? Collier wondered. She let out a bitter sigh of resignation and then she promised herself that she would clamp her mouth around her feelings from that moment on. Over and over she repeated the vow she had made as a nine-year-old child. The Brahmins of Boston would never laugh at her again.

Addison dug his fingers into the arms of his chair and tried not to look at her. That profile. So strong. That square chin. That damned pride she wore as casually as those slacks she had on. He shifted in his seat. The sun glinted off the gold in

271

her hair and gilded her deep tan. His heart lifted when he thought of how he was going to destroy her.

Judge Tewes shuffled the last set of papers in front of him and cleared his throat.

"Because of the seriousness of a charge of non compos mentis and the urgency apparent in Plaintiff's motion, and because of the parties involved in this particular action, I agreed to this preliminary hearing this morning. Such a procedure is not without precedent; in fact, it usually serves to expedite matters. The purpose of such a hearing is to allow counsel for the plaintiff to present the kind of evidence, both in expert testimony and physical proof, upon which he intends to build his case. If, at the end of his presentation, I find the evidence sufficiently strong as to warrant a formal trial, I will order a date to be so inscribed. If, however, I find the evidence fails to prove the merits of the motion, I will dismiss the action. Is this clearly understood by both parties?"

"It is, Your Honor," Ender and Fitzpatrick responded together.

"Very well, then, you may proceed, Mr. Fitzpatrick."

Dirwood Fitzpatrick got to his feet. "Your Honor, we intend to show through expert testimony, eyewitness accounts, photographs and the actions of the defendant herself that Collier Paget-Browne is unfit to retain control of the Paget-Browne family fortune, that she is unfit to continue in her capacity as president of Paget-Browne Enterprises, that she is incompetent in areas requiring sound judgment, and that justice would be best served if she were placed in a remedial setting and Plaintiff assigned the rights of guardian until such time as she is deemed fit to return to society and resume her responsibilities."

Collier stared straight ahead of her. As the man droned on, she pretended that this was all a dream, and that if she concentrated hard enough and used all of her will, she would wake up safe on her island again.

Addison leaned forward in his seat. Her mask had slipped. She actually looked unhappy. He sat back in the chair again and crossed his legs. He moistened his lips with the tip of his tongue. *Just wait,* he told her silently, gleefully. *Wait until the charges are read out loud. They'll sound much more effective than they looked on paper.*

"The defendant's own history is one of mental illness, which has claimed her mother, her maternal grandmother and her maternal great-grandmother. The defendant herself is suffering from this same illness, known today as schizophrenia, and we shall prove through expert psychiatric testimony that her erratic behavior and lack of judgment are direct results of this affliction. We shall also prove, through eyewitness accounts and through photographs, that the defendant has used illegal drugs, engaged in group sex and committed one of the most grievous of all moral sins—that of incest with her half-brother, Leland Taggert."

Collier bit down hard on her bottom lip. This was the cruelest blow of all. It took all of her self-control to remain seated in her chair. She tasted blood. She had broken the skin on her lip.

Leland was waiting for her in Rockport. At her insistence he hadn't accompanied her. As much as she wanted him with her, she couldn't risk providing Addison with any more ammunition for a case which was already so strong that she could hear the slamming of that windowed door each time she drew a breath.

Perspiration broke out all over Addison's body. He saw her with her legs wrapped around that other brother, her mouth open against his. The bastard. He would destroy them both. He thought of Mary Beth, that millstone around his neck, dragging him down. He thought of his sons, two of them now, Andrew and Edward. They were more than worth the agony it had caused him to produce them. His sons would save him. And ruin her.

"Eleven years ago, the plaintiff engaged the services of a private investigator to monitor the activities of the defendant. The photographs I am submitting to you, Your Honor, for your consideration, are the results of his surveillance."

Collier began to shake. She pressed her legs together to keep her knees from knocking. He had spied on her. Addison had had someone follow her around the world just to spy on her. She had probably even paid for the man herself. How much of her private life had been photographed by someone who had been stalking her all these years? She felt as if she had been raped, her life violated for eleven years.

She looked at Addison again. His face was flushed. A muscle was twitching beside his left eye. Was he embarrassed? Was he ashamed of what he was doing to her? He wouldn't turn to meet her eyes. Something had come over him. He seemed agitated. She frowned, wondering what was going on behind those icy blue eyes of his.

Addison crossed and re-crossed his legs. He could feel her staring at him. He tried to burrow deep inside himself so that she couldn't follow him, but the heat betrayed him. It surged up from his groin and spread through his body and stained his skin red. If she kept on watching him that way, she would know. A leaden hammer began banging away at his guts.

She heard Fitzpatrick read the names of the doctors prepared to certify her and lock her away. Neither her money nor her name would be able to save her then. Addison would win, just as Elinor had said he would. Then Fitzpatrick listed those ready to swear to her promiscuity and her drug taking. She heard the name of Paul Caitlin and she couldn't sit still any longer.

"Lies!" she shouted. "They're all lies!"

"Miss Paget-Browne, please sit down!" barked Judge Tewes.

"They're lying and they've paid people off with my own money to get them to lie for them!"

"Mr. Ender, please ask your client to sit down!"

"No!" Collier roared, pushing John Ender out of her way. "I will *not* sit down and I will *not* allow my attorney to muzzle me. I'm the one being accused and I'll be the one to defend myself."

"Miss Paget-Browne," Tewes said in a more reasonable tone, "counsel for the plaintiff is not through presenting his evidence. When he is, providing your counsel agrees, of course, I will hear what you have to say."

Somewhat mollified, Collier finally sat down again.

She was breaking. The façade was cracking. He was getting through to her. It was not his shame now but the promise of victory which continued to darken Addison's face. He felt so lightheaded he could have gotten up and danced. Her agony was freeing him and trapping her. He was close now, so very close. He smiled as Fitzpatrick droned on.

"Miss Paget-Browne," the judge was addressing her. "If you wish, you may speak now. Counsel for the plaintiff has finished his presentation."

Collier stood up, drawing herself up to her full height, and stared directly at Addison. She watched him flinch. That made her smile. When she began to speak, her voice was deep and strong and completely controlled.

"Your Honor, my brother Addison is attempting to label

me unstable, incompetent and mad. What some call unstable, others call adventurous. What some call incompetent, others call daring. What some consider to be madness, others prefer to call vision. I am neither unstable, incompetent nor mad. I am what most people would call a maverick.

"For every witness my brother calls upon to perjure himself by damning me, I will call a dozen to tell the truth and praise me. Am I to be committed to an institution for the crime of being born first? Am I to be held accountable for a father's love which saw him entrust his name and his fortune to a daughter because he had no son? Am I to be blamed for the illness of a mother when, for forty years, I have led a productive life, free of medication, free of doctors and free of hospitals?"

Addison was sweating again. He took out his handkerchief and blotted his forehead and his chin. She had tricked him. She hadn't crumbled at all. It has all been an act, all of it, just to get the judge's attention and his sympathy. She was turning everything around. The hatred curdled his saliva and turned it to bile.

"I have helped a large family corporation expand and prosper. Is this incompetence? I have built an art center to support young and talented American artists. Is this incompetence? I have encouraged the native population of a small Caribbean island to build a future for themselves. Is this madness? I have amassed one of the largest private collections of twentieth century American art, promoting obscure men who are now being hailed as geniuses. Is this madness?"

Addison was furious. Why wasn't Fitzpatrick saying anything? Why was the judge allowing her to continue? Why weren't they stopping her? He had to make her shut up. She was ruining it. Ruining it.

"How would you define madness, Your Honor? Wouldn't you consider applying that very label to someone who has spent a lifetime denying reality, denying the truth and choosing instead to extort, connive and cheat in order to regain what he wrongly believes he once lost? My brother, Addison, has spent his life using every available means to try to separate me from the inheritance he believes my father should have left to him. Your Honor, my father had no son until one hour before his own death. Should I be locked away because of my brother's delusions? Should I be asked to sacrifice myself because of my brother's destructive greed? If we define madness as the inability to distinguish between reality and illusion, Your Honor, who would you say is the mad one, he or I?"

Addison was out of his chair. He lunged for Collier, his hands reaching for her throat. His fingers dug deep into her flesh. His blue eyes were infused with blood and his mouth was drawn back in a savage snarl.

"I'll kill you, I'll kill you!" he shouted as both attorneys worked to pry him away from Collier. "I'll lock you up and they'll never let you out again. You bitch, I'll kill you for what you've done to me!"

"Mr. Fitzpatrick!" bellowed Tewes, slamming his fist down on his desk. "Control your client or I'll have him ejected from my chambers!"

Fitzpatrick flung Addison into his chair and held him there.

Shaken, Collier sank down into her own chair again and began to rub her neck. She was certain that in a few hours, ten deep red marks would appear and circle her throat like a jagged rope of beads.

Addison was panting. He shook the hair out of his eyes and fumbled for his handkerchief again. He wanted her dead. Nothing short of her death would satisfy him. His fingers burned from the touch of her skin. He could smell her all around him, on his fingers, on his face, in his hair. He thought about dying then. He thought about dying with the scent of her all around him.

"If you have all recovered from this disruption, I would like to proceed." Tewes trained his stern gaze on Collier. She faced him squarely, wondering, as their eyes met, if there wasn't the slightest hint of a twinkle in his. "Have you finished, Miss Paget-Browne, or did you wish to continue?"

She cleared her throat and swallowed hard before replying. "After my brother's outburst, anything I might add would only be redundant, Your Honor."

Tewes steepled his fingers together and leaned across his desk. "In a matter as delicate and complex as this one, I would prefer not to hand down an immediate decision. Therefore, I will take the case under advisement and render my judgment as to the merits of the action one week from today." He got up from his chair, signaling an end to the hearing.

With Fitzpatrick tugging him out of his chair and practically shoving him out of the room, Addison had only a moment to glance back at her. *Look at me, damn it,* he wanted to shout.

Look at the face of the man who will see you dead. He felt like weeping. She was ignoring him. She was leaning back in her chair with her eyes closed, ignoring him. He would punish her for that. He would make her pay.

Collier waited until Addison and Fitzpatrick had gone. Then she turned to Ender. "How strong is their case?" she asked. him.

The attorney shook his head. "Pretty damned strong, I'm afraid. We can deal with the expert testimony without too much difficulty, but it's the photographs that worry me. Addison must have paid that detective a fortune over the years to pile up that kind of evidence against you. You can read whatever you want into the pictures, but they're suggestive enough to convince your average judge and jury."

Collier felt dead inside. She had no emotions left to draw on now except her pride. "I feel dirty, John," she confided. "I feel like filth. And if we fight this out in an open court, I'm going to be humiliated all over again. I can't let that happen, not when I've spent my entire life trying to preserve the dignity and the sanctity of the name of Paget-Browne. I'm my father's daughter, John, and I won't allow my name to be sullied again. I won't go through another trial."

"What do you suggest we do then?"

"All Addison wants is money. I'm willing to pay him off, no matter what the amount, to get him out of my life once and for all."

"You're probably talking millions."

"I *have* millions, John. This is my life at stake. And if millions will stop him, then I'll give him millions. I will not risk being institutionalized. I will not risk having my father's company destroyed through Addison's incompetence. I will not have my art collection sold, the Center closed, the island disintegrate. Addison will not destroy me. He won't destroy what I've done. Even if it means relinquishing half of my fortune, I don't care. I'll pay any price to be free."

"But Addison wants the whole pie. If he believes he has a chance to get it, why should he settle for a slice, no matter how generous it is?"

"Because he's afraid."

"I don't understand."

"Addison will only push this if he's convinced I won't fight back. Now he knows I will. I can reach more people than he

can and I can pay them more than he can. But there's something
else. He's hiding something, John, and I intend to find out
what it is. We've been given a week?" John nodded his head.
"I'm giving you two days. Find Paul Caitlin for me."

Two days later, John Ender arrived at Collier's hotel with
a surly Paul Caitlin in tow. It had been fairly easy to locate
the onetime sculptor who framed paintings for a living and
lived in a room behind the shop he owned near the harbor.
Everyone in the area knew Paul Caitlin. He still boasted about
having made it with that rich bitch Collier Paget-Browne, hint-
ing that she'd given him the money to start up his own business.
Most people believed him. Since he never sold any of his
sculptures, how else could he have afforded his shop?

Collier had wondered how she might react when she confronted Paul Caitlin again. She had imagined herself feeling
everything from revulsion to rage. But when she opened the
door of her room and saw him standing there with John's hand
clamped firmly around his arm, she felt absolutely nothing.
Paul, on the other hand, appeared annoyed and ill-at-ease.
Collier thought she even detected a look of panic in his bleary
eyes.

He was obviously high on something. His movements were
jerky, his hands were trembling. Wearing a short sleeved print
shirt over a pair of patched jeans, with his blond hair and
beard long and straggly, he looked like a scruffy beachcomber
sorely out of place in such lavish surroundings.

Collier led the way through the bedroom into the large sitting
room and directed Paul to a chair near the window. She and
John settled themselves on the sofa opposite him. Without
wasting any time on preliminaries, Collier came straight to the
point.

"I need some answers from you, Mr. Caitlin," she said,
refusing to even consider calling him by his first name.

Paul Caitlin leaned back in his chair and casually crossed
his legs. "I don't have any answers to give you."

"That's where you're wrong."

"No, bitch!" he snapped, "that's where *you're* wrong."

"How dare you—"

"It's all right, John." Collier patted her attorney on the knee.
He looked so prim in his three-piece suit, wearing that scowl

of righteous indignation on his face. She felt sorry for him, having to be there and hear all this. "Mr. Caitlin's just a little hostile this morning."

"You're damned right I'm hostile," he retorted. "You had no business dragging me up here like this. I've got nothing to say to you."

"I think you do," Collier insisted, keeping her voice down.

"You ruined me!" he shouted at her.

"Did I?"

"You're goddamned right you did! I was good."

"You were mediocre."

"You made sure not one gallery would touch me."

"People would have stopped buying you sooner or later."

Paul's mouth dropped. He was fuming and she was sitting there as calm as you please. For a moment, he said nothing. He simply sat in his chair, studying the backs of his hands. Finally, he said,

"You willing to deal?"

His question took Collier by surprise.

"You willing to trade?" he persisted. "My information for your lifting the ban on my work."

"I don't think I care for that deal, Mr. Caitlin," she said.

"That's okay with me then," he shrugged. "But you don't get your answers."

Collier took out a cigar and lit it. "Let me think about it," she countered.

"Not good enough."

"Don't push me, young man," she warned him. "I can make life very uncomfortable for you."

"You already have."

"Think of it as only the beginning."

Something in the way her eyes were getting darker made him shudder. He began to lose some of his cockiness. This lady was no one to mess around with, and it was too bad he hadn't found that out a little sooner.

"Just what do you want to know?" he mumbled, looking down at his hands again.

"Did my brother pay you to get me up to your apartment that night?"

"You could say he was behind it," Paul said, picking at a scab on one of his fingers. "Some guy who said he was a private eye working for your brother came to me with the deal."

"And you were supposed to drug me and photograph me?"

"I drugged you, he took the pictures."

"That's all that happened?"

"If you mean did we all make it with you, the answer's no. He told us to just make it look real."

Collier took a deep pull on her cigar. At least they hadn't raped her. She was grateful for that.

"There goes some of the evidence," John muttered under his breath.

"And one witness," Collier added.

"You're not going to work your way through the entire list of witnesses, are you?" John's brown eyes were widening at the thought of it. "We've only got five more days before—"

"Shh." She held a finger to his lips. "Just wait. " She turned to Paul again. "How did you meet my brother?"

"I worked as his chauffeur for a few months."

"Did he know that you had been a student at the Center?"

"Yeah, he eventually found out about that." Paul looked uncomfortable. He began shifting around in his chair. "Your brother's one hell of a weird character," he told her, "one really kinky dude."

Collier leaned forward expectantly, resting her elbows on her knees. She was getting close. Close to what she needed to save herself. Close to what she would have to use if she wanted to win this awful battle with Addison. She glanced at John. He was starting to look embarrassed.

"Why do you say my brother's weird?" she asked Paul, hating the way he was controlling this now, feeding out his answers, bit by tantalizing bit.

"He used to get me to play these games." Paul was staring down at the floor now.

"What kind of games?"

"I had this room over the garage, you see, and every night at nine, I'd check to see if he was standing at one of the windows up in the big house. If he was, I'd open up the curtains and do this strip for him."

Collier grimaced.

John was now struggling to loosen the knot in his tie.

Paul began to scratch at his beard.

"Is that all you did for him?" persisted Collier.

"Look, can we work something out," Paul pleaded, "I don't—"

"What else did you do for my brother, Mr. Caitlin?" Collier shouted, finally losing her patience.

"I sucked him off!" Paul shouted back, his face flushing angrily. "That's right, the guy's queer. He's a goddamned faggot! He never touched me though, I'm no queer, he just wanted it done to him. Look, he paid and I needed the bread. Sometimes I'd use this whip on him, some fucking plastic whip left over from a costume party he'd had when he was a kid. Would you believe it? I'd whack him with this kid's whip and he'd be on his knees creaming all over the place."

John got up and went to pour himself a glass of water from the carafe in the bedroom. His face was now as red as his hair.

Collier grabbed an ashtray and viciously ground out her cigar. So this was Addison's terrible secret. This was what he had counted on keeping hidden from her. Poor Addison. Collier pictured him as an angry child, holding onto a plastic whip. Was this his way of punishing himself for being who he was, just as he kept punishing her because of who she was?

Did Elinor know about her precious son? Did she know that he was hiding his shame behind Mary Beth Kelly's skirts, behind the respectable veneer of marriage, behind the two sons he had produced to prove he was every bit a Paget-Browne, the true heir, capable of siring other male heirs?

Paul was squirming in his chair like a worm at the end of a hook. John came back to the sofa with a second glass of water and refused to meet Collier's eyes as he sat down again. Poor John, she thought. He was forty-seven years old, but from the expression on his face, he looked more like a teenager being told about the nastier facts of life for the first time.

Collier fixed Paul with an icy stare. "Would you be willing to testify for me instead of for my brother if this case goes to trial?" she asked him.

He stopped his fidgeting. "What's in it for me?"

"What's it worth to you?"

"Like I told you before, I'm a sculptor. I want to sell whatever I turn out. Spread the word that I'm not poison anymore, and we've got ourselves a deal."

Collier shook her head. "Sorry. What I did, I did for myself. It had nothing to do with my brother."

Paul hauled himself out of his chair and ambled toward the door. "Then I guess I'll be leaving now."

Collier's voice stopped him in his tracks. "I'll pay you

double what my brother paid you, if you put everything you've just told me down in writing." She turned to John again. "If you witness what he writes, it will be considered notarized, won't it, and therefore admissable as evidence?"

"It would be admissable even without my witnessing it," he told her. "But, Collier—"

She silenced him with a wave of her hand. "That's my deal, Mr. Caitlin, take it or leave it."

With one hand still resting on the doorknob, Paul began to waver.

Collier pressed her advantage. "How much did my brother pay you?"

"Five thousand bucks."

"I'll give you ten."

"When?"

"As soon as you've given me what I want. I need details, names, places, dates, anything you can remember. Then I'll give you a check."

Paul turned away from the door. "Where's some goddamned paper?"

After Paul Caitlin had gone, John dialed the number of the house on Commonwealth Avenue. When Addison came on the line, Collier took the receiver from John and sat down on the bed.

"I don't want to talk to you," Addison cut her off when he heard her voice.

"You don't have to talk, Addison," she said coldly. "Just listen."

"What for?"

"Because I'm sure you'd rather hear it from me than in open court."

Addison's mouth went dry. "All right," he told her, "I'm listening."

"I want you to drop your suit against me."

His snort of laughter set Collier's teeth on edge. "Now why should I do that?" he asked.

"Because I'm telling you to."

"Why? Are you that afraid we're going to win? Are you afraid that performance of yours the other day won't stack up against our evidence? I have no intention of dropping that suit, sister dear. I want what you stole from me."

"I think I can change your mind about that, Addison."

Something in her voice was making him nervous. She was clever. He had to be careful.

"I've just had a most informative little chat with Paul Caitlin, Addison." She paused to allow the effect of her words to sink in. "You probably don't remember him that well, considering all the chauffeurs you've had over the years, but he remembers you."

Addison gasped.

"As a matter of fact," she continued calmly, "he's just signed a document for me which I intend to show to Judge Tewes tomorrow. Or I could wait to see if this case ever goes to court and use it then. Not only will Paul's statement poke a giant hole in your case, Addison, but I'm afraid it's going to ruin you."

Addison's tongue was suddenly too thick for his mouth. "W-what are you talking about?" he stammered.

"I think you know what I'm talking about. And once the papers get hold of it and the Brahmins find out about it, there won't be a stone large enough for you to crawl under."

Addison gulped. She knew. She knew all about him. His whole body was shaking now and his stomach heaved ominously.

"Addison?"

Shut up, shut up, shut up, he wanted to shout at her. He had to think. She was right. If this leaked out, he'd be destroyed. They'd all be destroyed. He thought of his mother. She'd be slapped in the face by every society matron in Boston. He thought of his sons. They'd be bullied and tormented for the rest of their lives. He himself would be laughed out of the company. He'd be drummed out of all his clubs. No one would even be caught being seen with him in the men's room. They'd make him feel like dirt. Everything he'd done to protect himself and to preserve the lousy sanctity of the Paget-Browne name would go down the drain. And all because of her.

"Addison, are you still there?"

He had to say something. "I'm still here," he said in a voice scarcely above a croak. His brain was working furiously. What if she was bluffing? Caitlin was a doper. He could have told her anything. "Just what do you know?" he demanded, trying to sound strong again.

"You want me to spell it out for you, don't you?" Collier was deriving no pleasure from their conversation at all. All she felt was a sickening sense of shame. "Well, I'm not surprised, Addison, it's the same as your wanting to be whipped."

He caught his breath. So she *did* know. That bastard had told her everything. He buried his head in his hands. Tears burned the backs of his eyelids. He couldn't cry now. He couldn't give her the satisfaction of hearing him break down.

"I'll do whatever you want," he finally said, his voice cracking in spite of himself.

Collier relaxed her grip on the receiver. "My attorney will contact yours in the morning. Good-bye, Addison."

He dropped the phone and sank to his knees, sobbing.

Collier hung up quietly. She felt exhausted and she felt soiled. She wanted to open all the windows in the room, strip off her clothes and soak in a tub for a week. But even after doing all that, she doubted she would ever feel completely clean again. She let out a weary sigh. Perhaps all she really needed was a good, stiff drink.

"Let's get out of here, John," she said as she got up slowly from the bed.

"How about trying the bar downstairs?" he suggested, reading her mind.

"What a wonderful idea." She gave him a weak smile.

He took her arm as they walked to the elevator. "Now that Addison's obviously willing to drop the charges," he said, "you're not going to pay him anything, are you?"

"Just because he's lost this fight doesn't mean he won't try again. I intend to pay him, John, to keep him from being too angry a loser, and to keep him from trying something even worse the next time. As I told you once before, I'm willing to pay him anything if it guarantees me some peace."

Leland was with her at the hotel when John called the following afternoon to say that Addison had dropped the charges against her.

"He didn't even say 'thank you' when I handed him your check, though," John said with a chuckle.

"Did you actually expect him to?"

"One can always hope."

Collier had just bought herself what she hoped would be a lifetime of peace for the sum of five million dollars. Three million of it was to be paid directly to Addison, while the other two million were to be deposited in separate trusts for his sons.

When Collier hung up, Leland took her in his arms. "It's over, dear heart," he whispered, pecking her lightly on the mouth. "It's finally over."

"Is it?" she asked him. "Do you really believe it is?"

Diego

1971 – 1978

Chapter Twenty-Seven

The September sun shone into her face as she stood alone at the top of the steps. She shielded her eyes against the glare and anxiously scanned the crowd. She was dressed simply in an ivory wool suit with a long silver fox boa thrown casually across her shoulders. Her blond hair was gathered into a full, swirling topknot with wispy tendrils framing her face and curling at the base of her neck. Her sudden smile brought out the fine lines around her eyes and deepened the creases running from her nose to the outer corners of her strong, wide mouth.

Collier relaxed. He had finally arrived, walking briskly up the steps while a group of reporters hurried after him. He used his silver-topped cane more for effect than necessity, but it was his favorite defense against reporters who got too close to him.

"Forgive me, *querida,* but you know how these tapings can drag on." He kissed Collier on both cheeks and then tucked her arm through his. "You look very beautiful this morning," he murmured, bending closer to whisper the words in her ear. Then, he held the glass door open for her and she walked into the foyer ahead of him.

Today marked the fifteenth anniversary of the opening of the Collier Paget-Brown Center for Fine Arts. Thousands of young artists had walked in and out of these same glass doors. Their works had hung on the walls, filled the corridors and spilled out into the gardens. A new wing had been added to the building four years before to accommodate the continually increasing enrollment of art students from all across the country.

Collier squeezed the arm of the man standing next to her and he gave her a broad wink. Even out of the sun she felt warm. Warmed by his presence, warmed by his touch. For a moment he seemed distracted. Then she saw why. Leland was on his way over to them.

"Leland, *buenos días,*" he called out, shaking the younger man's hand. "Is this not a proud day for your sister?"

Leland grinned. "From the look on her face, I'd say the Center was the furthest thing from her mind."

Collier flushed. At fifty-one, she felt like a schoolgirl. And the man who made her feel that way was fifty-eight. She returned her brother's hug and kissed him lightly on the mouth.

"You're blushing, dear heart," he whispered.

"Don't those reporter's eyes ever miss anything?" she retorted.

"Not up this close, they don't. Even without my glasses, I can still spot something deeper than an island tan."

Collier still couldn't get used to seeing Leland in glasses. It was further proof that time was passing and they were aging. Sometimes the swift flight of the years frightened her to the point of panic. In spite of her money, in spite of her name, in spite of her achievements, time was the one thing over which she had no control.

She spent too much of her time these days reminiscing. That itself was a sign of incipient old age. She would keep going back over her life, sorting out all the details, putting them into the proper perspective and then trying to get comfortable with them. Each time she found the proper place for one memory, she found herself with another one to deal with. There seemed to be so many events to remember, so many people to forget.

Thaddeus had died in 1964. When Collier read his lengthy obituary in *The New York Times,* she learned that he had bequeathed his entire collection of artifacts to the British Museum in Athens. She immediately thought of Gulliver. He would never have to dust them again.

Paul Caitlin had died of an overdose of heroin in 1966. She still felt an occasional twinge of guilt whenever she thought of him, but the part he had played in Addison's attempt to institutionalize her somehow assuaged that guilt.

And then there was Jenny. Jenny who had taken her daughter, Colleen, Collier's godchild and namesake, back to live in the lighthouse at Eastern Point. The lighthouse had been abandoned in 1967 and the site had remained unused. And so it was home again to the thirty-four-year-old woman who had never really wanted to be anything more than a child after all. Leland had slipped into the role of part-time father with an awkwardness he never lost. He was more of a visiting uncle to his child, and yet, in spite of the arrangement, all three seemed strangely content. Jenny continued to successfully exhibit her batiks and soft wool sculptures in many of the East Coast's most prestigious galleries, and she had taught Colleen to paint.

Collier turned to face the photographers grouped about in front of her and gave them her best Collier Paget-Browne smile. It was the smile of a woman who has finally reconciled herself to having them in her life. She had spent all of her fifty-one years in front of the camera but, unlike a model, she had never once gotten paid for it. Her smile widened. Fifty-one years. She had lived for more than half a century, and she was still proving them wrong.

Once again, she found herself drifting back, remembering. . . .

Following her bitter confrontation with Addison, she had returned to St. Cristobal, living out the next few years in relative tranquility, with nothing more than peace on her mind, time on her hands, and monthly visits from Leland. But it was her very complacency, coupled with Thaddeus's death, which finally spurred her into action. She had looked around herself and found to her dismay that she had become what she had deplored most about her late husband: she had become a hoarder. She owned a museum filled with hundreds of works of contemporary American art and she shared it with only a handful of strangers one weekend a year.

She made her decision and acted swiftly.

For the next six years, she divided her time equally between her island and the mainland. She spent January to June on St. Cristobal and July to December touring the United States with selected works from her collection—ranging from her earliest Racine to her latest acquisitions, the optical paintings of Richard Anuszkiewicz, Kenneth Noland and Larry Poons. Each exhibit was mounted for two weeks in twelve major cities, and Collier appeared on all the major talk shows and news programs to promote her tours.

After six years and seventy-two cities, Collier had seen hundreds of thousands of Americans, and she had met Diego Luis Velasquez, the fiery Cuban poet whose writings had chronicled a revolution and inspired a nation. He was the man who had been called the "right arm of Fidel." He was the husband who had seen his wife shot down in the streets of Havana by Batista's men in 1959. He was the father who had watched the

eldest of his two sons die, at the age of nineteen, in the first
disastrous uprising Fidel had led against Batista at Moncado
in 1953. But he was also the Cuban patriot who wanted peace.
The man who, in 1966, turned his back on his comrade Fidel
and fled the country he had helped re-create to live instead in
exile in the United States. The man whose youngest son had
turned his back on his father to stand beside Castro.

They had met for the first time in August 1970 when they
were both guests on the *Today Show*. He was promoting his
latest book of poetry, *Lovestone,* and she was promoting her
final tour. They met again one week later when Diego was
being interviewed on *Meet the Press,* and Leland was one of
the panelists. After the show, the three of them had lunch at
the Tavern on the Green in Central Park. That evening, Collier
and Diego had dinner together in the dining room of the Plaza
Hotel. The following morning, they shared a limousine to La
Guardia Airport, from which he left for a speaking engagement
in Phoenix and she left for Austin, Texas. Collier was capti-
vated by the man.

To her, Diego Luis Velasquez was a conundrum, a fasci-
nating puzzle she wanted to solve. The more she knew about
him, the less she felt she knew, and the more she needed to
know. Stripping away the protective layers of Diego Velasquez
was much like peeling away the layers of an onion.

Their times together were infrequent and therefore all the
more precious. Where once Diego Velasquez had been considered an enemy of the United States, he was now a cherished
ally. His fourteen books of poetry, once banned, were translated
into English and printed and reprinted over and over again. He
was flown from one end of the country to the other to lecture
at universities, attend symposia on Latin American affairs and
to participate in protest marches organized on behalf of civil
and human rights. He was America's most celebrated exile,
and his face had appeared on the cover of every major magazine
at least once.

Once asked why he had renounced Castro and the revolution, he replied, "The revolution was to have produced a sweet
harvest, but the yield was bitter. I wanted only what we had
promised the people of Cuba at the beginning—an equal share
of the same dream. That dream was not to be. All of the
promises were soon broken. Like many of my compatriots, I
bore witness to the truth and was forbidden to even speak of

it. Stifled by enforced conformity, I began to choke on my own disillusionment. My words left me stillborn. I was no longer able to create. I put down my pen in favor of silence. When I realized that my silence meant my death, I left my country. And when I took up my pen again, I turned it against our tarnished dream."

They had begun their affair when he agreed to accompany her to Minneapolis with her exhibit. For the next five months, their affair continued in some of the finest hotels in the country. And then, in January, when her six-month tour was finally over, she took him down to St. Cristobal and introduced him to paradise.

"I am so close, *querida*," he said to her as they stood on the cliff looking out to sea, "and yet I wonder if I am far enough away."

His words brought tears to her eyes. He was looking to the northeast, to Cuba, and although neither of them could see the island, it lay there like a dark threat on a night when only the stars were out and the new moon was nowhere to be seen.

He took her in his arms then, and her fears began to ease. The tears she was storing for him didn't have to be shed just yet. His mouth on hers dispelled the terror his words evoked in her and his hands in her hair brought her peace again.

With him, she felt whole, reborn, an aging woman suddenly young again. Lying beside him in the bed no man had shared for nearly twenty years, she would touch his hand, feel his body close to hers, and know that the wait was over. The waiting had been more than worth it. It had prepared her for this most precious of all emotions.

Love.

For the first time in her life, Collier Paget-Browne was in love.

She wanted to offer him St. Cristobal for his home. She wanted to offer him its peace, its isolation and its serenity. But she said nothing. In his five years in the United States, he had called no city home for long. He still moved about as stealthily as the guerrilla fighter he once had been, breaking cover only to attack and then to just as quickly retreat. And like any fighter's woman, she followed him.

She taught herself to live within the perimeters he defined for their relationship. She learned to respect his silences and his moods, his need for solitude and his need for her company.

If there was any truth to the rumor that he was involved in a plot to overthrow Castro, she learned never to press him for an answer. She learned that questions only drove him deeper into himself, and so she kept him from getting lost inside himself by keeping him closer to her. She wondered at the absurdity of life which was now permitting her the rites of passage with a tender stranger, part enemy, part friend, whose past she had never shared and whose future was as uncertain as his present.

When she told him how frightened she was by his casual dismissal of death and his lack of concern about tomorrow, he taught her to live for today. He would read his poetry to her in an effort to reach her through his writing, and whenever they were apart, she would read those same poems herself, committing bits of them to memory.

"Breathe the fullness of today into your soul, for tomorrow is but a promise left in someone else's keeping..."

"No single moment will ever be repeated. Cherish each one for its own uniqueness..."

"With each new sunrise, another tomorrow is born and one more tomorrow becomes today..."

Diego exhilarated her and excited her, stimulating her as no man had ever stimulated her before. His personal system of checks and balances fascinated her. Brief flashes of humor were matched by silences. His warmth could be quickly cooled by a strange aloofness. Great spurts of energy often gave way to complete fatigue. Days of continuous writing were followed by days of reading, of solitary walks.

And so she was waiting, waiting for him to ask her to share his life. She had found what she had spent her youth searching for, and she wished she could turn back the clock and begin at the beginning with him....

The ceremony marking the fifteenth anniversary of the Center lasted for forty-five minutes. At the end of the other speeches, Collier stepped forward to make an announcement of her own.

"I want to take this opportunity to announce to everyone here, and especially the members of the press"—she trained her famous smile on them—"that I have decided to build a museum on the grounds of the Center."

A murmur ran through the gathering. She could hear note-pads being flipped open.

"The museum will house the art collection which is now in my private museum on the island of St. Cristobal."

There were isolated gasps of surprise from the three hundred assembled guests.

"This collection rightfully belongs to the American people and it belongs in America in a permanent home." She glanced up at Leland then. "Besides, I'm getting too old for this vagabond kind of life. I'll leave the traveling up to my brother from now on; he's used to it."

There were appreciative laughs from the audience and Leland gave her a peck on the forehead.

Her next remark was meant for Diego. "All I want to do now is return to my beloved island and watch the sun come up every day for at least a year without having to pack another suitcase."

"If you plan to move your entire collection to Boston," called out one of the reporters, "what will you do with the museum on the island?"

Collier laughed. "I'll start another collection, of course."

"You even managed to take me by surprise," Leland told Collier as he dined with her and Diego at their hotel that evening. "I find it hard to imagine the walls of the museum on the island covered with nothing but picture hooks."

"It won't stay that way for long," Collier assured him. "Give me a year off and I'll be back in New York again scouting around."

Diego had been unusually quiet during the meal and all evening Collier had been torn between asking if anything was wrong and respecting his mood. She could have kissed Leland for being the one to get it out into the open.

"Collier told me that you've spoken to your son again. Is that true, Diego?"

The man sighed and set down his wineglass. So that was it, thought Collier. She reached for Diego's hand and gave it a squeeze. His eyes had that faraway look in them, the look which meant he was dealing with one of his own inner battles and that he didn't want to be disturbed. But at Leland's question, he seemed to be grateful to let down his guard and answer it.

"Jorge has telephoned me twice this week. Each time he has expressed considerable concern about my mounting criticism of Fidel. Apparently, Fidel is now being criticized by some of his own supporters, and my campaign is further aggravating an increasingly uncomfortable situation. He asked me quite politely to assume what we would call a lower profile as a gesture of respect for a cause I myself once fought for." He combed both his hands through his thick white hair, something he always did when he was searching for the right words or when he was trying to arrive at a decision. "I think that for the first time, the father might do well to heed the advice of the son."

Collier and Leland exchanged glances.

"Like Collier, I, too, am tired. I, too, have been living the life of a vagabond these past five years. I feel much like a record which has been played too long and is no longer listened to as attentively as before. Perhaps a period of silence, which would permit me to continue with my writing, would enable me to emerge with a stronger voice, one made more effective by virtue of its absence."

He looked directly at Collier. "You have often hinted that the island of St. Cristobal is one place where a man might heal himself and grow strong again. If what I myself have experienced during my brief stays on the island is proof of what I can expect, I might consider offering myself into your hands for just such healing, *querida*. On one condition, of course."

"And that is?" Collier whispered.

"That we give the gentlemen of the press the answer to one of their most persistent questions. Shall we tell them, *corazón*, that you have consented to become my wife?"

"Looks like I've scooped them all on this one!" crowed Leland as Diego leaned forward to kiss Collier.

Collier and Diego were married in Boston on September 18 in the private chambers of Judge Harlan Tewes, one day before he was due to retire from the bench. Leland and Jenny acted as witnesses. At the end of the ceremony, Collier caught the judge's eye and held it. There was no mistaking the twinkle there this time. In fact, when he gave the groom permission to kiss the bride, she was convinced that she saw him wink.

Chapter Twenty-eight

Collier was stretched out on a lounge chair beside the pool. Diego finished slathering suntan lotion onto the backs of her legs and gave her a playful pinch on the behind.

"You are already the color of mahogany, *corazón*. How much darker do you wish to be?"

"I couldn't care less about the tan," she mumbled into the padded cushion. "It's only an excuse to have you put lotion on me."

He sat down on the edge of the chaise and kissed the side of her neck. "You should know by now that you need no such excuses. I seem to find enough reasons of my own to get my hands on you." Gently turning her head, he bent down and placed a warm, lingering kiss on her mouth.

As he began to kiss her face, his moustache moved in light, furry strokes over her skin, making her tingle. It aroused and excited her. It was so much a part of their lovemaking, so much a part of this man she loved. She turned onto her back and ran her fingers over his black eyebrows and the black moustache which had only recently begun to betray the first signs of graying.

"Did I ever tell you that you look just like Cesar Romero?" she murmured. "Except that you're even handsomer than he is."

"If I said yes, would you stop telling me that?" His lips moved from her eyelids to the tip of her nose.

Collier wrapped her arms around his neck and drew his face down to hers. Their lips met and held. As always, she could feel herself being lifted out of her body, tugged beyond the confines of her own skin and merging with his body beneath his own protective layer of skin.

"Are you happy, *querida?*" he whispered.

"If I said yes, would my happiness disappear?"

In answer to her question, he kissed her again.

"Do you know what frightens me, Diego?"

He shook his head.

"I'm so at peace with you. You make me feel truly loved. No man ever made me feel that way before, and it makes me afraid."

"You have too many fears, *querida*." He brushed back a loose strand of her hair. "Have I not tried to guide you beyond the shadows of your fears to more fully appreciate the light? Do not lose the joy of a moment by fearing the end of it, Collier. Cherish each one and then let it go, so that you may seize the next one."

"But I don't want any of these moments to ever end."

"Whatever we share together at any one moment can never end. As long as we are alive, we will have the feelings these moments inspire in us, and then, when the moment is gone, we still have our memories."

She pulled his head down to her chest and began to stroke his hair. She could lie that way with him forever, she thought, with her hands in his hair and his mouth against her skin.

"Your heart is like a hummingbird whose wings flutter so frantically in the air," he told her. "I love you so very much, Collier, and I wish I could find some way to soothe you. For a man whose life has been dedicated to words, I find myself helpless, unable either to write your fears away or to talk them away."

"I love you too, Diego," she sighed. "Whenever I realize how much you've become a part of me, I can't help being afraid. What we have together, I've never had before, and that makes me feel cheated. Sometimes I get so angry, wishing I'd met you when I was twenty instead of fifty. That way I could have had you for thirty years more."

"You would not have liked me much when you were twenty. I was twenty-seven then and I was an angry young man with a dream. I had a young wife and two young sons who understood very little about my dream. You and I lived on opposing sides of an ideological barrier then, and we would have been enemies."

"And yet, after all these years, you're still angry, Diego. You may be using a pen instead of a gun now, but you're as devoted as ever to that same dream. Only now it's you and Fidel who are on opposite sides of that ideological barrier. And that's where the real danger lies. You know it as well as I do, and you know that I have every right to be afraid."

Diego sat up then, and Collier let her arms fall to her sides. It frightened her to feel him pulling away from her.

"You're getting ready to fight again, I know it," she said, trying to keep her voice steady. "I've sensed your growing restlessness these last few weeks. Tell me I'm wrong, Diego. Tell me I've just been imagining it."

The look in his dark eyes made her heart stop. "You have not been imagining it, *querida*. It is true. But this was an inevitability neither of us denied existed. We promised each other one year of solitude. Instead we have had nearly two years together. It is time, my love. More than time."

He went over to the table where he had left his cigars and lit one. Collier watched him, her eyes greedily following each of his movements. He had grown handsomer during the two years of their self-imposed exile. He was tanned, his body fit from swimming and walking the beach. There was even a youthful spring in his step which hadn't been there when they first arrived on the island. St. Cristobal had infused him with a new life and a new vitality. Each step away from the island, each step closer to the outside world would be a step away from that life.

He came back and sat down again. "Do you realize that over two hundred and seventy thousand refugees have been airlifted from Cuba with the help of the American government in the past few years? Does that not tell you something of the turmoil within the country? Criticism of Fidel's policies grow more bitter and more open with each passing day. There has been such a drastic decline in labor productivity recently that the country is now in grave economic trouble."

"But you can't speak out again without putting yourself in danger," Collier protested. "Don't you enjoy feeling safe? Or does it make you feel guilty?"

"It is not a question of guilt, Collier, nor is it a matter of spending my life in safety. I have as much of an obligation to the people who have fled Fidel's rule as I have to the ones remaining behind. I must demonstrate to both groups that they are being supported and that perhaps some compromises can be worked out. All that I am advocating is a relaxation of some of the restrictions which have converted a country of proud fighters into a nation of subdued and frightened sheep."

He pulled her into his arms and began to stroke her back, but the specter of his leaving would not release its icy grip on her heart. Then, just as she felt herself beginning to relax, he spoke.

"I would love nothing more than to stay out here and stroke

your back and simply hold you, *querida*, but I have some more work to do before Cleavon arrives."

She opened her mouth to say something and just as quickly closed it again. It would do her no good to argue. Sadly, she watched him pick up his beach robe and walk into the house. She lay back on the chaise and closed her eyes. All she could see was the face of Cleavon Coombes.

His visits troubled her more than she dared admit to Diego. At forty, Cleavon was still single. While his younger brother, Clement, had married and given Horace five grandchildren in the space of seven years, Cleavon remained dedicated to the defense of his island. He had appointed himself the official watchman of St. Cristobal.

With Diego advising him, Cleavon had recruited all of the young men in Bonnyport and was turning them into a crack military unit. They spent five mornings a week rigorously training in the fields behind the town hall and three afternoons a week going out on maneuvers. Each man wore a uniform and carried a submachine gun, but no one would reveal the source of their equipment to Collier. Even Diego refused to talk about it.

"Cleavon's activities have absolutely nothing to do with any planned attack on Cuba," he had assured her when she first learned about the group. "He and his men simply want to feel like men. It would be absurd to think they are forming a task force to take over Cuba. They have forty-three men, Collier. One does not overthrow a foreign government with forty-three men. What they are doing is remaining in a state of readiness in the event of an act of aggression being directed against them."

"But why are you getting involved with them?"

"Because I am the only soldier they know."

"You *were* a soldier, Diego. You're not a soldier anymore."

"But as you yourself admit, *querida,* I am still at war. And these young men remind me so much of myself and Fidel when we were youths. These men are proud of their island and they are prepared to fight for it. You were the one who taught them about pride, were you not?"

Their clashes over Cleavon and his group were the only sources of friction between them. The rest of their times together were gentle, filled with love and tenderness and caring. In two years, Collier had never once found herself restless.

She thought of nothing but Diego, and she was content to do nothing more than simply be with him.

They took all their meals together. They made love in the afternoon when Diego insisted they take a siesta. They could sit together for hours in the library, saying nothing. While he worked on his poetry or labored over an article for a magazine, Collier would either read or curl up in a chair and listen to the recordings of Segovia and Montoya which he loved. And in the evening, after a late dinner, they would take a long walk on the beach, and then sit on the sand and watch the tide roll in and out.

They had left the island only once, and that had been to attend the dedication of the Collier Paget-Browne Museum of American Art in Boston. . . .

On their arrival at Logan Airport, the press greeted them with all the fanfare elsewhere reserved for returning royalty. To Collier's surprise and delight, Diego refused to answer any of their questions, insisting that the day was hers.

Collier led the members of the press and two hundred invited guests through the rooms of the two-story marble and glass building with all the pride of a grandmother showing off photographs of her only grandson. She was glowing. To her, the museum was her greatest achievement, the summing up of her life's work.

The building followed the same clean, horizontal lines as the Center, but instead of being filled with the works of students, it represented the work of America's greatest modern artists. Beneath a majestic crystal chandelier, in the center of the foyer where two curving staircases converged, stood a broad marble pedestal, partially covered by a white sheet. Collier stepped up to the pedestal and asked for quiet.

"No one has ever known if the Collier Paget-Browne Center for Fine Arts was named after my father or me. This time, there will be no such confusion." With a grand flourish, she swept off the white sheet to reveal a large bronze bust of her father.

"Ladies and gentlemen," she announced in a loud clear voice, "I hereby dedicate this museum to my late father, Collier Paget-Browne."

The applause echoed through the vast, high-ceilinged lobby and ricocheted off the museum's glass outer walls. Collier stood

with her eyes on the likeness of her father, which seemed to
gaze, proud and handsome, at the Charles River below him.
She swallowed the lump in her throat and blinked. . . .

"Miss Collier, how are you this afternoon?"

Collier started. She must have fallen asleep. Cleavon was
standing over her, dressed in his olive green battle fatigues.

"Cleavon," she inclined her head.

"You still disapprove of what we are doing, don't you?"

"You know I do."

"Your husband is very important to us, Miss Collier, and
although you may resent what he has done—"

"I detest violence, Cleavon," she cut him off curtly.

"We have no desire to engage in combat of any kind, but
if we are ever threatened, we intend to be prepared to defend
ourselves. It is more than a mere show of empty pride now, it
is a matter of survival. Three boatloads of Cuban refugees have
landed at Bonnyport in this last year. We have taken them in,
built homes for them, put the men and women to work and
put the children into our school. We have once again aroused
the anger of the government in Cuba by these simple human-
itarian gestures." He dropped his voice then. "Do not forget,
Miss Collier, it was the presence of Diego Velasquez himself
on St. Cristobal which alerted the Cubans to our very existence
in the first place."

Collier experienced a familiar sinking feeling in the pit of
her stomach. Was Cleavon right? Did Diego's presence on the
island pose a threat to all of them? It was something she had
never allowed herself to think about before. Had she betrayed
her people? Had she herself brought them closer to the enemy
they had feared for so long?

Just then Diego came out of the house. He was dressed as
he usually was, in an embroidered white gauze shirt, loose
trousers and sandals. He looked like an ordinary peon. What
belied the simple peasant image were his dark glasses and the
heavy gold wedding band that matched the one Collier wore.

"I will return in time for dinner, *corazón*." He kissed her
on the mouth and gave her hand a squeeze. "Now my advice
to you is to get out of the sun before you do any more damage
to your lovely skin."

She waited until the two men had left and then she went
for a swim. She spent the rest of the afternoon stretched out

on her bed, listening to the flamenco guitar of Carlos Montoya, and wishing Diego were there beside her instead of off tramping about in the bushes playing at being a soldier again.

When Diego returned to the house that evening, he seemed strangely subdued.

"Come," he said, taking her hand. "Let us take a walk on the beach."

At the edge of the cliff, he stopped and turned her around to face him. "I have seldom known a contentment greater than this—holding you in my arms and looking out at the sea. It is at moments like this that I wish I were not the man I am. I wish I could be content with this and only this, and ignore the stirring in my blood which says I must do more." Taking her hand again, he led her down the stone steps onto the beach.

"Another boatload of Cuban refugees landed late this afternoon near Bonnyport," he told her. "Among them was a man I have known since childhood. He is a doctor, and like me, he was once a loyal supporter of Fidel. Now he is a refugee. We talked for more than an hour together, and his stories, together with my own instincts have convinced me that I must speak out again. And I must do it soon. With my new book of poetry due to be released in three weeks, I will tell my agent that I will consent to a promotional tour—"

"But you said you didn't want one this time," she cried. "You promised."

"I must, *querida,* because the timing is right."

"And because of the tour, you'll have a ready-made audience for your attacks against Fidel," she lashed out at him, not bothering to disguise the bitterness in her voice.

"Collier, please do not berate me for what you know I must do." He reached out for her, but she shrugged him off. "Collier, come with me on the tour. Be with me. You did not think I would leave you behind, did you?"

She slowed her steps. She didn't know what she had thought. She had almost succeeded in forgetting about the launching of his new book, *Remembrances.*

"You can visit with Leland if you come with me. Philadelphia will undoubtedly be one of the cities on the tour, and I will arrange to appear on one of the programs at his station."

Leland. A sharp stab of regret made her wince. It made her conscious of that lonely place inside of her reserved for Leland. He had been the sole owner of Philadelphia's most successful

TV station WPLA for five years now. When his father had died and left the station to him, it was floundering and nearing bankruptcy. Leland resigned his positions at WNBC and *The New York Times*, kept his weekly program *We The People* on NBC, and returned to Philadelphia to live. He re-built the station, dedicating himself to the project with all the energy he had once reserved for his newspaper career.

She had only seen him once in the two years since her marriage to Diego and that had been in Boston at the dedication of the museum. He had attended the ceremonies with the young anchorwoman from his six o'clock news program. She was only one of the many women filling in the spaces in his life since the end of his affair with Jenny. Yes, it would be good to see her brother again. She needed to see him.

Diego was frowning. "I sense a sadness in you, Collier. Is it because of Leland?"

"I miss him, Diego," she slowly answered him. "I miss him and I feel that I've betrayed him in some way."

"I do not understand."

"There's a distance between us that was never there before. Even when I was married to Thaddeus and hardly saw Leland at all, the gap was bridged as soon as we were together again. It isn't the miles or the infrequency now that's causing this distance, it's something else. He's backed off, backed away, as if he thinks he'd be intruding if he came near me now." She stooped to pick up a piece of seaweed and absently began tearing it apart. "It hurts to think of him still living alone. He's been the most important person in my life. He's been loyal and loving and giving. He's stood by me whenever I've needed him. I miss him terribly, Diego, and I want him back in my life."

"Would you like me to speak to him, Collier? He has been a loyal friend to me as well. We have always respected one another. He might reveal himself to me."

Collier shook her head. "No one's ever spoken for me before, my darling, but thank you." She kissed him softly on the mouth. "I'll come with you on your tour and when we're in Philadelphia, I'll talk to him myself. At least that way I'll have a whole day to worry about something besides your on-going war with Fidel." She snuggled up to him and leaned her head on his shoulder. "I love you, Diego, I love you so much. I love looking at you. I love seeing you walking beside me, sitting across the table from me, sleeping next to me in bed. I love the way you pronounce my name. Did you know that every time you say my name, it makes me shiver?"

"Collier," he whispered in her ear. "Collier," he breathed again as he closed his mouth over hers.

"Let's go back." Her voice was husky.

"Sí, querida."

He kept his arm around her waist as they headed back up the beach.

Philadelphia was the third city on Diego's tour. While he was taping an hour's interview for WPLA's weekly news program *Between Us,* Collier and Leland went down the street for a cup of coffee. Facing him at last, being alone with him for the first time in two years, she suddenly felt shy. She kept looking up at him and then glancing away again, as if she didn't want him to catch her studying him.

He wore his glasses all the time now and they lent him an earnestness he seemed to have lost over the years. His handsome face was only lightly lined, and his thick, sandy brown hair showed only an occasional strand of white in it. She closed her hands around her mug and waited for him to speak first.

"I've been seeing a lot more of Jennifer and Colleen these past few months," he told her. "You wouldn't believe how beautiful that child is. She has Jennifer's black hair and my eyes and she's going to be a stunner. She's just turning twelve and I'm already jealous of those illiterate fishermen's sons who'll soon start circling the lighthouse. Jennifer's art is still selling incredibly well, but she's gotten away from batiks and wall-hangings. Now she's doing wood collages."

He sounded as nervous as she felt. She had known about Jenny's work. What she hadn't known was that she and Leland were seeing more of each other. She pretended to be intrigued by the chip in the rim of her mug while she waited for him to continue.

"I've been thinking about asking Jennifer to marry me."

Collier's mug came down hard on the table.

"I'm going to be fifty years old next year, Collier. Fifty! I run a successful TV station which demands more of my time than I want to give it. I still tape four segments a month for *We The People.* I spend at least five months a year traveling and writing articles, and whatever time I have left, I divide in half and give to my daughter. Nothing's changed all that much in twenty-five years, and yet I'm feeling something I've never felt before. It's called loneliness. I'm alone, Collier, and it's scaring the hell out of me."

He took off his glasses and went on.

"I don't want Jennifer to live in Gloucester anymore. I don't want her playing the role of princess in the tower and getting Colleen to do the same. The two of them are inseparable. If Jennifer paints, Colleen paints. If Jennifer works in wood, Colleen wants to work in wood, too. Jennifer just barely puts up with Colleen's going to school, and Colleen refuses to make friends with the children in town her own age."

"Well, that should ease your worries about the fishermen's sons," Collier laughed nervously.

Leland didn't crack a smile. "I want them to move away from Gloucester and live with me in the townhouse I've just bought here."

Collier took hold of her brother's hand. "Are you doing this because you love Jenny or because you're afraid of being alone? Or are you doing it because you're still playing the role of the prince who's supposed to save the princess from the isolation she's chosen for herself?"

Leland pulled his hands away. "I've always loved Jennifer in my own way," he maintained, "and if I want to marry someone, why shouldn't it be the mother of my own child?"

"You don't have to defend your decision to me, Leland," she chided him gently, "as long as you're sure."

She felt sorry for him. She had never seen him so helpless and in such pain before. Not even after Diana died.

"Collier," he said her name and then his voice broke. "Tell me how it feels to love someone the way you love Diego."

She was taken aback by his question. Stunned. For a moment her mind was blank, and then, like the lights on a pinball machine, the feelings and the answers flashed and popped and clanged until she couldn't seem to get the words out quickly enough.

"Sometimes I feel as if I'm living out a commuted death sentence. The happiness, the contentment, the sharing all seem to have a dark underside that is always there waiting. I live in terror of our being separated even for a few hours. My love for him is too intense. So is my need to protect him and keep him safe. I'm jealous of his past, and I want to be everything he needs now and could ever need in the future. Sometimes I forget that I had my own past without him. It's as if he's always been in my life. Then I realize how short a time I've really had him, and it frightens me all over again. Loving is still too new to me, Leland, and I'll probably spend the rest of my life learning how to handle it properly."

"I wonder if this love is a curse or a blessing, Collier," he murmured, more to himself than to her.

But she caught his words and she knew they were hers, back to haunt her.

"I wonder if I should envy you or pity you," he said.

His words began to chill her.

He put his glasses on again and there was something coolly detached about the look he gave her.

"I don't think I could ever learn to handle that kind of love," he confessed to her.

"So now you're the one who's willing to settle?"

He shrugged. "Maybe I don't deserve anything better than that."

Was this how it had been for her own father? she wondered. Fifty years old and in need of an heir. Collier couldn't shake off the cold feeling settling inside her. She saw her father sitting there instead of Leland—each of them willing to pay in his own desperate way. Both of them willing to settle.

"I suppose I shouldn't have even mentioned it to you," Leland was saying now. "I guess I just wanted to hear how the idea sounded out loud."

The moment when she could have said something came and passed, and she kept silent. Somehow, she felt she didn't have the right to interfere. Instead, she said, "Whatever you decide to do, you know I'll stand by you. All I want is for you to be happy, Leland."

Then she took a deep breath. "But I also want something else."

He looked at her sharply.

"I still want your love." Before he could say anything, she hurried on. "I still need your love, Leland, and I can feel it slipping away from me. I can feel *you* slipping away from me and it hurts. I want you to visit us on the island. So does Diego. I miss you, Leland. We both do. I feel as if you've cut me out of your life, and I couldn't bear it if you did."

Now it was Leland who took hold of *her* hands. "I haven't

cut you out of my life, dear heart. You've finally found someone to fill your life the way it should have been filled years ago." He kissed the backs of both her hands. "I've just been giving you the time to savor it in private. God knows you've waited long enough. Treasure what you have, Collier. Love Diego and let him love you. There's always plenty of time for brothers."

Where she should have felt relief, even gratitude, she felt only a peculiar trepidation. It was as if there was a subtle warning in his words, a warning which made her want to run back to the station and make sure that Diego was all right.

Just as she was reaching for her purse, she saw Leland glance up at the time. "They're through taping," he said. "We'd better head back."

She tucked her arm through his as they left the restaurant.

"Will you consider coming down to the island for a visit, Leland?" she asked him. "Soon?"

"I will. Eventually."

"Will you at least let me know what happens with Jenny?"

"You know I will. Eventually. It might take me a little more time to get up the nerve to ask her though. I've already been rejected once." He patted her arm. "Who knows, maybe we'll round the corner and I'll fall madly in love with the first person I see and propose to her instead."

But when they rounded the corner, the only person coming their way was an elderly woman walking her poodle.

Chapter Twenty-nine

They were lying together in bed. One of Collier's legs was flung across Diego and her head was resting on his chest. His fingers were wound up in several long strands of her hair. She pressed her mouth to the spot where she could see his heart beating and felt it pulse rhythmically against her lips. Then she lifted her head just enough to be able to look down at his beloved face.

He smiled up at her and she smiled back. He nudged her face closer to his and their lips touched. They deepened their kiss. They remained that way for several minutes, their mouths connected, breathing evenly, as if each was the other's life support system and they shared a common oxygen supply. When Diego finally broke the kiss, Collier felt abandoned.

"I must finish the lecture I am to deliver at the school tomorrow, *querida*," he said, carefully working his fingers free of her hair. "I am already far enough behind that I may have to postpone my talk for another day or two. You realize, of course, that these siestas are playing havoc with my work schedule."

"But they were your idea, *Señor* Velasquez." She put on her sexiest pout.

"And as much as I might grumble, I do not regret my idea for a single moment."

"Same time tomorrow then?" she teased him.

He laughed. "Same time tomorrow."

While he was getting dressed, Collier stretched out on the bed. She felt languorous. Well loved and well cared for. Content. Calm. It was only as Diego went out the door that she felt a slight stirring of anxiety.

Cleavon had asked him to speak to a general assembly of the high school students in Bonnyport once a week, and Diego had been lecturing to them weekly for nearly two months. Not only was he reading them his poetry, but he was teaching them about the world of the revolutionary, the idealist, the rebel with

309

a cause worth fighting and possibly dying for. What their history books had cautiously omitted Diego was putting back, teaching them about history from his own experiences. As much as his lectures distressed Collier, there was nothing she could do about it. This was not her island, but theirs. She was only a landowner, not a monarch.

Suddenly, she didn't want to be alone. She threw on a robe and went into the library. She put on a Segovia record, turned down the volume and curled up on the sofa facing the desk where Diego was hunched over his work. He glanced up at her and blew her a kiss. Smiling, she blew one back to him. He returned to his papers and she picked up her writing pad and switched on the lamp nearest her. She owed Jenny a letter.

She dated the sheet of pale yellow paper January 6, 1973, and then stopped. Nibbling thoughtfully on the end of her pen, she considered the date she had just put down. The first few days in January were impossible. It seemed that somewhere between December 31 and January 1, she always lost an entire year. She found herself writing down the old year during those first few days, her stubborn way of putting a temporary freeze on time.

She scratched in a "4" over the "3," wrote *Dear Jenny,* and then stopped again. Just as she had sensed a distance between Leland and herself, she had begun to sense a growing distance between herself and Jenny. Jenny's letters, usually so full of chatter about her work and about Colleen, had been growing shorter and less newsy, and coming far less frequently. Was it because she had been seeing more of Leland? Was it because he had finally proposed to her again and she had refused again?

In his most recent letter, Leland hadn't even mentioned Jenny at all. Only Colleen. Collier was confused. Should she phone them? She felt so cut off from the two people who had been so important to her for most of her life.

The telephone rang and Collier jumped. Her heart began to race. Amiel had strict instructions not to answer. It rang again. Diego reached for it and Collier held her breath.

"Sí?"

Collier put down her pen and paper.

"Qué quiere?"

She got up and went over to the desk.

"Hable despacio, por favor!"

She put her hands on Diego's shoulders. She could feel the tension knotting them.

"Hable—"

He slammed down the phone. His face was pale beneath his tan. Then it darkened again, this time with rage.

"If they think that by their telephone calls they will silence me, they do not know Diego Velasquez very well," he thundered, pounding his fist on the desk. "Their cowardly actions only strengthen my resolve. The fools! They will not frighten me as Fidel has frightened them. I will not be silenced."

"Diego, please," Collier whimpered, flinging her arms around his neck. His chest was heaving. She could feel the heat of his anger through the shirt. "This has to stop, Diego, I can't bear to see you this way."

"Then tell them to stop!" he bellowed.

She stiffened. Then she backed away from him. He immediately got out of his chair and put his arms around her.

"Forgive me, *corazón*," he said, his voice quieter now. "I sometimes forget that *I* must control the anger, not allow the anger to control me."

She leaned her head against his shoulder. "I'm so afraid, Diego," she whispered.

"I know, my love, I know," he soothed her. "But they are only voices, and voices over a telephone can harm no one. We must not allow them to continue to hurt us, Collier, either by arousing my anger or by causing you to be afraid. Nor can I allow them to discourage me. The voices and the threats can only harm us if we turn the anger and the fear inward upon ourselves."

He held her for another moment and then let her go. How could he be so calm again? she wondered, watching him sit down, reach for his half-smoked cigar and pick up his pen. How could he act as if the phone call meant nothing? She went back to the sofa and lay down. She didn't have the energy to write her letter now.

When the telephone rang again, Collier let out a yelp. Diego silenced her with a warning glance and lifted the receiver on the third ring. She put her hands over her heart as if to keep it from leaping out of her chest. Was that a smile on Diego's face? She immediately sat up. He put his hand over the mouthpiece.

"It is Leland," he told her.

"Leland!" She sprang up from the sofa and hurried into the bedroom to pick up the extension.

Her excitement evaporated, her relief vanished as soon as

she heard the controlled tightness in his voice."

"I'd like to come down to the island," he said in that strange, crisp voice. "Just for the day."

"Wh-when?" Collier stuttered, taken aback by his curtness.

"Tomorrow."

"I don't understand."

"I'll explain when I see you. Will you send the chopper for me?"

"Of course," she mumbled through lips suddenly gone dry.

When he hung up she just stood there, still holding the receiver up to her ear. She could hear Diego's breathing over the hum of the dial tone.

"Diego?"

"Sí, querida?"

"Diego, what's happening?"

"That I do not know." Even he sounded worried now.

The three of them sat around a table on the terrace, their iced drinks growing warm, the frosted glasses beginning to sweat as they lay untouched in front of them. Leland took off his glasses, combed his fingers through his hair and then folded his arms on the table.

"First, let me apologize for my brusqueness over the phone yesterday." He glanced over at Collier and gave her a faint smile. "I just couldn't afford to take any chances."

"What kind of chances?" she demanded.

"Of the line being tapped."

Collier's eyes widened. Diego's face remained impassive.

"That's why I decided to fly down, rather than risk a phone call or a letter." Leland turned to Diego. "I'm here because you and I are friends, and because you're married to the person I love most in this world. But I'm also here because I'm privy to all kinds of information, the kind of information that's available to very few people. I have a lot of contacts. They come to me, I go to them. We've been bartering information back and forth now for nearly thirty years. And what I've been hearing lately has me worried. It all involves you, Diego."

"Me?"

Leland nodded. "You're making Washington nervous."

"But why?" he demanded. "We are all on the same side now."

"That may very well be, but they've started to believe the

rumors of your involvement with several militant ex-patriot Cuban groups, namely, the International Organization for the Liberation of Cuba and the Cuban People's Army, both of which are based in Florida. Then there are a number of smaller groups scattered throughout the Caribbean as well as Cleavon's army right here on St. Cristobal."

"They know about that too?"

Leland nodded. "Apparently the CIA has a pretty thick file on you."

Collier gulped. She quickly hid her hands under the table so that neither of them could see them shaking.

"I see." Diego solemnly looked down at his own hands which were clenched and resting on top of the table. He fingered his wedding band for a moment and then, without meeting Collier's gaze, he focused his attention solely on Leland.

"As I have repeatedly explained to Collier and as I have often told you, my friend, as a Cuban ex-patriot, I am emotionally bound to any one of my fellow countrymen who seeks my counsel. That I have given money to equip invasion task forces is untrue. That I have provided the funds to purchase uniforms and small arms for isolated groups of islanders determined to safeguard what is theirs is another matter entirely. That I will admit is true. But I am not, nor have I ever been, in favor of a military takeover of Cuba. I am not in favor of another bloody coup which will further undermine the cause for which I am still fighting. I am opposed to spilling any more of the blood of my former countrymen. I do not preach revolution, Leland. I am a man of peace, dedicated to finding peaceful solutions to the problems besetting my country. I thought all of this was understood and by now taken for granted."

Leland looked frustrated. "We're splitting hairs, Diego. What you consider emotional ties and counseling, the United States government views as meddlesome and aggressive. They don't want an international incident right now."

"I have never advocated aggression, only compromise," Diego retorted. "Is it my fault that Fidel does not believe in compromise? Is it my fault that hundreds of thousands of my former countrymen are crying out for change? I am but adding one small voice to their cries."

"But yours is the voice everyone in America hears most. They listen to you on the radio, they watch you on TV, they buy your books and they read your articles. You're the one with the real voice and the real power, Diego. What I'm trying to tell you is that unless you temper your attacks, cut off your financial support and sever your connections with all of these quasi-military groups, the United States government will come down hard on you."

"I am not a citizen of the United States!" Diego jabbed an angry finger at Leland. "I am a citizen of Cuba. I do not live in the United States but on the island of St. Cristobal."

"That may be true, but they can prevent you from ever entering the States again. It might not curtail all of your activities, but it would keep you off American soil and keep you off the airwaves." Leland softened his voice then, and his eyes had a pleading look in them. "All I'm asking of you, Diego, is that you think about what I've just told you. Think hard and don't be too quick to dismiss it."

"I have a lecture to deliver at the school, if you will both excuse me," Diego announced, his voice tight, his features strained as he got up from the table. "Thank you, *amigo*, for your concern and your advice." He reached out to shake Leland's hand. "I will think seriously about what you have said, and then I will try to find some way around it."

Collier stared after him in disbelief. "It's really no use, Leland. He's determined."

"And stubborn," he sighed, "just like you. I guess that must make for some pretty interesting times."

She didn't know whether to laugh at that or burst into tears. Instead she took several long pulls on her piña colada, hoping that the rum would calm her down. But she was still trembling when she finished her drink. She reached for the one Diego had left untouched and started on that one.

"There's something you want to tell me, isn't there?" Leland asked.

Halfway through her second drink, she stopped, then nodded her head.

"I'm afraid."

"That's nothing new."

"Diego's been receiving threatening mail."

"Postmarked?"

"Some from Cuba. Jamaica. Different cities in the States."

"What kind of threats?"

"Your usual, common garden variety kinds. Death threats. Warnings. Don't step off your island again. Don't speak at any more American universities. Retract your statements to the press. Stop supporting insurgent groups. They all use the standard labels and call him by all the standard names. Traitor. Turncoat. Judas. Benedict Arnold. He's even begun receiving phone calls."

"What kind of calls are they?"

"Sometimes there's just silence at the other end of the line. At other times someone shouts in Spanish. Several times someone's played the Cuban national anthem over the phone. We've hung up, of course, but when we've picked up the phone hours later, the anthem's still playing."

"That must be costing someone a fortune."

"Be serious, Leland!"

"I am, Collier. Along with a few crackpots and some nationalistic zealots, you've got someone who's willing to spend a lot of money to make you both damned uncomfortable."

"The worst call came three days ago. Diego was in the library and I was in the bedroom. We both picked up the receiver at the same time. I heard three gunshots. I dropped the phone and ran into the library, expecting to find Diego lying dead on the floor. But he was standing beside the desk, his face chalk white, shouting into the receiver in Spanish." She shuddered and tried to push away the memory of that horrible moment. "Oh, Leland, even if these are just threats, I'm so afraid. Diego says I see too many shadows, but these aren't just shadows anymore. They're real."

"Whether these threats are real or not, Collier, the threat of a crackdown on Diego's activities *is* real. It might even be a good thing, kind of a blessing in disguise." At her quizzical look, he continued, "If he's barred access to the States, he'll have to remain on the island. No more exposure. No more radio, no TV, no open auditoriums. Without an audience he'll be less vocal and at the same time he'll be less of a visible target. Think about it, Collier, and work on him."

He glanced down at his watch and frowned. "I've got to get back. Your chopper pilot charges by the hour."

She didn't even attempt a smile. "This wasn't the kind of visit I had in mind when we talked about it in Philadelphia," she said unhappily as he helped her to her feet. The drinks were finally beginning to work and as she started to sway a little, Leland put his arms around her.

"As I told you, dear heart, we'll have time for proper visits again. Just be patient."

"I'll try," she told him, putting on her best brave smile.

"I'm afraid I have some more news for you," he said.

"If it's bad, I don't think I want to hear it."

"Jennifer's getting married in March. Two days before my birthday." He laughed with only a slight trace of bitterness. "How's that for a fiftieth birthday present?"

"Oh God, I'm so sorry." Poor Leland. How she ached for him.

"His name is Eric Sheldon. He's thirty-five and he's a sculptor. He works in wood and I think he'd qualify more as a whittler, but at least he and Jennifer have something in common. They've known each other for two years. During those few months when I was seeing more of Jennifer and Colleen, he was off in Africa, seeing what the natives could teach him about working in wood. He wants to adopt Colleen and that's the part I think hurts the most, but there's nothing I can do about it. At least Jennifer's agreed to let me see Colleen whenever I want, so that part of it won't change.

"It's best this way, Collier. I'm happy for Jennifer because she's marrying someone who'll be safe for her. And that's what she's always needed. They'll live out their lives safely and securely in Gloucester, selling their art and watching Colleen grow up to be just like them. I've finally let Jennifer go. She can finally be exactly what she's always wanted to be without having to apologize, without trying to change. I hope it works out for them. I really do."

Collier cupped his face in her hands and looked deep into his eyes. "Have you been very hurt by this, Leland?" she murmured.

"I suppose my ego was a bit bruised by her announcement, but no, Collier, I'm not hurting." He looked almost bashful as he admitted, "I never even got around to proposing to her again. After discussing it with you in Philadelphia, I realized how much of a desperation measure it really was and that I might have just been using them as you'd said. Then I got involved in negotiations to purchase a radio station and—"

"A radio station? Why haven't you told me?"

"Because we just closed the deal this week. It's a small station, and it has the distinction of being the only one in Philadelphia which runs its programing in five languages. Its focus is on all the ethnic groups in the area and we've already started talking about a sixth language." His face was animated again and his voice was deep with enthusiasm as he spoke.

"I've been so preoccupied with it that I haven't had much time to think about anything else."

"You're starting to sound more and more like a Paget-Browne," she told him with a genuine smile. "You're becoming an empire builder in your old age, Leland Taggert. I like that."

He flushed. "Why not? Work has been the only area of my life I've ever known how to handle."

The following morning, while Diego was taking a walk on the beach, Cleavon arrived at the house to meet with Collier at her invitation. They sat together in the living room over glasses of iced tea and Collier quickly came to the point.

"Diego's life is being threatened, Cleavon, and I need your help."

"How can I help you, Miss Collier?" he asked, setting down his glass.

"If I order the necessary supplies from the mainland, would you and your men ring the compound with wooden posts and electrified wire?"

He didn't hesitate. "Of course we would."

"Would you also build a series of small guardhouses to be set every few hundred yards along the perimeter of the compound?"

Once again he agreed.

"And would you be prepared to man the guardhouses twenty-four hours a day? I'll pay you well for this, Cleavon, I promise."

"I would agree even without payment, Miss Collier. Your husband has spoken to us many times about these threats against his life. But he seems fearless in the face of them, almost defiant. Like you, I believe he has placed himself in grave danger, and like you, I am willing to do whatever I can to protect him. Diego Velasquez has done a great deal for this island and for my people, and we are willing to repay him even if it means repaying him with our lives."

His fierce loyalty sent a rush of tears to Collier's eyes and she hastily blotted them away. "Thank you, Cleavon," she told him in a husky whisper. "I know we won't be able to protect him all the time. We can't seal off the beach and I don't think either of us is prepared to live in a bomb shelter. But for my own peace of mind, regardless of how strenuously he may object, I have to do something."

"You can count on all of us, Miss Collier, to do whatever we can."

Cleavon had scarcely left the house when Diego came back from his walk. When Collier sat him down and told him about her plans, he was incredulous.

"But you will be turning this paradise of yours into a virtual prison," he argued. "Barbed wire and armed guards on patrol? Collier, *corazón,* you cannot barricade my words by building fences around me. I will continue to speak out for the truth, and if my voice cannot be heard, then my writings shall speak for me. No one will succeed in silencing me. No one, not even you, can protect me from the fate which has already been decided for me."

Chapter Thirty

In spite of his mother's protests, if it hadn't been for Andrew and Edward, Addison would have divorced Mary Beth long ago. But she was still the ideal cover. She was also a good mother and the perfect hostess, throwing the kind of parties the Paget-Brownes had always been famous for. Now eighty-two, a crusty and cranky Elinor had finally turned over the running of her house to her daughter-in-law, retiring to her bedroom where she spent her days reading and napping, and her evenings waiting for her grandsons to entertain her.

If Mary Beth had been having affairs over the years, Addison didn't know and he didn't care. His money kept her busy and happy and out of his way. She still played the devoted wife, and she'd even pretended to be upset when he'd moved out of their bedroom five years ago and into the large, empty yellow bedroom which overlooked the front lawn and Commonwealth Avenue.

The flowered wallpaper had faded, as had the yellow curtains on the windows and the draperies around the wide tester bed. But the arrangement of the furniture was exactly as Collier had left it forty-seven years ago. Nothing of the girl herself remained, except for a cellophane-wrapped cigar he'd found lying on the dusty floor of her clothes closet. He'd tucked it away in one of the dresser drawers, just as a reminder.

Surrounded by her, his obsession was complete.

He no longer knew where the hatred ended and the love began. Both emotions were intertwined inside him, festering within his brain and moldering in his guts. Twisted mirror images of themselves. He had abandoned his god as his god had abandoned him in a mutual and irrevocable cutting of the cord. There would be no absolution for him now, no penance to be paid, no salvation. She had finally taken full possession of his soul. He was hers as surely as she was his.

He'd been impotent for five years. He'd fired the last of his chauffeurs and never had him replaced. It didn't matter much

to him because he seldom went out anymore. He took a taxi
to the office whenever there were papers to sign. His signature
still one line below hers. His hand trembling so violently that
he had to use his left hand to steady his right in order to scrawl
his name in the small space allotted him.

If she were dead, he'd be free. He knew it. In her death,
he'd find the salvation even his God couldn't grant him. If she
were dead, she'd have to release her hold on him. She'd have
to free his guts and his balls, but most of all she'd finally let
go of his soul. Her death would give him back his life.

He'd promised himself that as a penance for his ultimate
salvation, he'd destroy all of the scrapbooks and the photographs he'd kept of her. That would be his sacrifice. Never to
look at her face again. Never to see her body again. Never to
read through the lists he'd kept as a child to see that all the
items on those lists had been checked off. If he could be free,
he'd even agree to give up wanting her. But only if he could
be free.

He went to bed in her bed each night dreaming of his freedom and woke up every morning still in chains.

He woke early one morning and rang for his breakfast. As
usual, on the tray next to the silver coffeepot was his copy of
the Boston *Herald*. He snapped open the paper and began to
scan the front page. He had no use for the news and very little
interest in the world around him. It didn't matter to him that
this year was an election year and that the stumbling, bumbling
Jerry Ford was running against some born-again holy-roller
named Jimmy Carter no one had ever heard of before. He
couldn't have cared less about it being his country's bicenten-
nial.

All he cared about was her. Reading about her and that
commie-turned-fascist husband of hers.

An article at the bottom of the front page caught his eye.
It was datelined Jamaica. He read the article and his heartbeat
quickened. The People's National Party had just been re-elected,
returning Prime Minister Michael Manley to power with the
greatest majority of any party since Jamaica's independence
from Britain. Manley was known for his leftist leanings and
for his open friendship with Cuba's Fidel Castro.

Addison smiled. That should give her husband something
else to raise a fuss about. But who'd even hear him? Since the
U.S. government had taken away his visa and kept him out of

the country, he hadn't been causing as much trouble as before. It was the smartest thing they'd ever done. They didn't need rabble-rousers. Especially foreigners. Foreigners preaching to them about peace. What a liar he was! What a hypocrite! He'd been a soldier. What the hell did he know about peace? What did he even know about being a man? He wrote like a woman. His poems were nothing but sentimental trash.

Addison was seething. He thought of him with her. For five years now. That white-haired old man with the cane. Touching her, touching her golden skin. He remembered them standing side by side on the steps of the Center that one time, and then again at the opening of the museum she'd built. He'd watched him touch her. Watched until he'd wanted to puke.

He was panting now as he tossed the paper aside and got out of bed to lock his door. Opening the door to the clothes closet, he took a small, portable record player down from the top shelf. He put the record player on the floor and dropped the record onto the turntable. His palms were slick with sweat. He wiped them on the bottoms of his pyjamas and then he reached for the phone.

He'd gotten an unlisted number for this phone and he only used it for these very special calls. He dialed the number and sat down on the floor to wait. It always took a long time to be connected with the island, but the wait was well worth it. His breathing rasped with an exaggerated harshness against the plastic mouthpiece. He wiped his forehead with the back of his hand and continued to wait.

The knot in his guts grew tighter and tighter. He sucked in his breath. It was her. She was answering again. Protecting him, still protecting him. The sound of her voice sent spears of anger and yearning and loathing through him, stabbing at his guts, jabbing him in the groin. He let the needle drop.

Listen to this and let it drive you mad, he wanted to shout. *Go mad, damn you, and put an end to my waiting. You've kept me waiting for forty-eight years and I'm tired of it. Time is running out. Die, bitch, die and let me live!*

He set the receiver down on its side next to the record player. Then he stripped off his soaked pyjamas and walked naked into the bathroom.

The Cuban national anthem played on.

Chapter Thirty-one

Collier stood at the edge of the cliff and looked down at the beach below. Clouds scudded across the morning sky, playing tag across the face of the sun, alternately darkening and lightening the otherwise clear blue sky. A strong breeze plucked at her dress and she wrapped her shawl more tightly around her shoulders. It seemed unseasonably cool for February. Or maybe it was just age catching up with her.

She smiled and began to wave as soon as she spotted Diego and Cleavon coming into view. Diego waved back. Cleavon raised his rifle high in the air above his head. Collier could feel her smile fading away.

Even after four years, she still hadn't gotten used to seeing Cleavon carrying that gun. It was an M-16, the type of rifle used by terrorist groups. But Cleavon Coombes was not a terrorist. He was Diego's self-appointed bodyguard. Wherever Diego went, so did Cleavon and his M-16. There were still times when Collier found herself resenting the enforced closeness of the two men, and then she would chide herself for her foolishness. Cleavon and the men of Bonnyport who patrolled the compound with their carbines had given her exactly what she had wanted. Safety. Security. And Diego himself. They had celebrated their sixth anniversary in September.

Although the United States government had revoked his travel visa in 1975, there was no law preventing Diego from appearing on the occasional taped telecast or radio broadcast. Even Leland had been coming down to the island to tape interviews with him. The man himself was less visible, his words slightly tempered, but Diego's voice was still being heard.

His last volume of poetry, published in the United States in 1977 without the usual promotional tour to support it, still sold out its first printing within one month of its publication. It was then that Diego announced his intention to give up poetry and concentrate on his autobiography. The world had read enough of his innermost thoughts, he maintained; now he would tell them the story behind the shaping of those thoughts.

It often seemed to Collier that she saw less of Diego now than when he had been traveling. Not only did she share him with Cleavon and various American journalists, but she was continually playing hostess to groups of foreign journalists, university professors, students, scientists and ordinary citizens interested in simply listening to what Diego Velasquez had to say. With the United States closed to him, Diego had been bringing the world down to him instead.

She herself hadn't left the island in three years. She was too afraid of leaving Diego and too possessive of their time together to risk missing out on one precious moment of it. And so, contrary to her own best intentions, time was proving Leland right and not her. The walls of her museum on St. Cristobal were still bare.

Her life was filled now with a tentative kind of peace, one which was untested, but a peace nonetheless. She had come to accept their constricted existence within the gentle prison of the compound. She felt safe. Protected from a hostile outside world. Safe even from Addison. She had been right to pay him off all those years ago.

Up until four months ago, the only ripples in their otherwise placid lives had been the nuisance phone calls and the threatening letters Diego still received. But Collier had resigned herself to suffering one small snake in paradise.

And then, in October, Castro had stunned the world by paying a six-day visit to Jamaica to confer with Prime Minister Michael Manley. By the end of the visit, what had once been no more than an easy friendship between the two countries had developed into a more firmly declared alliance. The rest of the islands in the Caribbean reacted with predictable alarm to Castro's initiative. They saw the heavy foot of Communist expansionism treading too near their own door.

Throughout the landmark trip to Jamaica, one man had stood out from all the rest. He was Jorge Velasquez, Diego's son. Jorge was one of Castro's few remaining advisors, one of the few men whose loyalty was never questioned. Together they were beginning to implement their plan for a Cuban-dominated Caribbean. Diego was stunned and he was angry. But more than that, he was curious. He began to probe, reaching behind the rhetoric, beyond the bombast, to what lay behind this sudden alliance with Jamaica. And what he learned, he passed on to the rest of the world.

Cuba was in trouble.

Diego stepped up his attacks on Castro and used every one of his contacts to carry his word. The small snake grew larger and more fearsome. To Collier, that snake was a man called Jorge. A man who telephoned weekly now begging his father to back down, to pull back, to keep still.

But the father, who had listened to the son once, refused to listen now.

Jorge's pleas turned to threats.

Collier watched now as Diego started up the steps from the beach, Cleavon behind him. She felt especially happy today. The guesthouse in the compound was empty. She would have him all to herself.

He was taking the steps more slowly than usual, stopping for that extra couple of seconds on each one before pushing himself on to the next. He looked so tired. He had been working himself too hard.

He was puffing as he reached the top step. His moustache, now completely white, was beaded with sweat. His smile was almost apologetic when he spoke. "You would think I would be used to these steps by now, but here I am, short of breath and soaked with sweat."

Slinging his rifle over one shoulder, Cleavon turned his back to them and looked back down at the beach, his eyes darting from left to right and back again, scanning, always scanning.

Diego took a handkerchief out of his pocket to wipe off his face. Then, almost as an afterthought, he unwrapped the rumpled handkerchief to reveal one perfect seashell tucked away inside.

"I think I was able to find a shell even you, my astute collector, have managed to miss so far," he told Collier as he placed the long, curled, ivory-colored shell in the palm of her hand. "Cleavon tells me that it is called a sea olive and that it is rather a rare find on St. Cristobal."

"It's beautiful," she murmured, turning it over to examine it more closely.

"It seems this is all I am ever able to offer you, *corazón.*" His look was mournful. "Nature provides you with an abundance of flowers. There are no stores for me to buy you even the smallest trinket. What else can this husband offer you but a seashell and his love?"

"I'll gladly accept both your seashell and your love," she

told him with a tender smile. "They're more precious than anything else you could offer me."

He put his arm around her waist and they started back toward the house with Cleavon trailing several yards behind them. As they neared the guardhouse set close to the patio, Collier could sense Diego beginning to withdraw into himself again.

"You seem worried," she said, pulling him to a stop and making him face her.

"I am," he admitted with a solemn nod. "Jamaica and Guyana have just endorsed Cuba's military presence in Angola. Fidel's intrusion in the affairs of a Third World country is a matter of grave concern. The repercussions of his action could be enormous."

Prickles of fear ran up and down Collier's spine. "Leland warned me about this very thing years ago."

"And his astute observation has now, unfortunately, been proven right. From now on, the entire Third World will be manipulated by the United States and the Soviet Union. It will be used as their own personal testing ground in a dangerous game of brinksmanship."

Collier grabbed hold of her husband's arm. "Diego, you're already sixty-four years old. Can't you leave the fighting of these ideological battles to someone younger now? Let the youth of today fight for their tomorrows. The future is theirs, not ours anymore. Can't you be content knowing that you've fought more gallantly than most men and let the people whom you've touched carry on from here? Diego," she murmured, stroking his cheek, "all I want is to share a peaceful old age with you."

He laughed and planted a kiss on the palm of her hand. "You'll never be old, *querida*. You're as youthful now as the day I met you. The white does not even show in the gold of your hair. I find it difficult to imagine you in old age and I wonder what you will do with a man like me. It is I who am aging, my love, while you will never know the meaning of the word. You will always be young."

She was chilled by his words. "If I'm to stay young, I'll keep you young with me," she whispered fiercely, as her eyes filled with tears. "I've made quite an investment in you, you know, and I intend to hang onto you for a long, long time." She sniffed back her tears and laughed. "I've even stopped caring about art because of you. And here I thought I was going to keep contributing something to the world."

He took her face in his hands and his voice was serious. "We are really very much alike, you and I, and that is why I hope you can appreciate *my* need to continue to contribute to the world. And yet, what do my contributions really amount to in the end? A handful of books on a shelf, there for someone to buy in a bookstore or read in a library, and then promptly forget. Once I am gone, my contribution is over. No one remembers a stilled voice, Collier, and my voice is my contribution."

The chill began to spread all through her body.

"You're trying to prepare me for something, Diego." Her tone was accusing.

He seemed to hesitate, as if groping for the right words. "I have arranged for a tape to be delivered in time for tomorrow's emergency meeting of the United Nations Security Council."

Collier's knees grew weak.

"The Council is meeting to discuss Cuba's intervention in Angola and to decide on the measures to be taken. Since I am barred from presenting my argument in person, I am hopeful that my voice will at least have some effect on the outcome of their session."

"Castro will find a way to punish you for this, Diego," Collier warned him. "Jorge will take this speech of yours and turn it against you."

But Diego disagreed with her. "Jorge will do nothing. He is but another disembodied voice. He has more to worry about at this moment than the words of his aging father. Besides, how could he hope to harm me? You have provided me with this fortress, have you not? Come, *querida,* let me shower, then we will have lunch and talk only of how we shall spend our old age together."

He signaled the man in the guardhouse who opened the gate to let them through.

Without saying another word, Collier allowed Diego to lead her into the house. But when their lunch was served, she found she had no appetite.

Diego's speech called for a joint resolution to be issued by the Security Council and the National Assembly condemning Cuba's actions and demanding an immediate withdrawal of her forces from Angola. Secondly, he suggested forming a special committee made up of the great world powers to act on Cuba's repressive human rights policies. And thirdly, as much as it hurt him to do so, he advocated a world embargo against Cuba.

As expected, Diego's speech was condemned by the Soviet Union and its satellites, and applauded by the United States and her allies. As Collier had feared, the media demanded immediate access to Diego, and for the first time in their six years together, it was Collier who laid down the law. St. Cristobal was closed to the press. She would take no more chances.

Then came the call she had dreaded most. And this request she could not refuse.

Jorge Velasquez arrived by launch on a mild March morning to confront the father he had not seen in twelve years. Cleavon and ten of his men had ringed the dock, their rifles raised, poised and ready. When the launch tied up at the dock, each member of the crew was brought up on deck with his arms raised to be searched. Jorge was the only man allowed off the boat. Cleavon searched him and then led him up the stone steps to the compound, while the rest of his men guarded the crew.

Collier held onto Diego's hand as they waited for Jorge out on the patio. Diego looked pale, but his eyes were strangely bright, his carriage proud and straight. Only the slight twitching at the corner of his mouth betrayed his underlying edginess. Collier could feel her panic rising. Her dress was beginning to stick to her back. But she tried to ignore her discomfort for Diego's sake. She stood just as tall and as straight as the man she loved, while she braced herself to face the man she feared most in the world. How cruel, she thought. One more example of one's own flesh turned against oneself. Addison and Jorge. Two of a kind. Devourers of the flesh of their kin.

And then she was staring at him.

At forty, Jorge Velasquez was a strikingly handsome man. Tall and bordering on boniness, he was as dark as Diego must have been in his youth, with a trim black moustache and beard, and piercing brown eyes. He was dressed the way Fidel himself dressed, in fatigues and heavy black boots. He swept off his cap and to Collier's astonishment, he bent over her hand and kissed it.

She forced herself not to pull back. Twin spots of color flamed in her cheeks as she held herself in check, her head high, her eyes cold.

"You were fortunate not to be shot, Jorge," Diego told his

son with a forced lightness in his voice. "As you can see, I have my own loyal followers here."

Jorge was standing stiffly in front of his father. Neither man made a move to embrace or to shake hands. Each was quickly and silently taking the measure of the other.

"I have come to talk, not to fight, Father," came the deep voice in heavily accented English. "And that is what I would like to do right now, if we could have some privacy." He glanced first at Collier and then back at Diego.

"Come into the library, then." Diego pointed the way. Cleavon started to follow them. "No, Cleavon." Diego held up his hand. "This must be a private meeting between father and son. I have nothing to fear from my own flesh."

Collier swallowed hard as she watched father and son go into the house. As soon as the door to the house slid shut, Collier's knees gave out. Cleavon helped her into a wicker chair. Then he settled himself in a chair facing her and rested his rifle across his knees.

Within minutes she got up again. She had to get away from the claustrophobic closeness of the compound for a while.

She stood at the head of the steps and looked out to sea. The water was calm, the surface almost completely smooth. It seemed so tranquil, so peaceful. The longer she stared at the water, the more peaceful she felt. Seagulls dipped and soared. A pelican swooped low over the waves, his bill open, searching for fish. The air was balmy, and she took deep, full breaths of it into her lungs and felt the peace flow through her.

Then she spotted the launch. The Cuban flag at its stern fluttering in the breeze. The crew, their legs spread, their arms behind their backs. Ten of her own islanders standing on the dock, their carbines aimed directly at the men. All of them rigid, still, like petrified figures in a wax museum's chamber of horrors.

The view no longer held any peace for her.

"Collier!"

She spun around.

Diego and Jorge were coming toward her. She wanted to run to Diego, but she held back. Unconsciously, she pulled herself up straighter and allowed her features to slip into a mask. Once more Jorge took her hand and bent over it. This time there was no kiss.

"Señora," was all he said before he put on his cap again.

Turning to his father, he snapped him a stiff military salute. Diego merely smiled tightly and did not respond.

Collier watched as Jorge started down the steps. When she could no longer see the top of his head, she turned to face her husband again. They reached out for one another at the same time.

Diego's face was gray. His eyes were red-rimmed and the lines in his face looked deeper than before. Pain seemed to leap in sparks from his body.

"My poor beloved," she soothed him. "Was it very difficult for you?"

He gave her a long, shuddering kiss before he answered her. "It was not a meeting between a loving father and his loving son," he said with a sad smile. "It was merely a polite encounter between two former allies who are now acknowledged adversaries. We were respectful and we were cautious. He told me nothing which surprised me. I told him nothing which surprised him. He was simply an emissary, bringing me a personal message from Fidel. In short, Fidel is asking me, as a former compatriot and friend, to remember our friendship and to honor it. He assured me that the dream lives on, that it has never died. Only that it is taking longer than they realized to be fulfilled. He begged me to be tolerant. But most of all, he begged me to be silent."

"And what did you tell him?"

"I told Jorge to tell Fidel that his dream ceased to be my dream many years ago. But I also told him that if he put down his gun, I would set down my pen and give him my hand."

"Did he threaten you?"

A shadow crossed Diego's face and then was gone. "How does a son threaten a father? By denying him his love? No, *querida*, Jorge did not threaten me. I am sure he hopes that Fidel's cajoling words will work more effectively than any threat of his."

"And will Fidel's words work, Diego?" she asked, anxiously scanning his face.

He pulled her close. "We shall see, my love, we shall see."

It was a muggy April evening. Collier slid open the glass doors in the bedroom in the hopes of catching whatever feeble breeze she could. She was exhausted. The strain of the last few weeks, the heat and the oppressive humidity which always preceded a thunderstorm, had given her a violent headache. She took two aspirins and went to lie down on her bed.

"Does this mean that I am to be deserted for our usual walk?" Diego asked, coming into the room and seeing her lying down.

"I'm afraid so," she moaned, beckoning him over to the bed.

He sat down beside her and pressed his lips against her eyelids.

"How beautiful you are," he whispered. "I love to see you with your hair spread across the pillow like a cape. Your face is so lovely, so strong." He kissed her on the forehead, then he kissed her eyelids again, the tip of her nose, her chin and finally her mouth. "I adore you, *corazón.*"

"Then stay with me," she murmured.

"My head needs clearing. Ten hours over my papers is more than enough in a single day." He got up from the bed. "But I will cut the walk short tonight, *querida.* Will that please you?"

She nodded. Her head was light now from the pills and from the heat, and she was getting drowsy.

"If I'm asleep when you come back, wake me up. Promise?"

"I promise."

She turned onto her side and wrapped her arms around her pillow.

She awoke to the roar of thunder. Getting groggily out of bed, she stumbled over to the doors to close them before the rain came in. The glare from a bolt of lightning momentarily blinded her.

Suddenly she froze.

The sky was clear. It wasn't raining.

There was no lightning. The floodlights around the compound had been turned on.

But the thunder continued.

Confused, she stepped out onto the terrace.

Who had given the order to turn on the floodlights?

Panic seized her. She started to run. The gate was open. The thunder grew louder.

Only it wasn't thunder. It was gunfire.

It ricocheted through the night in screaming whistles and blunted thuds.

She was almost at the stone steps. Someone grabbed her from behind and threw her down to the ground.

She began to struggle, but his hands held her down. The

man flung himself on top of her. He was crushing her, squash-
ing her, driving all the air out of her body. She tried to scream,
but she couldn't. He was going to rape her. *Diego!* She needed
Diego.

"Diego." It came out as a strangled little whisper.

Diego. Where was Diego?

The man on top of her shifted his weight slightly. Shifted
it enough for her to look up and see his face.

Collier gasped.

Clement! It was Clement, Cleavon's younger brother.

He moved again and she was able to breathe more easily.
And then she saw it in his face. Clement wasn't going to rape
her. He wasn't trying to smother her. He was trying to protect
her.

"Dear God," she whimpered, "where's Diego?" Who was
protecting Diego?

The gunfire suddenly stopped. Collier lay on the ground,
winded and dazed. All she could hear were the shouts of the
men and the sound of a launch heading out to sea.

Now Clement was hauling her to her feet. She saw criss-
crossing beams of light coming from the beach below.

"Come back to the house, Miss Collier," Clement was telling her as she struggled to get away from him.

"Diego! I have to find Diego!" she cried.

"Please, Miss Collier, come back with me now."

But Collier didn't hear him. With an animal scream, she
kicked out at him, catching him in the groin with the flat of
her foot. As he doubled over in pain, she wrenched free and
started, half-running, half-stumbling, down the steps to the
beach. She tripped on the last step and sprawled headlong in
the sand. Picking herself up, she started to run.

The shouts filled up the night. The ground rocked and tilted,
spinning in and out of focus as Collier ran.

Diana!

Once again she saw the pieces of driftwood scattered all
over the beach. An arm. A leg. A body.

"Miss Collier, no!"

She would never know whose voice it was that rang out in
the night, warning her to stay away. All she would remember
was Diego.

Diego. Lying on his back on the beach. His arms flung out,
his legs open. His blood and bits of his flesh splattered across

the sand. Cleavon lay beside him, face down, one arm thrown protectively across Diego's chest. The blood of the two men mingling.

"No!" she screamed. "No! No! No!"

Her screams drowned out the roar of the sea and the shouts of the men.

She was on her knees, cradling his head in her lap.

"Diego."

She called out to him, begged the staring, vacant eyes to recognize her, to clear and grow gentle as they always did when he looked at her.

"Diego, please, Diego."

His face was untouched. Only a slight trickle of blood at the corner of his mouth. She pressed her lips to his, tasted his blood and the salt of her tears.

"Miss Collier."

She brushed the hair out of his eyes. "My darling, my precious love," she crooned. "I love you, Diego, I love you. I should have told you before you left tonight. I should have told you how much I loved you."

"Miss Collier, please."

She heard the voice, but it made no difference.

Now someone was bending over Cleavon, gently tugging him away, breaking his hold on his mentor and his friend.

Collier knew she was dying. When the pain exploded in her chest, she knew it was her heart. A great black hole opened up inside her and she began to slide down into it. Down, down, down she slid, pulling Diego after her.

And then she saw him. He stepped out from the shadows and opened his arms for her.

"Daddy," she sighed, feeling his arms close around her at last.

At last she was safe.

Collier

$\sim\!\sim$

1978–1980

Chapter Thirty-two

The swan boat drifted up to them. They got on board and found the only two remaining seats. He stretched out his legs, pushed back his hat and lit up a cigar. She let her hand trail in the cool water, while the sun beat down and warmed her all over. The boat glided down the Charles, under the bridges and past the rowing teams practicing on the water. A light breeze blew the ash from his cigar into the air. The smile he gave her outshone the sun....

They turned her onto her side. One of them shook out her pillow and plumped it up before they lay her on her back again.

The squirrel nipped the tip of one of her fingers as she was feeding it a shelled walnut. She let out a little cry, more of surprise than of pain. He bent down and took her finger and pressed it to his lips. He kissed away the sting, and his black eyes told her that she had nothing to fear from squirrels....

The bottle was nearly empty. It was quickly replaced with a full one. Once the flow was regulated, the glucose solution dripped steadily down the tube and into her arm again.

Why wouldn't the baby stop crying? She couldn't sleep. She covered her ears with her hands, but she could still hear him crying. She didn't want this baby. She wanted him. She wanted the car with the top rolled down and the wind in her hair. She wanted to kiss him and taste his cigar on his mouth. She went outside to look for the car, but the car was gone. He was gone. So she took out her own cigar and sat down on the floor of the garage to wait for him....

She began to fight them. Two of them couldn't control her anymore. They rang for help. It took four of them to hold her down.

The wooden hammer kept pounding on the desk. But their laughter grew louder and louder until it finally drowned out the sound of the hammer. Bright white lights flashed and popped in front of her eyes. She put her arms around the crying woman with the golden hair and the sad blue eyes and rocked her in

her arms as if she were a baby. Then the great red wave swep
toward them and carried the woman away....

When they couldn't hold her down by themselves, they had
to tie her down.

All the colors were running into each other. Great blurs o,
red, yellow, orange, green, blue and black. She put out her
hands to catch them before they spilled onto the floor. He began
to laugh. He told her to take her hands away, that the colors
were dry, and that they couldn't run anymore. She took her
hands away. The colors ran right to the edge of the canva
and then they stopped. She began to laugh with him....

They lowered her into the tub of cool water and buckled
the canvas top over her so that only her head protruded.

The sea crashed against the rocks, sending showers of spray
high into the air. The wind whipped up the tops of the waves
until they were white and frothy. The great yellow light turned
round and round atop the tower and made the nighttime as
bright as day. The small girl with the black hair spilling down
her back led her over to the telescope and let her look through
it. She could see two figures down below, two figures dancing
naked in the moonlight....

They unbuckled the canvas top and lifted her out of the tub
Then they dried her off and put her back to bed.

It was so hot. She took off her shirt and used it to fan
herself. She was sitting in the middle of a pile of skulls. The
skulls stared up at her through the great, gaping holes where
their eyes should have been, and they grinned their toothy white
grins at her. He told her that the skulls couldn't hurt her. Only
the scorpions could hurt her and the shadows flying across the
face of the sun, pelting the earth and making the day soun
like the Fourth of July....

They untied her hands and lifted her out of bed, and between
the two of them, they got her to walk.

She stared at herself in the mirror. Something was different
Her reflection was changing, splitting down the middle, divid
ing itself in two. A man was now reflected beside her in the
mirror. He was the darker side of her lightness. He tucked a
scarlet flower behind her ear. She placed a sprig of crimson
blossoms in his hand. He took her hand and told her that he
would never leave her....

They adjusted the electrodes and stepped back. The current
was turned on. A spear of electricity hurtled through her brain

The small woman with the angry face shouted for the little boy to hurry. Time was running out. With a piercing shriek, he balled his fists and charged. As he struck her, his black eyes filled up with tears. Backing up, he charged again. He was taller now, almost a man, but his eyes were still filled with tears. . . .

They took her into the small, white room again. Turning up the dial, they shot a stronger current through her brain. And then they waited.

She knew by the music that she had found him. The strains of the guitar led her to the edge of the crowd. He was standing in the middle of the crowd, barefoot, his long white robe ragged from his arduous journey. In his whiteness, lay his great age, while in his blackness, lay his youth. Around his head was a golden aura and when he spoke, he spoke to them about peace. . . .

She began to thrash around on the bed. One of them swabbed her arm. The other plunged the hypodermic needle deep into her flesh. She was soon asleep.

They lay together on the cloud. He read to her from a long paper which had no end. She closed her eyes and allowed his words to envelop her. When she opened her eyes, he was gone. But he had left the paper behind. Soon the paper began to wind itself up, growing thicker and larger, rolling itself into a giant cylinder. The cylinder started to roll. It rolled over his guitar and smashed it. The music stopped . . .

She was screaming. She flung herself off the bed and tried to break away from them. It took all four of them to carry her to the bath and buckle her in.

She found him darting in and out among the trees. He beckoned to her and she followed him. Together they ran through the forest. The sunlight dappled the ground and danced long shadows behind them. Whenever she lost sight of him, he would wave to her from another hiding place and she would run to him. But when the forest ended and the sea began, she lost him again. She heard the thunder roar and when she looked up, she saw the sky exploding. Bits of it fell to earth again as rain, spattering her and staining her red. . . .

"Diego!"

She was running. They chased after her.

"Diego!"

They caught hold of her. Each of them reached for a different part of her and held her down.

"Diego!"

They put her back on the bed and strapped her down. The hypodermic plunged into her flesh again and sent her back to sleep.

The sun was in her eyes. She shielded her eyes with her hand and scanned the crest of the hill. The giant glass box rose up in front of her. And the sun glinted off the glass and shone back into her eyes. He took her hand and led her up the steep steps, and opened the door of the great glass box for her.

Inside were the paintings. Hanging on gold chains from the high ceiling. Their colors ran together in the sun, spilling onto the floor and the glass walls and staining them red and blue and yellow and green. She dropped to her knees and bowed her head.

The bell rang. She raised her head. The man at the head of the long table stood up and the twelve other men stood too. He closed his book and tucked the great seal under his arm. The other men closed their books and picked up their smaller seals. When the man put a cigar in his mouth, twelve matches were held up to light it for him. He waved them away. She held up her match. The heat from the lighted cigar drove her back. The flame of the match burned her fingers. She dropped the match and picked up the seal he had left for her.

He was waiting for her outside. He took her hand again and led her back down the steps. Her feet touched the sand and she felt the water come up and lap at her toes. She turned to look up at the cliff and she saw the purple and pink and scarlet flowers winding their way up the side of the cliff.

The sound of the drums made her spin around. The sun was all around her now. Wherever she turned, she found the sun.

"It is time," he told her. "Now you may look at my face."

"But the sun will blind me."

"Look!" he commanded her. "Look at my face."

Slowly she lifted her head and looked.

He was smiling at her. His black hair glistened in the sun. His hard, chiselled features looked exactly like hers. She touched his face and his face came away in her hands.

His hair was brown now, his eyes brown, and the full mouth laughed and laughed. Even as he was melting, his mouth continued to laugh.

But the laughter stopped because the sandy-haired man with the small beard never laughed. He spoke with a strange, clipped accent which blurred and slowed and drifted into the lilting melody of a guitar.

And the white hair was too white for the blackness of his brows. She pressed her hands around this face to preserve it. But she found herself holding grains of dust and bits of sand.

She began to cry. She was crying because she had lost them all.

"Look at me."

She shook her head. She knew what she would see. Nothing. There would be no one there now.

"Look!"

One last time she raised her head and looked.

The glasses reflected her own face back at her. She took off the glasses. His blue eyes were speckled with gray. His brown hair was sprinkled with gold. And when he smiled, the smile remained. She reached up one last time, prepared to feel the dust and the sand. But when she touched his face, it was warm and smooth and it throbbed with life.

This time his face remained intact.

Her eyelids fluttered open. The room swam in and out of focus. When her vision cleared, the first thing she noticed was the window. A curtainless window set high in a heavy wooden door. And in that window was the face of a woman. Collier let out a frightened scream and the man slumped in the chair beside her leapt up and pulled her into his arms.

"Leland?" she whispered uncertainly.

He barely managed a nod.

"Leland." She said it with more conviction this time.

"Oh Collier, thank God," he murmured. "Thank God."

"Where am I, Leland?"

He hesitated for a moment. Then in a muted voice, he said simply,

"Fairwood."

"Fairwood?" She repeated the dreaded name over and over to herself. Squeezing her eyes shut, she tried to block out the pain the sound of that name evoked. Fairwood. The place she had run from all her life. The place she had finally come home to. When she opened her eyes again, they were filled with tears.

"I hurt, Leland," she told him.

"I know, dear heart, I know."

The tears rolled down her cheeks. "I don't think I can live with so much pain."

"You *will* live," he insisted. "And I intend to see that you do. As long as you need me, Collier, I'll never leave you. I promise."

Promises. They had all made promises to her and broken them.

Except for him.

She leaned back against the pillows and took a long look around the room. It was identical to the room Diana had once been in. Her worst nightmare had been realized. She had received her mother's legacy at last.

Her head ached and her body felt as if it no longer belonged to her. It was sore. It was bruised. She felt as if she had just returned to earth after an eon in outer space.

"How long have I been here?" she wanted to know, bracing herself for his reply.

"This is July. You've been here for three months."

"My God," she whispered, horrified. The shock jarred her, making her wince. She covered her face with her hands. *Three months. Dear God. So much time lost.* "Am I going to be all right now?"

"If you want to be."

She shuddered. She didn't like the sound of that. "Will I be like her then, in and out of here for the rest of my life?"

Leland shook his head. "What you've had is a nervous breakdown. You aren't mad, Collier. You've never been mad. You've never been like Diana at all."

"But I lost control of my mind for three months," she persisted. "Wouldn't you call that mad?"

"Speak to the doctors, Collier," he told her patiently. "They'll tell you. It was a breakdown, not insanity. You didn't want to deal with Diego's death, so your mind took a holiday for a while. It simply closed down. It went into hiding. You just didn't want to be responsible for yourself or for your life anymore. By breaking down, you allowed other people to assume that responsibility for you. The tough part begins right now, because now you know what the alternatives are. That's why I said you'd be all right if you wanted to be. If you don't want to spend the rest of your life in and out of a place like Fairwood, you're going to have to come to grips with the fact that Diego

Velasquez is dead and that Collier Paget-Browne is still alive."

Collier gasped. Hearing Leland say Diego's name out loud was like ripping away a piece of her heart. A cold wind of pain swept into her.

"You can do whatever you want with your life now," Leland went on. "You can fight back or you can give up. I've never known the old Collier to back away from a challenge. And this is one hell of a challenge, dear heart. What the new Collier will do is anyone's guess. But I want you back, and I'll fight both Colliers to keep you."

She was crying again. She wondered if she would ever get tired of the tears. Crazy, absurd, unconnected thoughts tore through her mind ... Where had they buried him? ... She had missed her fifty-eighth birthday ... Had they caught his murderers? ... Who had been signing for her at Paget-Browne Enterprises? ... Had they punished his killers? ... There had probably been no special weekend for the prize-winning students from the Center ... Was Fidel content now? ...

She thought of the paths open to her. She was afraid of going back almost as much as she feared moving forward. She glanced over toward the door. At the window in that door. And at the face of the woman in the window staring back at her.

She took a deep breath. "Take me home, Leland," she said. "I think it's time I went home."

Chapter Thirty-three

"Here's to the New Year."

"And a new decade."

Collier and Leland clinked glasses.

It was midnight and they were sitting together on the patio. The moon was high, floating a wide silver stream across the sea from the horizon to the shoreline. The air smelled of jasmine, oleander and frangipani. Their view of the gardens was unobstructed now. The guardhouses and the electrified fencing had all been dismantled when Collier had returned from Fairwood.

Collier put down her empty glass and stood up.

"Would you walk with me to the grove now?" she asked him.

"Of course." He quickly drained his glass.

They walked, hand in hand, through the gardens to the small grove of oleanders which overlooked the beach. It was here that they had buried Diego, beside Diana.

Collier knelt down and bowed her head. After a few minutes, she placed a single red hibiscus blossom on his grave, but she continued to kneel. When Leland bent to help her to her feet, she shook her head.

"I think I'd like to stay here for a little while."

"Do you want me to wait?"

"You go back to the house," she told him. "But don't you dare finish the champagne without me."

She spread her shawl on the ground and sat down, tucking her knees up under her. In the bright light from the moon, she could clearly read the inscription on the simple white marker:

DIEGO LUIS VELASQUEZ
March 12, 1914–April 5, 1978
Patriot and Poet. Husband and Friend

Her eyes filled with tears. She let them flow unchecked down her cheeks.

"I keep waiting for the pain to lessen, my darling," she said in a soft undertone, "but I'd be betraying you if it ever went away completely. I'm much better, though. I can say your name without starting to cry. I can even look at your photographs now. I look at each one and I try to remember where you were and what you were saying at the exact moment the picture was taken. I'm using your cane now, did you know that? I don't have any reporters to fight off, but I've developed a bit of arthritis in my left knee. Leland tells me I look very aristocratic. He says I remind him of England's Queen Mary. Leland's been so good to me, my darling. He even managed to get me copies of most of your taped radio and TV interviews. I listen to your voice and I see your face, and no one can ever convince me you're not alive."

She buried her face in her hands. As long as his voice could be heard, Diego Velasquez would never die. Even if she was the only one who heard it. Even if she was the only one who remembered.

Her time at Fairwood had protected her from the shock of Diego's death, but it had also deprived her of the opportunity of personally receiving and acknowledging the tributes a stunned and saddened world paid to her slain husband. Leland had saved most of the clippings, articles, letters and telegrams for her, and she had managed to personally answer each one of them.

From Cuba, there had been only silence. No acknowledgement of Diego Velasquez's death whatsoever. She had never even heard from Jorge. Not even a line in any of the state-controlled newspapers.

And yet, from the thousands of men and women still fleeing the Castro regime, came reports of photographs of Diego being set up in makeshift tents and hovels. In the satchels and the bags of the refugees, a well-worn book of poetry was taken out and read in the evenings. And it was said that wherever groups of young activists congregated, the name of Diego Velasquez was spoken with reverence.

She drew some comfort from what she heard, but somehow she still felt helpless, ineffectual. Diego deserved more. She lamented the fact that his autobiography had not been further along at the time of his death. That, at least, would have given her something to work with. In the end, she had put his notes, all written in Spanish, in a large brown folder and locked it away in the wall safe in the library.

She discarded the idea of erecting a monument to him and chose instead to do something constructive with her money. She would build a living monument to him. And so she set up a one million dollar scholarship—the Diego Luis Velasquez Memorial Scholarship—at the University of Miami, because of the large Cuban population in Florida. The capital was to be invested and each year the interest was to be given in the form of individual scholarships to former Cuban nationals or the children of former Cuban nationals, whether for academic excellence or for financial reasons.

"So you see, my love," she murmured through her tears, "you were wrong. Your voice hasn't been stilled. It's living on in the young, just as I told you it should."

But in spite of these small triumphs which she laid out as her stepping stones to a complete recovery, Collier still lived in turmoil. There remained one unanswered question which stirred and kicked inside her and prevented her search for peace from being complete.

Who had killed Diego? This was the question she tortured herself with, whenever she forgot to keep herself occupied, programmed. Whenever she allowed her thoughts to wander.

Nothing had remained of that night except for some spent cartridges and some footprints quickly washed away by the tide. The inhabitants of the island had been taken by complete surprise. As prepared as they thought they were, someone had been more prepared. The helicopter's fuel lines had been cut. The launch's gas tanks had been punctured. Pursuit had been impossible. The act had been carefully planned, expertly timed and carried out with the precision timing of the most sophisticated guerrilla raid.

The men Collier hired turned up nothing. She used her name and her money and her influence and came up empty.

She finally considered offering a one million dollar reward for information leading to the capture of the murderers. Leland convinced her otherwise.

"Think of all the crank calls, the letters, the cables, the visits, the bits of phony evidence," he warned her. "You'll be inundated. You won't have a moment's peace. Spare yourself the ordeal, Collier. It could send you straight back to Fairwood. Time has a way of answering questions. Why don't you give it some time? Please."

So she had abandoned the idea. The question was something she forced herself to live with, but the frustrating injustice of it was like a constant bitter taste on her tongue.

She took a handkerchief out of her dress pocket now and blew her nose. Then she got up slowly, shook out her shawl and wrapped it around her shoulders again. She breathed in the sweet night smells of the island. She and her island were almost friends again. They were gradually making their peace with one another.

Clement had taken over the group his older brother had left behind, and it was Clement the townspeople elected to be their Prime Minister when Horace Coombes died at the age of eighty-nine. When Clement's wife gave birth to a son that Christmas, they named him Cleavon Diego Coombes, and Collier was made a godmother for the second time.

As the stepped up onto the patio, Leland got up and helped her into her chair.

"Is your leg very stiff?" he inquired, watching her set the cane down beside her.

"Not bad." She smiled. "I think I just like the effect."

He filled her empty glass. "See, I told you I wouldn't finish it without you. Of course, it's probably flat by now."

They raised their glasses.

"To us, Leland," she said. "To you and me."

"To us, Collier."

They clinked again.

"Did I tell you that I received a lovely Christmas card from Jenny?" Collier said. How sad. There were only Christmas cards between them now.

"Colleen's enrolling in the Center next fall," Leland told her.

It was as it should be. Collier smiled. "She'll be nineteen then." Her smile was wistful. "Remember Jenny at nineteen?"

Leland didn't answer her, but Collier thought she saw his hand tremble as he lifted his glass to his lips. Would it have been any different if Leland hadn't forsaken others to devote himself to her? If he hadn't loved her so much and loved everyone else less?

"Collier?"

She glanced up.

"Why don't you write your memoirs?"

"Do you think I'm old enough?" she laughed.

"I'm serious. I've been thinking about this for a long time now."

"But I'm not a writer," she protested. "Diego was the writer.

You're the chronicler. I'm just the collector."

"Then write about the people you knew and the paintings you collected. Tell your own story your way, Collier. God knows every newspaper and magazine in the world has been trying long enough to get the exclusive rights to it. Tell it before somebody else does. The publishers will be falling all over themselves trying to land a contract with you. Think about it."

After he had gone to bed, Collier went into the library and sat down at the desk. She located one of Diego's cigars, lit it and then leaned back in the chair to think. Maybe Leland was right. Writing her memoirs would give her something to do, keep her busy, keep her mind alert. Keep her from thinking too much. It would also make her less dependent on Leland.

He couldn't keep commuting between Philadelphia, New York, Gloucester and St. Cristobal this way. It was wearing him out, especially since he had just purchased the floundering *Philadelphia Falcon*. She had to smile, remembering how he had turned down her offer to run the Hall chain of newspapers so long ago. He had been right. Her beloved Leland had built an empire of his own without her help.

Should she do it? She chewed thoughtfully on her cigar. Could she do it? She toyed with the handle of the top drawer for awhile. Then, with a decisive tug, she pulled it open. She took out several sheets of white paper and set them down on the blotter in front of her. She would try. She would do it for him.

Picking up the silver pen Diego had used, she took a deep breath. Then she scribbled,

"They called me mad. But I wore my madness with a difference. After all, I *was* my father's daughter. I even bore my father's name . . ."

She worked steadily through the winter and into the spring. When her first draft was nearly completed, she telephoned Leland in Philadelphia to tell him.

"Do you trust me?" he asked her.

"Of course I do."

"Then, let me act as your agent. I'll sell your book to the top house in New York." He let out a whoop of glee. "Collier, my dear, you're going to set the publishing world on its ear."

She suddenly began to have second thoughts. "I'm telling the truth as I see it, you know," she said, "and I'm afraid a lot of people are going to have their eyes opened and their feelings hurt. Some idols are going to be toppled. Somehow, I think the book should be published only after I'm dead. That way, just my estate will be sued for libel."

"It can't be libel if it's the truth, dear heart."

She still had her doubts. "I don't think my father would have approved of what I'm doing, Leland. Our name is going to be tarnished, and it's a name I've upheld proudly for nearly sixty years now."

"Your name will endure no matter how muddied it gets. FDR is still a hero to everyone who worshipped him—in spite of Lucy Mercer. So is John Kennedy. Look at Nelson Rockefeller. People have short memories, Collier. Today's scandal is tomorrow's old news."

"It's cathartic, Leland," she admitted to him. "I'm finally taking out a lot of old ghosts and giving them a good airing."

"Then don't you dare quit. Keep on going," he urged her. "And in the meantime, I'm going to scout around for a buyer."

By August, her rough draft was finished—all twelve hundred handwritten pages of it. She gave Leland permission to break the story to the news media. Once again, she was a woman beseiged. Everyone wanted interviews, but she refused them all. She divulged nothing. This was her life they were talking about. It was her story. When and if she was ready to release it to them, she would.

At the end of the month, Leland flew down to the island. It took him three days to read through the draft, taking copious notes as he went along. Collier spent the entire time working off her nervous energy by swimming in the pool and going for long walks on the beach. It took all of her self-control not to ask him about the book when they met for meals.

The afternoon he finished the manuscript, he called her into the library. He handed her the bulky brown folder and she put it back in the wall safe underneath Diego's uncompleted autobiography. When she turned to face him, she was trembling.

"Well?" she finally asked.

He took her hand and pulled her down onto the sofa. "Right now, it's rough," he told her. "It's going to need a lot of work, but with the help of a good editor, you're going to have a blockbuster on your hands."

Collier gasped. She didn't know whether she was elated or terrified by the prospect.

"I have every major publishing house in New York bidding on the book right now," he said proudly. "Let's just hope you'll be able to handle the fallout once it hits the stands."

She groaned at this. "I hope I'll be dead by then."

"You'd better not be dead. Think of the promotional tour you'll be sent on. Think of the notoriety." He gave her a wink.

She made a face. Suddenly she found it stifling in the library. She got up to open the glass doors and then she sat down again.

Again she was assailed by doubt. "I'm really not sure about this anymore," she said hesitantly. "I keep thinking of what I've written and the questions people are going to ask because of it. I'm wondering if perhaps I'm not too old for this now. I've put down everything I thought should be put down, and now that it's done, I almost want to put it away and forget about it."

"But you can't!" he protested. "The world's been waiting a long time to hear the story of Collier Paget-Browne as it really happened, and not how a bunch of journalists and biographers thought it happened."

"What you say is true, Leland, but I wonder how much more I really owe this world. Writing this book provided me with the kind of release I never expected to find."

"All the ghosts were finally laid to rest?"

"Not only that. I think it helped me grow up. I can look back at my father now and see how badly I wanted to be like him and do the same things he did. As a result, I never gave myself credit for the things I did instead. I also realize that I've spent my life searching for the kind of love he gave me. I looked for it in Milo, in Thaddeus and even in Diego, and of course, I never found it. Diego once said that my life had meaning because of the monuments I'd built to myself." She gave her head a rueful shake. "He was wrong, Leland. I built those monuments out of devotion to my father, and to atone for having failed him. I wasn't the son he'd wanted. I wasn't even the son he was training me to be when he died. Well, I've atoned enough. The rest of my life belongs to me, without apologies to anyone."

"Even if it means shelving your book?" he asked her.

"Don't look so unhappy," she teased him. "I'm sure it's been done before. I've managed to dodge everyone's questions for sixty years, why give in now and provide them with all the answers?"

"I never thought you enjoyed the chase that much."

"Neither did I, until now." She sighed then, and rested her head against his shoulder. "Give me some time to think about it, Leland. As you well know, women are notorious for changing their minds." She snuggled closer to him. "Oh, by the way, I just received an invitation from the Kincaid Gallery in New York."

Leland groaned.

"They're mounting an exhibition of—"

He held up his hand to silence her.

"What's the matter?"

"I thought I heard something."

"That's impossible." Her heart began to pound. "The staff was given the day off. There's a wedding in town."

"It sounded like a boat."

"But today's Thursday. The supplies from the mainland always come on Friday."

Leland got up and Collier did too. He took her by the hand and hurried her out through the gardens and down to the edge of the cliff.

"My God," she gasped.

A small yacht was tied up at the dock. A man was walking toward the stone steps leading up from the beach. Collier and Leland exchanged glances. Together they eased their way over to the head of the steps to wait.

Collier moistened her lips with the tip of her tongue. The afternoon sun was suddenly too strong. It seemed to be growing hotter and glowing brighter. She opened the neck of her shirt as wide as it could go. Her hand, so tightly clutching Leland's, was getting wet and clammy.

When she spotted the top of his head, she took a step backward.

He was panting, his face running with sweat.

Collier's hand slid out of Leland's.

He stood at the top of the steps and began to mop his face with his handkerchief.

Her legs were beginning to buckle.

He could hardly catch his breath.

She couldn't breathe.

He stuck his handkerchief back in his pocket.

She wanted to run, but her legs refused to support her.

He finally got his breath back. "Aren't you even going to welcome me to your island?" demanded Addison.

Chapter Thirty-four

All three of them simply stood there.

Addison tried to control the twitching in his body as he studied her. In the half-light of the afternoon, she was still the girl in the photographs. Blond hair swirled in a soft cloud to frame her face. Tall, slim and proud. Her shoulders squared. Her chin thrust out. She made him feel small and ugly and old.

His heart thudded and skipped. It made awful rattling noises inside his rib cage. His mouth was dry. He flicked at his lips with a scratchy tongue. He grimaced, seeing the other one standing beside her with one hand on her shoulder. Protecting her. As always.

Collier stared at the small, dark man. Beneath his suntan, his skin looked gray and dry. He flicked his tongue in and out of his mouth like a lizard. His blue eyes kept darting about as if to snatch up bits and pieces of the surroundings. Revulsion rose and fell like a wave inside her. She closed her eyes, willing him to vanish, but when she opened them again, he was still standing there, wearing that same twisted sneer on what could have been a handsome face.

"I buried my mother yesterday," he said in a toneless voice.

Collier could only continue to stare at him. She felt absolutely nothing. He could have been talking about a stranger. He looked as if he were in a daze.

"You came all the way down here to tell me that?" She finally found her voice again.

"Time ran out for her," he continued as if she hadn't spoken. "We never thought it would be that way. She promised me you'd be the one time ran out on first. She couldn't wait any longer. Why couldn't she have waited just a bit longer?"

Collier glanced over at Leland. His face was hard. A muscle twitched in his jaw. She wondered what he was thinking. His hand felt like a lead weight on her shoulder.

"I've come to talk to you," the automaton with the short black hair was saying.

"What about?"

"In the house." He cocked his head in the direction of the house. "I'll tell you in the house."

Collier stood where she was and refused to move. "I have nothing to say to you, Addison. Whatever you have to tell me, tell me now, and then get off my island!"

If he had been an animal, he would have bared his fangs at her and frothed at the mouth. "I said I'd tell you in the house!"

His eyes were glittering. They were like the eyes of a mad dog. Collier's hands flew to her throat. She remembered how his hands had closed around her throat once and tried to squeeze the life out of her.

Leland was tugging her arm. "Let's go into the house, Collier." His voice was quiet but firm.

He was behaving as if Addison were holding a vial of nitroglycerin in front of him and any sudden movement or loud noise would make him drop it.

Collier nodded, giving in. She took Leland's hand and they started back.

Addison walked behind them, greedily devouring her property with his eyes. The envy and the hatred and the rage boiled up inside him. He was beginning to shake again. He reached into his shirt pocket, pulled out a small silver pillbox and popped a pale yellow pill into his mouth to calm him down. He'd nearly been sick on the way over from Jamaica. He'd never gotten used to handling a boat, especially on his own.

Collier led the way from the patio into the library and vaguely indicated a chair for Addison to sit in. She and Leland sat down together on the sofa.

Addison took out his handkerchief and wiped off his forehead. He tried not to look around him. He concentrated on her face instead. It took all of his self-control not to leap out of his chair and clamp his hands around her neck and feel it snap beneath his fingers. He could still feel her skin on the pads of his fingers.

"Well?" Collier's patience was wearing thin and her nerves were on edge. "What do you want to talk to me about?"

He cleared his throat. "You can't publish your book."

Collier started. Her grip tightened on Leland's hand.

"You can't publish your book," he repeated. "You'll ruin all of us. I know what these books are like. They're full of lies and gossip and everyone gets hurt. My mother's dead. Let her rest in peace. My son Andrew's getting married in two months. He's marrying into one of the wealthiest families in Boston. You simply cannot publish your book."

"Don't you dare tell me what I can and cannot do," she retorted, her fears forgotten as her anger flared to the surface.

"Give me the book."

Collier's mouth dropped open.

"I want that book."

"No."

He looked like a child about to throw a tantrum. "Give me that book. I want to see what you've written."

"Never! It's none of your business."

Instead of raising his voice as she was doing, he lowered it, and an ugly smile replaced the petulant pout of a moment ago.

"You're quite wrong, sister dear, that book *is* my business."

Collier was becoming alarmed. She looked at Leland and tried to read the expression on his face.

Addison licked his lips. He couldn't seem to work up enough saliva to wet them. His tongue felt like sandpaper. His fingers were itchy.

"Are you going to show me the book or not?"

Leland was frowning.

Collier hesitated.

Leland was leaning forward now, his hands braced on his knees.

Addison looked at Collier's eyes. They were turning from blue to black and then back to blue again. He felt his control slipping away from him. He slid his right hand into his jacket pocket.

Leland sprang.

Collier let out a scream.

Addison was on his feet, the gun in his hand.

"In the air!" he shouted at Leland. "Put your hands in the air!"

Collier covered her mouth to stifle another scream.

Leland slowly raised his arms above his head.

"Now get me your book!" ordered Addison.

Collier sat there frozen.

"Now!"

With a great effort, she got up and walked over to the safe. She skidded past each number in the combination and started over again. After the fourth try, she was finally able to open the safe. She took out the brown folder and closed the door again.

"Put it down on the desk."

She did as she was told.

"Now sit down again. Both of you."

She collapsed against Leland.

"Get your goddamned hands off her, you bastard!" shouted Addison. "Keep your arms in the air."

Leland raised his arms again.

Addison waved the gun in Collier's face. "Move over to the far side of the sofa."

Again she obeyed.

She sat there with her heart thumping wildly, refusing to meet his eyes. He was mad. And they were at his mercy. There was no one to help them. No one.

Had he known about the wedding? Had he known the compound would be empty? Impossible. How could he have known? Then she recalled the detective he had hired all those years ago. Nothing seemed impossible anymore. A trickle of perspiration slithered down her spine.

"Is this the only copy?" He was pointing the gun at her again.

She said nothing.

"Is it?" The cords were standing out in his neck.

Mutely she nodded her head.

"You're sure?"

Again she nodded.

He tucked the folder under his arm. "This should make for interesting reading on a cold night," he smirked. He was suddenly waving the gun at both of them. "Now get up. We're going for a walk."

"Addison, please—"

"Shut up! You've had it your way all your life. Now you're going to know how it feels to do something my way. Get up! Both of you!"

"Don't touch her!" Addison shouted as Leland reached for Collier's hand. "Keep your arms in the air and walk."

He walked them out of the house and through the gardens.

He was in control now. He began to smile. The folder was heavy. It felt good. What had she written about him? Did she know? Had she put it all down? The bitch. She was at his mercy now. He could do whatever he wanted with her.

A tongue of heat leaped up from between his legs. He was mesmerized by the sight of several long strands of her hair fluttering like golden feathers in the breeze as she walked ahead of him. Her swaying movements fanned the flame and ignited all the secret parts of him. His bloodstream became a convoluted passageway of fire, searing upward toward his brain. But it was in his groin that the flame burned brightest.

It was life he felt pulsing through him. Life! It would all be over soon. He'd be free. He'd be able to live again.

"Stop right there."

Collier and Leland were standing at the edge of the cliff, directly above the spot where Diego had died.

"What do you intend to do with us, Addison?" Collier asked the stranger who was her brother.

"I'm not going to do anything. You're going to do it all by yourselves."

She didn't understand. She glanced at Leland. What was he thinking about? Why wasn't he saying anything?

"Why are you doing this?" she demanded, fighting for time.

"Because, sister dear, all your life you've had it all your own way. You had everything and I had nothing. You stole what belonged to me. *I* was the son, not you. I was his rightful and natural heir. You were bought. You were an imposter. My mother told me I had time on my side and that I should be patient and wait. We waited and waited, but you always won. Well, now it's finally over. She couldn't wait and now neither can I."

"Even if I die, you still won't get what you want," she told him coldly. "You're not in my will, Addison. My death won't net you one cent."

"I don't want your money anymore, Collier Paget-Browne the second, I just want your life. Your life for my life. I'd say that's a pretty fair trade. Or should I say, your death for my life?"

He waved them closer to the edge.

"I'm not going to shoot you, you know. You're going to jump. Both of you. Two tired old lovers in a suicide pact. You've spent your lives together, so it's only fitting that you die together."

"Leave Leland out of this, Addison. Your quarrel is only with me," Collier pleaded.

"Don't fight your lover's battles for him," he sneered. "I couldn't very well leave him alive with you dead, now could I?"

He pointed the gun at Leland now. "Hold her hand, Leland Taggert. Hold onto the hand of your whore-of-a-mother's child, the child who stole my birthright from me and turned my mother's marriage into a sham. Take her hand I said!"

Leland reached for Collier's hand and gave it several hard squeezes. He relaxed his grip for a moment and then squeezed her hand again. Startled, Collier glanced up at him. He was staring at the folder under Addison's arm. She frowned. What was he trying to tell her?

"Well, are you both ready now?"

Collier began to tremble. Leland was still trying to tell her something. Her mind worked frantically to figure out what it was.

"Don't look so frightened, sister dear," Addison taunted her. "It won't be as painful as you think. It's a far sight better than being shot."

Collier's head came up sharply. Leland's pressure on her hand increased. Again she looked up to see him staring at the folder.

"Why couldn't you have died with your goddamned husband and saved me all this trouble?" Addison grumbled, glaring hatefully at Collier.

Her eyes widened. What had he meant by that? Leland signalled her again. At last, she understood. She studied the folder. She had given Addison the folder containing Diego's notes. She tried to think. She had to think clearly. Leland was letting her know that the folder was their only chance.

Addison's hand was beginning to tremble. He had to do it now. He had to get it over with once and for all.

Collier finally knew what she had to do. She looked up at Leland to give him the message. Something strange was happening to his face. It was darkening. His eyes were turning stony. His expression was fearsome. Abruptly, he dropped her hand.

Addison took a shaky step backward. He was losing his grip on the gun.

Leland grabbed Collier around the waist and pulled her up against him. Then, in a voice so low that she could barely hear him, he said,

"You had Diego Velasquez killed, didn't you, Addison?"
Collier gasped. What was he saying?

Addison's fingers tightened around the gun.

"Didn't you, Addison?" Leland demanded.

Collier felt her body growing weak. Leland's arm kept her
standing upright.

"Yes, I had Diego Velasquez killed!" Addison shouted.

Collier moaned.

"Who said there's no such thing as the perfect crime?
committed the perfect crime. No one's ever figured out
whether it was the FBI or the CIA or some of Castro's own
henchmen. No one except for you, Leland Taggert. Mr. Clever
Reporter!"

Collier was getting dizzy. The familiar black dots had begun
to explode behind her eyes again. "Why?" she whimpered, a
she sagged against Leland. "Why?"

"I wasn't really after Velasquez," Addison snarled at her
"I wanted *you*. I wanted *you* dead. He just made it easier
Everyone would have thought it was another political assas
sination if you'd both been killed."

Collier began to cry. All of the past pains came flooding
back and once more she was living through the agony of what
had happened that night.

"You walked together on the beach every night. Only that
night he was alone. But they went ahead with the plan anyway,
the bloody fools. They were afraid to wait around for a second
chance. They couldn't risk it. Once you'd found out about the
helicopter and the launch, you would have been prepared for
them the next time. One of my men almost made it up to your
house, but two of your faithful natives shot him. He crawled
back to the boat in time to die."

Collier was howling with pain. She covered her ears. She
didn't want to hear anymore.

"It was a disaster!" Addison was shouting at her again. "He
was dead but you were still alive. The only consolation I had
was knowing that you'd been hospitalized. At last! At last I
actually believed you'd been driven insane. But you gave us
only three months of peace. Three lousy months! Not much of
a death sentence, was it? Where was the madness we'd been
waiting for? You'd managed to cheat us once again!"

Collier felt Leland shaking her. He was hurting her. How
could he be treating her so roughly? She tried to stand up. She

tried to clear her mind of the pain so that she could think. She tried to remember what it was she had to do. She choked on her tears and her body went limp again.

"I've been waiting for fifty years, goddamn you, Collier Paget-Browne!" Addison shrilled. "I'm not waiting any longer. You're going to jump right now. Both of you. Now!"

Leland had Collier by the back of the neck. She struggled to get control of herself. She took a deep breath. Then she took another one. She wiped her eyes with the back of her hand and moistened her lips with the tip of her tongue. The pain was blinding her. She could hardly make Addison out.

"Addison." His name came out sounding like a cough. "Addison," she tried again, "I gave you the wrong folder."

His blue eyes blazed as he turned on her. "What kind of a trick are you trying to pull? I told you to jump and I meant it. Or do you want me to have to shoot you!"

"I gave you the folder with Diego's notes by mistake," she said in a quavering voice. "Both folders were in the safe. I gave you the wrong one."

"If you think you can trick me—"

It wasn't going to work. Leland tightened his grip on her. Collier tried again. "Open the folder and look for yourself. His notes are written in Spanish."

Addison threw the folder onto the ground. "Open it up for me," he ordered her.

Leland released her. She nearly stumbled and fell, but she finally managed to stoop down. With trembling fingers she untied the broad brown ribbon and lifted the flap.

Addison stood there with his legs apart, both hands clutching the gun.

Leland clenched and unclenched his fists while he waited for the right moment.

Forgive me, Diego, she whispered, as she dug a handful of pages out of the folder.

"Show them to me," barked Addison, keeping his gun trained on Leland.

Collier glanced back at her brother who was waiting for her cue, and drew in one final steadying breath. "Here, look for yourself," she called up to Addison.

Then, still crouching, she flung the papers into the air.

He was distracted just long enough.

It was all the time Leland needed. He tackled Addison and

both men fell heavily to the ground. The gun skidded out of Addison's hand. Both of them reached for it.

Collier collapsed, covering her face with her hands. Once again, the world was tipping. This time it was tilting behind her eyes. It was growing blacker. Great pinwheels of green light began to spin and whirr as her world grew even darker.

She heard the sound of a man screaming. It echoed in her mind and ricocheted through the caverns of her brain.

The screams grew fainter as he fell from the cliff to the beach below.

She waited for the gunshot. With her head bowed, she waited to die.

And while she waited, she tried to find some prayer to say for herself.

He touched her hand and she screamed.

"Collier?"

The sound of his hoarse whisper made her scream again.

"It's all over, dear heart."

She opened her eyes and looked up. With a grateful sob, she allowed Leland to pull her to her feet again.

She was sitting on the sofa in the library, shivering. Leland put down the phone.

"The Miami authorities are on their way," he told her.

They had left Addison's body where it was. Sprawled in the sand, just inches from the spot where Diego had lain.

She told Leland where to find the jacket and he got it for her. He draped it around her shoulders and went to pour them both a brandy.

Her fingers stroked the faded crest on the breast pocket of the navy blue blazer. It had been so many years since she had felt its comforting warmth around her. As she sipped her brandy, she wondered if she should tell Leland about her magic healing ritual. It was the one secret she had not revealed in her book. No, she decided, she was entitled to at least one secret, even from him.

"Addison." She said his name out loud and Leland gave her a curious look.

"There was so much evil in him," she said, "so much hatred. And yet, I pitied him, Leland. Elinor perverted him from the day he was born. She robbed him of his chance to ever grow up and become a man." She gave a hollow, little laugh. "Addison and I obviously had our roles reversed, didn't we?"

How could she pity him now? He had killed the man she had loved. And if she hadn't had a headache that April night, she would have been killed too. She couldn't stop shivering. Even the brandy wasn't helping.

Diego, my beloved, I have my answer now. But she wondered if it would bring her the peace she needed. They were all gone now. She had won. Or had she? Addison had accused her of always winning. Had she won or had she simply outrun them?

She turned to look at Leland. He was the man who had come closest to her image of the perfect father love she had been seeking. He had demanded nothing of her, but to simply love and protect her. He was the only man who had kept all of his promises to her.

"I want to go home, Leland."

"This *is* your home."

She shook her head. "I want to go home to Boston. There's a house on Commonwealth Avenue that belongs to me and I've been waiting for fifty years to claim it. It's always been my real home, Leland. It belongs to the Paget-Brownes."

Addison's widow would be dealt with easily. Of that she was certain.

"But what about the island?"

"I'll leave everything the way it is and I'll use it as often as I want. I'll always need a paradise to escape to."

She lit a cigar and exhaled the smoke slowly.

Leland made a face and Collier laughed.

"You'd better get used to cigars," she told him. "All empire builders smoke cigars."

"Not this one."

Once again Avery Leggett's words ran through her mind. Her Leland had already proven himself an able empire builder. How would he be at handling hers?

"Just take one puff," she coaxed him. "Just one. For me?"

He took the cigar and sniffed it suspiciously. "All right," he said, "but only one. And only because it's you."

He blew one perfect smoke ring into the air.

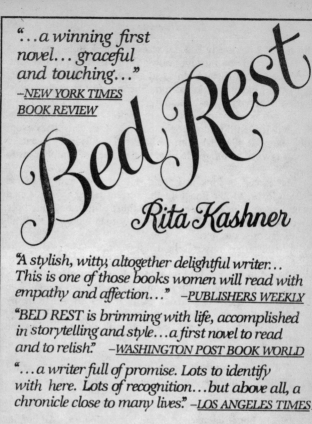

"...a winning first novel... graceful and touching..."
—_NEW YORK TIMES BOOK REVIEW_

Bed Rest

Rita Kashner

"A stylish, witty, altogether delightful writer... This is one of those books women will read with empathy and affection..." —_PUBLISHERS WEEKLY_

"BED REST is brimming with life, accomplished in storytelling and style... a first novel to read and to relish." —_WASHINGTON POST BOOK WORLD_

"...a writer full of promise. Lots to identify with here. Lots of recognition... but above all, a chronicle close to many lives." —_LOS ANGELES TIMES_

__05285-1 $3.25

Available wherever paperbacks are sold or use this coupon.